THE ECHOES OF THE ELK'S ESTATE

THE ECHOES OF THE ELK'S ESTATE

THE LIAM AND BOO SERIES

BOOK TWO

WILLIAM MIERZEJEWSKI

Your Author Journey Begins Here

DISCLAIMER

"This is a work of fiction. Unless otherwise indicated, all the names, characters, businesses, places, events and incidents in this book are either the product of the author's imagination or used in a fictitious manner. Any resemblance to actual persons, living or dead, or actual events is purely coincidental."

Quantity Purchases:
Companies, professional groups, clubs, and other organizations may qualify for special terms when ordering quantities of this title. For information, email info@ebooks2go.net, or call (847) 598-1150 ext. 4141. www.ebooks2go.net

Published in the United States by eBooks2go, Inc. 1827 Walden Office Square, Suite 260, Schaumburg, IL 60173

ISBN: 978-1-5457-5735-2

Library of Congress Cataloging in Publication

TABLE OF CONTENTS

....

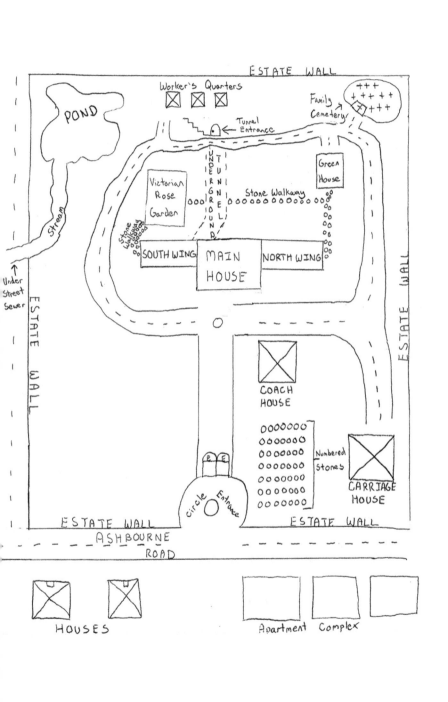

MAIN HOUSE

UPPER LEVEL

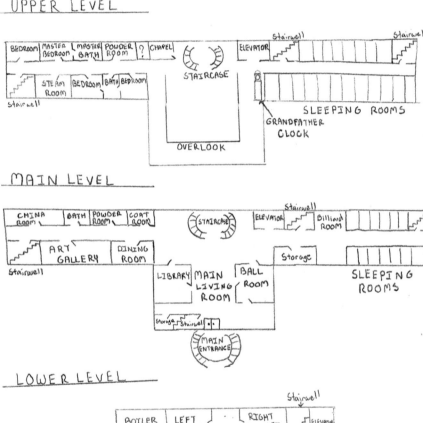

MAIN LEVEL

LOWER LEVEL

CHAPTER 1

....

IT STARTS WITH A DREAM

For several months after the events in Iron River, Liam would wake up every night in a panic. He was experiencing horrific night terrors. The night terrors as Liam would describe them seemed to replay his experiences with the beast. Sometimes the dream would be Liam and his friends driving along Route 2 as the beast advanced quickly toward them. Another dream replayed Liam running away from the beast and sheltering inside the church. But the dream that seemed to replay the most was his time in the cave where his friend and protector Nick Rosalie stood as a shield and ended the nightmare that plagued a community for generations.

Liam and Boo's parents, Annie and Will, tried their best to comfort their children after the events of last summer. Boo suffered the same trauma as her brother—nightmares, a loss of security, and problems with controlling her anxiety. Through some initial counseling with a behavior therapist, Boo seemed to recover faster than her brother. Liam took longer to rehabilitate his mind and spirit. Though not fully recovered, his parents felt that the worst was behind them. The behavioral therapist worked diligently with Liam and assured him that surviving the event was one step. The next step was surviving its memories and not allowing those memories to haunt and plague his future. After some time, Liam seemed to finally relax and put the beast and the nightmares to rest.

All that could be heard in the twilight of this particularly warm and humid summer night was the running of the ceiling fans and air conditioners in their bedrooms. Inside Annie and Will's bedroom,

Annie slept comfortably while Will tossed and turned in his sleep. He was dreaming but not about the events of Iron River. His dream was in a familiar setting. Something from his childhood.

During Will's childhood years, his mother, Bethany, worked as a housekeeper for the Catholic Church at Elk's Estate. Elk's Estate was located in Elkins Park, Pennsylvania, and was built by the extraordinarily wealthy Elk family at the turn of the twentieth century. The estate itself extended along a twenty-acre area. The main entrance to the estate was off the beautiful oak tree–covered setting of Ashbourne Road. A turn off the main road led into a tree-covered half-circle drive-up with tall black iron gates on either side that intersected in the middle with a large archway with the letters "E.E." across it. The gateway led to a 100-yard drive-up with oak trees and pines edged alongside the road to the main house. Arriving closer to the main house, the road led past a separate colonial coach house. The road separated at the entrance of the main house and formed a large circle, which extended along the other half of the property. This road led along the Victorian Rose Garden, outdoor event areas, a few cottages, and a small pond. The main building was the Elk's family mansion, which was also known as The Retreat House to the Catholic Church during their ownership. The exterior of the building was mainly constructed of concrete and gray stone and topped with an orange tile roof. The size of the mansion would rival most local elementary schools. The main entrance to the mansion included two circular gray stone staircases that led up to a vast walkway and two large oak doors.

This is where Will finds himself in his dream. He looks around the property from the vantage point of the front entrance. The weather is gloomy, bleak, and cloudy. There's a continuous breeze. He can't feel the wind, but he can see the movement of the trees and the fall of the autumn leaves. He hears the wind race through the trees and alongside the mansion while it sprinkles thousands of dry crinkled leaves that bounce and roll along the road. He also hears echoes from someone's indistinct voice. He walks back down the stairs. Not a soul in sight. From the bottom of the stairs, he sees one of the oak doors opening. He tries to race up the stairs. He wants to move quickly, but every step seems more difficult to reach and climb. Through his incredible effort he finally reaches the top of the stairs. He knocks on the door and says, "Hello?" No answer.

He walks through the entrance and into the grand hallway. To his left is a small hallway with a flight of stairs, which leads down to a lower level. Will looks down the stairs. Nothing can be seen. Just pitch blackness and a complete void of life. To his right is an entrance to a long hallway. He can see all the way down this hallway. The pendant-hanging lights move anxiously back and forth as though they were being moved by the wind or disturbed by something. Again, he says, "Hello? Can anyone hear me!" No answer.

He moves forward into the main living room. The forty-foot ceilings are spectacularly decorated with hand-crafted paintings that resemble the classic masterpieces of the Italian Renaissance. The furniture from the era of the late nineteenth and early twentieth century is both beautiful and old. He remembers this room and how he used to run through and play as a boy. He hears someone's echo past the main living room. He walks through the living room looking up and around to see if anyone is there. No one on the second floor or the main floor. He moves into another hallway that leads to another set of circular staircases. The voices are getting louder and begin to sound familiar.

The green carpeted circular staircases run on either side up to another set of double doors. He begins to walk up the stairs, and he notices the wallpaper. It's the same as it was when he was a boy. He thinks, *I remember playing on these steps with my toys while Mom was busy vacuuming and dusting. God, I remember how she would get so mad at me for running up and down these stairs. Rightfully so. That's how I got this mark on my wrist. By cutting myself on the sharp decorative railing.* He reaches the top of the staircase, and the double doors open.

He enters a gathering of some type. There are tables and chairs on either side of the wood-paneled room. The room is full of men wearing suits and tuxedoes. Vocal jazz music plays in the background and echoes off the high ceilings. One of the men approaches Will, puts his arm around Will's shoulder, and says, "Hey, Little Ski! Glad you were able to join us." Will, being confused and bewildered replies, "Little Ski? No one has called me that in years. That was what the guys at my dad's firehouse called me. My dad's nickname was Ski. Who are you?" The man laughs and says, "Good memory, Little Ski, but I guess not too good. I was a friend of your dad. You met me on a few occasions when your dad was still with the fire department. My name is Stan." Will looks at Stan and answers, "Oh yes, I remember. I would see you at some of the union parties. What are you doing here? And what happened to this place? This room used to be the old Catholic chapel where the priest held mass." Stan replies with a slight grin, "Yeah that all changed after some guy came here and made this some type of banquet hall room. Some of the locals and long-term residents are still not too happy with it. But we are here to congratulate you on becoming a firefighter and following in your dad's footsteps. We even heard you'll be promoted to an officer soon. We are all just so proud of you, especially your old man." Will, looking astonished answers, "I've been with the department for several years now. My old man? Stan, he died years ago. He never saw me graduate." Stan laughs at Will's reply and answers, "Of course I know that, Little Ski. We are all in the same boat as your old man. See, just look for yourself. He's over there in the corner with some of his buddies."

Will looks over his shoulder in the direction of Stan's pointed finger. Will sees his father sitting in the corner, smiling and raising a cocktail glass to him. That's when Will wakes up and almost jumps straight out of bed and onto the floor. *What the hell was that all about? I often dream about The Retreat House. Some are good, some aren't so good, but this one was so crazy and vivid. I haven't seen my father since his death fifteen years ago.*

CHAPTER 2

. . . .

TRAVEL PLANS

Will shouts and rises quickly out of bed. Annie wakes up startled from Will's reaction to his dream. She exclaims, "Jesus, honey! What's going on? Are you okay?"

Relieved after figuring it was a dream, Will replies, "What? It's nothing, my love. Just a dream. But God it seemed so real."

Annie questions, "Was it about my parents' lake house again?"

Will starts to lay back into bed again and answers, "No. Tried to block that place from my brain for a while now. No, this was about that Retreat House I told you about."

Annie replies, "What, that place where your mother worked when you were a kid?"

"Yes. That place. I dream about that place from time to time. Haven't been there in over twenty years. It was such a happy place in my childhood. Kind of like my sanctuary away from the rest of world."

Annie replies, "Maybe this is your mind's way of healing after the events of last summer. Think of the ripple effects it's had on the family."

"Maybe you're right. Maybe it's my mind's way of reflecting on a happy time in my life. But it's been on my mind lately, especially since we're heading out to Philly in a couple of days."

Annie replies, "I think it's great what your sister is doing out there. From what you described, it sounds like such a wonderful place. Something worth saving."

Will says, "It's certainly worth saving. Can't wait for you and the kids to see it. You'll be amazed by this place. I'm glad we decided to head there for our family vacation this summer."

Annie started to get comfortable again. Before falling back to sleep she says, "Me too, honey. Now let's get some sleep. We've got a lot to do tomorrow. Good night."

"Good idea. Good night, my love."

Liam wakes up to the smells of his dad making breakfast and his dog, Lady, jumping onto his bed and licking his face. Liam exclaims, "Okay, Lady. Stop! I'm up! I'm up. No! I'm not taking you for a run until later in the morning. And that's a maybe." Liam wipes off his face and gets out of bed.

The morning sun is rising from over the neighboring houses as he looks out his bedroom window. He hears the familiar sounds of the neighborhood. The next-door neighbor working on his car inside his garage. The landscaping company trimming his other neighbor's grass. The distant sound of a police car or an ambulance siren drifting off in the distance. He says to himself, "Good morning, Chicago. What treats do you have in store for me today? I guess we will find out after breakfast. Smells like Dad is cooking a feast. Smells like bacon and biscuits."

Liam puts on his slippers and starts to head downstairs as Lady runs quickly past him. Boo was already up and helping Dad by being the taste tester. Liam walks over to his sister to see what's on her plate. Liam says, "Looks like Dad is outdoing himself. Scrambled eggs, bacon, and biscuits with gravy. Wow!" Liam tries to steal a piece of bacon from Boo's plate, but being protective of her precious bacon, she slaps Liam's wrist and says, "Not happening! Go get your own."

Liam walks into the kitchen to find his dad in his glory—making a signature breakfast, brewing coffee, and listening to country music. Liam grabs a plate and says, "Wow, Dad! You must have slept well. You're cooking up a feast in here."

Will replies, "One weird dream in the middle of night. No biggie. The rest of the night I slept like a baby. Thank God for it. The day before we ran all night at work. Needed some good rest before we start our vacation. Figure I'd cook up what we had left in the fridge, especially since we'll be leaving soon. We got lots to do, kid."

Liam fills his plate and asks, "What, like chores?"

Will answers, "You better believe it. After breakfast I can use your help doing the yard work."

As Will continues to talk to Liam, Annie walks into the kitchen after walking up from the basement. She slides past Will and Liam, snags a piece of bacon from Liam's plate, grabs a cup from the cabinet, and pours herself a cup of coffee. Annie says, "First load of wash is started. After breakfast I'll get the suitcases out of the attic. While you and Dad are taking care of the yard work, Boo and I will be cleaning the house and doing the laundry. And I'll have to bring you with me when I drop off Lady at Nana's house."

Liam rolls his eyes and asks, "Why do I have to go? Can't you just take Boo? I promised my friends we would play some baseball at the park."

Annie answers, "You know that you're Lady's favorite. She gets all nervous when we drop her off at Nana's house. Poor thing always acts like we are abandoning her, and we'll never return."

Liam laughs. "Well, we almost didn't make it home after our last summer vacation. So, who's to say? Maybe she senses something."

Annie takes a long sip of her coffee. "First of all, true story. Second, not going there. Let's leave the past where it belongs. And lastly, I've got no problem if you want to hang out with your friends as long as you get all of your work done."

The whole family sits down at the dining room table to have breakfast. Liam looks at Will as he's drinking some of his coffee and asks, "So, Dad, just yard work, housework, and drop Lady off at Nana's? Anything else?"

Will answers, "That's basically it. That's all the help I'll need from you, son. Then I need to get fuel for the van and roll past Mr. Krazel's house. Have to drop off some tools I borrowed to repair the shed."

Liam sees a good opportunity and says, "I might hang out with my friends later and possibly do pizza and a movie at their house. Do you want me to drop it off for you?"

Will answers, "That's sounds like some good teamwork, son. Let's plan on that."

Getting a little irritated, Annie interjects, "Not so fast! Will, I don't want Liam staying out too long with his friends. I don't want any late-night stuff. We have an early call."

Will stares at his wife for a moment, looks at Liam, and says, "Duly noted. Don't worry, honey. I'll make sure he gets his chores done. Plus, it's his last opportunity to see his friends for the next couple of weeks. But your mom is right. We do have an early call. So, be home no later than 9:00 p.m. Okay? Deal?"

Liam smiles. "Deal. What time are we leaving tomorrow?"

Will answers, "No later than 7:00 a.m. Maybe sooner since that stretch of I-80 around the Illinois–Indiana Border can be a headache to get through. The plan is to drive to our hotel just outside of Cleveland. Hopefully arrive in time for dinner. Then the following day drive until we arrive to your Uncle Pete and Aunt Claire's house."

Boo asks, "Where do they live again?"

Will answers, "In Doylestown, Pennsylvania."

"Will Neil and Ellie be there when we arrive?"

"I talked to your Aunt Claire about your cousins, honey. Neil and Ellie should be home. They're looking forward to seeing you."

Will finishes the rest of his meal quickly. He tends to eat like a firefighter. Even when he's off duty he eats like the bell is going to go off. Soon after, the rest of the family clears the table and begins their chores. Will grabs the van keys from the hallway closet hook, gives Annie a kiss, and says, "I'll be back soon. Gonna fuel up the van. I already have the tools in the van. I'll save Liam a chore and drop off those tools and get some snacks for the road. Text me if you need anything else."

Annie smiles. "Will do. Love you, be careful."

"You know me. Always. Love you too."

CHAPTER 3

....

FAMILY FUN DAY. CHORES, CHORES, AND MORE CHORES

Will pulls away and out of the driveway as Liam waits patiently alongside the garage. Liam thinks, *Okay. So, Dad said that all I have to do is help with the yard, help Mom with Lady, and then I can finally have some time with my crew before I leave for a while.* He continues to gather his tools. *Lawn mower, check. Weed whacker, check. Blower, check. Extension cord, check. And a yard bag, check. Okay, got everything. Let's get this party started.* Liam tries to turn on the lawn mower with the pull string several times. The lawn mower doesn't start.

Great. Now the lawn mower won't start. If I can't get this damn thing working, I'll never get done. Wait...wait...stop and think. The fuel. I forgot to refill the fuel since last time. Liam walks to the back of his family's garage. He reaches up toward the top shelf where his father keeps all the different types of fuel. He reaches for the can and it's empty. *Great. Now we'll have to make time to get fuel at the gas station. But wait! Dad has a spare gallon gas can around here somewhere. Don't see it. Maybe it's in the storage locker in the other corner.*

Liam walks over to their other corner toward the storage locker. He opens the latch door. He sees the red gallon gas can and can see fluid being level toward the top of the container. *Yes, now I'm in business. Nothing is going to slow me dow—* He pauses in mid thought as he looks toward one of the top shelves in the

9

locker and finds the flashlight he had with him the night of the final confrontation with the beast. He thinks back to running through the cave with the beast hot on his trail. A chill goes down his spine. How terribly afraid he was. Not just for himself but for his little sister and for his friends as well. Liam can hear Mr. Rosalie's voice, "Keep going! Remember, just a few more yards until you enter the silver mines." He remembers begging Mr. Rosalie to stay with him. He remembers running toward the surface and the explosion behind him. His thoughts are again interrupted with the echo of a familiar voice. It was his next-door neighbor Tim.

"Hey, Liam. What's the haps, dude?! Liam…. Earth to Liam!" Tim tries to get Liam's attention while he walks toward his own garage.

Liam finally breaks away from his past, turns, and says, "Oh hi, Tim. How are you? Everything is good. Just helping Dad with the yard work." Liam begins to walk toward Tim.

Tim replies, "Sounds like a plan. You and the family are leaving for your trip soon, right? Your dad mentioned it to me. Wanted me to stop over every few days and pick up mail."

Liam answers, "Yeah, the plan is to leave tomorrow. You look like you're on your way to work. Teaching some summer classes?"

Tim answers, "Yup. Just for a couple more weeks though. Then I'm taking the rest of the summer off. Planning to head back to Michigan, visit the family, and do some fishing. I know that your family isn't going back to UP Michigan anytime soon."

Liam replies, "Yeah, the grandparents thought it was a good idea to just sell the place in the early spring. Too much history. A lot of good memories and some bad ones too."

"I hear you, dude. Seems like they made the right decision. That whole thing up there was a major story. People back in mainland Michigan near my folk's hometown were still talking about it when I visited around the holidays. Unreal, anyway man, I'm off to work. I hope your family has a fun, safe, and uneventful vacation, if you know what I mean. Just mention to your dad to leave me a key so I can drop off the mail."

"Sure thing. No problem, Tim."

Tim walks into his garage, fires up his motorcycle, and rolls down the street.

Within an hour, Liam completes his yard work. After doing more yard work with his dad over the previous summer, Liam got the yard work timing down to a science. Before he packs up from his chore, he admires his handiwork. He thinks, *Looks pretty good to me. Next step is to pack up this circus and help Mom with Lady.* Liam packs up all the tools and equipment and puts everything back into the garage. He runs into the house from the side entrance all pumped up a ready to get done with his next task. Liam yells down to the basement where he can see the shadow of his mom folding clothes, "Hey, Mom! I'm all done and ready to help with Lady!"

Annie answers as she peeks up the stairs, "No need to shout, kid. Your father is the one who's deaf due to all of those sirens in his ears. I can hear just fine. And don't you dare step further into this house with those grass-covered shoes. Take them off and leave them by the door. Boo just finished washing the surfaces. I just finished cleaning the floors and am currently between laundry loads. Plus, you're all sweaty, kid. Why don't you get a fresh set of clothes, throw that sweaty stuff into the laundry basket down here, and then we will head out."

Liam was used to his mother's very long-winded answers and orders. He did as his mom asked, and after some time, Liam and Boo were getting Lady ready to leave. Boo comes over to the side entrance and reaches for Lady's walking leash and says to Liam, "Dad just texted Mom. He'll be home in a couple of minutes. He just finished getting road-trip snacks, fueling up the van, and getting sidetracked with Mr. Krazel." Boo looks down at Lady and says, "Wow! Lady seems really nervous!" Lady, their wonderful and overall protective golden doodle, was never more than a room away from the family. She especially began to form a more special bond with Liam and Boo over the years. Boo would make time to play with her in the yard, and Liam would take her on walks and runs around Dunham Park.

Mom heads back upstairs from the basement and says to Liam and Boo, "Okay. I just put my loads of wash into the washer and dryer. Time to go and get this done."

Liam replies, "Doesn't Dad get upset when you leave the dryer on when no one's home?"

Mom answers, "Your father is just like Fire Marshal Bill from *In Living Color.*"

Boo looks puzzled and asks, "Who's Fire Marshal Bill?"

Mom rolls her eyes. "Never mind. It's well before your time. Back when TV was funny. But that's another story. Plus, I don't have anything to worry about since your father is on his way home. Let's head to Nana's house and drop off Lady."

With the arming of the security system, the closing of a door, and the turning of a lock, the family heads toward the car in the garage with Lady by their side. They are off to Nana's house.

CHAPTER 4

....

PLEASE TAKE THIS WITH YOU

"We are lucky it's the weekend, kids," Annie says as she drives down I-294 toward the southwest suburbs. She continues, "We are making good time. Looks like we will be arriving at Nana's house in about ten minutes." Annie gets into the far-right lane as she begins to exit I-294 and enters the I-55 ramp. Annie's parents own their home in Bolingbrook, Illinois. That's where Annie and her brothers were born and raised. Not too far from there is where Annie and Will met while attending college. They both worked at a movie theater together in Woodridge. Will was attending Benedictine University while Annie was attending Joliet Junior College. As Annie tells it, she tried to give Will not-so-subtle hints while they were working together, but Will was clueless. It took Annie a long time, but obviously it worked out in the end.

They turn down Annie's old street and begin to see her childhood home. The driveway was always a good gauge on who was home. They could tell Nana Tina was home. Grandpa Daniel wasn't home. They pulled up to the driveway where they saw Nana waiting for them at the front door. Boo took Lady's leash as she exited the car and said, "Come on, Lady. Let's go! Looks like Spartan is waiting for you." Spartan was waiting for Lady and the rest of the family at the front door as well. He's such a good watch dog—a large male German shepherd who had a bark of a lion but the heart of an adorable little puppy. Tina often jokes that she saves money every year by having Spartan and not having a home security system.

Tina opens the door with a smile and says, "Hey, everyone. Come on in. I'm baking some banana bread for you and the kids." Lady greets Tina and Spartan affectionately, and Tina says, "Hi, Lady! No banana bread for you. I learned since our last visit. Can't leave fresh bread on the counter unoccupied with you two around. Thick as thieves, you and Spartan. Go on now! You and Spartan head out to the backyard and play!" Spartan and Lady run side by side with each other toward the back door as Nana opens it.

Liam walks in with Annie and Boo, and they all take turns giving Tina a big hug. With a big smile Tina says, "Thank you for visiting me before your summer road trip. I'll miss both of you. Hope you have fun with your dad's family in Philly." Tina looks at Annie and asks, "You're leaving tomorrow, right?"

Annie answers, "That's the plan. Bright and early. Will wants to get past that horrible Indiana corridor before traffic gets bad."

Tina replies, "Now that's a good idea! Can't tell you how many times your father and I had nightmares on the stretch of road when we would take you on road trips."

The timer on the oven goes off and the wonderful aroma of banana bread fills the house with a sense of home. Tina hears the timer and says, "Now, who's up for some banana bread and milk?"

Boo answers, "I am! Can I have it with peanut butter and blueberry jam too?"

Tina laughs and replies, "You like to have my banana bread just like your father. Of course. In fact, I just canned some blueberry jam this week. It's in the back pantry. Second shelf to the right."

Boo runs off for the jam and peanut butter as Liam makes himself comfortable at the kitchen table waiting for Tina to serve him. At Annie's house, it was customary to help yourself, but Tina liked to take care of her grandchildren.

Boo runs back with her supply of goodies and takes a seat next to Liam, while Tina gathers plates and cups. Tina serves Liam and Boo and looks over to Annie who is restless and standing in the hallway entrance to the kitchen. Tina asks Annie, "Would you like some, dear?"

Annie answers, "No thanks. I'm good. Trying to stay away from the carbs, and I brought my own coffee so I'm good."

Tina rolls her eyes and says, "Why are you worried about carbs, dear? You were blessed with your father's metabolism, not mine. You can thank God for that one. That man can eat four hot dogs at every meal and wash it down with three cans of pop and never gain an ounce."

Annie replies, "True, but you know I'm always self-conscious of those things."

"Fine. More for me and your kids." Tina looks at Annie and back at Liam and Boo and says, "If you need anything else, kids, please help yourselves. I want to talk to your mom for a few minutes. Stay here please."

Tina gets up from the table and walks past Annie and over to the living room. Annie follows her. They both take seats next to each other on the coach and recliner. Tina begins the conversation and asks, "So you're heading to the East Coast for your summer vacation? It definitely feels different this year. How are you doing with everything that has happened?"

Annie replies, "Doing fine, I guess. Sure feels weird not going to the lake house this summer. We've been going up there for so many years." Annie pauses, drinks some of her coffee from her thermos, and continues, "I understand why you and Dad sold the property. So much happened up there. Before you left, did you find out more about the parties involved?"

Tina takes a deep breath and looks up at the ceiling. "Thank you for understanding. It broke my heart and more so your father's heart to sell the place, but we knew it was for the best. The town isn't the same, but it's in the process of healing. Took a while to sell the place given the newfound history of the area. Your father and I dropped the price three times before we finally found someone willing to purchase it. The next-door neighbors, Larry's family, decided to keep the place for their grandchildren. They close it during the winter months. Larry's wife lives with her daughter's family now and goes up to the lake with them in the summer. She doesn't feel safe up there alone. The Rosalie family paid to have a memorial built for Nick next to the public library. They are keeping the pizza place and antique shop open and running. And Bobby, God bless him, took the chief of police job."

Annie replies, "Wow! That's a big move for him. How did that come to be?"

"Well, after what happened with the old chief and the sergeant, some of the senior members took early retirement, and he was next in line for the job. They eventually hired some new officers."

Annie asks, "I heard from Dad that the old lady who lived down the road passed away. The one who gave Liam the silver cross. Is that true?"

"Mrs. Miller. Angela. Yes, that's certainly true. To my understanding, she passed away peacefully in her sleep one night. Her family sold the property to a young family that was looking to buy cheap and fix it up. House flipper types. They also paid for some type of name memorial at her church. I believe it's on a bench outside of the church. In loving memory type of deals."

Annie responds, "That's so lovely for her family to do that in her memory. She deserves it. Dad also said that there was a fire at the old mansion where you-know-who lived."

"Yes indeed. Not just a small fire. The entire mansion was burnt to the ground. You could feel the heat of the flames from the other side of the lake! Heck, someone told Dad that they could smell the smoke all the way east toward Crystal Falls. The fire started in the middle of the night. By the time anyone saw or smelled anything, the fire had engulfed most of the first floor. Since it was a volunteer fire department, it took a long time to finally get water on the fire. I heard that the Michigan State Police oversaw the arson investigation. They found one of those torch bottle cocktail things inside."

"Oh my God!" Annie exclaims. "Do the police know who started the fire?"

Tina answers, "Not a clue. Police questioned a few of the neighbors, but all of them were probably in bed when the fire started. I guess the town didn't feel justified. Rightfully so if you ask me. God help that town heal and recover. That reminds me, I have something for you."

Tina gets up from her recliner and walks upstairs. During that time, Boo and Liam finish their banana bread and begin to bring their empty plates and cups over to the sink. Tina walks back down with something small in her hand. Annie sees it glimmer and shine from the reflection of the sun from the front-door windows. It dangles back and forth from Tina's hand as she hands it over to Annie. Tina says, "We found this while we were packing everything up. Found it in between the sofa cushions. It's the silver cross and chain that Liam received from Mrs. Miller."

Annie is astonished at the finding. "Wow! Liam looked everywhere for this before we left the lake. He couldn't find it anywhere. Why are you giving this to me? Why not Liam?"

Tina smiles. "Figure it will be safer with you than Liam. He tends to be forgetful and lose things. Please take it with you. If anything, it provided protection for you and the family last time."

Annie smiles, acknowledges the appreciation of the gift, and puts it around her neck. "Thanks, Mom. It's in safekeeping, believe me. I promise it will be with us for the rest of the trip."

Tina feels rest assured, smiles, and gives her daughter a big hug. "You should be on your way. That way you can be home before traffic gets bad."

Boo and Liam enter the living room. Liam asks Tina and Annie, "So what are you two talking about?"

Annie answers, "Nothing much. Just catching up with things before we begin our trip. Time to leave, kids. Give Nana a hug and kiss and let the dogs in before we go." Annie pauses as she closely looks at Liam and continues, "Make sure you talk to your dog before we leave Liam."

Boo and Liam each take turns giving Tina a great big hug and kiss. Liam turns away from the living room and toward the back door to let the dogs back into the house. Liam exclaims to both dogs who are continuing to run and chase each other, "Lady! Spartan! Come on! Time to come in and time to leave!" They both run toward the back door and back into the house. Liam looks down at Lady, and before he says goodbye, Lady jumps into his arms and doesn't want to let go. She continues to whimper.

Boo walks over as well to say goodbye to Lady. "What's the matter with Lady? She seems really sad and anxious this time."

Liam replies, "Well, this is the first big trip we are taking without her."

"Yeah, but she seems really upset. Maybe she senses something?"

Liam replies, "Maybe, but you know how attached she is to all of us. Goodbye, Lady. We love you. I wish I can take you, but hotels don't allow dogs unless you have paperwork."

Annie walks over to both Boo and Liam. "Time to go, guys. That way you can get home for your friends, Liam."

Liam replies, "You're right. Time to go."

They all start to leave out the front door. Lady runs after them. Tina holds Lady back before she runs out the front door. Tina says, "Just go. She'll be fine after you leave. Plus, she has Spartan to keep her company. Enjoy your trip. Love you."

They make their way to the car as Lady watches from the front living room window. As they pull out of the driveway, Liam turns and waves to Lady and Tina. Annie looks through her rear-view mirror and grabs the silver cross with one hand and holds it tightly as they make their way back onto the highway.

CHAPTER 5

....

WE DIDN'T THINK WE SEE YOU

The family pulls up to their driveway and slowly backs into their garage. The day is moving fast; it is midafternoon already. As Annie backs up the car, they see Will talking to their next-door neighbor Tim. Once in the garage, they all exit the car, and Annie exclaims, "Hey, honey! Were you able to get everything done?"

Will looks at Tim, "You see, dude. This is why you're single. Girlfriends don't ask so many questions. Wives are always on your case." They both laugh.

Annie says, "You forgot that wives also hear and see everything. Heard everything you said."

Will rolls his eyes. "Yes, dear. I did all my chores. We are all set for the trip. Tim and I are planning to chill in his garage and have a cigar if you don't mind."

Annie rolls her eyes. "I suppose that's okay. This time I'll close all the windows before that horrible smell gets in the house."

Will looks at Boo and Liam and asks, "So how was your trip to Nana's house?"

Boo replies, "Good, Dad. I'm hungry. I'm going inside."

Liam replies, "She scarfed down a big piece of banana bread at Nana's, and yet she's still hungry. It was good, Dad. Got to and from Bolingbrook in pretty good time. Lady didn't like us leaving her. She didn't want to let go of me."

Will replies, "I'm sure. Still planning to meet up with your friends today?"

Liam answers, "Yup, that's the plan. The crew sent me a text on our way home from Nana's asking if they'll see me before I leave. They're at Dunham Park now. Haven't answered back yet. Mom said to check in with you before I give them an answer."

"Of course, buddy. Go see your friends. If you're planning to have dinner with them, just let us know. Be home before 9:00 p.m. Got an early start tomorrow."

"Thanks, Dad. Will do." Liam texts the crew on his phone: "On my way. Where am I heading?"

Ryan answers, "'Bout time you respond. We figured you got into trouble and your mom confiscated your phone. Grab your gear and meet us at the diamond next to the playground."

Robert responds to the thread. "Started to lose hope, man. Honestly, we didn't know if we would see you."

As quickly as he can, Liam grabs his backpack and his bike and heads over to Dunham Park. He couldn't wait to see his friends. You may recall Liam's group of friends. If not let's catch up.

Among these friends are Timmy, Tommy, Maddie, Robert and Ryan. Timmy and Tommy are a pair of brothers only separated in age by two years. Tommy is the same age as Liam. Both are excellent athletes. They play baseball together at their local park district. Maddie is the baby sister to Timmy and Tommy. Even though she is a couple years younger than Timmy, she always wants to do whatever her older brothers are doing. She is kind, sociable, and always involved in her Girl Scout Troop. Robert is also the same age as Liam. Not as athletic as the other lads. More of the nerd of the group but always fun and a great sense of humor. He is often the prankster of the group, especially toward Timmy and Maddie who are always an easy target. Robert loves his comics and the classic monster movies, mostly the ones that would air on a local show called *Svengoolie*, which of course he would DVR every week.

Both Robert and Liam are involved in a local Cub Scout Troop and hold the same rank of Bear. Robert is always down to play video games with everyone, and on occasion his friends would return the favor by playing some of Robert's strategy card games. Lastly, there is Ryan. The big kid in the group. He is the same age as Tommy, Robert, and Liam. They often joke that Ryan is a descendant of Viking bloodline. You may recall that Ryan and Robert were along with Liam and Boo during their thrilling adventure in UP Michigan last summer. They were both doing well and recovered much faster than Liam and Boo. Ryan is still heavily involved in sports, and Robert still loves his horror movies and comic books. Robert started working with Timmy and Tommy, who are both excellent artists. They are developing a graphic novel based on the adventures of last summer with Robert writing the storyline and most of the dialogue. Timmy and Tommy work on the illustrations and page layout.

Liam rides his bike down Giddings Street and sees his crew well into a baseball game. It is a typical summer scene. The summer sun hangs halfway to the west, breaking in and out between partly cloudy skies. The air is warm but pleasant with a slight cool breeze out from the west. The air smells of fresh-cut grass, as the local park district has just finished cutting the baseball fields. Ryan is up to the plate. Tommy is pitching. Timmy is playing first base. Maddie is in right field, and Robert is in left field. As Liam arrives, he hears Ryan shout out to Robert saying, "Hey, dude! With me being a righty and you playing left field, this isn't going to work out well for you!"

Robert exclaims, "Shut up, dude! I'll be fine!"

Ryan replies, "I'm not too sure of that, bro! You know that Maddie can field a ball better than you can! Why don't you switch places with her!"

Liam rides his bike around home plate and along the third-base line. Ryan shouts out, "Time! The man of the hour finally decided to show up!" Ryan looks at Liam and continues jokingly, "Did you do all of your chores for Mommy and Daddy like a good little boy?"

Liam answers, "I agree with Robert. Shut up, bro. A lot of talk. Let's see if you can actually hit the ball. Last time I checked you were having problems hitting Tommy's curve ball."

Ryan replies, "Okay, smartass, why don't you go out to center field and help your boy-wonder out there and field this ball I'm going to hit into deep left center field."

Liam grabs his mitt and says to Ryan, "Okay, let's see if the big man can call his shot. It's been like a hundred years since a fat guy called his shot and made it come true."

Liam runs out to center field as he hears Ryan say, "First of all, no one insults a Viking and gets away with it. Second, this isn't fat. I'm just a larger and stronger man than anyone of you!"

Tommy asks Ryan, "Are you done running your mouth, dude? I would like to throw the ball before my hands develop arthritis!"

Ryan replies, "Yeah, yeah all right then. Let's see what you got, Tommy."

Liams runs out to center field and says hi to everyone along the way.

Robert says, "Hey, Liam! How you been, man? Ready for your trip tomorrow?"

Liam replies, "As ready as I'll ever be. Gonna miss you guys. How's that graphic novel going with Timmy and Tommy?"

Robert replies, "So far so good. Are you interested in taking a look at it?"

"Not particularly. I would like to keep that stuff in the past and out of the memory bank as much as possible, if you don't mind."

Robert replies, "Understandable. Okay let's see if Ryan is a man of his word."

Tommy reaches back and throws his curve ball right down into Ryan's strike zone. Ryan licks his lips, steps forward with his left foot, and swings with full force. Ryan looks forward and waits to see the baseball launch into left center field. He doesn't feel the contact of the ball and hears the baseball bounce off the back cage. Tommy shouts, "Strike 1!"

Ryan picks up the ball, throws it back to Tommy, and says, "Okay. Nice pitch. I got two more chances to get it right. Let's see what you got."

They both get ready. Tommy looks at everyone, steps into his stance, and gets ready in his windup. He reaches back and throws the pitch. Right into the strike zone and a perfect inside corner curve ball. Ryan tries to hit it with a huge lumberjack swing. He misses yet again. Tommy shouts out, "Strike 2!"

Ryan picks up the ball again, throws it back to Tommy, and says, "Getting better, I see. This guy thinks he's the next closer like Liam Hendrix. Okay, Tommy, let's see if you can do it for a third time."

They both get into their stance. Ryan tightens his grip on the bat. Tommy gets his fingers in the proper place and winds up. The pitch is another curve ball, still in the strike zone, heading toward the high outside corner. Ryan takes his swing and *BAAM!* He hits the ball straight out to left center field. Liam starts running back to catch up to the ball, but it is too late. The ball goes well over Liam's head and drops another fifty feet away from him. Liam sees the ball and sprints toward it. Robert gets ready to be Liam's cut-off man. Liam picks up the ball, and he sees Ryan running from second to third base. Liam throws the ball to Robert. Ryan runs past third base and heads toward home. Robert winds up his throw and launches it to Tommy who is now waiting at home plate for the throw. The pitch is way offline and lands in between first base and home plate. Ryan slides into home plate and jumps up with a cheer. "Who's the man! Who's the man! Yes, ladies and gentlemen, the man, the myth, and the legend has called his shot, and the crowd goes wild!" Ryan shouts at his friends.

Robert runs back to left field while Liam takes a decent position in center field. Robert looks at Liam and asks, "So how long will you be gone, buddy?"

Liam answers, "About two weeks. Gonna go visit my aunt and uncle and the rest of the family from my dad's side. Honestly, it's the first trip out there since I was really little. My dad was born and raised in Philly. Some of his side of the family still live out there."

Robert replies, "Your grandpa was a firefighter out there, right?"

"Yup. That's right. After he retired from the fire department, they moved to Chicago so my grandmom can be with her side of the family."

After a few rounds of each of them taking turns at the plate, Ryan shouts out, "Hey, anyone hungry?"

Robert replies, "We know you're always hungry, fat boy!"

Ryan exclaims, "Shut up, wimp! Again, my weight gives me strength as you recently witnessed. So how 'bout it?"

Robert replies, "Sure, I'm down, but my dad is busy this evening so no yummy pizza at my house. Leftovers tonight."

Timmy asks, "Doesn't your mom know the recipe?"

Robert replies, "Nope. Sorry. My dad has a secret recipe and makes the dough from scratch. Plus, you know my mom is a shit cook. We only eat leftovers or takeout when Dad is at work."

Tommy says, "How 'bout we go over to that barbeque place off Gunnison? They always give discounts for the local baseball players."

Maddie replies, "Yeah that's a good idea. I think they will even give us a bigger discount since we all play at Dunham Park. Liam, what do you think?"

Liam replies, "Sounds great. Don't have to be home for a while, plus it's our last night out until I come back. Let's do it!"

CHAPTER 6

....

ON THE ROAD AGAIN

They pack up their gear, mount their bikes, and head down Giddings Street. As the group of friends approaches Austin Avenue, they head north a couple of blocks until they reach their destination. They all park their bikes along the sidewalk and walk inside. Ryan looks around and says, "Thank God. Only a couple of people in line. I'm starving!"

Robert exclaims, "Yeah and you look it too!"

Ryan says, "Shut up or next time I won't help you out when you're being chased by some cursed beast."

Robert takes a big gulp and says, "Sorry, you're right. Well played."

Ryan is the first to order. "I'll have the slow-cooked beef brisket burrito with North Carolina sauce, fries with cheese, and coleslaw." Ryan looks back at Robert and says, "Don't say a word, bro. I told you I'm hungry. Don't judge me."

Robert says, "Consider it done, dude."

Ryan turns and looks at the owner of the restaurant who's working at the front counter. The owner is a middle-aged gentleman named Mitch. Polish descent. He is of average height and skinny with dark-blond hair. Mitch looks at the group of friends and says, "Well, if it isn't my favorite group from Dunham Park. How you kids doing?"

Ryan says, "Fine, Mitch. We are all starving. Gonna give us that discount?"

Mitch rolls his eyes and smiles. "Do you even have to ask? Of course."

They each take a turn, order their food, and sit down to enjoy their dinner.

Robert looks at Liam and says, "You okay, bro? You look a little down."

Liam takes a break from his delicious meal and replies, "Yeah, I'm good. Feel like I'm going to miss you guys is all."

Tommy who is sitting next to Liam gives him a hug and says, "Aww isn't that just so sweet. Thanks, buddy."

Ryan replies with a mouth full of food, "Thanks, man. But you'll only be gone for like two weeks, right?"

Liam answers, "That's about right. At least we finished the baseball season with the park before we left."

Tommy says, "Dude, you know your dad wouldn't take you out of the season to go on a trip. He's cool enough to try to plan his vacation around your sports schedule."

Liam replies, "This is true. He's pretty awesome that way."

Maddie asks, "Did your folks say what you're going to be doing out there?"

Liam answers, "Yeah, they want to do some of the touristy stuff. Independence Hall, Betsy Ross House, Liberty Bell, Penn's Landing, that type of stuff."

Ryan interjects, "And cheesesteaks, right?"

The group laughs.

Liam answers, "Of course, and hoagies and soft pretzels. You know, the local cuisine. My folks said we're planning to help my aunt Claire with some preservation project she's working on."

Timmy asks, "What kind of project?"

"I still don't know all the details. It's some old mansion where my grandmom worked when my dad was a kid. Place is supposed to be impressive. Been left abandoned for several years now."

Ryan looks at Robert who is sitting next to him. "Sounds a bit spooky. You're sure you don't want us to come along and protect you?"

They all laugh.

Liam says, "Not a bad idea. I would love for you guys to come, but after last summer, I don't think your parents will be too keen on taking a trip with us."

They finish their meals, say their goodbyes, and get ready to head their separate ways. Tommy, Timmy, and Maddie all start riding down Austin Avenue toward home. Ryan and Robert are the last to say goodbye to Liam. Robert says, "Have fun, buddy. See you in a couple of weeks."

Liam replies, "Thanks, dude."

Ryan asks, "Do you want us to ride with you back home?"

Liam answers, "Nah, I should be good. At least home has streetlights and people around. Unlike UP Michigan."

Robert exclaims, "Yeah and there's no moon tonight either so you should be fine." Liam and Ryan both laugh, and Robert continues, "Sorry, had to do it." They all say their goodbyes and head for home.

The next morning, it's bustling early. Liam wakes up to the sounds of his dad carrying the luggage down the stairs. Liam gets out of bed and asks his dad if he needs help with anything. Will responds, "Yeah sure, kid. There're still a few bags in my room if you can bring them down. And I think your mom might need help packing lunches."

Boo arises from her slumber. She enters the upstairs hallway and says, "What's going on around here?"

Will answers, "Glad you're awake, honey. Try to help your brother with the bags please."

Boo responds, "Dad it's like six in the morning. I didn't even know what the world looks like at this hour of the day. Now you want me to do work?"

Will laughs. "Welcome to the working world, kid. I'm usually leaving for work around this time. Now, if you would please." Will walks off with the luggage and toward the rear entrance of house.

Boo turns to Liam and says, "Have fun with that, older brother. Your sister won't lift a finger around here until I have my shower, pick out my clothes, and try to wake up for a little bit." She enters the bathroom next to Liam and slams the door shut.

Within no time, Will has the van all packed up. Annie has lunches packed as well. Annie and Will are old pros to getting on the road quickly. They have taken so many trips up to Michigan over the years that leaving for a road trip was almost routine. Boo and Liam step into the middle row of the van. The back seats are taken down, and the back is filled with luggage. In between the front seats and the middle seats are their sleepover bags for the hotel and a cooler filled with snacks and lunches. Annie is next to enter the van complete with her headphones and a large travel cup of coffee. Will is the last to leave the house after taking several minutes to do another safety check from top to bottom.

As Will enters the van, Annie asks, "Are you happy with the twelve-point safety check of the entire house, dear?"

Will rolls his eyes as he sits down in the driver's seat. "You know me too well, honey. Been to too many calls with my job when families didn't check the house before leaving. Don't want to worry about it while we are gone."

Annie replies, "Okay. Just checking. Do you need me to be your navigator?"

Will starts up the van, drives out of the driveway, and heads north toward the highway. Will replies, "That's probably not a bad idea. Just tell me which way would be faster to hit I-80 from here. And then I should be fine."

Annie takes a moment to look at the possible travel routes on her phone. Will continues to approach the highway. "I need an answer soon, hon. Am I going through the city or around it?"

Annie answers, "Stand by. I'm still checking. Got it. Looks like we are heading into the city, hon. The map says the quickest route is the Dan Ryan through the city, take the Skyway toward Indiana and out to I-80."

"Got it. Sounds good. Same route that we take to go to Notre Dame."

It's a beautiful summer day to be traveling. Crystal clear blue skies, no clouds, low humidity, and a misty breeze that feels like it came off the lake. Will enters the highway and puts on his classic rock channel on the radio. It begins to feel like the road trip has officially begun. They drive past one of the overpasses that displays the travel time. Will says, "Looks like Mom is right, guys. Only fourteen minutes to downtown." They make a few turns along the stretch of the highway. Very little traffic. Eventually the city comes into full view. Downtown looks beautiful with the morning sun reflecting off the many downtown high-rises. They pass through Hubbard Street Cave as downtown passes by on their left. They make their way past the stadium where the White Sox play.

They eventually make their way to I-80 via the Chicago Skyway and head east toward Notre Dame. The traffic is moderate with construction as per usual but not bad considering previous experiences. When they begin to pass by South Bend, Liam sees the golden dome of Notre Dame from outside his window. "Hey, Dad, are we still planning to meet up with the uncles and cousins to the football game in the fall?"

Will turns down the radio to answer Liam. "That's the plan, kid. They like to go to a game in late September or early October. Before the weather gets too cold. I think we are going to the Notre Dame vs. Navy game."

Boo takes a break from her reading and joins in the conversation. "What's the plan for today, Dad? When are we stopping?"

Will answers, "The plan is to drive as long as we can till lunch. Eat while we are on the road. Mom and I will change drivers and eventually stop for the night just outside Cleveland."

Liam replies, "Any chance that the Guardians are playing tonight, and we can go?"

Will laughs. "It's like you can read my mind, kid. I already checked. They are playing the Tigers in Detroit tonight. Away game. Would have been a good idea. Mom doesn't have any interest. It would have been just us while Mom stays back at the hotel."

Boo asks, "So if the Guardians are out, what's the plan for tonight?"

Will answers, "Just take it easy, kid. The plan is to have dinner out. You guys pick the place. And then you can go to the hotel pool for a while tonight if you'd like."

They make their way without incident to the hotel for the night. Annie puts the van into park, exits the van, and gets a big stretch. She exclaims, "Not too bad, honey. Made pretty good time."

"Not bad at all, hon. It makes a huge difference if we get through that Indiana/Illinois border stretch of I-80 without it getting backed up. Easy drive really." Will asks both Liam and Boo, "Okay, kids. After we get checked in, we can go out for dinner. Where would you like to go?"

Liam looks at Boo since she has better ideas. Boo answers, "I'm in the mood for nachos and burritos tonight."

Will replies, "Perfect, there's a Chipotle right down the street from here."

Boo asks, "Wow, how did you know that?"

Annie answers with a smile, "Because your father knows all, honey."

Will laughs. "Somewhat true. But your mom and I took a few road trips out to visit Uncle Pete and Aunt Claire before you were born. That's where we would eat. Keep it simple."

They check into the hotel, go out to eat, and enjoy a relaxing evening at the hotel pool. Everything has seemed perfect on this road trip up to this point.

CHAPTER 7

....

FOLLOW THE SIGNS

The twilight of the evening at the hotel seems normal and very comfortable for most. Everyone is in bed and asleep for the night. Boo has the queen-sized bed next to her parents. Liam is of the age now that sleeping in the same bed as his sister just seems a bit too weird for him. So, he decides to sleep on the sofa bed. Annie is fast asleep and doesn't move a muscle. Will is asleep but restless as he tosses and turns. He is having another dream.

He finds himself back in the old mansion. He is outside the doors where the old chapel used to be located. The doors are now closed. Will tries to open the doors, but they're locked. He knocks on the door and exclaims, "Hello! Anyone there? Dad? Stan?" He hears someone walk down the tiled hallway behind him. The footsteps are loud and moving quickly down the hallway. He quickly turns around only to see the shadow of a figure moving. He tries to move quickly down the circular staircase, but every step seems slow and a struggle. He finally makes his way down the stairs and out into the hallway. Will looks down the hallway and only sees a glimpse of the figure from behind as it passes by a mirror. The figure looks familiar and haunting—tall, thin, and wearing an old gardening hat. Feeling scared and cautious, Will doesn't shout out anymore.

He slowly makes his way down the hallway as the figure drifts out of view. He makes a left turn and notices the old elevator that looks like it's still in operation. He looks down at the buttons. The downward button is illuminated, and the elevator dial shows that it's on its way down from the upper floor. He begins to hear creepy echoes and voices coming from the elevator as it descends toward his floor. He is frightened and moves farther down the hallway that leads to the billiard room. The room has old-fashioned wood paneling from floor to ceiling. There's a fireplace illuminated with a small fire in the far corner surrounded by tall chairs, a large coffee table, and footrests. There's a billiard table in the middle of the room and large paintings of tall ships at sea scattered on the walls throughout the living space. No one is in the room. The elevator dings as it approaches the floor, and the door begins to open. Will tries to move quickly and sees another large hallway that stretches over 100 feet or more. Will thinks, *I remember this place. These were the rooms my mom would clean after the weekend retreats.* He walks down the hall. All the doors are closed. The lights flicker on and off. He begins to hear those same creepy echoes coming from the billiard room. He turns to look back at the billiard room. A great shadow fills the room, and a giant wind blows through the corridor. The fire goes out immediately in the fireplace. The shadow removes all light from the room, and all that's left is pure darkness. He can hear the wind sweep through the corridor but still can't feel it. He begins to hear those familiar eerie echoes again as they seem to move farther down the corridor toward him.

Will moves as quickly as he can toward the exit at the far end. He notices one door open as he passes it. Will peeks inside the room and sees a man lying in bed. But he can't see his face. Will moves further into the room and hears a heart monitor. He looks at the man in the bed. It's his father! Will looks at the heart monitor. He hears the heart rate, but the telemetry reading on the monitor is flatlined. Will's dad turns to him, smiles, and lifts his hand toward his son. Will moves to his father, and the entry door slams shut! Will, being both frightened and astonished, grabs his father's hand and asks, "Dad! What the hell is going on? What's out there? Why are we here?" His dad grips his hand firmly and says, "I still have that strong grip, son. I'll never let go. You remember how strong my grip was the day before I died. I'm here now. Listen for it and follow the signs." Will gasps and exclaims, "Listen for what, Dad? What's going on he—?" Just then, he feels a cold chill go down his spine as he stops mid-sentence. Someone is behind him! Will turns quickly and sees The Shadow Man standing right in front of him. He can only see the outline of him. The man is the figure of darkness and a complete void of light. The figure laughs, beams his radiant green eyes at Will, and says, "Welcome home, Will!"

Will wakes up with a gasp and a startle. So much so that he wakes up his wife.

Annie startles. "What's the matter, honey? Another dream?"

Still catching his breath and in a cold sweat, Will says, "That man. He seems so familiar. What did Dad mean? Listen for what?"

Annie feels worried for her husband and tries to reassure him. "Honey, calm down. Try to be quiet or you'll wake up the kids. It was just a dream. Was it back at that place again?"

"Yes. But it was in a different part of the building that I haven't thought about in a long time. Dad was there. He looks like he did the last day he was alive. Honey, it was horrifying."

Annie replies, "It's okay, honey. Try to relax. I'm right here. If anything, I'll take over more driving tomorrow if you want."

After a few minutes, Will calms down and relaxes his mind. "Thanks, honey. I will try to get more sleep if I can. Good night."

CHAPTER 8

....

WE'RE HERE!

L iam wakes up from a relaxing night's sleep to his parents getting the bags ready to hit the road again. Boo wakes up too.

Annie asks, "Morning, guys. How did you sleep?"

Liam answers, "Slept better here than at home."

Boo answers, "Me too. Maybe it's the swimming last night that helped us sleep better."

Annie says, "I think so. Both of you were splashing around and swimming for over an hour last night. Glad everyone got a good night sleep."

Will replies, "At least most of us."

They make their way down to the lobby to pack up the car and have the hotel breakfast before hitting the road. Liam swore that his father's favorite part of the road trip wasn't the traveling. It was waking up to a full-course breakfast complete with eggs, bacon, sausage, biscuits and gravy.

As they were enjoying their breakfast, Dad looks at his watch and says, "Finish up soon, guys. We should have hit the road by now. The goal is to reach Uncle Pete and Aunt Claire's house in Doylestown before dinner." Will sips on his coffee and continues, "I'm looking forward to it. Being 'home' and all. Haven't been back on the East Coast in several years."

Boo asks, "Why haven't we visited sooner, Dad?"

"It's been difficult to find time to go, honey. Daddy would use most of his vacation time up at the lake house and road trips out west to visit your grandparents out in Colorado."

They finish up their breakfast and hit the road, back onto I-80 east toward Pennsylvania. The weather for day two of their travels is a bit gloomy. Overnight, the clear skies made their way out of the area, and dark clouds and rain stretch as far as the eye can see. As they drive, Will asks Annie, "Honey, can you look up a weather radar and see how long this rain is supposed to last?"

Annie takes a break from her audiobook, looks up the radar, shakes her head, and says, "Do you want the good news or the bad news?"

Will answers, "Good news first."

"Okay so the rain should stop by the time we reach Doylestown. The bad news, this rain will continue for the rest of the way."

Will replies, "Great. Nothing like riding along the Pennsylvania Turnpike in the rain."

Annie asks, "I'm somewhat familiar with the route. Do you want me to drive?"

"That sounds fine, honey. I'll drive until we get past Pittsburgh, and you can take over from there."

The family make their way slowly toward Doylestown. The mixture of the rain and blocked stretches of I-80 under construction made for a lot of stop-and-go traffic. They make their way through Pennsylvania, past Pittsburgh, and toward Penn State University. Looking tired from driving, Will looks at Annie and says, "Hey, honey. Let's plan to do lunch near Penn State, fuel up, and switch drivers."

Annie says, "Sounds good to me. That's the best place to stop around these parts."

Boo looks puzzled and asks, "Why is it such a good place to stop, Mom?"

"Look around, sweetheart. Most of Pennsylvania is nothing but mountains, forests, winding roads, and farms. And more importantly, not a decent bathroom or restaurant for hundreds of miles."

Liam takes a break from his game and looks out the window at the acres of mountainous forests. "Looks like Mom is right."

Annie nods her head. "Believe me when I tell you that the valley around Penn State is the best place to stop for clean bathrooms and restaurants between here and Doylestown. We learned that the hard way before you kids were born."

Will laughs. "Very true, honey. Very true."

After the family makes their stop near Penn State for lunch and fuel, Annie takes over as the driver. Before she starts the van, she looks at the radar and the cloudy skies as they begin to depart. She says, "Good news for my driving shift. Looks like the storms have moved up to the north so it should be a smooth ride from here. Next stop, Doylestown."

They make their way ever so closer to Doylestown. Annie asks Will who was starting to fall asleep, "Honey…honey…honey!"

Will wakes up startled. "What is it, honey? Have we made it there yet?"

"No. Not yet but we are heading toward civilization again, and it's been a while since I took these Pennsylvania highways. Need a little bit of help."

Will answers, "Okay no problem. Let me get my bearings here." Will looks at his phone to pinpoint their location and tells Annie, "Okay. Got it. Looks like the best way is to take I-80 east until we get to I-476 and head south. We will go past Allentown and head toward Norristown."

Annie replies, "That's where they have all of that shopping around there."

"Yup. That's right, dear. The King of Prussia Mall and Plymouth Meeting Mall are right around there."

Annie says in a proud voice, "See, I know my way around."

"Yeah, you know your way around any mall when it comes to shopping."

"What was that, honey?"

Will answers, "Nothing, honey. Never mind. From there we can take the Turnpike to either take the 202 or Route 611."

"Which road has that water ice stand? Thinking maybe a nice treat for the kids would be nice."

"That will be Route 611. Thinking Rita's Water Ice?"

Annie says, "Yup. Didn't much care for those soft pretzel shops that you rave about, but I do like the water ice stands."

Boo hears the mentioning of a treat and enters the conversation asking, "What is water ice, Daddy?"

Will laughs. "It's basically the same thing as Italian ice, honey. You know how Daddy will bring home Italian ice from the stand in Little Italy, right?"

Boo answers, "Yeah, I remember. I like the lime, and Liam likes blueberry."

Will replies, "Well it's basically the same thing. It's a local treat. They have water ice and custard."

The family make their way toward Willow Grove, Pennsylvania. Will points out the old Willow Grove Naval Air Base as they pass it on Route 611. "You see that military base, kids?"

Liam looks out the window as Boo replies, "Yeah, Dad. What about it?"

Will answers, "That's where your Papa (Will's dad) did his reserve time in the military."

As Liam looks out the window he says, "That's cool. Wasn't Papa in like three different branches of the military?"

Will replies, "He sure was, kid. He went into the navy right out of high school. That's how he met Grandmom. Went to Vietnam when Grandmom was pregnant with Aunt Lindsey. He later did the rest of his reserve time right here with the Marine Reserve and the Air Force Reserve. The water ice stand is just a few minutes up the road from here."

They reach the water ice stand and have a nice treat before they head to Claire's house. Boo has the lime, and Liam tries the blueberry. Annie has vanilla custard, and Will has chocolate. As Will tastes his chocolate custard, a smile comes over his face. "God this brings back memories. A little taste of home for sure. We would stop by the water ice stand near our house after baseball games. Aunt Claire worked there." Will receives a text from Pete that says: "Hope your travels have been well. I'm home from work early. Claire will be home by dinner. Neil and Ellie are on their way home. See you soon."

Will looks up from his phone and says, "Okay. Finish up, everyone. Got about twenty more minutes to go before we reach our destination."

Will decides he will drive the rest of the way. They all hop back into the van and make their way up Route 611 toward Doylestown. They eventually see the sign for Doylestown and make their way through their downtown area. The downtown area is a quaint little town filled with colonial-type storefronts and buildings. They drive past an old library, coffee houses, a movie theater, a couple of pizza places, and cheesesteak stands. As Liam looks out the window he asks, "Hey, Dad, will we have some free time to explore their downtown area?"

Will replies, "Sure thing, kid. According to Uncle Pete, Ellie spends a lot of time down here with her friends. She'll be happy to give you a full tour. She doesn't have her driver's license yet, but Neil does. If anything, there is a bike trail from Aunt Claire's house that takes you right to Downtown Doylestown."

From the downtown area they make their way down some narrow and curvy two-lane tree-covered roads until they reach their street. Annie looks out her window as Will starts to pull into their driveway. "There it is kids. This is the place."

Pete and Claire live in an older colonial house that sits on a couple of acres of land. The home has a classic historical look to it but also a sense of modern décor and a well-maintained landscape. They all exit the van. Will says, "So, kids, what do you think?"

Boo says, "It's looks cool, Dad. Where am I sleeping anyway?"

Will answers, "You'll be sleeping in Ellie's room. She's got a bunk bed, and Liam will be in Neil's room I think."

They approach the front door as Pete begins to open it. Pete and Claire are both older than Annie and Will by at least ten years. Pete works in the insurance business. He always seems well put together. Liam couldn't recall if he had ever seen his Uncle Pete with anything less than a golf shirt and khaki shorts. Pete walks outside, gives Will a big hug, and says, "Welcome home, brother! Good to see you." He then turns to Annie and gives her a hug as well. "Hey, Annie. Good to see you, sis. It's been too long." He turns to Boo and Liam and says, "This can't be Liam and Boo! The Liam and Boo I knew were about a foot shorter than you two."

With a big smile, Boo says, "Hi, Uncle Pete!" She gives him a big hug and asks, "Are Ellie and Neil home yet?"

Just then, there's a honk of a horn, and a beautiful older cherry-red mustang convertible pulls up in the driveway. Neil is at the wheel, and Ellie is riding in the passenger seat. Everyone looks in their direction. Will asks Pete, "You actually let my nephew run around in your first love?"

Pete laughs. "As long as he takes care of it and doesn't do anything stupid, I don't mind. I've been working all the time and using the company car. The pony needs a good ride occasionally."

Neil and Ellie exit the car and walk toward the group. Neil is seventeen years old and just about to enter his senior year of high school. He's the athletic type. He plays lacrosse and soccer and works hard to keep up with his excellent grades. He's tall like Will and has long hair, which is the style with most of the boys his age. His plan is to get accepted into a premiere engineering program for college.

Ellie is carrying her helmet and a skateboard. She's short like Claire with long jet-black hair, which used to be brunette before she started to dye it. She's wearing a David Bowie T-shirt, black baggy pants with a long chain going from a belt loop back into her pocket, and big aviator sunglasses. She is a fair student, but her passion isn't in her grades. Her passion is playing in the high school band, skateboarding, and art.

Liam and Boo each take turns saying hello and giving hugs to their cousins. Will and Annie each give them a hug. Will says, "Good to see you, kids. It's been a while. I like the look, Ellie."

Ellie smiles. "Thanks."

Pete walks over to his mustang and inspects it for any marks or scratches as Neil rolls his eyes. Neil exclaims, "The car is fine, Dad."

Pete replies, "Just checking, son. All fueled up."

Neil replies, "Yeah. If you want to stop worrying about your car, you can always buy me another car."

Pete replies, "We can talk about that when you get a job, son. Plus, all our extra money is going toward your college fund right now. You're welcome, by the way." Pete looks at Ellie and asks, "How was your day, honey? Did you have fun with your friends at the skate park?"

Ellie answers, "Yeah, Dad. It was cool. Band practice went well, and then Simon and I went to the skate park."

Pete answers, "That's good. Well, drop your stuff off into the house and help the family unpack the car. When your mom gets home from work, we are going out to dinner."

Neil grabs a few bags from the back seat of the van. "Where are we eating?"

Pete answers, "That pub house we like in Downtown Doylestown. Mom wants us to have a good meal tonight. Tomorrow, it looks like you're going to help her with the Elk's Estate."

CHAPTER 9

....

WE SHOULDN'T GO IN THERE

It is a warm summer evening in Downtown Doylestown. The streets are alive and crowded with locals enjoying the festivities. The family enjoys their meal at the Doylestown Pub and later goes to the ice cream shop across the street from Ellie's favorite record store. That same evening down Route 611 in Elkins Park, two friends make their way toward the front gate of Elk's Estate. The iron gates are closed with a chain and lock in the middle. A metal sign is attached to each gate stating, "NO TRESSPASSING. AREA IS CONDEMED." Reggie takes out his flashlight, looks at the sign, and scans the front driveway. Nothing out of the ordinary. He hears the wind blow through the trees and the sound of an owl nearby. He shines his light further into the property and sees the lifeless old mansion. Reggie looks over at Jerald and says, "Dude. Maybe this isn't such a good idea. Maybe it's best to just go home."

Jerald, getting a set of bolt cutters out of his backpack looks at Reggie and says, "Dude, don't chicken out, bro. We all heard the rumors of the main house. We're not going in there. The mission is the coach house."

Reggie shines his light over to the coach house and says, "That's a coach house? That thing is bigger than most of the houses in the neighborhood. Man, these people must have been filthy rich."

Jerald walks over to the gate with the bolt cutters and says, "Yup, that family sure was loaded. Some old money from back in Europe or something. They've been dead for years. Now help me. Shine your light on the chain."

Reggie does what Jerald asks. Jerald tries his best to cut the chain, but it's no use. The chains are too thick, and his bolt cutters are too small. Reggie asks Jerald, "What's the problem? Can't you break it?"

Jerald struggles, gets frustrated, and says, "It's not cutting dude. Damn it! Maybe we can squeeze through the chains. That's if you can suck in that gut of yours."

Reggie exclaims, "It's not my fault. My mom says I have a slow metabolism."

Jerald replies, "That's bullshit and you know it. Eating that football-sized burrito tonight didn't help your metabolism either."

Reggie says, "You ate one too. Jerald."

"Good point, but I'm not the one with a shitty metabolism either. Let's try to get in."

Reggie and Jerald take turns helping each other slide in between the gates. Jerald makes it through without any trouble. Reggie gets through but it's a process. Eventually he fits his way through, and they begin to walk down the main driveway. The wind continues to blow, and the owl is heard in the distance. Through the wind, Reggie thinks he hears someone's echoing voice. Startled, he screams out and moves closely to Jerald. He exclaims, "What the hell was that? Jerald, I heard someone I swear. Screw this, man! Let's get out of here!"

Jerald grabs Reggie by the arm as Reggie starts to move back toward the main gate. Jerald says, "Reggie, just chill, man. I didn't hear anything. It's the wind and your mind playing tricks on you."

Reggie takes a deep breath, calms down, and says, "Okay. Okay. I'm cool. It's cool. Jerald, answer me a question. Why do I listen to you?"

Jerald smiles and answers, "Because I've known you since we were little, and I'm older by a year."

Reggie replies, "I forgot, you're a big mean sophomore at school now. I'm just a lowly freshman."

Jerald exclaims, "That's right! And don't you forget it. Now that's our mission right there."

Jerald points to the main door of the coach house. Reggie shines his light at the main door and says, "It looks like it's open! How did you know?"

Jerald answers, "That charity group was here a couple of days ago. I got a good view of the place from my front window back home.

It looked like someone forgot to close it up. Figure there might be something in there worth selling on eBay. These old rich folks must have had lots of shiny expensive things all over this place."

Reggie agrees as Jerald continues, "We go in. Check it out. Hopefully find something and we are back home in no time. Come on!"

They both make their way to the coach house. Reggie shines his flashlight down to the ground as he feels something solid. He notices several flat stones on the grass with numbers on them. He thinks, *This place is so weird* as he continues to walk along the path. The house is completely dark, and plywood boards have replaced most of the windows. The night is illuminated by the light coming from the moon and Reggie's flashlight. A slight fog coming from the small pond on the edge of the property sweeps over the house. The wind continues to blow even harder than before. Reggie says, "This place is full of all things creepy." They walk up the front stairs of the coach house, which leads to a long outdoor porch. The wood planks holding the porch together are old and weathered. With each step there's a loud creek and echoing cracks in the base of the wood. Jerald inspects the front door. It's an old-fashioned double door with stained-glass windows. The door to the right is halfway open. The door to the left is shut tight. Jerald opens the door fully and begins to walk into the house.

Reggie shines his light up and down the porch. He hears another echo of someone's voice. It sounds closer now! He quickly shines the light to the other side of the porch and sees someone vanish around the corner! Reggie freaks out. "That's it! I'm done! Time to go home and play video games. I've had enough fun for one night!"

Jerald runs out of the front door and grabs Reggie by the shoulder as Reggie begins to make his way down the stairs. Jerald exclaims, "Reggie! Dude! Chill, man. What did you see?"

Reggie answers with a slight stammer, "Ther-ther-there is someone that van-vanished. He was at the end of the porch. I swear!"

Jerald takes the light from Reggie and shines it back to where Reggie saw the figure. He scans the area and says, "Reggie! Chill out, bro! It's just your imagination. And keep your voice down. If someone is outside the property walking their dog and hears all this commotion, they'll probably call the cops."

Reggie takes a deep breath again and says, "Okay. I'm cool. Just a few minutes and we are out of here, right?"

As he gives Reggie the flashlight, Jerald answers, "Right. Just a few minutes. Come on. Let's stop wasting time."

They both walk up to the front door again. Jerald walks in first and pulls Reggie in behind him. Jerald says, "Come on, dude. You have the flashlight. You lead the way, and I'll be right behind you."

Reggie shines his light around the first floor. The front room is a vacant living room. No furniture. Just some cleaning equipment in the middle of the room. Reggie smiles and says, "See, dude? Nothing here! Let's just leave."

Jerald pushes Reggie further into the building and says, "Come on, bro. This is a big house, and this is just the living room. Lots of places to still check out."

Reggie shines his light in both directions. To his left there's a hallway that leads to another room that has some painting materials. To his right there's another hallway that leads into what looks like a kitchen. Reggie says, "Okay. Fine. Which way do you want to go? Left, or right?"

Jerald says, "Neither. I figured the first floor won't have anything. Let's go upstairs and check out the second floor." He points to the staircase located at the far end of the front living room. Reggie shines his light to the staircase, and they walk through the living room. Reggie stops at the bottom of the staircase and shines his light up the stairs. Jerald bumps Reggie on the shoulder and says, "Come on, dude! What are you waiting for?"

Reggie answers, "Noth-noth-nothing. How 'bout this? I give you the light and I'll watch your back?"

Becoming more frustrated, Jerald rolls his eyes and says, "Yeah, you'll watch my back by running out of the damn house and leaving me behind. That ain't happening. You go first."

Reggie starts to walk up the stairs toward the second floor. Each step creaks loudly and echoes through the empty first floor. Reggie hears what sounds like a scratching noise coming from one of the second-floor windows. Reggie makes his way up to the second-floor landing. A loud thump is heard from the direction of that same window. Reggie screams, "Ahhhh! That's it. I'm done! Something's here I know it." Reggie tries to run past Jerald but Jerald grabs Reggie by his shirt and yanks him back up to the second-floor landing.

Jerald exclaims, "Dude. Stop it! There's nothing here. The sound that you heard is the tree branches from large tree in the front yard hitting the side of that window."

Reggie gives a big sigh of relief as he flashes his light toward the window. "Okay. We are on the second floor. What now?"

Jerald looks around and instructs Reggie to shine his flashlight in all directions. The second floor has a large area landing with two floor-to-ceiling windows facing the front of the house. The glass is still in place on one of the windows, while a board is secured from the outside to the other. There's a large old-fashioned chandelier with cobwebs hanging a few feet below the base of the ceiling. The hallway divides into three separate areas. The hallway has several old paintings and pictures hanging from the walls. Reggie shines the light into the room to the right. The outside moonlight pierces the darkness in the bedroom. He sees some old furniture covered by old white sheets. He says, "Hey, Jerald. Looks like this room has some old stuff."

Jerald turns toward Reggie, smiles, and says, "Perfect. There's got to be something left in the drawers or something. I'll check out this room. You check out the room down the hall."

Reggie shines his light down the hallway into the back bedroom. He stammers, "Y-y-you want me to check it out by myself?"

Jerald walking into the other bedroom says, "Look, just take a quick look and get back to me. I'll be right in here. Plus, it means we can leave quicker."

Reggie nods in approval. "Okay. Okay. Just a few minutes."

They each walk toward the separate bedrooms. Reggie walks past a ring on a long chain. He shines his light up the chain and sees a hatch that leads to an attic. Reggie shakes his head and says, "Definitely not going into the creepy old attic tonight." Reggie can hear Jerald remove the old sheets from the furniture, open drawers, and rummage through items. Reggie flashes his light around the bedroom. It's a standard bedroom with a single bed, old bed posts, a dresser covered by a sheet, old pictures on the walls, and a mirror hanging over a small sitting powder table. Reggie says to himself, "Look at this place. Looks like no one has touched anything for a long time." He makes his way around the room, shining his light on each of the old, framed pictures. He notices black-and-white pictures of a family. Children playing throughout the grounds, family photos, pictures of religious figures, group photos of Catholic nuns and priests. Reggie calls out. "Hey, Jerald! Your grandma worked at this place back in the day, right?"

Jerald takes a break from shuffling through the drawers and says, "Yeah. Grandma worked here when this place was owned by the church. She worked in the kitchen and helped with housekeeping. Why do you ask?"

Reggie answers, "I'm seeing these old pictures. Just curious. Find anything good yet?"

Jerald replies, "Yeah. Found some old jewelry stuffed behind the drawer."

Reggie answers, "Cool," as he takes off the old sheet covering the dresser and starts to look through the drawers.

As Jerald places the items into his backpack, the wind from outside the house begins to increase. Almost like a whirlwind. The wind blows so hard it takes off one of the boards securing the second-floor window. The board flies into the air, out past the large oak tree and down to the front lawn. Jerald exclaims, "Damn that wind is bad! You find anything good, Reggie?"

Reggie answers, "Haven't found anything yet! You think we should head out of here? Sounds like a storm is coming."

Just then, Reggie hears an echo of a person's voice. It's a deep angry male voice. Startled he says, "What's that? Who's in here?"

The echo answers, "You don't belong here." The voice seems closer now.

Reggie quickly exits the room. He moves too fast and trips over himself and falls in the hallway. The flashlight falls in front of him. Jerald comes out of the other bedroom with his backpack and exclaims, "Reggie, what the hell's the matter with you?"

Reggie grabs the flashlight, stands up, and shines the light at Jerald.

Jerald asks, "Dude! What's all the commotion?"

Outside a storm begins to roll in. The storm-filled clouds remove the illuminating light from the moon. The wind blows harder now. Lightning and thunder begin to rip through the sky. Rain starts to fall. Reggie answers, "Jerald! There's something here. It's a voice! A deep awful voice! It said we don't belong here!"

Jerald replies, "What are you talking about? I didn't hear a voice. Did you see anyone?"

Jerald is standing in the hallway with his back to the window. Reggie is looking at Jerald. There's a flash of lightning. Reggie looks out the window, there's a dark figure floating outside the window! The figure looks like he's wearing a hat. Reggie tries to warn Jerald as he backs up and stammers. Jerald asks, "Reggie, what is it, bro?"

At that moment, the window shatters. Glass flies everywhere, and Jerald is pulled out of the window! He bounces off of the tree and hits several branches on the way down. He screams as he plummets down to the bottom of the tree. As he lands, the back of his head hits a large stone at the tree base. He lies there motionless.

Reggie screams in terror as he runs down the stairs. He looks back upstairs and sees the dark figure walk toward the top of the stairs on the second-floor landing. Reggie is frozen in fright. The dark figure looks like a three-dimensional shadow. The void of light and life.

The Shadow Man looks down at Reggie and says, "Welcome home, Reggie."

Reggie screams in horror, "Ahhhh!" He runs out the front door and to Jerald. Rain is pouring down. Lightning and thunder continue to strike and shatter through the turbulent air. Reggie crouches down at Jerald's side. Reggie exclaims, "Jerald! Jerald! Come on, dude! We have to get out of here!"

Jerald remains motionless. Reggie realizes that Jerald isn't breathing. There's a loud crash of thunder and an orange flash of lightning. The lightning strikes the large oak tree. Reggie is startled to his feet from the loud bang. A large tree branch comes crashing down and lands on top of Jerald. Reggie flashes his light onto the large branch on top of Jerald. Rain is now a downpour. Reggie flashes his light back at the house. The Shadow Man is standing on the front porch looking at Reggie. Reggie scrambles to his feet and runs for his life out toward the main entrance. He tries to squeeze between the gates. He gets stuck! He pulls himself out as best he can. The Shadow Man grabs ahold of one of his feet! Reggie screams in horror as The Shadow Man says, "You can't leave now, Reggie. Jerald needs his friend to stay with him at his new home." Reggie continues to scream as he pulls his foot away from The Shadow Man. His shoe comes off and is left behind as he finally breaks free from the gate and runs home.

CHAPTER 10

....

THERE'S BEEN AN INCIDENT

The family makes their way home from an evening of fun festivities. They all enjoyed their meals, spending time together, telling old stories, and having ice cream. The evening's events couldn't have been timed better. By the time both families make their way home, the weather starts to turn for the worse—thunder, lightning, heavy rain, and winds. Will, who is driving his vehicle, follows Pete and Claire back to their house. Will says, "God! What a storm! This one seemed to come out of nowhere!"

Annie who is riding up front asks, "Are you doing okay driving, honey? These roads back here are incredibly dark."

Will answers, "Yeah. That is something I never got used to. How dark these roads get at night. Why don't they put streetlights out here like they do back home?"

Annie answers, "Because we live in the city, honey. It's just like the lake house. Out in the country, they don't have the streets illuminated like they do in the city."

They carefully make their way back to Pete and Claire's home. As they park the car, they wait for Pete to open the front door. The thunder, lightning, heavy winds, and downpour continue. As Pete opens the front door, the rest of the family exit their vehicles and run into the house. Claire meets everyone at the door and says, "So sorry. If I knew it was going to be like this, maybe I would have just made a nice home-cooked meal. But if you want there's plenty of towels in the upstairs hallway closet. Make yourselves at home. Oh, and I almost forgot to tell you the sleeping arrangements. Will and Annie, you have the guest room. Boo, you are sleeping in Ellie's room. She has the bunk bed. And Liam, you're sleeping on an air mattress in Neil's room."

Liam looks back at Will and whispers, "An air mattress for two weeks."

Will shrugs his shoulders. Liam looks at his Aunt Claire and asks, "Aunt Claire, would you mind if I just sleep on the couch in the living room? Not too fond of air mattresses."

Claire answers, "That's fine if that's what you want to do. But Uncle Pete and I figured that you would like to hang out with Neil in his room. He has plenty of video games and often plays online with his friends. I'm sure he has an extra headset you can use."

Liam smiles. "That sounds great! Maybe I'll give this air mattress thing another chance."

It is late by the time everyone gets settled in for the night. Everyone goes into their respective bedrooms. The heavy storms make their way through the area and now just a steady rain could be heard from the roof and windows. Boo walks into Ellie's room. The walls are hot pink with several music band posters on the walls. The bands range from modern artists to rock hair bands from the 80s. Inside her room, there is a computer desk that houses a laptop and a TV connected to a retro video game system, a chair, a record player that can play vinyl, cassettes and AM/FM radio, the bunk bed with Ellie's personal items on the bottom bunk, and a nicely made top bunk with fresh sheets and pillows. Ellie says, "Okay, cuz. Make yourself at home."

Boo replies, "I like your room, Ellie. It's really cool. Where did you get all these posters?"

"Some online, some from your dad, and some that my parents stored in the garage."

Boo looks at the record player and says, "That looks like the one my dad has in our garage."

Ellie replies, "Yeah, he found this one for me and sent it over to the house. Your dad is cool about finding me cool retro things. What kind of music do you like?"

Boo says, "Judging from the posters around the room, a lot of the same music you like."

Ellie smiles. "I've been listening to a lot of David Bowie recently. Care to listen?"

Boo smiles as Ellie turns on some music. Boo continues to talk to Ellie before they both go to bed.

Liam makes his way into Neil's room. The walls are dark blue with a red-and-white stripe going through the center of the walls. The walls have several decals from all the Philadelphia sports teams. His room has a computer desk that houses a desktop computer and small flat-screen TV connected to his new video game system. There is a bookshelf with several books, video games, comics and sports memorabilia, Neil's bed, and his office chair with his headset wrapped around the arm rest. Neil asks Liam, "You too tired to play with some friends online?"

Liam smiles. "Never too tired for that, dude."

"Okay cool. Let me find my extra headset and we can sign in."

Liam looked around the room and finds his air mattress. "Thanks for sharing your room."

Neil replies, "No worries, dude. But I get it. I usually stay up late on the weekends and play online with my friends. If the light is too much, feel free to sleep downstairs. So how good are you with online play?"

Liam answers, "My buddy Robert is a huge fan, so I have plenty of experience. In fact, he should be online right now!"

Neil hands Liam his extra headset. "Cool, let's find him, invite him to my group, and have some fun."

Liam wakes up in the morning to an air mattress that seems to have an air leak. He is lying in a fold of his bed as his body rests on the hard floor in between the two sides that still have air. Liam is alone in the room and smells breakfast and coffee being made. He carefully makes his way out of the bed, stands up, and looks out the bedroom window, which faces the backyard. The backyard is deep and well-maintained. It's a couple of acres of land that extends to a marsh forest area in the back of the property. The heavy rains and storms from the night before are completely gone. The morning weather looks beautiful with blue skies, a few white puffy clouds, and the sun beaming down off the grass, which reflects the raindrops from the night before. Liam looks over at the office desk and notices the time on Neil's digital clock. It is close to 9:30 a.m. Liam walks out to the hallway. Boo is walking toward the main bathroom on the second floor. With a towel and her hygiene bag in her hand, she says, "'Bout time you woke up, sleepy head."

Liam answers, "I can't believe I slept so long. Slept like a baby all night. That's after Neil and I played online for a while."

Boo replies, "Well if I were you, I would get downstairs and have some breakfast. It sounds like we are going together as a family out to that mansion."

Liam exclaims, "Already. I thought we were going to see the Phillies or check out Center City or something."

Boo answers, "Don't kill the messenger. That's what I heard. The bathroom is free, and I'm next. See ya."

Liam makes his way downstairs to the sweet smells of breakfast. To his amazement his dad isn't the one cooking. Will and Annie are sitting at the kitchen table with Ellie and Neil. Claire is cooking breakfast. Annie says, "Good morning, sunshine. You slept in, didn't you."

Liam answers, "Yeah, I guess. Where's Uncle Pete?"

Claire answers, "Uncle Pete had to go into the office today. Had to do some estimates for some of his clients. Breakfast is ready. Help yourself."

Liam grabs a plate from the cabinet and walks over to the stove. He takes a couple of scoops of scrambled eggs, investigates the next frying pan, and asks, "Aunt Claire, what is this?"

Claire looks over to her brother Will and asks, "You never fed my nephew scrapple before? Shame on you!"

Neil says jokingly, "What's wrong with you?"

Ellie replies, "Yeah, seriously. He doesn't know what scrapple is?"

Will answers, "It's not a thing back in Chicago. There's like one store that carries that stuff and it's hard to find."

Claire shakes her head. "You are in for a treat, Liam. Scrapple is a bricked organ meatloaf that you slice and fry with your eggs. Trust me it tastes better than it looks."

Will replies, "She ain't lying, kid. It's really good, and Aunt Claire bought some fresh bagels too."

Liam asks, "What are you having, Dad?"

"Having some eggs and scrapple same as you. Along with a raisin bagel with cream cheese and lox."

Liam asks, "What are lox, Dad?"

Annie answers, "It's gross smelly fish, and it's disgusting to watch your father eat it."

Neil and Ellie both laugh.

Will answers, "Don't knock it until you try it. This stuff isn't the same back home. Lox is smoked salmon. The fresh bagels and the smoked salmon are excellent, sis. The coffee is good too. Where did you get it?"

Claire answers, "Believe it or not, Wawa."

Will exclaims, "Wawa! You're kidding!"

Claire replies, "Nope. Not kidding. Wawa sells their own bagged coffee now. I get it every time I fill up the car.

Liam asks, "What's a Wawa? You two are speaking a different language around here."

Claire laughs as she answers, "We got a lot to teach you. But there's time. Eat up. We are leaving in forty-five minutes."

Within the hour they get into their vehicles and head toward Route 611. They head south for over thirty minutes as they drive through Willow Grove and Jenkintown. They reach Elkins Park and turn down Ashbourne Road. Claire is leading the way in the Mustang convertible with the top down. Will and Annie are with Liam and Boo in their vehicle behind her. Ashbourne Road is a curvy two-lane road surrounded by a vast number of trees, beautiful homes, and old masonry two-story apartment buildings. As they continue down the road, Will is startled by the sight of two police squad cars with lights and sirens behind him. He pulls over quickly as Annie asks, "What did you do, Will? Were you speeding or something?"

Will answers, "Not really, honey. Don't know what the problem is."

Claire sees the police cars and pulls over as well. Will looks through his rearview mirror as Liam and Boo look behind to see the police. The police enter the opposite lane of traffic, cruise past their vehicles, and head toward the estate. Will says, "What the hell is going on?" Will waits for Claire to get back on the road. Both vehicles make their way back onto the road toward the estate. As they approach the estate entrance, they notice all the activity. Police have the semi-circle driveway blocked off with a police squad car blocking the entrance. The gates are open, and there are several police squad cars in the main drive. Claire and Will park their cars along the side of the road. Claire exits the vehicle to get a better look. Will says to Annie, "Honey, why don't you stay here with the kids and let me find out what's going on."

Annie says, "Okay, honey. Just let me know."

Will and Claire walk up the semicircle drive and approach the officer guarding the front gate. Will asks Claire, "Do you know what's going on, sis?"

Claire answers, "No. I'm in charge of the volunteer group so I usually arrive early. No one else should be here yet."

They approach the officer who walks around his police car toward Will and Claire. The officer says, "Will, is that you?"

Will takes a good hard look at the officer, pauses, and says, "Kenny! Is that you?"

The officer says, "Sure is. Good to see you, old friend!"

Kenny is an old childhood friend of Will. He's the same age as Will. He's bigger framed man with red hair, freckles, and a mustache. Kenny and Will shake hands and give each other a hug. Claire asks, "How do you two know each other?"

Kenny answers, "I went to elementary school with your brother before he moved out to Chi-town."

Will says, "Kenny, I thought you wanted to be on the fire department. What happened?"

Kenny chuckles. "Hard to get that job. You know that. Elkins Park PD was doing a massive hiring a few years ago."

Claire interjects, "So, Kenny. Officer. What's happened here? I'm the head volunteer of the restoration group."

Kenny looks at Claire. "Oh yeah. That's right. Your mom worked here back in the day, didn't she? The community is happy to see something being done with the estate after all these years. But, unfortunately, there was an incident last night."

Claire and Will looked past Kenny. They can see other officers walking around, rolling out yellow police tape, and marking evidence. They also see a white sheet covering what looks like a human being. They see the county coroner van parked along the drive and getting ready to move the body. Will says to Kenny, "Looks like it was a little bit more than an incident, Kenny. Does anyone know what happened?"

Kenny looks around. "Well, it's all under investigation right now. Can't say much. But the victim was a young local kid. Teenager. Lives in one of the apartments across the street with his grandma. One of his buddies was with him." Kenny points in the direction of the apartment buildings. "You can see our detective questioning one of the kids over there. The kid's grandma was given the unfortunate news early this morning. Haven't seen her come out of her unit since."

Claire looks over to the young man being questioned by police and says, "That boy looks familiar. I think he hangs out with... Oh God!"

Will asks, "What is it, sis?"

"You remember Dotty? Mom's old friend?"

Will thinks for a moment and says, "Oh yeah. The lady who worked with Mom at the estate. What about her?"

Claire answers, "Dotty has been helping with the restoration project. I recognize that boy. He hangs out with her grandson, Jerald. I think Dotty's grandson was the victim!"

CHAPTER 11

....

THE INVESTIGATION IS ONGOING

K enny asks, "So you knew the victim, Claire?"
"A little. I've been spending a lot of time with his grandmother, Dotty. Jerald is her grandson. He would come over to help every once in a while when we were working on the property. He would help his grandmother with the stairs. She's been having a difficult time with her knees recently. He brought his friend over to help once or twice. I think his name is Reggie. Do you think it would be okay to go and talk to Jerald's grandmother, Kenny?"

Kenny looks at Will and Claire as he finishes taking a few notes in his notepad. "I suppose it would be okay. Maybe the sight of a familiar face will be good for the poor thing."

Will extends his hand to shake Kenny's and says, "Thanks for your time, Kenny. We won't keep you. Good to see you again."

Kenny replies, "Sure thing. Good to see you too. If you'll be in town for a bit, let's meet up for lunch and couple of rounds."

Will answers, "Sure thing, buddy. Stay safe."

Will and Claire make their way back to their vehicles as Kenny walks back around his squad car to talk to another officer on the property. Claire is greeted by Neil and Ellie, and Will is greeted by his family.

Neil asks, "What's going on, Mom?"

Ellie asks, "Yeah really. Looks serious. What happened?"

Claire looks at Will and then looks back at Neil and Ellie. "There was an incident last night. Someone died."

Liam and Boo overhear the conversation between Claire, Neil, and Ellie as they listen from the back seat of their vehicle with the windows rolled down. Annie asks Will, "Oh my God! Someone died? Who?"

Will answers, "Some local kid. Sounds like it was the son of an old family friend who lives right down the street. He was very young. A teenager."

Claire overhears as she approaches Will and Annie and says, "Yes. I knew the grandmother. She used to work with my mother at the estate here. I'll have to call the volunteers and cancel for today."

Annie says, "Claire, why don't you give me the list of volunteers. The kids and I can help with contacting them. That way you and Will can visit with this woman."

Claire looks at Will. Will gives a nod of approval and Claire answers, "That sounds like a plan. Let's drive up to the apartment building. It's just up the road here, and I can see some open spots. We'll park there and figure this out."

The two vehicles drive up the road and pull into the apartment building parking lot. They drive past an Elkins Park Police car and an officer walking back to his vehicle. They see the young man sitting on the front steps that lead to the sidewalk. A few onlookers and curious neighbors are standing out on their lawns observing the unusual activities. Claire and Will park their vehicles and everyone exits. Claire walks over to Annie and gives her a piece of paper from her folder and says, "Here's the lists of all the volunteers. Thank you."

Annie says, "No worries, Claire. The kids and I are more than capable of doing this while you visit your friend."

Will and Claire walk up the stairs to the front entrance of the apartment building. The front door is a security door that's locked. Will looks over at the buzzer lists and asks, "Hey, sis. What is Dotty's last name?"

Claire says, "I think it's…Rose. Yeah, that's it. Dotty Rose." Will finds the button for the Rose apartment and presses the button. There's a pause for a few moments and then a voice in the speaker next to the buzzer list says, "Go away! No more today! I told the police everything that I know!"

Will steps aside and lets Claire answer back. Claire holds down the speak button and says, "Dotty. Sweetheart? It's Claire. Bethany's daughter. We were on our way to the estate when we heard what happened. My brother Will is with me. Can we come up please?"

There's another brief pause. Will shakes his head, doubting if Dotty will open the door. Suddenly, there's a buzz and Claire opens the door. They both make their way inside the building.

Liam, Boo, Ellie, and Neil help with the phone calls. As they finish up, they all start walking around the parking lot as Annie stays with the vehicles. They walk toward the front of the building and see the young man still sitting on the steps near the sidewalk. Liam says, "Looks like that dude had a rough night. Hasn't moved since the police finished questioning him."

They notice the police officer who was questioning the young man talk into the radio and begin to drive off back toward the estate. Ellie asks, "Do you think we should go over and talk to him?"

Neil says, "Hard to say. Maybe we should leave him alone. Doesn't seem to be our problem."

Boo says, "Well, it sounds like he knows Aunt Claire so let's try to find out if we can help him." Boo begins to walk over to the young man. The young man continues to sit there motionless with a blank stare. Boo notices that his clothes look torn up and muddy, and he is missing one of his shoes. The rest of the group begins to walk over toward Boo. Boo says, "Hey. My name is Boo. What's your name?"

The young man says in a low voice, "Reggie."

Boo replies, "What happened to your other shoe, Reggie?"

"The Shadow Man got it. Along with Jerald."

Boo questions, "Who's The Shadow Man?"

Liam overhears the conversation first and says, "Wait, what happened? Who's The Shadow Man?"

Boo says, "Liam, everyone, this is Reggie."

Neil says, "Hey, Reggie. You okay, man?"

After a brief pause, Reggie looks at Neil and says, "No, man. I ain't okay."

Ellie asks, "Reggie, what happened to your shoe?"

Reggie answers, "It was left behind. There was nothing I could do. The Shadow Man grabbed hold of it."

The group looks around at each other. Puzzled at what Reggie is saying, Liam steps closer to Reggie. "Reggie, who's this Shadow Man?"

Reggie pauses before he speaks. He starts to get upset and choked up. "It's hard to describe him. I only saw glimpses of him. Saw him outside the coach house, then I saw him outside the second-floor window. That's when he took Jerald."

The group looks at each other even more puzzled. Boo asks, "He was hanging out of the second-floor window?"

Reggie replies, "It's hard to say if he was in the tree or maybe he was floating in midair."

Neil says, "This Shadow Man was floating outside a window? That's impossible."

Reggie replies, "It's only impossible if you're human. That thing might have been human at one time. Whatever it is, it ain't human now."

Liam asks, "What does he look like, Reggie?"

Reggie answers, "Like a shadow of a tall adult man. He's wearing some type of large hat. Like one of those big gardening hats. He's darkness. Pitch black. Like a 3D shadow. Glowing green eyes. Has a deep voice and he knew my name and Jerald's name."

Ellie says, "Okay. I'm a little creeped out now. You're telling us that a large shadow attacked you last night?"

Liam interjects. "Did you tell the police what happened?"

Reggie replies, "No. No, I didn't. I was too scared. I didn't want them to know all the details. I kept my answers brief." Reggie stands up and begins to walk away from the group saying, "I've had enough of this. Everyone wants me to answer their questions. I'm done. I'm going home."

Liam walks next to Reggie and says, "Reggie. Wait. Please. Let us try to help you."

Reggie continues walking. He gets more frustrated, stops walking, and turns around to face Liam and the rest of the group. "No one can help me! That thing has been around here for a long time. It's a local legend. Most of the neighborhood knows that this place is haunted. Long history there. Jerald's mom would tell us stories about The Shadow Man and the echoes of the Elk's Estate. We just thought she was off her rocker or just trying to scare us, so we wouldn't go over there. I should have listened! If I were you, I would leave this place and never come back!"

Reggie continues to walk down the street toward his apartment building. The group stays back. Neil says, "Forget it. Like I said before. Not our problem. Kid has a laundry list of problems. He needs to sort it out himself."

Boo replies, "I just feel bad for him."

Ellie says, "Like Neil said, there's nothing we can do."

Boo looks at her brother and says, "Liam and I have some experience dealing with dark forces. Maybe we can help him."

Liam looks back at his sister and shakes his head disapprovingly. Liam says, "Sis. That was a beast. A freak of nature. This is something supernatural it seems."

Ellie interjects, "What the hell are you talking about?"

Liam looks at Neil and Ellie who look puzzled and asks, "Your folks never told you what happened, did they?"

Neil says, "No."

Ellie replies, "What beast?"

Liam replies, "We have a lot to talk about."

The police officer who questioned Reggie parks his vehicle next to the circle drive and walks up to Kenny who is still guarding the front gate. Kenny sees the officer and says, "How you doing, Eric? Get any info from that kid?"

Eric is an older detective who has been on the force for over twenty-five years. He's tall and still in very good shape given his age and time on the job. His hair is dark hair with shades of gray and parted to one side. Eric answers, "Not too much, Kenny. Kid seems like he's in shock over what happened. I had the medics come by and check on him. They said he was fine. Didn't want to tell me why both he and his buddy were lurking around the property during a heavy thunderstorm."

Kenny replies, "Kind of figured. Haven't he and his buddy been in trouble before?"

Eric answers, "Yeah, they were caught by one of our young officers, Ethan, in the early spring. They were trespassing in a school one night."

Kenny points to the apartment where Liam, Boo, Neil, and Ellie are still standing and says, "You see that group of kids?"

Eric answers, "Yup. Sure do. Saw them with a couple of adults when I started to make my way back here. Why do you ask?"

Kenny replies, "Those kids are with that woman Claire who runs the volunteer group here. Apparently, she knows the victim's grandmother."

Eric asks, "Interesting. How are things going around here?"

"Okay, I guess. The chief walked over a few minutes ago. Said they were done with the evidence collection and photos for now, and we were packing up shortly."

"Sounds like a plan. I can always come back and check things out when things calm down. Fresh set of eyes."

Kenny asks, "If anyone comes by the station and ask what's happening what should I say?"

"Just tell them the investigation is ongoing."

Within the hour, the coroner is ready to move to their county examiner's office. They are the first to leave the estate. The rest of the officers follow suit after packing up their equipment. Kenny is the last officer at the estate. He closes the iron gates and secures them with a lock and chain. As he walks back to his vehicle, the wind starts to pick up and he hears the echoes of voices. Kenny pauses. "Hello! Anyone else here?" He looks around the property through the iron gates. Doesn't see a soul. He shrugs his shoulders, gets into his vehicle, and drives away.

CHAPTER 12

....

MRS. DOTTY ROSE

Will and Claire make their way up a few flights of stairs. Will is used to stair climbing given his profession. His older sister, Claire, is starting to get out of breath as she makes her way to the third-level landing. Will says, "Come on, sis! I thought you used to be a track star and play field hockey at your high school."

Catching her breath, Claire says, "Will…that was a long time ago. I'm too tired after my shifts at the hospital to go to the gym."

Will answers, "I hear you. But I also hear excuses. Yes, this is it. Apartment 3B. I thought you said that Dotty is having trouble getting around."

Claire reaches the third-floor landing and replies, "Yes, she is. She's lived here for several years since her husband passed away. She wasn't having trouble until recently. That's why her grandson was so vital to her."

"I'll let you do the introductions, sis. Here we go."

Claire knocks on the door. There's a brief pause and then a voice saying, "Hold on! I'm coming! Is that you Claire, honey?"

Claire responds, "Yeah, Dotty! It's me, sweetheart. I have Will with me."

After a few turns of some locks, Dotty opens the door and welcomes Claire and Will into her home. Claire steps alongside Dotty who is walking with her walker and gives Dotty a big hug saying, "Dotty, I'm so sorry. I know how much Jerald did for you. I can't imagine how you feel."

Dotty starts to get choked up as she holds Claire tightly. So tightly that Dotty almost loses her balance. Claire exclaims, "Will! Quick! Grab a chair."

Will runs over to the dining room table, grabs a chair, and brings it over behind Dotty before she completely loses her balance. Will grabs ahold of Dotty and says softly, "It's okay, Dotty. I have one of your chairs from the dining room right behind you. If you reach back, you can grab the arm rest and I'll help bring you down slowly."

Dotty does as Will instructs her to do and very carefully has a seat in her chair. Will comes around and gives Dotty a hug. Dotty hugs him back and looks at Will with focused eyes. "There's my big strong firefighter. God, how you grown up so well. You are the spitting image of your father when he was your age, except for the mustache of course. It was the style at the time, and your father wore it so well." Dotty focuses her eyes on the empty space to her right, nods her head, and continues, "I know how proud your father must be. I feel better now. My strength has come back to me. Please help me up." Will helps Dotty to her feet and Dotty says, "I put some coffee on, and there's cake in the kitchen."

Dotty makes her way slowly over to the kitchen as Will and Claire follow her. They walk through her living room and dining room. The apartment is outdated with old furniture but well maintained and clean. Dotty says to Will, "You seem to know how to help a nice old woman like me. Seems like you've had a lot of practice."

Will laughs as he responds, "We help lift and move the elderly and sick more so than fight fires, Dotty."

Dotty smiles. "Is that a fact. Sounds like the job has changed a bit since the time your dad was on the job. Please have a seat."

Claire says, "Dotty, honey, why don't you have a seat. Will and I are very capable of helping each other. Please."

Dotty sits down next to Will.

Claire asks Dotty, "Can I get you anything?"

"Yes, coffee please with a healthy portion of cream and sugar." Dotty looks at Will and says, "I'm sure if it were any other day, your sister would give an ear full about how I should watch my sugar intake. But not today."

Claire hands Dotty a cup of coffee. "Yes, ma'am, I would. Has anyone checked your blood pressure and sugar today?"

Dotty responds, "Yes, the medics came up after the cops gave me the news. They checked on me right before they checked on poor Reggie."

Claire responds, "Well, how were your numbers, Dotty?"

"As good as it could be expected, honey." Dotty looks at Will and continues, "Your sister is a good nurse. Always looking out for me. She's an angel." Dotty looks to her left and concentrates on an empty space in the room and continues, "Well…an angel. Here in this realm of course."

Claire takes a seat at the table with a cup of coffee. She hands another cup over to her brother and asks Dotty, "Did the police give you any other information?"

Dotty answers, "They told me what they could, honey. That's all. Told me that he died sometime overnight during that horrific thunderstorm. I didn't even know that he left the apartment. I fell asleep in my recliner watching some reruns. They told me that the investigation is ongoing."

Will asks, "You've been raising him, Dotty?"

"Ever since he was a young boy. Jerald never knew his father. He was my daughter's boy. She wasn't fit to raise him. Right before she bailed and left town for good, she left him with Roger and me one night and never came back. Haven't seen her since. Don't even know how I could reach her to tell her that her boy is gone."

Will asks, "What happened to your husband, Roger?"

Dotty answers, "Cancer took him from this world a few years ago. Jerald was the only thing I had left." Will stands up and rubs Dotty's shoulders. "I'm sorry to hear about all this, Dotty. You and your husband did what you could for him."

Will looks over to the dining room wall and notices some old pictures. He walks over to the pictures. "These look like some old pictures of Elk's Estate. Here, this picture has Mom in it."

Dotty replies, "Yes, those were good times. Some of the best times in my life was working at the estate with your mother."

Will points to one of the Catholic sisters in the picture and asks, "Isn't that Sister Mary Frances?"

Dotty looks at the picture and says, "Sure is. What a wonderful woman. She was our boss during our time at the estate. She was there until they shut the place down. She's still alive, believe it or not. She lives at a nursing home for retired sisters in Willow Grove."

Will replies, "I remember her well. She helped raise me when Mom was busy cleaning and maintaining the estate."

Dotty replies, "She sure did. A lot of the sisters helped raise you. You were like a son to them, Will."

Claire stands up from the table. "Don't forget, I helped raise you too, Will. When Mom and Dad were both working it was left up to me to take care of you."

Will says jokingly, "Yeah don't remind me. I still remember the screams."

Claire replies, "Don't listen to him, Dotty. I was good to him. Dotty, I'm going to use your bathroom and check your medication prescriptions and their quantities. I'll be back in a few minutes."

Claire walks toward the living room. Before she walks to the bathroom, she hears some commotion outside. She looks out the living room window and sees the kids talking to the young boy, Reggie, as he shouts something back before walking away. Will looks over at Claire and asks, "Everything okay, sis?"

Claire responds, "Looks like our kids were trying to make friends with Reggie. Reggie didn't seem too happy. He's walking away. Everything's fine. I'll be back in a few." Claire walks to the bathroom and closes the door.

Will looks at the different photos and notices one that is somewhat peculiar. Will pauses, points at the photo, and asks Dotty, "Was this taken at some type of Halloween party or something?"

"Which one, honey?"

"This one here. You're all dressed up in the psychic outfit and a crystal ball in the middle of the table. Looks pretty legit to me."

Dotty laughs. "That's because it is legit, honey."

Will questions, "Excuse me? You're telling me that you're a...?"

Dotty continues, "A psychic. That's right, honey. Some would call it that, others would say I'm gifted with a key to another realm."

Will's eyes widen. "You're kidding, right?"

"I'm afraid not, honey. My powers and gifts are not what they used to be, but they are still there."

"Did my mother know about this?"

"Sure did. But your mother is too much of a good Catholic soul to dabble into this stuff."

Will continues asking, "Who are the other people in the photo?"

Dotty answers, "Most of them were people who worked at the estate. You may not recognize the young lady sitting next to me. I'll give you a hint. She's not wearing her veil in that picture."

Will concentrates on the picture and replies, "Sister Rachel!"

Dotty replies, "Bingo. She's still active in the church. She's older now of course. She taught at Saint Basil Academy for a few years before that closed too. She works at the nursing home where Sister Mary Frances resides."

Will exclaims, "I can't believe a nun would sit in a psychic reading."

Dotty laughs. "Sister Rachel is a good Catholic soul, but she is also a free spirit and very open-minded. The gifts of being a young woman at the time. She knew very well about my abilities."

Dotty concentrates again on some empty space to her left and asks Will as he walks back over to the table, "Now honey, I have to ask you this so please don't be upset."

Will asks curiously, "What's that?"

"I know your sister never saw the man at the estate. She was far too old. You were very young when you were basically living at the estate while your mother worked."

Will grows uncomfortable. "What are you talking about, Dotty? What man?"

Dotty replies, "Most children, very young children, can see things behind the veil of our realm. It's that new developing mind that allows it. Most forget the things they have seen beyond our realm, but sometimes things from the other side leave an imprint in their thoughts and dreams." Dotty reaches over, touches Will's hand, and closes her eyes.

Will becomes more uncomfortable asks, "What are you doing, Dotty?"

Dotty opens her eyes and says, "You did see him once when you were very little! You were playing with some of the children from the other staff in the coach house close to the entrance of the property. It was a summertime holiday gathering. You were playing hide-and-seek. You snuck your way up to the attic. Someone left the attic door open and pulled down the ladder. You hid next to some boxes, and you saw him from across the gloomy attic space. He was wearing an old gardening hat. His face. He had a beard and a horrifically deep voice. He screamed at you and asked what you are doing up here! He came toward you. He was angry, enraged, and tried to grab you. You ran toward the hatch, but you fell down the ladder. The children came to your aid and so did the Sister Rachel after you hurt yourself. You spoke of a man in the attic but not one was found."

Will pulls his hand away and trembles at the recalled story Dotty just told him. Will exclaims, "That can't be true! That was just a recurring nightmare from when I was a kid."

Dotty answers, "I'm afraid not, honey. It was real. He is real. His shadow is near."

Will stands up and trembles at the words being spoken to him.

Dotty continues, "It's okay, honey. You have protection. Remember to follow the signs. Look at the time."

Will looks over to the time on the microwave. 11:11 a.m.

Will turns and starts to walk away from Dotty and toward the apartment door entrance. "Dotty, I have to go now," Will exclaims.

Just then, Claire comes out of the bathroom and says, "Dotty, honey. Your medications are looking okay. Looks like you have enough for a couple of weeks. Just check in…where are you going, Will?"

Will exclaims, "We are leaving. Now!"

CHAPTER 13

....

NICE TO MEET THE FAMILY

Will quickly stomps his way down the stairs and toward the front entrance of the apartment building. He doesn't say anything to Claire as Claire questions, "Will…Will…Will! Could you slow down a minute and tell me what's going on? Why are you acting this way?"

Will turns to Claire as he opens the front door and says, "How much do you really know about Dotty, sis?"

Claire walks out as Will continues to hold the door. "What do you mean?"

Will continues to walk to his car. "Did you know about her so-called abilities?"

Claire answers, "Will, I honestly don't know what you're talking about, but I can tell you're upset. Let's talk for a minute."

Will stops walking, takes a deep breath, and looks at Claire. "Sorry. You're right. We'll talk, but let's wait until later. Maybe after the kids head to bed. Until then, let's head back to your house for the day."

Claire answers, "That sounds like the right idea. There's simply nothing we can do at the estate today. And honestly, who would want to? I'll have to talk to the Elkins Park Police to see if we can get access to the property sometime soon. Until then, let's head home."

Will continues to head over to his vehicle and looks at Annie who's been waiting patiently for her husband to return. Annie looks at Will and says, "Hey honey…what's wrong? You look upset."

Will quickly shrugs it off and replies, "Oh it's nothing, I'm fine. Let's head back to Claire's house."

Annie shakes her head. "I've known you for a long time, Will. And when you have that look on your face and say everything is fine, it most certainly isn't fine."

Will walks toward the group of kids still hanging out on the front lawn discussing something. "Okay, kids! Time to go!" Will heads back over to the car as Annie sits in the passenger seat. He gets inside and turns on the car. Annie is looking at him. He tries to ignore her for a moment, but then he looks back at her saying, "You and my sister always know when I'm upset, don't you?"

Annie answers, "Oh, honey, and so does the rest of the world. You may be a big and tough firefighter, but you always wear your emotions on your sleeve."

Will chuckles. "Is that right?"

"Yup. One thing you are not is a liar, honey. You're honest to your core. That's why my brother always beats you in card games."

Will laughs and then beeps the horn to get the attention of the kids.

Liam and Boo look back at their car, and Boo says, "Man! Dad isn't kidding. He wants to leave now."

Liam replies, "Yeah you can always tell when Dad is upset. Let's go before he gets more upset."

Ellie and Neil start heading back to their vehicle as well. Ellie says to Liam, "Hey, Liam, so when are you going to tell us the rest of the story? You know about what *really* happened in Michigan last year."

Liam replies as he continues to walk toward the cars, "Let's all talk about it when we get back to your house. Deal?"

Ellie smiles. "Deal."

Everyone gets back into their vehicles and makes their way out of the parking lot and out toward Ashbourne Road. Claire takes the lead as Will follows right behind her.

They drive past the estate. The estate's half-circle entrance goes past Liam's side of the car. Liam looks at the entrance and sees the black iron gates closed. He looks past the iron gates and for a split second he believes he sees a shadow of a tall man standing below the large oak tree in front of the coach house. The figure remains motionless. Liam looks back as Will continues to drive past. Liam looks again, but this time out through the rear window. Boo notices Liam taking notice of something and says, "What is it, big brother?"

Will looks through his rearview mirror, notices Liam, and asks, "Everything okay, buddy?"

Liam turns around, looks at his sister and at his father's reflection in the rearview mirror, and replies, "Yeah, Dad. Everything is fine. Just taking a second look is all."

In Claire's vehicle, Neil is riding shotgun and Ellie is riding in the back seat. Neil looks over to Claire and jokingly asks, "So, Mom, do you think we're ever going to be able to work on the estate again? It would be such a shame to have my calendar open up. I'm asking for a friend."

Ellie laughs as Claire answers, "I'm sure we will be able to work on the property soon. I'll wait until tomorrow to contact the police. I'm sure they have their hands full. Plus, the hours that you're putting into the estate goes toward your community service hours. So, you're welcome, by the way. I'm helping you pad that resume for college applications."

Neil replies, "Fair enough, Mom. Fair enough. But can't I do these community service hours closer to home. I still don't understand. What's the big deal with this place?"

Ellie says, "Yeah Mom really. I could do my hours volunteering at our downtown library."

Claire replies, "Oh! Yeah right. So that way you can sneak away and hang out with Simon at the coffee shop, the pizza parlor, the used record store, and the retro arcade place that are within a block of the library. Nice try, dear. This is a big deal to me, okay? I grew up there, and I have a lot of fond memories. It breaks my heart to see the place almost in ruins. I want to see the property back to a healthy and maintained level. That way the village can see that my volunteer group is serious, and we can get that official historical landmark seal and get grant money to help maintain the property for a long time."

Ellie shakes her head. Unhappy that she's not spending as much time as she would like with her best friend, Simon, she texts Simon: "We're on our way back to Doylestown."

Simon texts, "That was quick! What happened? Did the place burn down overnight lol."

Ellie snickers and replies, "Worse. Some kid died there overnight. Cops and detectives were there. Shut down the whole place. We couldn't even step foot onto the property."

Simon replies, "No way!!! That's wicked. Sucks for the kid though. We still planning to hang out later today? You can ride your bike down the trail and meet me at the record store."

Ellie replies, "You're already there?"

Simon replies, "LOL. Sure am. Couldn't wait around for you all day. Figure I can shop and then hopefully meet up with you for coffee and arcades. What do you say?"

Ellie replies, "I don't think I can. Something's come up with my little cousins. Gonna try to find out what."

Simon replies, "Drag. You're no fun. Sounds intriguing though. And sounds mysterious. Anything you want to clue me in to?"

Ellie texts: "Nothing for right now. But it sounds interesting. I'll clue you in when I see you. Peace out."

Ellie puts down her phone and Claire asks, "Who was that, Ellie? Simon again?"

Neil says jokingly, "Yeah, correction, Mom, that was her *boyfriend*, Simon."

Ellie replies, "Shut up! He's not my boyfriend. It's not like that. He's my best friend."

Neil laughs. "Yeah, right. Whatever."

Ellie looks at her mom and asks, "So Mom, did Uncle Will or Aunt Annie ever tell you why that lake house in Michigan was sold and their side of the family doesn't own it anymore?"

Claire looks through her rearview mirror and asks, "Why do you ask? Did Liam and Boo say something?"

Ellie thinks for a moment. Neil glares at Ellie. Ellie answers, "Not really. They just mentioned that their grandparents sold the property and they're not going back up there anymore is all."

Claire replies, "Gotcha. The only reason I heard was the traveling distance was getting too difficult for the grandparents. That's all I know."

Ellie replies, "Okay Mom. Just curious."

Neil continues to look at Ellie and shakes his head in disapproval as she shrugs her shoulders and silently says, "What?"

Both vehicles make their way to Route 611 and head north back toward Doylestown. Back at the estate, the figure that Liam thought he saw still stands below the large oak tree. He's tall, thin, and wearing a hat. The wind begins to pick up. One can hear the slight sounds of echoes in the distance. The echoes are several voices. The words that are whispered into the wind are too low to understand and comprehend. The figure stands there for a moment and says, "So, Will. I finally get to see your family in the flesh. Your son looks just like you when you were a little boy. I'm sure they'll enjoy their stay here. Like all our other residents." The figure lets out a deep and evil laugh and vanishes out of sight. His shadow disappears into the wind, and the echoes go silent.

CHAPTER 14

·····················

PIZZA AND ARCADES

It's now later in the day, and the family is back at Pete and Claire's home deciding on what to have for dinner. All the family are gathered in the kitchen thinking about possible options. Pete says, "Well, Will, you're our guests, so you decide on what you would like for dinner."

Will thinks about it for a few minutes and looks over to Annie and the kids and asks, "What are you guys in the mood for?"

Annie shrugs her shoulders as she continues to look at her phone and says, "Whatever you want, hon. As long as we go soon. Starting to get hangry."

Liam and Boo look at each other and are unable to offer suggestions.

Will thinks for a minute and says, "How 'bout that pizza and hoagie place in Downtown Doylestown?"

Pete replies, "You don't want something fancier than that?"

Will laughs and answers, "Nope. Remember, Annie and I don't like fancy. That's your department. We like a casual place where we can relax and have a good meal. Plus, I can finally have a decent cheesesteak hoagie. Been craving one since I came back here."

Ellie smiles and says, "That sounds like a great idea. My friend Simon should be down at one of our haunts. I can take Liam and Boo with me after dinner and meet up with him."

Neil interjects, "Hey, what about me? Am I invited to hang out with you guys?"

Ellie answers, "Maybe if you're finally nice to me and you stop saying that Simon is my boyfriend."

Neil laughs. "Deal. Scout's honor. I'll be on my best behavior."

The family all leave the house and enter their vehicles. On the way to the restaurant, Boo asks, "So, Dad...question?"

Will says, "What's that, honey?"

Boo replies, "What exactly is a cheesesteak hoagie? Sounds kind of gross."

Annie laughs and says, "I thought that same thing, honey, when your father took me to a hoagie shop in his old neighborhood when we visited years ago. Trust me, it's good. You like your beef sandwiches with cheese back home. This is similar to that."

Will interjects, "Yeah. But better."

Liam asks, "So, Dad, who makes the best cheesesteaks?"

"That's a good question. I'd say that is open for debate. There's a couple of places in South Philly that are popular. But my favorite is the place I used to go to when I was a boy."

Liam asks Annie, "Was that where Dad took you, Mom?"

Annie answers, "Sure was. Dad grew up in Northeast Philadelphia. Where was that place, hon?"

"It was a few blocks from my childhood home. Off the corner of Levick and Algon."

Liam asks, "Any chance we can go and check that place out while we are here?"

Will answers, "Wish we could, buddy. The place closed a few years ago. But this place tonight sounds good."

The family arrives at the restaurant. It's a beautiful summer evening. The temperature has cooled off after a warm day. The sun is setting, and there's a pleasant breeze coming out of the west. The restaurant is a typical pizza and sandwich shop around these parts. The restaurant is small, crowded, but a few tables with their checkerboard red-and-white tablecloths are still available. The front counter has several pizzas hot, fresh and ready to order by the slice. Liam and Boo walk past all the pizzas. The combination of the yummy smells is both inviting and enticing. Boo says, "I don't think I'm going to try that cheesesteak thing that Dad brags about. This pizza looks too good."

Liam replies, "I think you're right, Boo. This pizza looks too good to pass up. What's weird though, I'm used to pizza in squares not triangles."

Boo says, "Good point. And look at the sizes of the slices. They're huge!"

Ellie walks up to Boo. "Which slice are you thinking?"

Boo answers, "Any recommendations?"

Ellie replies, "Yeah, the pepperoni and the veggie-lover pizzas are my favorite."

Ellie remembers that her friend Simon might still be in the area. She pulls out her phone and texts Simon: "Dinner plans? Family is at our pizza shop on the corner."

Simon immediately replies: "At the arcade. Be there in a few minutes."

The gentleman behind the counter recognizes Ellie and says, "Good evening, young lady. Where's your friend? Brought the family I see."

Ellie answers, "Hey, Mario. Simon is on his way. This is my family from Chicago."

Mario says, "Chicago. The home of the thin slice and deep dish. My name is Mario Monet. Nice to meet you. Are you here to test my pies or enjoy the local cuisine?"

Will laughs and says, "Local cuisine for me. But I think my kids are going to test your pies." Will orders his cheesesteak hoagie, the slices for Liam and Boo, and orders a pepperoni pizza for the family to share. They sit down comfortably and enjoy each other's company. Mario brings over a large circular platform to house the pizza before it's brought over to the table. He then brings over the cheesesteak hoagie for Will and says, "Okay, young man. Let me know how my sandwich compares to those tourist traps in the city."

Will laughs. "Will do, Mario. Thank you. Looks wonderful." Next, Mario brings out the pizza and places it in the center of the table.

There's a ring from the front entrance bell. Simon walks through and notices the family sitting at their table. Mario notices Simon and says, "If it isn't one of my favorite customers. How are you doing, young man?"

Simon says, "Hey, Mario. Good today. Played at the arcade for hours. Stirred up an appetite."

Mario replies, "Hours? How many quarters did you go through?"

Simon laughs as he says, "It's not like it was back in the day, Mario. You pay a flat fee, and you can play all day as much as you want. In fact, I'll probably go back there after I've had some"— Simon walks over to the table where the family is sitting and grabs a big slice of pepperoni—"pizza for dinner. Can you ring up a soda, too, Mario and put it on their tab? Thanks. Hey, lovely family. What's going on?"

Ellie smiles and laughs at Simon, as Claire says, "Doing just fine, Simon. Please join us. Maybe next time you should ask first before taking."

Simon replies, "Sorry, Ellie's mom." Simon looks at Pete and says, "Good evening, sir."

Pete replies, "Evening, Simon. Please join us. Seems like you join us for dinner about three times a week nowadays. Simon, this is our family from Chicago. This is Will, Annie, Liam, and Boo."

Simon replies, "Yes of course. The family from Chicago. At last, we meet. Nice to meet all of you."

Simon grabs his soda from Mario, pulls up a chair next to Ellie, and finishes his slice of pizza quickly. By now there's only one slice of pizza left in the pan. Neil tries to take the last slice, but Simon quickly moves in before Neil can get his fingers on it. Simon says, "Anyone gonna have the last slice? Thanks."

Mario comes over to take the pan away, looks over at Will, and asks, "Well, sir. How does my sandwich taste in comparison?"

Will finishes his big bite from his hoagie and says, "It tastes like home, Mario. Thank you, sir."

Mario smiles. "No problem, sir. My pleasure."

Simon looks at Ellie and says, "You gonna join me over at the arcade?"

"Sure, but my cousins are coming along too. Want to show them around."

Neil quickly interjects, "And your brother too. Hey, Dad, can we have some money?"

Pete looks over to Claire for approval and pulls out his wallet. "Fine. Here's money for your little cousins too."

Will says, "Come on, Pete. Let me cover the kids."

Pete says, "Nope. Already taken care of, brother."

Will smiles and says, "Fine. Then dinner and coffee afterward are on me."

Pete smiles back and says, "Deal." Pete looks at Ellie and Neil as they stand up and walk over to Simon who's already halfway to the door. "Hey Neil...Ellie! Look after your cousins and meet us at the coffee shop in about an hour, okay? Have fun."

The group makes their way out the door, down the street, and into the arcade. Pete, Claire, Will, and Annie pay their bill and make their way over to the coffee shop.

Simon looks over to Liam and Boo and says, "Welcome to our home away from home."

Ellie pipes in. "So, Boo what do you think?"

Boo replies, "Looks like a classic selection of arcades to me. Awesome place."

Simon asks Liam and Boo, "You guys hang out at arcades back home?"

Liam answers, "Sure do. Our dad has been a fan of arcades since he was a kid. He'll occasionally take us to one of the biggest arcades around after a trip to Brookfield Zoo. It's right down the street from there."

Simon asks, "Is that so? So, what are your favorite games?"

Boo answers, "Mine are racing games."

Neil interjects into the conversation as the group walks past a row of pinball machines. "And mine is pinball. See you guys later."

Neil finds his favorite pinball machine and starts playing. Liam answers Simon, "Mine are fighting games."

Ellie looks at Simon, and Simon replies, "Is that so? So you have practice in the ways of the warrior, do you? Let's test those abilities. Select our game and fighter, sir." Ellie smiles, looks at Boo and says, "You guys have fun. I'll show Boo the racing games. See you in a bit."

Liam finds his favorite fighting game, takes his position, and selects his fighter. Simon follows suit. Simon says, "A fine choice, Liam. But I'll have to warn you. I've beat this game several times, and your cousin has never defeated me."

Liam smiles, looks at Simon, and says, "Okay. Challenge accepted. Game on." Simon and Liam go back and forth between rounds. Simon tries all of his best moves, but Liam counters perfectly. Liam wins two out of three fights! Shocked, Simon looks at Liam and says, "So, Liam. You are skilled in the ways of the warrior after all. Well played. Who taught you the ways?"

Liam laughs and says, "Thanks. My dad. Been training me in these games for years."

The group enjoys their evening at the arcade while Claire, Pete, Will, and Annie enjoy their coffee while sitting outside the coffee shop. The adults laugh, converse about their kids, and reminisce about past memories. As they are sitting outside, the temperature drops, and the wind begins to pick up. Will looks up at the dark sky and takes a deep breath in through his nose. "Smells like rain, folks. I didn't know that they were calling for storms."

Pete looks at the clouds to the west and says, "They weren't calling for any storms, but it looks like it's starting to lightning out toward the west. Maybe it's a good idea to get the kids and call it a night."

Annie replies, "Sounds like a good idea. I'll text Liam and let him know it's time to head home for the night."

Southwest of Doylestown, down Route 611, the storm is already wreaking havoc on the town of Elkins Park. Reggie is home. He's in his bedroom trying to play video games and forget about the frightening events over the last twenty-four hours. Lightning and thunder crash as the storm gets closer. A flash of lightning, a few seconds go by, and then a roar of thunder. A few seconds later, another big flash of lightning then a louder crash of thunder just a second behind it. The storm is getting closer. Reggie hits pause on his game and looks out his bedroom window. He sees the flashes of lightning, the winds bending the trees across the street, and the rain hitting his window. There's another big flash of lightning and a huge crash of thunder that hits so close to Reggie's house that Reggie sees an orange glow outside his window. The lights flicker for a moment, then the power goes out in Reggie's home. Reggie looks around his dark room and says, "Great. Just what I need right now." Reggie looks out the window as his eyes adjust to the darkness. The storm rages on outside. Across the street is the eight-foot stone wall that encircles and barricades the boundaries of Elk's Estate. Reggie looks out toward the stone wall of the estate. He thinks he sees something standing on top of the stone wall. It looks tall but he can't make it out. There's another big flash of lightning and Reggie sees The Shadow Man standing on top of the stone wall looking in his direction. The Shadow Man waves to Reggie! Reggie screams, shuts the blinds, runs over to his bed, and covers his head with his pillow. The storms go by as Reggie stays in his bed alone in the dark. He begins to cry. He weeps for his friend Jerald. As he sobs for the loss of his friend, in a scared stammer he says to himself, "Jerald's g-g-gone. The Shadow Man is going to g-g-get me sooner or later. My folks don't believe a word I say. No one can help me! Oh, God, I'm so s-s-s-scared. Please help me."

CHAPTER 15

....

CRAZY OLD MAN JACK

As the storm rages on outside, a local drifter named Jack tries to take shelter from the storm. Jack is an older man with long, unkept white hair, a long salt-and-pepper beard, and extremely sun-damaged skin. The locals call him Crazy Old Man Jack. Jack lived his entire life in and around Elkins Park. He was raised by his folks in a small house just a mile away from Elk's Estate. He remembers being a young boy and walking past Elk's Estate when the original Elk family owned the property. This was before the property was later purchased by the Catholic Church. For several years, Jack worked as a groundskeeper for the estate.

Since the property was so vast, the upkeep of the property was his full-time work. Jack lived on the property in one of the small cottages on the far edge of the grounds. Life was simple but peaceful for him. The pay wasn't fantastic, but it was enough to support him, and he couldn't complain about the free cottage living that overlooked the pond. When the Catholic Church finally sold the property, Jack was forced from his home, and he was left to his own defenses. Jack hoped he would be able to stay and live on the property for the rest of his life. He was never good with his finances and didn't have much saved to afford a place of his own. He settled to a life living as a drifter. He took odd jobs working for cash to help local homeowners with their landscaping. Every month he picked up his social security check from a PO box from the local post office.

Some of the locals would help Jack from time to time. They would hear him coming down the block with his raggedy old wagon holding all his landscaping tools and equipment. He would go around and ask to work on other's property. Some would accept and give him cash for his troubles. Others were troubled by his look and appearance and sent him away.

Tonight, Jack makes his way around the stone wall surrounding the property. On gloomy nights like this, Jack would take refuge underneath the large storm drain that runs underneath one of the residential streets. The property itself is closed off with the stone wall and chains with locks on all the gates, but no one thought to block access to the property from the storm drain.

Jack makes it to the storm drain. Wet, tired and miserable, he drags his squeaky-wheeled wagon underneath the drain so his tools and equipment can dry off. He says to himself as he laughs, "These dirty old clothes of mine needed washing anyway. Lucky for me, I guess. My tools will be okay here. But I need somewhere dry to rest for the night. Let me look around."

Jack grabs his trusty flashlight and backpack from his wagon and walks through the storm drain and into the interior section of the property. Rain, thunder, and lightning still crash down from the heavens above as Jack makes his way toward his old cottage. The cottages date to when the Elk family originally owned the property. The cottages were living quarters for some of the staff who worked in the main house as housekeepers or kitchen staff. Customary for the time, Elk's Estate had a tunnel that went from the main house back to the cottages so the family and guests wouldn't see the workers as they moved back and forth along the property. The tunnel ran on a downward angle from the main house. The cottages, along with the other buildings on the property, have been boarded up and secured by the local authorities. Lucky for Jack, the local authorities were too cheap to remove or change the locks on the door that leads to the tunnel. He also knows that the floors of the tunnel will be dry as we walks upward toward the main house.

Jack walks past the pond that borders the cottage grounds. He flashes his light along the dark waters as thousands of tiny droplets hit its wavy surface. As the wind blows and Jack struggles to keep his hat on, he hears the echoes of voices being carried in the wind. He freezes, pans his flashlight around, and exclaims, "Hello! Anyone there! Hello! Damn place. Love it but it still gives me the willies." Jack pans his flashlight and sees his target. A few yards away from the front porch of his old cottage are the stairs that lead down to a tunnel entrance. Jack chuckles and says to himself, "Bingo. I still got my old keys that unlock that door."

He makes his way down the stairs to the door and reaches into a side pocket in his cargo pants, feeling for his set of keys. He focuses his light on the door lock. The flashlight starts to fade and turn off just as he tries to put the key into the lock. Jack says, "Damn flashlight! Batteries must be getting wet. Come on baby, just hold out for a few more minutes." Jack hits the side of the flashlight a few times, and the light turns back on. Jack puts the key into the lock and unlocks the door. He opens the door pushing against mud and running water along the entrance. He makes it inside and says, "Okay, home sweet home for tonight."

Jack walks up the tunnel for about ten yards and finds a solid dry patch of ground to sleep in for the night. The tunnel is made of a concrete floor and large stone cement walls. The tunnel is supported by old wooden lintels that stretch from one side to another. He flashes his light forward toward the tunnel entrance of the main house. He just sees a long tunnel. Jack thinks, *Damn! I still wish I had that key that opened the door to the main house. Lost that stupid thing years back somewhere on the grounds. I could live like a king in the main house, and no one would be the wiser.* Jack puts his flashlight down. He takes off his drenched long-sleeve shirt and hat and places them onto the dry floor. Next, he takes out an old sheet and a towel from his backpack. He places the sheet onto the floor and uses the towel to dry his face and hair. He then rolls up the towel and plans to use it for a pillow.

Jack settles down nicely onto the floor, turns off his flashlight, closes his eyes, and tries to drift off to sleep. Outside the storm carries on. A gust of wind comes from the outside entrance of the tunnel. Jack hears the echoes again as the wind travels past him and up the corridor. Jack is startled, opens his eyes, and turns on his flashlight to look around. "Damn it! I know someone is here! Who's there and what you want?" Jack pans his lights toward the outside entrance as the crash of thunder vibrates the tunnel corridor. His heart rate starts to pound, and his breathing starts to increase. He pans his flashlight back toward the long corridor up to the main house entrance. All he sees is a shadow!

Jack thinks, *What the hell?* Jack exclaims, "Is someone down there! Show yourself!" Jack's flashlight begins to burn out and then turns off. Jack hit his light and says, "Oh God. Work dammit!" The flashlight comes back to life for a few seconds. The shadow only gets bigger as it moves down the tunnel toward him. The flashlight goes out again! Jack stands up and hits the side of his flashlight again. It turns back on but only for a few seconds to show The Shadow Man positioned upside down right in front of him! Jack only catches a glimpse of the figure before he walks backward and trips over his backpack. Jack falls to the ground. The Shadow Man says in his deep dark voice, "Welcome home, Jack."

Jack exclaims, "What the hell are you?" Jack scrambles to pick up his flashlight, but it's slightly out of reach. The Shadow Man stands over Jack and begins to laugh. Jack pulls himself forward and tries to grab his flashlight, but he feels something wrapped around his legs and starts to pull him to the outside entrance! Jack thinks it's a snake or a rope as it wraps around him tightly and drags him quickly out of the tunnel. Jack screams, "Oh God! What the hell is this? Please let me go!" The Shadow Man walks alongside Jack as he gets pulled outside. The tunnel entrance door slams shut.

The Shadow Man says, "This is your welcome home party, Jack. My guests and I have been expecting you." Jack, bewildered and terrified, looks at his legs and tries to figure out what has him in its grasp. Lightning flashes and Jack sees large vines of lily pads wrapped around his legs and pulling him toward the pond! Jack screams, but it's no use. The thunder drowns out his cries for help. The Shadow Man continues to walk alongside Jack and says, "I know this is what you want, Jack. I know you wanted to stay here. Most people don't want to leave. Now, I'm making your dreams come true. You'll fit in nicely with our other guests."

Jack screams some more as his legs begin to submerge into the shallow waters of the pond. The vines continue to reach deeper into the depths of the water. Jack screams until his face is below the water's surface. His face drifts underneath the surface of the water and down into the blackness of the depths. The Shadow Man stands along the shore and laughs. He then walks away and back toward the main house. He laughs some more and says, "I can't wait for my other guests to arrive. They'll enjoy their stay, especially Will and his family."

CHAPTER 16

....

WAIT! WHAT HAPPENED?

The family reconvenes together in Downtown Doylestown. Simon joins the rest of the group and says, "What's the plan gang?"

Pete replies, "There's a storm brewing out to the west." Pete pauses, looks at his phone, and continues, "The radar shows the storm came out of nowhere and is moving northeast toward us, so it will be best to head home. How did you get here, Simon?"

"I rode my bike down the trail from home to downtown."

Will interjects, "We can fit your bike in our van, and we can all make our way home."

Simon looks at Ellie and asks, "Spend some time with you and the fam back at the house?"

Ellie answers, "Sounds like a plan. We can play some video games or something."

The family make their way to their vehicles. Simon puts his bike into Will's van and then rides back home with Pete, Claire, Neil, and Ellie. They arrive back home as the winds and rain continue to gain momentum. They make their way into the house before the main body of the storm arrives at their doorstep. Simon says, "Well, it's good to be home."

Claire replies, "Yeah, Simon. If you hang out anymore at our house, I swear I'm going to claim you on my taxes."

Pete looks at Simon and says, "You're welcome to stay as long as you want, Simon. Just let your parents know what's going on, okay?"

Simon answers, "Of course. Already texted them and told them I'll be home after the storm passes."

Will, Annie, Pete, and Claire make their way to the kitchen for some more coffee and conversation. Neil, Ellie, Liam, Boo, and Simon walk upstairs to Neil's room and close the door. Simon walks over to Liam and Boo and says, "So, Ellie says there's something interesting and mysterious about you two."

Ellie says, "We haven't dived deep into what happened yet, but Liam promised he would tell us the story."

Liam replies, "Before we get into it, let's put on the TV and drown out our conversation."

Neil turns on the TV, and Simon says, "A secret story. You're right, Ellie. Now you have my full attention."

Liam looks at Boo. "What do you think?"

Boo looks back at Liam. "Tell them the truth. It's up to them to believe it or not."

Liam walks around the room and collects his thoughts. The thunder and lightning continue to get closer. Rain begins to hit the window harder and heavier. Liam looks out the bedroom window and out toward the backyard. The rain falls quickly from the glass down to the gutters.

Simon says, "Now this is entertaining. I'm on the edge of my seat."

Liam looks at everyone and says, "Last year, Boo and I were attacked by a werewolf. We were trying to help a few new friends. A lot of people died in the process. This older gentleman, Mr. Rosalie, saved our lives. We lost him too."

Neil says, "Oh come on! Really? I'm calling bullshit!"

Ellie laughs, and Simon says, "Good one, Liam. You're a good storyteller. It's Ellie's and my favorite genre."

Boo interjects and exclaims, "He's not making it up! It's all true. If you don't believe me, look up Iron River, Michigan. You'll definitely find some shaky and blurry clips of a beast attacking people."

Liam interjects, "It's all true. I'll give you some of the names of the people involved. You'll find their obituaries. Most of them died within a day or two of each other."

There's another bright flash from a lightning strike and a crash of thunder outside. Simon, Neil, and Ellie stop laughing and now look serious. Neil says, "You're both for real, aren't you? You're not making this up?"

Simon says, "Holy shit! A real-life werewolf like straight out of the movies?"

Liam answers, "Yes. Boo, me, and a few other friends survived."

Ellie asks, "Like, how did you kill the werewolf? Silver bullet or something?"

Boo answers, "We didn't kill the werewolf. Mr. Rosalie did. Blew himself up in a mining cave surrounded by iron and silver with a stick of dynamite."

Simon says, "Wicked!"

Neil interjects, "Wait a minute! This kind of makes more sense than the bullshit story our parents told us."

Liam asks, "What did your parents tell you?"

Neil answers, "Basically that Aunt Annie's folks suddenly sold the house. Didn't make much sense to us. Sounded like your side of the family really enjoyed it up there."

Liam replied, "Yeah. My grandparents sold the house, but that was after the events that happened last summer. We haven't been back since."

Simon says, "Dude. You and your sister are like straight up monster hunters." Simon looks at Ellie and says, "Why didn't you tell me that your little cousins are this cool? They're little kids, but they're slaying monsters. That's badass."

Ellie says, "Yeah, really. I would have if I knew, but this is the first I'm hearing it." Ellie looks at Simon and says, "And it sounds like there's something strange happening at that abandoned mansion in Elkins Park."

Simon replies, "The one that your mom is trying to help keep open?"

Neil answers, "Yeah, the one we've been working on over the summer for our community service hours."

Simon looks at Ellie and asks, "What do you mean strange?"

Ellie answers, "We went out there, and we couldn't get access to the property. Police, yellow tape, detectives, county morgue van, ambulance, you name it."

Simon replies, "Yes. You mentioned some of this in your text message! What happened?"

Neil answers, "Some kid died in the middle of the night inside the property line."

Boo interjects, "It's true. The really strange part of this story was meeting that other kid."

Simon asks, "What other kid?"

Boo answers, "This kid named Reggie. He was with the kid who died."

Simon asks, "What did he say to you?"

Boo answers, "Nothing much. He seems to be still living in the moment or something. Kind of like he was playing the scene over and over in his head."

Neil says, "It's called 'shocked,' Boo."

Boo replies, "I know what shocked means, Neil. I experienced it after the werewolf attack."

Ellie says, "Really smooth, bro."

Neil replies, "Shut up!"

Boo continues, "He mentioned something about a Shadow Man. He said The Shadow Man got him or something like that."

Simon is really intrigued, looks at Ellie, and says, "Ellie, is this true! This kid saw The Shadow Man?"

Ellie answers, "Yeah, that's what he said. Figure I would run it past you and see if you know anything about it."

Liam reenters the conversation. "Why would Simon know about The Shadow Man?"

Simon says, "Ellie and I like this ghost stuff, and we try to do research on the subject from time to time. We ride our bikes out to old, abandoned buildings, try to do research on the property, set up a voice recorder, asks questions, see if anything comes through, have our cameras rolling on our phones, that sort of thing."

Neil exclaims, "That's what you two nerds have been doing this whole time? Why didn't you tell me about this?"

Ellie answers, "Because you can't keep a secret to save your life. I know it would get to Mom and Dad and then I'll be in deep shit."

Liam asks, "Have you and Ellie ever found any evidence on ghosts from your research?"

Simon answers, "We had a few things. Noises in the house. Things falling or possibly being thrown around. My voice recorder captured some strange voices in a low frequency. Some pretty cool stuff."

Ellie says, "Yeah it was enough to convince me to believe in this stuff and to continue doing research. Simon asked me if I ever saw anything creepy at the main house back in Elkins Park."

Liam asks, "Did you experience anything, Ellie?"

"Nothing. Pardon the pun but dead silence."

Liam looks over at Neil. "How 'bout you, Neil, anything?"

Neil replies, "No. Nothing. But I wasn't looking for anything either."

Liam looks at Simon. "You heard of this Shadow Man?"

Simon answers, "Only a few things online. Nothing from a formal website or something. Just a few mentions of The Shadow Man through some social media platforms about local ghosts and legends."

Liam asks, "What's been said about this thing?"

Simon replies, "It's supposed to haunt the grounds of the property. Some of the locals around Elkins Park claim to have seen a shadow figure from time to time. Supposed to be tall, thin, wearing a large hat, like a gardening hat, and some claimed to have seen green eyes."

Simon asks Ellie, "When do you think you'll be going back to the property?"

Ellie answers, "Not sure. I think my mom has to wait for the green light from the Elkins Park PD before we can do anything else. What are you thinking?"

Simon answers, "I think I'll volunteer my services next time you go there. Try to do some field research if you will. Any idea on how we can contact this kid, Reggie?"

Neil says, "He's a local kid. He lives in the apartment buildings across from the property. Don't know which building or unit. He stormed away while we were trying to talk to him."

Ellie interjects, "There's some type of connection between the victim, who was Reggie's friend, and one of Mom's friends who used to work at the estate. Maybe I can find the kid through Mom's social media account, see if her friend has a profile and then find Reggie in the process."

Neil asks, "Won't you need Mom's password?"

Ellie rolls her eyes. "I know Mom's password. She uses the same password for everything."

Neil replies, "Wow. I guess all of the truth is coming out tonight, sis."

Liam looks at Boo and then looks at the rest of the group. There's another quick flash of lightning that hits so close to the house there's an orange glow outside the window. Immediately after, there's an exploding boom of thunder that shakes the house and flickers the lights. The group looks startled for a moment. All except for Liam who focuses his attention on the group. "It sounds like we have some work to do. Neil, try to find out when we are going back to the property. Ellie, you work your magic online and see what you can find out. Simon, try to do more research on the property and this Shadow Man. If we agree, we will try to find out what's happening on that property and help this kid Reggie. And more importantly, don't tell the grown-ups. Agreed?" The group looks at each other and nods. Simon and Ellie smile at each other. Simon says, "Sounds like we have a real-life ghostly mystery to solve. Let's do it!"

CHAPTER 17

....

WORKING THEIR MAGIC

The storm stays in the area for the remainder of the evening. Simon's parents eventually drive over to the house to pick up Simon and his bike. The bleak weather from the night before washes away overnight. Liam wakes up to a bright and beautiful sunny morning and to the smell of breakfast cooking downstairs. Liam rubs his eyes, gets out of bed, and walks out to the hallway. Boo exits the bathroom. Liam looks at Boo. "Smells good. What's Aunt Claire cooking today?"

Boo, now in fresh clothes, was busy combing her damp hair. She answers, "Not sure. Haven't been downstairs yet. Dad said to get ready for the day. He was planning to take us into the city."

Liam asks, "Did he say what we were doing?"

Boo answers, "He was mumbling something about experiencing history."

Liam walks past Ellie's bedroom door. Ellie is up but still in her pajamas. She is working on her computer and browsing through some social media pages. Liam walks into the room. Ellie smiles and says, "Morning, monster slayer. How did you sleep?"

Liam smiles, laughs a bit, and says, "Good. Didn't wake up at all. No nightmares either. Able to find anything?"

Ellie replies, "I'm logged in under my mom's account. I found some potentials for sure. I narrowed down the search to a few people who are both friends with my mom and grandmom. I'm looking through their friends and family lists to see if I can spot our new friend."

Liam replies, "Okay cool. Let me know if you find anything,"

Ellie chuckles. "Will do, boss. I'll be down in a bit to have breakfast. Simon will probably get back to me later today. Knowing him, he was probably up late playing video games online. He's still in bed. Guaranteed."

Liam walks out of Ellie's room and downstairs into the kitchen. Will, Annie, Pete, and Neil are all sitting at the kitchen table. Will looks at Liam and says, "Hey good morning, sleepy head."

Annie takes a sip from her coffee and says, "Morning, honey. How did you sleep?"

Liam says, "Good, Mom."

Pete stands up and gets a plate for Liam and says, "Aunt Claire is making some eggs, and she picked up some fresh bagels from the bakery this morning. Help yourself."

Liam replies, "Thanks, Uncle Pete. What are you having on your bagel?"

Pete smiles. "I just like cream cheese on my bagel, buddy."

Liam exclaims, "You're not having that lox stuff that my dad likes?"

Pete replies, "Lox is a smoked salmon, buddy. It's good for ya. A good East Coast breakfast. But I must be in the mood for that meal. Just ask your old man. That's what he's having."

Liam looks over to his dad who was eating a big piece of lox from his raisin bagel and gives Liam and thumbs up.

Claire walks toward Liam and says, "Don't listen to your dad, honey. He's crazy. That's stuff is disgusting. Come with me, honey. Take your pick of bagel and take as much scrambled eggs as you want."

As Liam decides on his bagel, Neil walks over to his mom to get more eggs. He asks, "Hey, Mom. Any idea when we will be able to get back to the property?"

Liam looks over to Neil as Neil winks back at him with a smile. Claire answers, "Good question, honey. I have to call back that detective today and find out. Planning to call him after breakfast. But before you get seconds, let me serve your cousin."

Claire puts some eggs onto Liam's plate and says, "Why don't you start out with these eggs, honey, and I'll bring over your bagel when it pops out of the toaster."

Liam takes his breakfast over to the kitchen table and sits. Liam looks at his dad and asks, "What's the plan today, Dad?"

Will looks up at Liam. "I want to take you to an important place on our nation's history son. You, Boo, and mom. I've got reserved tickets to do a tour of Independence Hall! And while we are down there, we can check out the Liberty Bell and Betsy Ross's house. Mom mentioned you were learning a little bit more about the Revolutionary War in school."

Liam replies, "What about the rest of the family?"

Will answers, "Uncle Pete and Aunt Claire have been down there plenty of times with their own kids. Plus, Uncle Pete has to do some work on the computer. Aunt Claire has some errands to run, and it sounds like Neil and Ellie are busy today. Plus, if you're up for it, we can check out a baseball game today. There's a home game in the midafternoon."

Liam smiles. "Sounds great, Dad. Thank you."

Annie laughs and says, "Trust me, Liam, he's not doing it for you. He has selfish reasons."

Will smiles and replies, "I'm not doubting your statement. I want to see my hometown team too. It's been a while."

Liam finishes his breakfast and makes his way upstairs to get ready for the day. Liam walks past Ellie's room when she exclaims, "Liam! Come here really quick!"

Liam walks up to Ellie's computer, and she says, "I found him! Here's our guy. Here's Reggie."

Liam looks at the screen. "Yup! That's him. That's Reggie all right. Were you able to find his address somewhere?"

Ellie replies, "I can't find much. He's not friends with my mom. But he's friends with this lady my mom knows. I think she's the lady that my mom and your dad talked to when we visited the apartment building."

Liam asks, "What are you thinking?"

Ellie replies, "I'll talk to Neil and Simon. If we can make it happen, maybe Neil can drive down to the building, and Simon and I can talk to this lady and find out more about Reggie. Get his address, visit him, and talk to him. Find out more about what happened."

Liam replies, "What are you gonna tell your parents?"

Ellie smiles and says, "Don't worry about them. We will give some excuse to leave the house with the car. Sounds like my mom and dad will be busy most of the day anyway."

Liam smiles back. "Sounds good, cuz. Work your magic."

After everyone finishes with breakfast, Liam, Boo, Will, and Annie make their way to their vehicle and head into the city. Ellie is finishing up her research on the computer. She tries to text Simon. No answer. She waits a few minutes and tries to call him. Her call goes to voicemail. Frustrated, Ellie thinks, *He's probably still in bed sleeping.* Just then, she gets a call from Simon. She answers, "Hey, bud. What's up?"

Simon answers, "Sorry, didn't mean to miss your call. I slept in late. After I got home, I logged into the network and was playing online with some of the crew from the band. Fell asleep with the controller in my hand."

Ellie laughs. "So, what you're really trying to say is you didn't do any research on The Shadow Man."

Simon replies, "I didn't say that at all. In fact, I've been hard at work for the last hour. I've been trying to find out more about our shadow character. Ran into a lot of dead ends. Pardon the pun. But I found out some really interesting stuff about the history of the estate. At least as much as I can online."

Ellie asks, "What are you thinking?"

Simon answers, "I know that the Elkins Park Library has that whole local history section."

Ellie replies, "And I thought I was a big nerd. Do you think they will have more information at the local library?"

Simon replies, "You've read my mind, gorgeous."

Ellie exclaims, "This can work out perfectly! My brother can drive. We can stop by the Elkins Park Library on the way down to the estate. We can find out what we can there. Also, I found our mystery person. That kid Reggie. We can hit the library first, then talk to this lady who knows Reggie, and then hopefully talk to Reggie himself."

Simon replies, "Works for me. Let me know when you're on your way. I'll be ready."

Meanwhile, Pete and Claire are talking in the kitchen. Pete is on his laptop sending an email while Claire is cleaning up from breakfast. Ellie approaches Neil and tells him about her plan. Neil approves and approaches his parents. Neil walks into the kitchen and says, "Hey, Dad! Question."

Pete replies, "Answer."

Neil says, "It's supposed to be a really nice day. Do you mind if I take the convertible out for a ride?"

Pete answers, "That depends, son."

Neil replies, "On what, Dad?"

Pete takes a break from typing on his laptop and answers, "It depends on where you are planning to go and if you can bring the car back with a full tank of gas this time."

Neil laughs. "Nowhere special, Dad. Ellie asked if I could take her over to the skateboard park in Jenkintown with Simon. Figured afterward we can get something to eat in town."

Pete looks at Neil, then looks at Claire and asks, "What do you think, honey?"

Claire says, "I don't care. It's not my convertible. I'll have to call back that detective and run some errands, so I'll be busy most of the day."

Pete looks back at Neil. He smiles, stands up, reaches into his pocket, walks over to Neil, and hands over some money. "I can use the peace and quiet this afternoon. With everyone out of the house, I can focus on work. Bring her back with a full tank and run it through the car wash too. The rest of the cash is for you and Ellie. Not for Simon. Let that freeloader pay his own way."

Neil replies, "Thanks, Dad. Will do. You got a lot of work today?"

Pete replies, "Sure do. A lot of clients are filing claims due to the storm damage. These storms have been brutal. But anyway, have fun."

Neil grabs the keys, and Ellie follows him out to the convertible. Neil turns the ignition and asks, "Where to first, sis?"

Ellie replies, "First stop, Simon. Next stop, Elkins Park Library."

Claire finishes cleaning up the kitchen and reaches for her phone on the counter. She looks up the contact information for the Elkins Park Police Department. She finds the non-emergency number and calls it. The phone rings a few times and a then a young voice answers the call saying, "Elkins Park Police Department, this is Officer Adams speaking, how can I direct your call?"

Claire answers, "I'm sorry who is this?"

Officer Adams answers, "This is Officer Ethan Adams, ma'am. How can I direct your call?"

Claire replies, "My name is Claire. I'm in charge of the volunteer group for Elk's Estate. I want to talk to someone in charge to ask if we can get access to the property."

Officer Adams pauses for a moment while he thinks of an answer. As Ethan is looking around the department office area for help, Kenny walks across the front desk. Kenny says, "Hey good morning, kid. How was the night shift?"

Ethan replies to Claire, "Ma'am, I'll have to put you on a brief hold." Ethan puts Claire on hold.

Kenny asks, "Who's on the phone, kid?"

Ethan answers, "First, the night shift was fine. No calls. I had the front desk duty. And no one called in about Crazy Old Man Jack."

Kenny replies, "I guess that old man found somewhere to hide from the weather last night and sleep it off. I wonder where he goes when the weather is bad."

Ethan replies, "If it's not sleeping off his miserable life here in lockup overnight, I don't know. Nor do I care."

Kenny says, "Man. Good attitude, rookie. Who's on the phone?"

Ethan answers, "Some lady. Says she's in charge of the volunteer group for the Elk's Estate. She's wondering when she can get access."

Kenny answers the phone saying, "Good morning, ma'am. This is Officer Mills. How can I help you?"

Claire says, "Yes I'm trying to talk to someone in charge over there to find out when I can get access to the Elk's Estate."

Kenny answers, "I'm not sure, ma'am. This is Claire, right? I met you and your brother outside the estate entrance. This is Kenny, Will's old friend."

Claire, getting frustrated says, "Yes, everyone seems to know my brother. Very popular guy. Can you direct me to someone who might have an answer please?"

With the phone still up to his ear, Kenny looks around the office and sees Detective Rhinelander sitting in his office looking over some files. Kenny says, "Yes, ma'am, I'll have to place you on a brief hold." Kenny places Claire on hold and uses the intercom system to place a call directly into Detective Rhinelander's office.

The phone rings and Detective Rhinelander answers, "Yeah, kid. What can I do for you?"

Kenny replies, "Hey, Eric. This is Kenny."

Eric replies, "Oh hey, Kenny. What's up?"

"I got a lively woman on the other line who loves to be placed on hold several times while she gets bounced around the office trying to get an answer. Figure you're the perfect person to answer her question, Detective."

Eric rolls his eyes. "Okay send it over."

Kenny says, "You got it, sir."

The phone rings in Eric's office. He answers, "Detective Rhinelander."

Claire says, "Great. At least I'm getting closer to a sergeant on duty or something."

Eric replies, "There's no sergeant on this shift, ma'am. The chief is in the process of selecting a new one."

Claire asks, "Can I just talk to the chief then?"

Eric answers, "Unfortunately no, ma'am. The chief will be away from the office today, so I'm the highest-ranking officer on duty. So, what can I do for you?"

Claire answers, "Detective. My name is Claire. I'm the person in charge of the volunteer group for the estate. I want to get in there as soon as possible to continue my work with my crew."

Eric pauses and asks, "Can I ask what's the rush, ma'am? The place has only been there for a century."

Claire takes and deep breath due to frustration and says, "Detective, I want to complete as much of the cleanup in the building before the end of the month. That's when the committee from the historical society is planning to evaluate our work and determine if they are going to invest the money and resources into the property."

Eric says, "Ah ha. I see. And what happens to the estate if the committee decides against it?"

Claire answers, "Then the building will continue to deteriorate until it either falls down or burns down."

Eric looks down at his paperwork on his desk and pauses in silence for a moment. "Well, it looks like you're in luck, ma'am."

Claire asks, "How's that, Detective?"

"Well, I'm about to close this case and rule it out to be accidental. I'm still waiting for the final report from the coroner's office, but everything looks like this kid's death was accidental. I might be in and around the grounds of the estate for the next few days so I can wrap this up, but you can have access to the property starting tomorrow morning."

Claire says, "That's sounds great, Detective, thank you. We will be back out there tomorrow for sure."

"You're welcome, ma'am. I'll connect you with Officer Adams and coordinate a time. Good luck and have a good day."

CHAPTER 18

....

DOING SOME DETECTIVE WORK OF OUR OWN

Ellie and Neil make their way to Simon's house. It's a beautiful summer morning in Doylestown. Ellie and Neil have the convertible top down. The warm summer wind blows steadily through Ellie's think dark hair. Neil asks, "So after we pick up Simon, what's our first stop again?"

Ellie replies, "The Elkins Park Library. Simon has an idea on how we can find out more about the property. He says that library has a local history section."

Neil laughs. "Wow what a nerd! You two are a perfect match."

"Shut up! Again, Simon isn't my boyfriend."

"You say that now, sis. Time will tell."

Neil and Ellie drive up to Simon's driveway, and Neil honks the horn. Simon makes his way out of the house. Simon is wearing a monster movie T-shirt, jean shorts, white socks, and black shoes. Neil says, "Your boyfriend even dresses like a dork."

Ellie answers, "Whatever."

Simon jumps into the back seat of the convertible. "I always like doing that. Makes me feel like I'm in some type of 80s comedy movie. So, the plan is to check out the library first, right?"

Ellie says, "Yeah, that's the plan. Afterward, I figure you and I can talk to the lady my mom knows and try to find out more about Reggie."

Simon says, "Sounds like a plan, monster slayers." Simon puts on his aviator sunglasses and says, "Okay, Neil. Let's ride."

Neil rolls his eyes and looks at Ellie. Ellie rolls her eyes.

Neil, Simon, and Ellie make their way south on Route 611 toward Elkins Park. They drive through Willow Grove and Jenkintown. Neil drives past a Wawa gas station and says to Ellie, "Remind me to stop there on the way home. Dad's orders."

Ellie replies, "Got it and noted."

After a few more minutes of driving, Neil pulls up to the Elkins Park Public Library. Neil parks the car. Neil and Ellie both exit the vehicle as Simon attempts to jump out of the back seat from hoping on top of the trunk and off the vehicle with both feet. He stumbles and makes a crash landing, falls chest first, and completely wipes out onto the parking lot surface. Neil laughs and says, "You're as graceful as you are athletic. What as dork."

Ellie comes to aid her friend and says, "Shut it, Neil! Last time I checked, Liam is more athletic than you are."

Neil says, "Yeah, whatever."

Ellie helps bring Simon to his feet. "You okay, bud?"

Simon replies, "As long as I have you wrapped in my arms, of course I'm okay."

Ellie laughs and says, "Okay, Romeo."

The three make their way into the Elkins Park Library's main entrance. It's a beautiful colonial building complete with large white columns encircling the main entrance and old window shutters around each window surrounded by its red brick traditional masonry. As they walk in the main entrance, Simon directs Neil and Ellie toward the local history section of the library. Neil asks Simon, "How did you know about this place?"

Simon says, "I'm a nerd, remember? Plus, I love this old stuff. You can find out some interesting things. Things that haven't made it to the internet."

They walk past an archway with "The History of Elkins Park" along the top. The section has several shelves of old books, a table dedicated to the old, preserved newspapers from the *Elkins Park Inquirer*, an archive of old maps from the settlement years, and a digital newspaper section to browse through. Ellie says, "This is cool. How should we go about this, Simon?"

Simon looks around, inhales deeply through his nose, and says, "Ah, the smell of old books and newspapers. I wish they would put this scent into a candle or something." Simon cracks his knuckles and continues, "Figure many hands make the work light. Ellie, you start in the old book archive. Neil, you make your way through the digital newspaper clippings, and I'll maneuver my way through the old newspaper archives and maps."

They all agree with that plan and make their way to their assigned stations. Ellie finds books that were preserved from the original Elkins Park Elementary School that was established in the late 1700s. This section was titled, "The educational books from the times of the settlement." After several minutes, Ellie looks over toward Simon who's already at his table putting on a pair of white gloves. Ellie asks, "What are you doing, dude?"

Simon replies, "The library asks you to apply gloves while handling the newspapers. Helps keep our greasy fingers off the paper and help preserve it for longer. Find anything yet?"

Ellie answers, "Found some interesting things but nothing about the estate."

Ellie continues to walk down the rows of old books when she sees a small sign that reads, "The Elk's Estate Archive." She sees a man in the aisle looking at the row of books next to archive. He's an older gentleman wearing a US Navy baseball hat, a yellow button shirt, jeans, and a gray Member's Only Jacket. The man looks at Ellie and says, "Sorry. Let me get out of your way." Upon closer examination, Ellie notices that the man looks sickly. His skin looks pale and jaundiced. The man is very skinny. So much so that he no longer fits in his seasoned clothes that are at least two sizes too big from his former natural frame. He smiles at Ellie through his glasses that are resting midway along his nose. Ellie looks at him as though he's a familiar face and says, "No worries, sir. I'm just looking for some info on Elk's Estate. Do I know you from somewhere?"

The old man replies with a smile, "You've seen me around, I'm sure. But if you're looking for information about the Elk's Estate you've come to the right place." The old man points to a row of books on the top shelf and continues, "In fact, make sure you look at these. Interesting stuff."

Ellie says, "Thank you. I know I met you somewhere. You look so familiar."

The old man laughs and coughs slightly. "Don't worry about it, kid. I'll see you around." The old man does an about-face and begins to walk down the aisle. He turns his head and extends his arm. He ways goodbye with a slight shake of his hands and exits the aisle.

Still feeling strange about the encounter, Ellie walks to the end of the aisle to get one more look at the old man. She reaches the end of the aisle and doesn't see the old man anywhere. Ellie turns and heads back to the row of books that the old man pointed out to her. Excited, she calls for Simon to come over and look at her discovery.

Simon asks, "What did you find?"

Ellie replies, "I think I found the motherload. Check it out!"

As they scan through the row of books, they find old copies of classic literature and other books that look like diaries.

Simon says, "Well this is interesting."

As they are looking at the books, one of the Elkins Park librarians walks past them. She asks, "Hello, do you need help finding anything in particular?"

Simon turns to answer, "Yes, ma'am. We are thinking of doing a podcast regarding the old Elk's Estate and are looking for more information. What can you tell us about this collection?"

The librarian asks, "I'm sorry, where are my manners? I didn't introduce myself. My name is Grace. And you are?"

Simon and Ellie introduce themselves formally as Grace introduces them to the collection. Grace answers, "Well, it is nice seeing young people interested in our town's history. What you see in front of you are books from the private library of Arthur Elk. You will also find some old diaries from his family. Mainly from his children."

Ellie asks, "So Arthur Elk was the rich dude who built the estate?"

Grace smiles. "Yes indeed. Arthur Elk was a very successful businessman who immigrated from England to the states in the late 1800s. He was a descendant of old money who came from English royalty. When he came over to the States, he settled in Elkins Park and began building his private estate."

Simon asks, "Where did he make that kind of money to build such a grand estate?"

Grace answers, "He invested heavily into the expansion of the United States railroad system during the great mass expansion in the early 1900s. That's how he made most of his wealth."

Simon says, "You seem to know a lot about this family, ma'am."

Grace smiles and says, "Yes indeed. One of my aunts was one of the Catholic sisters who used to work at the estate until it shut down completely. She helped with the preservation and acquisition of this private library and diaries to the library."

Simon says, "That's very interesting as well. Who was your aunt?"

Grace answers, "She's retired but is still active in the Catholic Church. Still goes by her 'Sister' name. Sister Rachel of the Dominican Sisters. Now, I must catalog a few new books for our library. But if you have any further questions, please feel free to ask."

Simon and Ellie both say thank you and Neil walks down the aisle and toward them. Neil asks, "Who was that?"

Simon says, "She's a librarian with a wealth of knowledge that may come in handy."

Ellie says, "I'm really interested in looking at these old diaries. Did you find anything, Neil?"

Neil answers, "Believe it or not I did. Some old newspaper reels about the construction of Elk's Estate from the old *Elkins Park Inquire*."

Simon says, "Cool, let me look at that with you while Ellie checks out these old diaries."

Ellie takes a few diaries off the shelf, sits down in a quiet corner, and starts reading. Neil and Simon walk back toward the digital newspaper archive. Simon asks, "Okay, dude. What did you find?"

Neil says, "Take a look for yourself."

Simon starts reading the article titled, *"The Elk's Family Breaks Ground on Their Luxurious Estate."* Simon continues, *"Wealthy railroad businessman Arthur Elk breaks ground today on the annexed 26-acre area. Mr. Elk plans to maintain his current residence in downtown Philadelphia until the grand estate is built from the ground up. Mr. Elk has hired an esteemed architect, George*

Walter Ruth, from England who has a long-lasting relationship with the Elk family. This grand estate, which will be completely designed by Mr. Ruth and Mr. Elk, will include a gilded age main mansion with 42 rooms, an art gallery, and frescos. Mr. Elk along with his wife, Clara, and his two daughters, Margaret and Eleanor, plan to live at the mansion upon its completion. The estate will also include a Tudor coach house with an outdoor pool, a Victorian rose garden complete with stone statues and steps, servant houses next to a large pond, and a large stone wall that will surround the property. It has been reported to this Inquire *that Mr. Elk is planning to have a state-of-the-art electrical generator built in the basement of the grand mansion.*"

Simon looks at the article and says, "Sounds like a really nice place."

Neil says, "It is, dude. It's something from the old world. Believe me when I tell you that no expense was spared when they built this place."

Simon replies, "Cool, man. Let's check back with your sister and see what she has found."

Simon and Neil find Ellie who is sitting quietly reading through one of the old diaries that she placed on the reading table. Simon asks, "Find anything interesting yet?"

Ellie says, "I think so."

Simon asks, "What did you find?"

"I'm reading through an old diary from Margaret Elk. She talks about the family living at the estate. The grandness of it all. Living in the Gilded Age. The elegant parties held throughout the year. Her dresses and the precious jewelry and how close she was to her sister Eleanor."

Neil says, "Sounds about right. But it all sounds normal. Find anything else?"

Ellie replies, "Yes. Here's the interesting thing. Margaret says in her diary that her sister was supposed to marry one of the sons from another wealthy family who was in business with their father. She mentions how Eleanor didn't have feelings for the man, and she especially didn't want to get married to him. Margaret mentions that Eleanor had feelings for a young groundskeeper by the name of Abbott Michaels."

Simon says, "Ah! One of those forbidden romances it seems. Does it say anything else?"

Ellie replies, "Towards the end of this particular section of the diary, it describes how Eleanor, who was eighteen at the time, and Abbott who was twenty-two, had strong romantic feelings for each other, but Margaret advised Eleanor to either keep it a secret or end it quickly before their father found out."

Neil says, "Sounds like an interesting story. Anything else in the diary?"

Ellie answers, "One last thing. It describes Abbott as a tall thin man with long, curly black hair, a thin beard, athletically built due to the nature of his work, and very handsome green eyes."

CHAPTER 19

....

SO, YOU'RE BILL'S GRANDKIDS

Simon says to Ellie, "It all looks like the pieces of the puzzle are coming together. I have a library card already set up for this library. Why don't we check out these old books and diaries and see if there's anything else we can find."

Ellie says, "Sounds like a good idea. If you and I split up the books, we can comb through the material twice as quickly."

Neil is on his way back to Simon and Ellie carrying a few large printouts. Simon asks, "What else did you find, dude?"

Neil replies, "I paid a couple of bucks and used the printer to have the physical copies. Found a couple of follow-up articles about the estate, a copy of the original blueprints, and some maps of the grounds."

Ellie smiles. "Look at you being all resourceful."

Simon says, "I'll say. Especially with blueprints. Most of the time if you want copies of blueprints or property dimensions, assessments, and land survey plats, you must go to a county building to acquire them."

Neil laughs. "How the hell would you know anything about that?"

Simon says, "I'm thorough when I do field research."

"Wow! Okay. Whatever. I got them anyway. Maybe it's due to the age of the building."

Simon replies, "It's a strong possibility. Let's get the other stuff checked out and then head over to that lady's house."

Simon, Neil, and Ellie make their way to the checkout counter of the library. There, they find Grace who was back working behind the counter and finishing up with another customer. After the customer leaves, Grace calls them over to the counter and says, "Hello again, young people. Find everything you need?"

Simon says, "Yes, ma'am. Sure did."

Grace replies, "Well that's wonderful. Now, which one of you has a library card?"

Simon reaches into his wallet for his library card and asks Grace, "Ma'am, you mentioned that your aunt worked at the estate as one of the sisters?"

As Grace takes Simon's library card and continues to scan the books, she replies, "Yes. That's correct, young man. Sister Rachel of the Catholic Dominican Sisters. Wonderful woman. Very spiritual and down to earth."

Simon asks, "Does Sister Rachel still live close to the area?"

Grace smiles. "She sure does. She helps take care of some of the older sisters at a nursing home nearby."

Simon continues to ask a few questions. "That's interesting, ma'am. With us doing a research project about the estate, do you think she would be open to talking to us? It would be great the gather that real life, first-hand experience."

Grace replies, "I'm sure she would be fine with it. Tell you what, let me write down her number, and I'll let her know to expect your call."

As Grace writes down Sister Rachel's number on the library receipt, Simon says, "Thank you, ma'am."

"You're welcome. Have fun with your project."

Simon, Ellie, and Neil walk out of the library and back to the car. Ellie smiles, looks at Simon, and says, "I think we found out more here than we were expecting."

Simon says, "I agree. In fact, I'm really impressed with your tall and rangy brother. Scarecrow uses his academic brain outside of school after all."

Neil responds, "Shut up, dork! Where to next, sis?"

Neil drives back to the main road from the parking lot. Ellie says, "Make your way to Ashbourne Road and toward those apartment buildings."

Neil replies, "Got it."

Simon asks Ellie, "So where does this lady live?"

Ellie replies, "She lives right across the street from the estate in one of the apartment buildings. We were there once. That's where we met Reggie. But, in total, there's like six apartment buildings, and they all look alike. I couldn't remember which one we were at."

Simon asks Neil, "Do you remember which building it was, Neil?"

Neil replies, "Honestly, I wasn't paying much attention. I was playing on my phone most of the time."

Ellie interjects, "But I did some detective work and found out her name and address."

Simon laughs. "Broke into your mom's social media account and phone again, didn't you?"

Ellie smiles. "You know it!"

Neil drives the convertible back onto Route 611, down toward Ashbourne Road. As they drive alongside the estate, there's no activity. No police vehicles, ambulances, or commotion. The only movement is the wind blowing through the trees. They drive past the main half circle entrance.

Simon notices the main gate and says, "Looks like they have that place sealed shut."

Neil asks, "What do you mean?"

Simon replies, "I know you're paying attention to the road, so you didn't see. There's a big chain and a lock on those large, black iron gates."

Ellie tries to take notice as Neil continues to drive past. She says, "Looks like Mom will have to clear it with the police before she can get access to the property. Hopefully that works out for her."

Neil looks at Ellie. "The apartments are coming up. Which one, sis?"

"We are looking for 6336 for the address and unit number 3B. Looks like it's this one. Yup. Turn in here."

Neil finds an open parking spot and parks the vehicle. They all get out of the convertible and walk up to the main entrance. Simon asks Ellie, "So, what are the chances of this woman even being home?"

Ellie says, "The chances are good. From the sound of it, this lady is old, retired, and has a hard time getting around."

They walk into the main foyer from the outer door of the apartment building and look at the mailboxes and search the buttons. Neil asks, "Which one are we looking for, sis?"

"3B. Last name Rose."

Simon finds it first and presses the button. They all wait a minute and try to be patient as they await a reply. No answer. Neil presses the apartment button next, and they can hear the button's vibrating noise echo through the hallway on the other side of the security door. Patiently they wait as they get no answer.

Ellie looks at Simon. "What do you think?"

Simon says, "Who knows. Maybe she's out for the day or has a doctor's appointment or something."

Neil says, "Screw it. Let's just leave."

Neil starts to leave the foyer entrance first. Simon and Ellie follow. Then they hear from the intercom, "Who's there? Is someone there?"

They run back to the press-to-talk button. Ellie is the first to press and answer saying, "Yes, ma'am. Mrs. Rose. This is Ellie. Claire's daughter. I was wondering if…"

Dotty replies, "Yes, Ellie, and you brought your brother, Neil, and some other young man. Please come up. We've um…I'm sorry…I've been expecting you." There's a buzz that vibrates from the door lock, and Neil opens the security door.

The three walk up the stairs to the third floor. Simon struggles after reaching the second-floor landing. Neil laughs. "Sounds like you should incorporate more cardio into your field work."

Simon replies, "Sounds like you're breathing a lot too, bro."

They all hear laughter coming from the top floor as they make their way up. Dotty is waiting at her apartment door, keeping it open with her foot and her walker at the ready next to her. Dotty says, "In my youth, I could climb these stairs without thinking twice. And do it with a load of groceries too." Dotty looks at her guests. She then looks to her side, looks back, and says, "You must be Ellie and Neil. Nice to finally meet you both." Dotty looks at Simon. "Now, this one I do not know. What is your name?"

Simon replies, "The name is Simon, ma'am. The best friend to our lovely lady, Ellie, and a sort-of friend to this scarecrow, Neil."

Dotty says, "Nice to meet you, young man. Now, please come in. And Neil, honey, please hold the door open for me. This damn thing is heavy, and it shuts quickly."

They all make their way into Dotty's home. They walk into the living room. Dotty says, "Now, please make your way into the kitchen. I just started brewing a pot of coffee. Don't worry about me. I move slowly nowadays. I'll be in there in a minute."

Simon, Neil, and Ellie walk through the living room and dining room and enter the kitchen. They all take seats at Dotty's kitchen table. Simon says to Ellie, "This lady is giving me a creepy vibe. Like for real. Can we make this quick?"

Ellie says, "Shut up, Simon. We made it this far."

Simon replies, "But this place smells like old lady."

Neil laughs and Ellie exclaims, "Both of you, shut up!"

As she enters the kitchen, Dotty says, "I'm sorry, honey. My place usually doesn't smell like an old lady. I usually sleep with my windows open at night. But these damn storms have been coming out of nowhere."

Simon is shocked, and says to Ellie, "Nothing wrong with her hearing."

Dotty starts making a cup of coffee for herself and says, "That's right, honey. My body has been giving up lately. But most of my senses still work very well. Anyone want a cup?"

They all say no as Dotty takes a seat. "Neil, could you help me sit down in this chair? It's a bit low."

Neil stands up and helps Dotty into her chair. Dotty smiles. "Your face reminds me of your grandfather. You and your uncle Will have a strong resemblance to him."

Dotty looks over to her side and back to her guests. "I'll assume you're here because you want to know more about the estate and that little boy Reggie."

Simon looked puzzled. "How did you know that?"

Dotty smiles, chuckles, and says, "I have my ways, honey. I have my ways."

Ellie says, "I'm so sorry to hear about your grandson, Jerald. To my understanding, he's Reggie's friend?"

Dotty replies, "That's right, honey. Jerald and Reggie had been friends since kindergarten. Jerald wasn't a bad kid growing up. He would cause a little bit of mischief. And of course, Reggie was just along for the ride. I'm sure that boy is lost without my Jerald."

Neil asks, "He seemed lost and scared. Someone who could use our help. Can we have his contact information?"

Dotty answers, "Sure thing, honey. He lives right down the block. 6442. Unit 3A."

Ellie takes down the information and says, "Thank you."

Dotty smiles, looks to her side, looks back at Ellie, and says, "You never got to meet your grandfather did you, honey?"

Ellie replies, "No, unfortunately. He died before I was born."

Dotty looks over to Neil. "But you, honey. You were very young when he died. You were at his funeral."

Neil looks at Ellie and Simon. Both look puzzled. Neil replies, "How do you know these things?"

Dotty laughs. "I have my ways, honey. I was very a close very friend to your grandparents before they moved."

Simon asks, "Are you psychic or something?"

Ellie exclaims, "Simon! What the hell?"

Dotty laughs and replies, "It's okay, honey. Some would call it that; others would say that I have a key to another realm. I'm sensitive to the things beyond."

Simon exclaims, "No way! You're a legit psychic? Like you know the future or can read our thoughts?"

Dotty chuckles. "No, honey. If I had a clear picture of the future, I would have figured out the winning lottery numbers and moved down to sunny Florida years ago. You can say that I'm sensitive to the world just beyond."

Ellie asks, "How does that work?"

"I am given images and can sense things that most can't. That's how it works. For example"—Dotty looks over to Neil—"you saw your grandfather the day before his funeral. You saw him just on the other side of your grandmom's kitchen window. He waved to you, and you waved back. Your grandmom and your parents were going over the funeral arrangements in the kitchen. You pulled out a chair for him and asked him to sit down. Gave your grandmom and your parents one hell of a spook."

Dotty then looks over to Ellie and says, "You never met your grandfather in the physical world, but you saw him when you were young."

Ellie is shocked. "I don't remember that. You must be making this stuff up!"

Dotty smiles. "Nothing made up, honey. Most children lose this sense as they get into their later toddler years. You used to carry around this Christmas ornament that had his picture in it."

Neil exclaims, "She's right! I remember you carrying around that ornament."

Simon, Neil, and Ellie and amazed by the events that Dotty discusses. Neil and Ellie are speechless and look freaked out! Simon exclaims, "This is way too cool. This lady is the real deal. What else can you tell us?"

Dotty looks to her side, looks back at her guests, and says, "All in good time, honey. There will be more to talk about soon. But for now. Why don't you go over to Reggie's house. Right now, that boy is hiding in his room, waiting for someone to help him."

Simon says, "Ah come on, just a few more questions!"

Neil and Ellie, who are shocked and spooked by their interaction, start to make their way back toward the apartment entrance door. Ellie walks back, grabs Simon's arm, and says, "Time to go, Simon!"

Dotty says, "Yes indeed. Time is important. I almost forgot. Please remember this."

Ellie asks, "What's that, Mrs. Rose?"

"Follow the signs and keep track of the time." Dotty points to the clock from her oven, 11:11 a.m.

CHAPTER 20

....

REGGIE'S ON BOARD

Simon, Neil, and Ellie head down the stairs and out of the apartment building. Amazed by these events, Simon says, "How cool was that?" Simon looks over at Neil and continues, "Dude, I saw the hair stand up on the back of your neck!"

Neil says, "Dude! That would freak out anyone."

Simon laughs, looks at Ellie, and says, "And Ellie, I saw goose bumps on your arms, and I know that chills went down your spine."

Ellie replies, "That was no doubt freaky. It's not every day you hear that your dead grandfather is still lingering around." Just then, Ellie gets a text from Liam asking: "How did you make out?" Ellie reaches for her phone while she, Neil, and Simon continue to walk back to the car.

Simon sees Ellie looking at her phone and asks, "Who's that?"

Neil laughs and interjects, "It's her boyfriend."

Ellie replies, "Shut up! No, I don't have a boyfriend. It's Liam."

As they get inside the car, Simon asks, "What does he want?"

Ellie answers, "He's looking for a status update." Ellie replies to Liam's text: "Going well so far. Found a lot of good info at the library. Had a freaky encounter with that old lady who knows the family. On our way to Reggie's house."

Neil backs out of the parking spot and heads out to the main road. Neil asks Ellie, "What address are we looking for again, sis?"

Ellie replies, "6442. Unit 3A."

"Got it."

Ellie looks back at her phone as Liam replies, "Sounds like you're on track. We are still near Independence Hall. Heading to the baseball game soon. Your mom has been in contact with my dad. Sounds like we are all going to the main house tomorrow. Just FYI."

Ellie answers back, "Good to know. See you tonight. A lot to go over."

Neil finds the correct building and heads into their parking lot. Ellie looks up to the third-floor window and sees Reggie looking outside toward the estate. Ellie exclaims, "Mrs. Rose was right. Reggie is home. Just saw him in the window."

Neil parks the car, and they all exit and head to the main apartment entrance. They walk into the foyer and find the buzzer for 3A. Simon presses it and waits for a reply. After a brief moment, there's a young voice that says, "Who is it?"

Simon holds down the press-to-talk button and asks, "Hey, is this Reggie?"

Reggie replies, "Maybe. Who the hell is this?"

Ellie pushes Simon aside and presses the push-to-talk button. "Hey, Reggie. This is Ellie. We met the day after the incident at the estate. My family and I were outside Mrs. Rose's building."

Reggie replies, "What do you want?"

Ellie answers, "Would you let us come up to talk to you?"

There's no answer. Simon, Neil, and Ellie look at each other, wondering what to do next. When there's a vibrating buzz that triggers the lock on the security entrance, Neil opens the door, and they all make their way up to the third floor.

Simon has to catch his breath. "I hate cardio, and I hate gym class. Why does everyone we need to talk to live on the third floor?"

Neil laughs. "See? You are getting some more cardio in your field research. Good job."

As they reach the third-floor landing, they see Reggie standing in front of his open apartment door. Reggie says, "I thought I told you before. No one can help me. Why are you back here?"

Ellie replies, "Reggie. If you don't remember, I'm Ellie, this my brother, Neil, and this is my friend Simon."

Neil says, "Sup."

Simon says, "Nice to finally meet you."

Reggie says, "So what do you want?"

Ellie answers, "Reggie, you have firsthand knowledge of that estate. It turns out that my family and Jerald's family know each other and have a strange connection to that place. We want to know more about the estate and help you in the process."

Reggie nods his head. "Okay. Why don't you come in." Reggie welcomes them into his home.

The three follow Reggie into his bedroom. Ellie asks, "No one else is home, Reggie?"

Reggie answers, "Nope, both my parents work all day. It's just me here on the homestead during the day until school starts up again."

Simon asks, "I'm assuming high school? What year?"

Reggie replies, "I was going into my freshmen year of high school. Jerald was going into his sophomore year. He was gonna show me around and keep me under his wing."

Ellie says, "Sorry for your loss, Reggie."

They all walk into Reggie's bedroom. All the walls are covered with movie and video game posters. Simon says, "Cool room, dude! I see you like the same forms of entertainment that I like. You play a lot of games online?"

Reggie says, "Yeah, I play. Thanks, man."

Neil looks outside Reggie's window and over to the tall stone walls that surround the estate. Neil says, "You have a nice view of the estate from here, dude."

Reggie says, "Yeah, I know. I keep the window curtains and blinds open during the day. But when the sun goes down, it's lights out. Curtains and blinds are closed."

Simon asks, "Why's that?"

"Look, man. I appreciate that you want to help me and stuff, but I'm telling you that Shadow Man is no bullshit."

Ellie interjects, "We believe you. That's why we are here."

Reggie asks, "So what's your interest in this place?"

Ellie replies, "My mom has been working in and around the estate for a while. She's in charge of the volunteer group. My grandmom worked at the estate back in the '80s, and my mother and uncle made that place their second home while growing up. Since our families are involved in the maintenance of the property, we want to know more about what's going on there. Plus, my concern is that my mother and uncle are strangely attached to this place. Like it has a hold on them or something."

Reggie says, "So your mom has been working on the estate? Has she had any strange encounters?"

Ellie answers, "Not that we are aware. My brother and I have also been around the estate and up to the main house several times. Nothing out of the ordinary."

Reggie says, "What about your grandmother? She ever mention anything?"

Ellie shakes her head.

Reggie looks at everyone and continues, "I've seen the volunteer group working in and around the grounds. Right from that window over there. But it doesn't surprise me that no one has experienced some weird shit."

Simon interjects, asking, "Why's that?"

Reggie replies, "Because all the work they've been doing is during the day and in good weather. At night, especially when those bad storms break out, that's when shit gets spooky over there."

Ellie asks, "Can you tell us about the night that Jerald died."

Reggie shakes his head, walks around the room, pauses, and says, "Okay. Fine. Jerald and I were looking for some old stuff that we could make some money on. We were in the coach house alongside the main entrance. I saw The Shadow Man outside the window. Then it was all downhill from there. You already know the results of that night."

Simon says, "Did you find anything in there?"

Reggie answers, "I didn't. But Jerald found some old jewelry and stuff. Didn't make it out of the building with anything."

Neil asks, "Was there anything else?"

Reggie replies, "Yeah, there was an entrance to an attic. Didn't want to go up there."

Simon asks Reggie, "Why do you keep the blinds and curtains closed at night?"

Reggie says, nervously, "Be-bec-because, I sa-saw The Shadow Man standing on top of that ugly wall across the street. Staring into my bedroom window with those glowing green eyes and waving at me. I don't know what to do."

Simon, Ellie, and Neil look at each other. Ellie answers, "We are trying to figure out a plan as we speak. We actually found some information about the estate at the library. If you're not busy, we can go through this stuff together and see what we can find."

Reggie nods his head. "I didn't have any plans for the day. I've been too scared to go to sleep with The Shadow Man out there. I've been staying up most of the night, drinking energy drinks and playing games online. I usually just sleep in all morning. But this is starting to get old quick." Reggie pauses for a moment and continues, "Sure, I'll help you. You're helping me. Let's see what you got."

Neil goes out to the car and gathers the printouts, books, and diaries. He comes back with the material and places everything on Reggie's desk in his room. Ellie says, "Here's what I'm thinking. Reggie and Simon, see if there is anything interesting in those old blueprints and survey plat of the estate. Maybe we can find something. Neil and I will comb through these old books and diaries and see what else we can find."

Reggie approves as Simon says, "Got it, boss." Neil takes a couple of books, and Ellie picks up a few diaries.

Reggie looks at Simon. "What do you want? Blueprints or the survey map of the property?"

Simon answers, "I'll take the blueprints. Since you're really familiar with the area, why don't you check out the plat of survey."

Reggie approves, and they both get to work. Reggie grabs a highlighter from his office drawer and highlights a few items on the map. Simon combs through the blueprints and keeps saying things like, "Wow, interesting, now that's strange, cool."

Reggie looks over at Simon. "Sounds like you've found some interesting things too. Care to divulge?"

Simon chuckles. "Yes, sir. Planning to during our team meeting."

Reggie questions, "Team meeting?"

"Yeah, figure it's best for each member of the team to do their research and present all their data during the team meeting. Kind of part of the scientific method and all. Sorry, I'm bit of a nerd."

Reggie laughs. "Don't tell anyone outside this room, but I'm a bit of a nerd too."

Ellie looks over at Neil. "What are you reading?"

Neil answers, "Some local author wrote a book about the Elk's family and the estate. It's an old book. Published back in the '70s but figured it was worth a look. What about yourself?"

Ellie replies, "I'm still reading the rest of the diary from Margaret. Figure I'll read through this and start looking through the next diary. It's taking longer to read. Her handwriting was beautiful, but it's all in old cursive. I overheard Simon saying that we should have a team meeting after we search through the material. Like that plan, let's stick to it."

Neil replies, "Okay sounds good."

About an hour has passed since the group began their research into Elk's Estate. Reggie goes back and forth between the plat of survey and his computer. Simon writes down outlined notes on a piece of paper. Neil and Ellie continue to look through their source material and write down notes as well. Ellie looks around the room and says, "Okay, is everyone ready to talk about what they found out?"

They all agree.

Ellie looks at Simon first and says, "So, Simon, what did you find?"

Simon excitedly says, "What *didn't* I find! This place was well ahead of its time! Turns out this place was one of the first buildings in the area to have its own alternating current (AC) generator. I looked online, and this generator that they installed was state-of-the-art when this place opened. There's also some interesting stuff here about underground tunnels. Looks like the Elks family installed tunnels in and around the property to help the workers of the estate get to and from their living quarters when inclement weather was a factor."

Ellie says, "Cool. Reggie, what did you find out?"

Reggie says, "I told my new friend Simon here that I'm bit of a nerd too, especially with Earth science. In the plat of survey, it shows the boundaries of the entire property. This particular copy must have been updated after the Elk family purchased the land. This copy shows the layout of all the buildings and the large stone walls that surround the property. There's also a note on the side of the printout that describes the stones used to create the wall. The main stones used were lodestone, ironstone, and magnetite.

These stones are highly magnetic and extraordinarily expensive, especially given that they were used to create a large stone wall over a twenty-acre property. I also found something else that's interesting. There is a large sewer drain that goes underneath the street. Big enough that we could walk through it if we bend down. If we needed to get quick access in and out of the property, we can use this storm drain."

Ellie says, "Really interesting stuff. Good work." Ellie looks over at Neil and says, "How about you, brother? What did you find?"

Neil answers, "There were some intriguing things in the book. It discusses the family. Mr. and Mrs. Elk and their two daughters, Margaret and Eleanor. Seems like a tragic story. Mrs. Elk, Clara, died before the construction of the estate was complete. She was diagnosed with tuberculosis. Mr. Elk moved into the grand estate with only his two daughters. Never remarried. Mr. Elk hosted several large galas and events while he resided there. Many famous people walked through the halls of Elk's Estate during its time. His one daughter, Margaret, married into a family that was connected to Mr. Elk's railroad investments. The other daughter died tragically on the grounds of the estate when she was only eighteen years old. Mr. Elk spent most of his days on the estate never wanting to leave. He was later considered mentally unstable and was committed to a sanitarium in Upper Darby. Margaret and her husband continued to live on the estate. Margaret and her husband, Henry, had one child, Misty, but her daughter died after she fell through the elevator shaft when she was only ten years old. Margaret and Henry continued to live on the estate until they died. There's a small family cemetery and tomb in the back corner of the estate where the Elk family is buried. With no living heirs, the Catholic Church purchased the property from the state. That's all I got out of it since it's an old book. The Church didn't give up the property until the early 2010s."

Simon says, "Not bad, scarecrow. Not bad. What did you find out, Ellie?"

Ellie pauses and says, "The two diaries I read were from the daughters. One from Margaret. One from Eleanor. I've already discussed the one from Margaret. The one from Eleanor is very interesting."

Simon interjects, "Do tell, I'm waiting."

Ellie laughs and says, "Eleanor was the older sister by two years. Eleanor was in love with the groundskeeper, Abbott Michaels. She talks about how sweet, kind, and handsome Abbott was. She talks about how they would leave notes for each other around the property and sneak away to have romantic rendezvous."

Simon says, "Wicked. Sounds like one of those corny romantic novels."

Ellie replies, "Shut up, Simon! Let me finish. Anyway, she talks about some of the strange people her father would have over during different times of the year. Usually late at night. She also talked about the jewelry she loved the most were the items she received from Abbott. They planned to run away together against all her father's wishes. In her last entry, she says that she plans to run away with Abbott during one of her father's late-night gatherings."

Reggie looks around at everyone. "If I had to bet money on this, I would put my money that The Shadow Man is Abbott Michaels."

Simon says, "Looks that way for sure."

Neil asks Ellie, "Hey, sis. Did you hear anything else from Liam or from Mom and Dad?"

Ellie looks at her phone and says, "Yeah. A few messages. I kept my phone on silent so I could concentrate. Dad is asking when we are planning to come home. Dinner will be at five. Pasta and meatballs tonight. Mom says that everyone will be going to the main house tomorrow to continue their work. And Liam says that he should be home with the rest of the family for dinner."

Reggie asks, "Okay, so what do we do now?"

Ellie asks Simon, "You plan on staying for dinner tonight?"

Simon answers, "I can't pass up your mom's homemade meatballs. They're the best."

Ellie replies, "Sounds good. Mom and Dad just set a place for you at the table anyway."

Ellie looks over at Reggie. "Reggie, what are your thoughts on pasta, meatballs, and a sleepover at our house?"

Reggie smiles. "I love pasta and meatballs. I'm up for a sleepover. I'll let my parents know that I'll be sleeping over at a friend's house. They're usually too tired after work to care anyway. Maybe I'll actually get a good night's sleep tonight."

CHAPTER 21

....

PASTA, MEATBALLS, AND TEAM PLANNING

Neil, Ellie, Simon, and Reggie all get ready to leave Reggie's home and head back to Doylestown. Reggie packs an overnight gym bag while Ellie and Neil gather all the source material they collected from the library. Reggie asks Simon, "Do you think I should pack an extra controller just in case we have time to play online tonight?"

Simon replies, "Absolutely. Not too sure what the rest of the crew has in mind after spaghetti and meatballs."

Reggie asks, "So Ellie and Neil's mom makes homemade meatballs?"

Simon answers, "Sure does. She makes them as big as a snowball too. She adds a little sugar, basil, and parmesan cheese to her sauce."

Reggie says, "Sounds delicious. Haven't had a homecooked meal in a while. My parents have been working so much. They come home exhausted. We've been doing a lot of frozen dinners and pizza."

Reggie zips up his overnight bag, grabs his cell phone, and says, "All set to leave when you are."

Neil, Ellie, and Simon follow Reggie out of his home and walk back toward the car. As Neil puts the keys into the ignition, Ellie reminds Neil that he needs to stop by the gas station on the way home. Neil asks Ellie, "Is the plan to stop by the Wawa in Jenkintown on the way home?"

Ellie answers, "Yup. That's the plan."

Neil makes his way out of the parking lot, back onto Ashbourne Road, and continues north on Route 611.

Simon asks, "Did I hear Ellie mention Wawa will be a destination in our near future?"

Ellie replies, "That's right. Our dad wants the car back with a full tank of gas."

Simon says, "Awesome. I can go for one of their hoagies and a large drink. Good plan."

Reggie says, "That sounds great. I'm starving."

Neil shakes his head, laughs, and says, "Can't you nerds wait till we get home?"

Simon says, "Absolutely not. You're stopping there anyway. Plus, your mom doesn't do appetizers, and I don't do field research on an empty stomach."

Neil laughs. "Yeah, sounds like that's why you have a little bit of a weight problem."

Simon says, "Shut up, scarecrow!"

Reggie laughs. "Now this is my kind of group. Always busting each other's balls. I love it."

Everyone laughs. Then Ellie says to Simon, "My mom does appetizers. She always has a salad."

Simon replies, "Salad is not an appetizer. Veggies are not filling and can't be considered appetizers."

Reggie asks, "What about those veggie trays at parties with the dip in the middle?"

Simon asks, "What about them?"

Reggie answers, "That's a tray of veggies, and I consider that an appetizer."

Simon chuckles. "Valid point, my new friend. Even better is when the party has bread with spinach dip next to the veggie tray. Now *that's* an appetizer."

Reggie laughs. "Now you're speaking my language."

Neil pulls up to the Wawa next to one of the fuel pumps. Reggie and Simon exit the back of the car and start to head inside together. Simon says, "Please, sir. Allow this round of hoagies and drinks be on me."

Reggie smiles and says, "I won't stop you. Next time it's on me."

Simon says, "Deal." Simon looks back at Neil and Ellie and yells, "You guys want anything?"

Neil yells back, "Yeah. Iced coffee for me."

Ellie yells back, "Same!"

Simon yells, "Don't worry, I know how my girl likes her coffee!"

Simon and Reggie enter the convenience store, and Ellie walks over to Neil. Neil smiles and says, "Looks like your boyfriend found a new friend."

Ellie smiles. "Not my boyfriend. But yeah, sure looks like they hit it off." Ellie looks at her phone and loads up her mobile map app. She types in her home address and says to Neil, "Looks like it will take us just about thirty minutes to get home right now."

Neil asks, "That seems about right considering rush hour is starting. Have you heard anything else from Liam?"

Ellie answers, "Not yet. I'll text him." Ellie texts Liam: "Hey! On our way home with that kid Reggie. He will be joining us for dinner and sleeping over. How are you guys doing?"

There's a brief pause, then Liam texts Ellie back: "Doing well. Game is almost over. It's basically a blowout game. Dad said we can leave at the end of the inning and listen to the rest of the game on the radio. He wants to get home in time for dinner."

Ellie texts: "Cool. See you then."

Neil finishes filling up the car just as Simon and Reggie exit the convenience store with their food and drinks. Simon and Reggie slide into the back seat. Simon says to Neil, "Good call on the Wawa stop, dude."

Neil laughs and puts the key into the ignition. "Thanks. My dad likes to stop at this place on the way home. Gas is cheaper, and he likes their coffee. Now, please don't leave a mess in the back seat like you did last time, Simon."

Simon takes a bite out of his hoagie and says, "Don't worry. I remember how mad your dad got at me last time. I got plenty of napkins."

Neil exits the Wawa and heads north along Route 611.

The four arrive back to the Doylestown residence before dinnertime. They all exit the vehicle and hear a riding lawn mower. Reggie looks around and says, "Your folks have a nice place."

Neil says, "Thanks."

They walk up to the main entrance when they see Pete come around the corner with the lawn mower and begin to work on the front lawn. Pete waves, stops the motor, and walks toward the group. "Hey, kids! How was your day?"

Neil says, "Good, Dad. Been fun."

Pete replies, "Well that's good." Pete looks over to Reggie and continues, "I don't know if I ever met your friend. Who is this?"

Ellie answers, "Oh, Dad. This is Reggie. He lives near Elk's Estate. We met him the day Uncle Will and Mom met that old lady in that apartment building."

Pete replies, "I see." Pete extends his hand to shake Reggie's hand. "Nice to meet you, Reggie. Will you be joining us for dinner?"

Reggie answers, "Yes, sir. You have a beautiful home here."

Pete smiles. "Thank you, Reggie." Pete looks at Ellie and Neil and says, "I thought you guys were heading to Jenkintown. You didn't mention heading all the way out to Elkins Park."

Simon interjects, "Sir, I can explain. I've been playing video games with Reggie online. He wanted to meet up with all of us. So, it was my idea."

Pete answers, "I see."

Neil says, "But we stopped and got gas for the car on the way home."

Pete looks over to the car and says, "Excellent. It looks like you forgot to take it through the car wash though."

Neil replies, "Damn! I knew I forgot something. Sorry, Dad."

Pete replies, "No worries, son. You can wash the car later."

Pete looks back at Reggie and says, "Well, Reggie, make yourself at home. I have to finish up the yard. Dinner will be soon."

Reggie replies, "Thank you, sir."

Pete walks back over to the riding lawn mower and continues his work as the group makes their way into the house. The house smells like home sweet home when they walk through the door. The aroma of meatballs fills the hallways and rooms. Claire has music playing in the kitchen as she works over the four-burner stovetop making noodles and sauce. The group walks into the kitchen.

Neil says, "Hey, Mom. We're home."

Claire says, "Excellent. Glad you're home."

Ellie says, "This is our friend Reggie. He's joining us for dinner."

Claire says, "Sounds good. I'll just have to make one more placement at the dining room table."

Simon says, "Did you already make my place at the table?"

Claire answers, "Simon, I just assume that you are basically living and eating here, so I always make a place for you regardless."

Simon says, "Thank you. Sometime after dinner, I'll have my folks swing by and pick up Reggie and me. He's staying over at my place tonight."

Claire replies, "That sounds fine."

Ellie interjects and says to Claire, "And Simon and Reggie want to come with us tomorrow to help with the estate."

Claire asks, "Is that right?"

Reggie and Simon say in unison, "Yes."

Claire answers, "Well, that's wonderful. In fact, I have an assignment for both of them. They can help by cleaning up the outside grounds tomorrow."

Reggie looks over to Simon, and Simon nods his head in approval with this plan. Reggie smiles, looks back at Claire, and says, "That sounds fine, ma'am."

Claire says, "Thank you for your wonderful manners. Dinner will be soon. The rest of the family is on their way home. Make yourself at home, Reggie. Just follow Simon's lead. He has no problem with that."

Simon laughs.

Neil says, "Thanks, Mom. We are all going to hang out in our room and play some video games until dinner."

The group goes upstairs into Neil's room. Simon says to Ellie and Neil, "Sounds like the plan is on for tomorrow. Reggie and I can cover a lot of area, especially since Reggie is familiar with the estate grounds. I'll head downstairs really quick."

Ellie asks, "Where are you going, Simon?"

Simon replies, "I left all the research material in the car. I'll go down and grab it." Simon walks downstairs and into the front entrance foyer when he sees the rest of the family pull into the driveway. Simon walks outside and greets the family as he gathers the material from the convertible. Will is the first to exit the vehicle, followed by Annie, Liam, and Boo.

Will says, "Hey, Simon! You joining us for dinner again?"

Simon says, "Yes, sir. How was your day in the big city?"

"Oh, just fine. Great time. A little bit of history and baseball. Can't beat it."

Liam and Boo walk over to Simon as Annie makes her way into the house. Will follows Annie inside as Liam and Boo continue to converse with Simon. Liam asks, "Is that all of the stuff you found at the library?"

Simon says, "Sure is. Got a lot of stuff to cover. Sounds like your Aunt Claire already has assignments for us tomorrow."

Boo asks, "What's the plan then?"

Simon answers, "Let's try to find out what we can over dinner, and then all of us can converse in private afterward."

Liam agrees. "Sounds like a good idea. How's that other kid, Reggie?"

Simon replies, "He's actually really cool. I feel he fits in nicely with the group."

Simon takes all the material upstairs, and soon after the family gathers together for dinner. The dining room table has a full complement of guests. They all take turns filling up their dishes with spaghetti and meatballs and taking their seats. Claire says, "I'm glad we purchased a dining room table that includes a table extension. Comes in handy during the holidays and occasions like tonight. I made a salad as well, so everyone help themselves."

Simon and Reggie sit next to each other. They both look at the salad on the dining room table, look at each other, and laugh. Pete, at the head of the table, asks, "What's so funny, boys?"

Simon, who continues laughing, says, "Nothing, sir. Just an inside joke."

The family discusses the events of the day. Liam looks at Claire and asks, "Aunt Claire?"

"Yes, honey. What can I help you with?"

Liam asks, "Are we all going to that estate you mentioned tomorrow?"

Claire replies, "That's correct. Got permission to proceed. We will meet up with the rest of the volunteer group tomorrow morning after breakfast."

Simon asks, "You mentioned that Reggie and I will have assignments cleaning up the grounds, right?"

Claire answers, "That's correct."

Ellie asks Claire, "What will the rest of us be doing, Mom?"

Claire pauses and thinks for a moment. She takes her phone out of her pocket and continues, "Good question. I sent an email to the volunteer group with all of the assignments. Let me see." Claire checks her email. "Okay, I have Marcus and Katie working with Boo and Annie on the lower level of the estate. I will be on the main level with Ellie, Anton, and Liam. And the upper level will be Will, Pete, and Neil."

After hearing the names, Will smiles and asks Claire, "Is that the same Marcus, Anton, and Katie who used to work with you at the estate when we were kids?"

Claire smiles and answers, "Yup. Sure is. The very same."

Will happily exclaims, "That's wonderful! Haven't seen them for so long."

Boo looks at Claire and asks, "You worked at the estate too, Aunt Claire?"

Claire says, "Yup. Sure did. In fact, for most of us, it was our first job. Grandmom helped us get the job. She worked overtime during the weekend Catholic retreats at the estate. My friends, the people I mentioned, and even your dad helped wash dishes and clean tables from the guest dinners."

Will interjects, "They got a lot of free labor out of me. I was too young to be employed, but Aunt Claire and her friends were teenagers at the time. I just had fun hanging out with Aunt Claire and the rest of the older kids. Marcus and Anton are twin brothers. Their mother worked at the estate with Grandmom. And Katie was Aunt Claire's best friend in high school."

Claire replies, "Yup. She's still my best friend. Helped her get the job at the estate so we could hang out on the weekends and make some extra money."

The family and guests finish their meal, then they all make their way into the kitchen to drop their dishes into the sink. Claire says to the Neil, "It's your turn to clean up from dinner, son."

Neil disapproves and shakes his head.

Will notices Neil's reaction and says to Claire, "Hey, sis. Why don't you give Neil the night off. I'll take care of it."

Claire asks Will, "You don't mind doing the dishes?"

Will answers, "Don't mind at all. Least I can do after a wonderfully homecooked meal. Firefighters are basically semi-professional cooks and dishwashers. Plus, Neil can enjoy his cousins and friends."

Claire looks at Neil and says, "Okay fine. But you have dishes tomorrow evening. No exceptions."

Neil smiles and replies, "Got it. Thanks, Uncle Will."

Will replies, "No problem, kid. Go enjoy your company."

The group of kids make their way up to Neil's room and shut the door. They gather in a circle. Simon says, "Okay. We all have our assignments for tomorrow. What's going to be our game plan?"

CHAPTER 22

....

I'LL BE THERE TO CATCH YOU

Neil, Ellie, Reggie, and Simon share all the information they discovered at the library with Liam and Boo. Liam is amazed with the amount of information they were able to discover and gather together. Liam looks at Simon and asks, "What are your thoughts, Simon?"

Simon looks at Reggie and then back to Liam. Simon pulls out the map of the property and throws it over Neil's bed as the group gathers around it. Simon answers, "I figure Reggie and I can take a better look at those stone walls and the rest of the estate grounds. They have a very interesting composition. Since we will be less supervised by the adults, Reggie and I can sneak around to some other sections of the property. Maybe take a good look at the secret tunnel and the old generator in the basement of the main house."

Reggie shakes his head and appears to be nervous. He walks away from the group and Liam says, "Are you okay, Reggie?"

Reggie answers, "No, man, I ain't okay. That coach house is where I lost Jerald to The Shadow Man. Not too keen on going back in there."

Simon says, "You said it yourself, Reggie. You never seen any paranormal spooky shit happening over there during the day. Plus, you and I will stick together."

Ellie interjects into the conversation, "Yeah, and my mom has radios for everyone. So, if you run into a jam, just call for us and we'll come running."

Reggie thinks about it, takes a deep breath, and calms down. "You're right. We got each other. I'm in. What else do we have to do?"

Liam says, "It sounds like all of us will be separated around the main house and the entire property. While we are doing our chores and assignments, we should try to find out whatever we can. Other clues and information that will help us understand more about what's going on there."

The group continues to discuss different plans of actions and contingencies. As the evening carries on, Simon contacts his folks and lets them know that a friend will be sleeping over at his house. Simon's parents arrive in their vehicle. Simon gathers the rest of the material from the library while Reggie makes his way downstairs. Ellie, who's next to Simon, says, "You can leave that stuff here tonight if you want."

Simon disapproves, shakes his head, and replies, "Reggie and I can go over a few more things tonight. Then we will see you bright and early in the morning."

Ellie replies, "Sounds good. Be ready by 9:00 a.m. My Mom and Dad will be picking you guys up."

Simon answers, "Don't worry, bright eyes. We'll be ready for anything."

Ellie laughs and pushes Simon toward the stairs leading down to the front entrance foyer. Reggie and Simon make their way to their ride. The rest of the house gets ready for an early bedtime.

The summer day finally cools off. Claire decides to open some of the windows and turn off the air conditioning. Liam, Boo, Neil, and Ellie are already turned in for the night. Pete is in bed reading his book. Annie is doing the same in her bedroom. Will is exiting the washroom when he sees his sister walk up the stairs. Claire says to Will, "That's gonna be it for me tonight. It's cooling off nicely outside. I turned off the air. My plan is to open our windows upstairs and let mother nature cool down our house and save our electric bill."

Will replies, "Sounds like a good idea. Back home we hear way too much airport noise. We can't leave the bedroom windows open overnight without a 747 flying over our house and waking me up. I love that your area is so quiet at night."

Claire enters her bedroom and shuts the door. Will enters his bedroom and opens the windows. He looks over to Annie who is peacefully reading her book before she goes to bed. Will looks over to Annie's nightstand and sees a silver cross and a necklace. Will asks, "Is that what I think it is?"

Annie questions, "What's that, babe?"

Will points at the silver cross and says, "The cross that Liam got from that old lady in Iron River. I thought he lost that."

Annie laughs and says, "He did lose it. But my mom found it while she was cleaning up the lake house during the big move. I've been holding on to it for safe keeping."

"Gotcha. When do you think you'll give it back to Liam?"

"When he shows that he's not so forgetful and takes more responsibility."

Will smiles. "Good luck with that, hon. I'm going to sleep. Love you and enjoy your book."

Annie leans over and gives Will a kiss and says, "Love you too. Sweet dreams."

Will falls fast asleep. He enters a dream state and finds himself back at the estate.

He's back outside the main house. Will looks around. The sky is gloomy and threatening. A storm is approaching. He hears thunder in the distance and sees flashes of lightning. He looks at the row of trees along the main drive up to the main house. The trees are bending to the wind, but he doesn't feel the wind run through his hair, his face, or his body. Will turns back to the main house and runs up the circular stairs that lead to the main entrance. One of the doors is left open. He enters.

Will looks down one hallway. He sees rusty dried-up leaves rush across the floor being picked up from the wind and the hanging lights swing back and forth. He looks down the other hallway that leads to the downstairs lower level. Will walks toward the stairs and sees nothing but darkness. He looks closer as he begins to hear echoes coming from the basement. Suddenly, he sees flashes of light coming from downstairs and the echoes of people screaming. Will backs away from the stairs and walks into the main living room. The lights throughout the estate begin to flicker. Will thinks he hears whispers of people coming from down the other end of the main level. Will shouts, "Hello! Anyone there? Hello?" No reply.

Will walks through the main living room space and looks up at the large painting on the ceiling. He looks over to the hallway viewing area on the second floor and sees a woman dressed as a nun. Will says, "Hello! Ma'am? Sister?" The nun walks away from the overlook and vanishes down the hallway. Will tries to run after her but has difficulty getting anywhere fast. Every step seems difficult and exhausting. He finally enters the room at the other end of the main floor that leads to another set of grand circular stairs up to the second floor. He climbs the stairs and sees the doors that lead to the old chapel. He remembers the prior dream and thinks, *This is the room where Dad and his friends were having a party.* He climbs to the first landing. One of the doors is open. He looks inside and sees the old chapel as it was when he was a young boy. Will sees a young priest blessing the whole room with holy water and saying, "I bless this house and cast out all evil spirits away from this place. This is a holy place now! I command this in the name of the Father, and of the Son, and the Holy Spirit!" The chapel turns completely black behind the altar. The shadow continues to fill the room! Will exclaims, "Father? What the hell is going on here?!"

The priest looks back and says, "Get out of here, Will. Be gone, my son! It's not safe here. I can't stop it!"

Will, horrified, runs backward and stumbles over his own feet. He lands on his back and looks up the rest of the staircase and sees the nun from before looking down at Will from the second-floor landing. Will exclaims, "Sister? Sister, please help me. I don't know what going on?" The nun doesn't say a word and walks away from Will and down the hallway. Will gets up and tirelessly makes his way to the second-floor landing.

He looks down the long hallway where he sees the nun running down the hallway screaming, "This house is cursed! This house is cursed! We can't stop it!" Will is frozen in fear. He doesn't know what to do or where to go. The darkness from the chapel room makes its way up the stairs toward him. The darkness spreads like a black shroud of mist and fog crawling along the ceiling, walls, and floor. Will hears the sound of whispers get louder as the shroud of darkness gets closer. Will turns toward the second-floor overlook and sees his father! Will's father is dressed in his normal clothes as if he were alive—a button short-sleeved shirt, jeans, and a baseball cap. Will exclaims, "Oh Jesus. Dad! Thank God you're here!" Will walks closer to his father who's leaning up against the overlook railing. Will continues, "Dad, its coming! The priest can't stop it! The sister can't stop it! What are we gonna do?"

Will's father smiles and says, "It's okay, kid. I'm here now. Don't worry about it. We will have to figure it out together."

Will replies, "What do you mean, Dad?" How are we going to figure this out?"

Will's father smiles and says, "It's okay, kid. Just remember to follow the signs, and I'll be there to catch you when you fall."

Will asks, "What do you mean, Dad? I don't understand!"

Will's father raises his hand toward an old grandfather clock down in the hallway as the shadow of complete darkness continues to edge closer to Will and his father. The echoes of the voices keep getting louder and louder. Will looks down at the clock and observes the time. 11:11.

Will looks back up toward his father. His father is gone! Will screams, "DAD!" Suddenly, the echoes stop, and it becomes very still and quiet. Will turns around. The shadow of darkness begins to take form in front of him! It forms into a tall, slender shadow of a man with two glowing green eyes and a large hat. Will is terrified and frozen in fright. He breathes heavily and begins to panic. The Shadow Man inches closer to him and laughs. The Shadow Man says, "Welcome home, Will." Suddenly, a great wind comes rushing down the hallway and lifts Will up and over the banister. Will begins to fall several feet, screaming as he quickly descends to the first floor!

Just then, Will wakes up in a scream and startles Annie out of her restful slumber.

CHAPTER 23

....

WELCOME TO THE ELK'S ESTATE MAIN HOUSE

"Ahhhhh, oh God! Dad! Where am I? What's—" Will screams out as he crosses back into the consciousness of the living world. The bedroom is dark with only the twilight from the moon shining through the window. Annie wakes up scared and anxious by her husband's reaction. She quickly turns on the lamp on the nightstand, shakes Will on his shoulder, and says, "Will! Honey! Jesus! You, okay?"

Will, still frightened by his horrific encounter, looks over to Annie and says, "Honey. Thank God. I'm okay. I'm okay. God, that was one of the scariest dreams I ever had."

Just then, there's a slight knock on the door. Annie, still trying to comfort her husband, turns toward the door and says, "Yes. Come in."

The door opens slightly. Pete pops his head from behind the door and asks, "Everything okay in here?"

Will shakes his head yes and he wipes a couple of tears away from his eyes. Annie answers, "Yeah. Everything is okay Pete. Just a bad dream." Pete replies, "Seems likes an outright night terror from that reaction." Will laughs a bit and says, "Yeah you can call it that. It was something. I'm good. Thanks brother." Pete replies, "No worries. Have a good night you two." Pete closes the door and walks back into his bedroom.

Annie continues to look at her husband as Will slows down his breathing and begins to relax. Annie asks, "What was happening in that mind of yours?"

Will answers, "Another dream about the estate. This one was so creepy and vivid. Just scared the shit out of me is all."

Annie pauses for a moment. "Honey. When you woke up you screamed, 'Dad.' Was your dad in the dream?"

Will answers, "He sure was. Well, he was there for a part of the dream. I can't believe how much of the dream I can remember. It was like he was alive again and I was talking to him as if he were in the room with me the whole time."

Annie asks, "What was he doing there?"

Will laughs a little. "He was giving me a message and providing me some comfort or something. There was something about an old grandfather clock that he pointed to when we were in that hallway. That part I can't remember. It was crazy. And the darkness."

Annie questions, "What about the darkness?"

"Nothing. Don't worry about it. It's just a dream anyway." Will turns to his wife, gives her a kiss, and says, "Good night, honey. Get some sleep."

Annie replies, "I'll try. You do the same. Good dreams for the rest of the night please. Good night." Annie turns off the lamp and they both drift off to sleep.

Liam wakes up to the sounds of an alarm clock going off in one of the bedrooms. He wakes up to a beautiful sunny morning. The morning light touches the floor and bounces off the walls as Liam breathes the fresh morning air from the open window in his room. The fresh morning air is mixed with the sweet aroma of breakfast cooking downstairs. Liam looks at the alarm clock in his room. It reads 8:00 a.m. He gets out of bed and looks at the crystal clear blue sunny sky from his bedroom window. He begins to walk out to the hallway and sees Boo beginning to walk downstairs. Liam says, "Morning, Boo. How did you sleep?"

Boo replies, "Better than dad apparently."

Liam asks, "What do you mean?"

"I heard something last night. Some commotion but just turned over and went back to bed. Did you hear anything?"

Liam shakes his head. "Nope. Slept like a baby."

Boo laughs. "Well, apparently Dad had a bad dream last night. Woke up Mom and Uncle Pete. I heard the adults talking about it this morning. But anyway, I'm hungry and Aunt Claire made some french toast and eggs for breakfast. Bye." Boo walks downstairs and toward the kitchen.

Liam walks down the hallway and peeks inside his parents' room. No one is inside, and the bed is already made. Liam then investigates Ellie's room. Ellie is up at her computer and having a cup of coffee. Liam walks into Ellie's room. "Hey, Ellie. What are you doing?"

Ellie turns and smiles at Liam. "Nothing much. Just seeing if there's anything else I can find out before we leave."

Liam looks at Ellie's coffee and asks, "Are you drinking coffee?"

Ellie says, "Yeah. Simon and I go to the coffee shop in town all the time. By the time you reach high school, believe me, you'll need some extra pick-me-up. Couldn't find out anything else. Nothing groundbreaking at least. I'm ready to leave when the rest of the family is ready."

Liam answers, "Sounds good."

Liam begins to walk out of her room when Ellie says, "Hey, Liam!"

Liam stops, turns, and looks at Ellie. "Yeah?"

Ellie replies, "When that beast attacked you in Michigan, how did you deal with being scared?"

"I was never so terrified in my life. Honestly, I wouldn't have made it through if it weren't for Boo, my friends, and the people who helped protect us."

"Do you think it's natural that I'm a little nervous about going back to that place?"

"Absolutely. But remember, we got each other. We got this."

They both smile, and Liam walks downstairs to have breakfast.

After a yummy breakfast, the family gets ready to leave. Annie is gathering her things, and she gets a feeling like she left something upstairs in the bedroom. She walks upstairs and enters her bedroom. The morning sun is glistening through the window and reflecting a sparkling light off the nightstand. She notices the shimmering light and walks over to the nightstand. It's Liam's silver cross. She picks it up and says to herself, "I think it's time to give this back to him." Annie walks back downstairs and sees Liam by the front door almost ready to leave. She gets Liam's attention saying, "Hey, honey. Could you come here for a minute?"

Liam answers, "Sure, Mom. What's up?"

Annie leans over to make eye contact with Liam. She looks down to her folded-up hand and reveals Liam's silver cross. Annie says, "I had a feeling I was forgetting something."

Liam looks at her hand and exclaims, "My silver cross! Where did you find it?"

Annie smiles and says, "You can thank your Nana for that. Found it while she was packing up the lake house. Please take good care of it this time." Annie hands Liam the cross, and he gives his mother a hug.

"Thanks, Mom. Will do." He puts the silver cross necklace around his neck and tucks it under his shirt.

The families begin to enter their respective cars. Pete looks over to Will before Will steps inside his van and says, "Hey, Will! Do you mind following me over to Simon's house and having the boys ride with you? Otherwise, it will be too crowded in my car."

Will says, "Not a problem. You lead the way."

Ellie sees Boo walking over to the van with her scooter and says, "You're bringing your scooter, Boo?"

Boo answers, "Yup. Figure if it's okay with Mom I can take a ride around the estate."

Ellie says, "I'm sure it will be fine. Good idea. That access road is a long way around, and there's no cars around to worry about. Tell you what." Ellie walks over to her garage, grabs her skateboard, and says, "I'll take the tour with you on this."

Boo smiles. "Sure! That's sounds fun."

Ellie and Boo place the scooter and skateboard into the cargo section of the van, and they make their way into their respective vehicles.

Both vehicles head down the street toward Simon's home. Pete stops his car along the side of the street and points at Simon's house. Will pulls his van into the driveway. Simon and Reggie are waiting by the front door. Simon smiles and waves at the family. Simon and Reggie leave the house and close the door behind them. Simon is carrying a backpack, while Reggie is carrying a small gym bag. Liam opens his door and steps out to let Simon and Reggie into the van.

Simon says, "Morning, monster slayer. Ready to do some more detective work?"

Liam gives Simon a death glare and says softly, "Dude. Shut it. Parents don't know we told you, remember?"

Will overhears and says, "Did you call Liam a monster slayer?"

Reggie laughs as he climbs aboard.

Simon pauses and begins to stammer, "Ye-ye-ya know. He and I were talking about monster movies, and he likes the old flicks about monster slayers is all."

Will chuckles. "Gotcha. Okay."

Simon looks at Liam with a sigh of relief as he climbs aboard.

Both vehicles begin to make their way to Route 611 as they head south toward Elkins Park. Inside the van, Liam looks back at Reggie and Simon and whispers, "What's in the bags?"

Reggie smiles as Simon leans toward Liam and whispers back, "Some ghost detecting equipment and some other stuff."

Liam asks, "What other stuff?"

Simon quietly answers, "Other stuff we may need. Flashlights, extra batteries for the flashlights, some of the books, maps and journals from the library, and survival snacks."

Reggie laughs a bit and whispers to Liam, "Yeah, we basically cleaned out his parents' cabinet and garage fridge. We got enough munchy food and soda to keep us wired for the entire day and night."

Simon turns to Reggie. "Hopefully not until nighttime. That's when bad shit happens, remember?"

Reggie answers, "How could I forget."

Liam continues to quietly question Simon. "What kind of ghost detection stuff?"

Simon replies, "Leave that up to the professionals, little slayer. I've been researching ghosts with Ellie for some time. Bought the same detection stuff that they use in some of my ghost shows. We got it covered."

Both vehicles turn off Route 611 as they reach Ashbourne Road. They follow the road, drive past the stone walls, and up to the main circle drive of the estate. There, they see an Elkins Park

Police vehicle parked at the main gate. They stop their vehicles and see a police officer exit his squad car as he waves to them. It's Will's old friend Kenny. Kenny walks over to the main gate with a set of keys to open the lock keeping the thick, heavy chain secured to the two black iron gates. Kenny opens the locks, wraps the chain around one of the gates, opens both gates, and waves both vehicles inside. Pete and Will drive past Kenny as Will waves at his friend. They both drive up the long path up to the main house. Annie looks out her window and says, "This place is amazing, honey. You grew up here?"

Will answers, "Sure did. Ran up and down these hallways for years. Good memories."

Pete and Will park their vehicles along the side of the main road close to the circular stairs that lead to the main entrance. Everyone exits the vehicles. Claire looks at Will's family and says, "Welcome to the Elk's Estate."

Everyone looks at the immense house. They turn toward the entrance they had just driven through as they hear and see the Elkins Park squad car pull up behind them. Kenny parks his vehicle, talks on his radio for a minute, and exits the car. Will walks over to his friend; they shake hands. Will says, "Hey, Kenny. Fancy seeing you here."

Kenny laughs. "Fancy that, Will."

Will asks Kenny, "So, they have the police watching over this place?"

Kenny nods his head. "Yes, sir. That's correct. We're in charge of keeping an eye on it and securing the place and grounds, especially after what happened to that boy." Kenny looks over at the group and notices Reggie. "Is that the kid who was with the boy who died?"

Will answers, "Sure is. Turns out there's a family connection between his family and my own. Don't worry. We'll keep a good eye on him."

Kenny says, "As long as you keep an eye on him. I feel like he and that boy were up to no good when the incident occurred. My bosses decided to leave it alone considering the circumstances. If you run into any trouble, you call me."

Will replies, "Understood."

Claire walks over to Kenny and says, "Good morning, Officer."

Kenny says, "Morning."

Claire asks, "Are there any specific instructions since the incident?"

Kenny answers, "Just call us when you have completed your work. We will have a squad car return to secure the doors and gates. All that we ask is no work after sunset."

Will asks, "Why's that?"

Claire says, "Those were the rules I had from the police even before the recent incident."

Kenny answers, "That's the orders from my bosses. Something about safety after dark and the estate being a liability issue for the township. But anyway, I'll go upstairs and unlock the main doors."

As Kenny walks up the circular stone staircase, the group gathers and begins to discuss their plans. Will asks Claire, "What time is the rest of the group getting here?"

Claire looks at her watch and hears a couple of vehicles make their way through the main entrance. "Speak of the devil. Looks like they're right on time as per usual."

Two other vehicles approach and park behind the other vehicles. Three people exit the cars and approach the rest of the group. It's Marcus, Anton, and Katie. Marcus and Anton are twin brothers. Both are the same age as Claire and Katie. Marcus and Anton are both tall, thin, and athletic. They open the trunk to gather their belts and tool kits. Katie resembles Claire in many ways. Both Claire and Katie are around the same height, which is short, both are brunettes, and similar facial features. It has been a running joke for Claire and Katie growing up. They were able to convince people that they were actually sisters by wearing similar outfits and having the same hairstyles.

Marcus, Anton, and Katie see the group, notice Will, and smile. Will walks over to them and says, "Well, it's been a minute hasn't it!" They each take turns giving Will a hug.

Marcus looks at Claire and says, "This can't be your little brother. This is a grown-ass man in front of me."

Anton laughs and says, "I remember that little kid with the bad haircut, running around here with his toys and constantly annoying us."

Claire smiles and says, "Time has gone by. He's all grown up now."

Will gives Katie a hug and says, "Hello, sweetheart, you're as beautiful as ever."

Katie exclaims, "It's so good to see you. Now please introduce your family. I heard about them and saw some of the pictures your sister posts online."

Will walks up with Marcus, Anton, and Katie to the rest of the group. Will asks Marcus and Anton, "So what are you two up to nowadays?"

Marcus answers, "We work for each other now. Both of us have our contracting licenses. I work in electrical contracting and demolition. Anton does plumbing and other maintenance work."

Will says, "Well good for you. That's amazing."

Anton replies, "Indeed. Business is good. We have work lined up until the holidays. We heard about you following in your dad's footsteps with the fire department. Good job."

Will smiles. "Thank you."

Marcus replies, "He's got to be looking down at you and being the proudest daddy ever."

Will laughs. "Apparently." Will looks at Katie and asks, "What about you, Katie? I heard something a while back that you were pre-med?"

Katie says, "I was pre-med when I first went into college. Claire and I took a lot of the same classes together. Mainly the sciences. But she was always better and smarter than me in those subjects. I went the other route. I went pre-law. Work for a law firm in downtown Philadelphia."

Will replies, "Wow! Look at you. I'll keep that in mind when I need some free legal advice."

Katie laughs and says, "I guess I can give a few free consultations."

Claire goes to the trunk of her car. She looks at Neil and says, "Neil, honey, help me with these radios please."

Neil helps his mother while Claire grabs some paperwork, and Pete carries a cooler out of the trunk. Claire hands everyone a small handheld radio and begins her instructions. "Well, good morning, everyone. Thank you for being patient these last few days. We have a lot of ground to cover today, so listen carefully. We will be working in four different teams. Three teams will be in the main house. One team per floor. The fourth team will be cleaning up and policing the grounds for any trash. That team will consist of Reggie and Simon. And I'll be periodically checking on you two to make sure you're actually doing some work. I have a landscaping crew arriving tomorrow to clean up all the overgrown grass, bushes, and trees. The first team will be on the lower level, which will consist of Marcus, Katie, Boo and Annie. The second team will be on the main level, which will include Ellie, Anton, Liam and myself. And lastly, the third team, the upper level, will be Will, Pete, and Neil. There's a lot of stuff on that upper level to move down to the main level, so that is where I need the muscle. I packed a picnic lunch for everyone. And there's plenty of snacks and refreshments." Claire looks at Simon and Reggie and says, "But you two. Be conservative with your partaking, if you please."

Simon laughs. "Don't worry about me. Reggie and I have that covered."

Claire rolls her eyes. "Okay. Marcus will be working on some electrical work on the lower level, and Anton is still in the process of replacing some broken pipes on the main floor. Each of you will have a list of chores to accomplish, and if you have any questions, just let me know."

Will laughs. "That's why my sister was always the honor student in school. She's always been the thorough one in the family."

Claire replies, "Better believe it. Any questions? Okay let's get started. The morning is getting away from us quickly. Everyone follow me up to the main entrance. It's the only door that is open right now. Any other doors and windows you open must be locked and secured before we leave."

Simon asks, "Do you need us to come inside too?"

Claire answers, "Yes. I have a box full of trash bags, gloves, and trash pickers to give you up in the main hallway."

Simon sarcastically replies, "Great. Sounds like a lot of fun."

The group all walk up the stairs and through the entrance of the main house. Little do they know that they all have walked into a trap!

CHAPTER 24

....

I'LL GIVE YOU
THE FIVE-CENT TOUR

Everyone makes their way up the gray stone circular stairs up to the main entrance doors. The view from the outside shows a dark entrance. They each take turns walking through the doors. The mansion is dark and quiet. The groups' footsteps echo through the long corridors and high ceilings. Light from the bright sun outside illuminates patches of what are otherwise dark passageways of this once vibrant home owned by a very wealthy family. They all remain in the main foyer, which leads into three separate paths. Simon says, "This place is amazing! But a bit spooky. You guys don't have to work in the dark, do you?"

Claire rolls her eyes. "No, Simon. We don't have to work in the dark. In fact, Marcus, can you fire up the main generator please?"

Marcus nods his head. "Sure thing." Marcus grabs a flashlight out of his tool kit and makes his way down the main living room and vanishes down a hallway on the far side of the first floor.

The group slowly makes their way through the foyer and into the main living room. Will is the last to enter. He looks toward the main living room. He then looks down at the two hallways that branch off on either side from the foyer. The hallway to his right is a long corridor. It's just like his dream. He thinks, *Wow, nothing has changed in so many years!* Next, he looks to the smaller hallway to his left, which leads to a coat room, washroom, and a stairway down to the lower level. He turns left and slowly walks down the hallway and glances down the stairs that lead to the lower level. He can see a few steps leading down the stairs and then nothing but an abyss of darkness. He remembers flash images from one of his dreams: the flashes of light that beamed from the lower level and the screams.

Liam turns back and doesn't see his dad behind him. He turns around and walks from the main living room back into the foyer. He sees his father down the hallway and makes his way toward him. As Liam approaches his father, he says, "Hey, Dad. Everything okay?"

Will continues to look down the staircase that leads to pitch blackness. In Will's mind, he replays the flashes of light and the screams.

He begins to pull back as he hears his son repeat, "Hey, Dad! Is everything okay?"

Will comes back to reality and turns back toward Liam. "Hmm? Sorry, son. What did you say?"

"Everything okay, Dad? I asked you a couple times. Figured something was wrong or maybe you were daydreaming."

Will looks at Liam and then back down the dark staircase. The darkness lifts immediately with the illumination of lights up and down the corridor and down the staircase. Will looks back at Liam and says, "Looks like Marcus turned on the generator. Let's catch up with the rest of the group."

Liam asks, "You okay, Dad? You seemed spooked when I came close to you."

Will shakes his head. "Oh, it's nothing, son. Just picking up pieces of memory lane is all. Now let's catch up with the rest of the group."

Liam and Will walk into the main living room where the rest of the group is waiting for them. Claire looks back at Liam and Will saying, "There's the rest of the party. Did you get lost?"

Will shakes his head. "Nope just looking around."

Claire smiles. "I'm sure you were. But please allow me to give all of you the five-cent tour of the main house."

Simon replies, "Yes please. This place is incredible."

Annie says, "That would be lovely. I agree. This place is unbelievable. It reminds me of the mansion from one of my old English shows."

Will says, "I told you, honey. It's just like one of your shows."

Anton looks at Will. "You watch those shows with your wife, Will?"

Will shakes his head and says, "No. Of course not. Just sports and sci-fi shows for me."

Anton grins. "Not judging. Hell, I watch those shows too. I admire the elegance, and it reminds me of this place."

Claire says, "So, everyone. You are now in the main living room of Elk's Estate. The pillars in each of the corners are solid gray-and-white marble that lead up twenty feet to the overview of the living room from the second floor. Another twenty feet above the overview you'll notice the large Italian fresco painting on the ceiling. That was hand-painted from and Italian artist before the Elk's family moved onto the property. The large chandelier that hangs down from the forty-foot ceilings is all crystal. Thank God the roof, which is secured by hand-crafted orange tiles, held for as long as the building's been open, or the fresco and the chandelier would have been destroyed."

Anton replies, "Lucky indeed. Mother Nature has been giving this place a beating, especially with all those severe storms they've been having in the area. But Mother Nature couldn't help a few pipes burst on the main floor."

Claire replies, "That's part of the work Anton will be completing today. That way, we can have running water finally. Which reminds me, if you need to use the potty, there's a portable potty located just outside the main house. Walk this way please. You'll notice most of the floor is original ceramic tile. Black and white like a chessboard. That was Mr. Elk's favorite game. He often played chess with some members from English royalty when they visited from overseas. The Elk family was certainly wealthy and powerful."

Claire leads the group through this large and extravagant room and points out the two open doors that lead to other rooms from the main living room. Claire points to both open doors on either side of the living room and says, "From the living room, you'll notice the other rooms. This house has a main artery and then branches off into a south and north wing. The room to the south is the library. None of the original books from the Elk's family library are here. Most of them are with the Elkins Park Library or sold at auction by the Catholic Church when they sold the property. The room to the north is the ballroom. That's the room with many mirrors. Most of which are unharmed, but some have been broken over the years." Everyone from the group takes turns looking into the rooms, and Claire continues the tour.

Claire leads the group out of the main living room and pauses in another corridor branch. This corridor branches off into two long hallways and to another room in front, which leads to another grand spiral staircase to the upper level. She turns to the group and says, "This is where the main house branches off into its respective wings. From this hallway, you can go down the south wing. The south wing will lead you to the dining room, the art gallery, and the china room. The north wing has an elevator, which is right around the corner. Next to that you'll find another set of stairs, a billiard room, and forty sleeping rooms, which were used by the Catholic Church when this estate housed members of the local parishes and communities during weekend retreats. Twenty rooms on the main floor followed by another twenty rooms on the upper floor. The room in front of us contains a grand staircase that leads up to the old Catholic chapel, the overlook of the main living room, and the rest of the second floor."

Simon, who's standing next to Reggie in the branch corridor, says to him, "Have you ever been inside this place?"

Reggie replies, "Nope. Been living across the street from this place my whole life. Never stepped foot into the main house. Jerald had a hard enough time trying to get me inside the coach house off the main drive."

Simon says to Claire, "One thing I'm not seeing is a lot of furniture, art, and all of the fancy expensive stuff that the Elk's family probably had during their reign."

Claire smiles. "Well of course not. Most items including the furniture, artwork, and expensive items were acquired by the Catholic Church when they took over the property. The church owned and operated this estate until the early 2010s. Until suddenly they abandoned the property and took most of the items with them to be moved elsewhere. Some other items were either sold or donated to local organizations. I've mentioned the books at the Elkins Park Library. Some of the original artwork was donated by the Catholic Church to the Philadelphia Art Museum."

Boo asks, "Which place is that? Daddy showed us around when we did our tour of Center City."

Liam laughs. "Boo, it's the place that has the 'Rocky' steps. Remember? We raced Dad up the stairs, and Dad almost took a header because he missed a step."

Boo laughs. "Oh yeah. That was fun."

Claire leads the group into the room in front and up the grand spiral staircase up to the first landing before reaching the second floor. They pause as they reach the landing and look inside the doors that lead into the old chapel. Claire leads them into the chapel. The finely wood paneled trimmed room that once housed several dark wooden pews and an altar is now empty. Behind the altar along the far back wall are two large stained-glass windows, which beautifully illuminate Catholic artwork. Along the left wall is a large canvas painting of Saint Michael—eight feet long and four feet wide—that extends down to the floor. Claire says, "Welcome to the old chapel."

Will looks around the room. He reflects on the dream he had with his father. He pictures everyone in the room. Stanley coming up and talking to him. Everyone sitting at their tables wearing tuxedoes and his dad raising his glass to him. Liam looks up at his father who looks like he's distracted again. Almost in a dreamlike state.

Liam says, "Hey, Dad?"

Will replies, "Hmm? What's up, son?"

Liam answers, "Looks like you were daydreaming again."

Will says, "Sorry. Just picking up the pieces again. This is where the nuns would hold their Christmas Eve mass every year. You heard me mention that before." Will turns to Claire and says, "You remember, sis? Mom and Dad would take us every year. The only thing left in here since our time here is that painting of Saint Michael."

Claire smiles and says, "Good memories for sure. The priests and nuns who lived here would host a private Christmas Eve mass and reception for everyone who worked here. The mass and the after party were lovely. Small and elegant. Everyone knew everybody. They would have a brilliant reception afterward in the lower-level reception hall next to the kitchen. Coffee, cake, and music."

Will interjects, "It really was a great time. One of my favorite memories from my childhood. What happened to the pews and the altar, sis? Did the church take that stuff when they left?"

Claire answers, "They did not. The chapel stayed here preserved as the church left it. Pews, statues, altar, crosses, you name it. All that stuff didn't move until the estate was purchased and briefly owned by a wedding venue. A wealthy family with a wedding venue business wanted to update, renovate, and host weddings here. Kind of like a wedding venue and hotel all in one. A good idea in theory with all the good intentions in place. They wanted this room to be an extra wedding reception hall so they could host another smaller wedding in case the ballroom was reserved."

Liam asks Claire, "What happened to the wedding venue?"

Annie interjects, "Yeah. Seems like a wonderful idea. I would have booked this place for our wedding if given the chance."

Claire answers, "It was a great idea. In fact, Pete and I had our wedding pictures done here. Isn't that right, honey?"

Pete replies, "Yes. It was wonderful. The church still owned the estate at that time. We took most of the pictures outside along the main entrance and the wood trellis corridor in the Victorian Rose Garden."

Claire looks back at Liam and continues, "To answer your question. The details are slim to none. After they started renovating, they removed all the items left by the Catholic Church. The church was insistent that they keep the items in place for an unknown reason. The venue was adamant about their intentions. Shortly after that, the project was terminated and the venue abandoned the property, leaving the property to the legal authority of the state. Let me show you around the upper level."

Claire leads the group to the upper level and around the overlook that encircles the first floor. Claire says, "Welcome to the overlook. Here you will see the beautiful view of the entire main living room. This was one of my favorite spots, especially during the holidays. The estate had a forty-foot Christmas tree in this living space. I used to love to lean over this overlook and admire the beauty of thousands of colorful lights and ornaments. My mother always admired that built-in grandfather clock along the overlook."

Will looks over to the clock and remembers his dream. He thinks about his father pointing out the clock, and a chill goes down his spine. Annie notices her husband shiver and asks, "You okay, honey?"

Will answers, "I'm fine, hon. No worries. Just got a cold chill is all. These old mansions you know."

Annie replies, "Okay. Just checking."

Claire looks at Will and Annie and asks, "Will, Annie, do you have a question?"

Will answers, "Nothing, sis. Just amazed that the old clock is still here and working."

Claire replies, "Yes. In fact, it didn't work until recently. Had an old friend from high school who lives in the area look at it. He enjoys repairing old clocks as a side business. Sorry, not to get off the subject, but the layout on this floor is very similar to the main floor. The south wing will lead you to the Elk family bedrooms, which also include a steam room and several elegant washrooms. The north is just like the main floor minus the billiard room."

Just then, the group hears the elevator bell chime. The doors open and it's Marcus. Marcus slightly exits the elevator while keeping the majority of his body inside while he holds the door. Marcus says, "Hello again, everyone. How's the tour going, Claire?"

Claire laughs and replies, "Just fine. I could quit my job and be a professional tour guide for this place. I love it so much. Actually, this is perfect timing. Let's make our way down to the lower level and get started. Who wants to ride on the elevator? Some will have to wait for the next ride."

Annie pauses. "Is this elevator safe?"

Marcus replies, "If it wasn't safe, I wouldn't be riding on it."

Claire interjects, "Yes, that elevator shaft used to hold an old elevator, which was the best in the market during the time of the original construction. The Church installed another elevator back in the early '90s. We had an elevator company come out to repair it, and a state inspector came out to license it."

Liam says, "All of this stuff sounds expensive."

Claire says, "Yes, it is. Which is why we are grateful for all the charitable donations we received from the community to resurrect the property."

Marcus says, "In fact, the elevator works so well its yelling at me to close the door, so if you would please."

The adults take the elevator down to the lower level while the younger crew take to the stairs. Simon says to Neil, "It looks like you and the volunteers have been busy, scarecrow."

Neil laughs and replies, "You can say that. We've been doing a lot of work to help our mom with this place."

Simon asks, "So what's on the lower level? All the dead bodies?"

The group laughs as Neil replies, "Haven't seen any dead bodies. Not yet anyway. Mainly it's the kitchen, some offices, the boiler room, and a lower reception hall."

Liam, Boo, Neil, Ellie, Simon, and Reggie exit the stairway to the lower level where they are met by the rest of the group. Claire looks around at everyone as though she's taking attendance. She says, "Okay. Seems like we have everyone. You are now in the main hallway for the lower level." Claire points behind the group as she continues, "Behind you is the main food storage locker, the walk-in freezer, and the outside door that leads to a loading dock." Claire directs the group down the hallway, turns to face the group, and points to her left and her right. She directs, "To my right is the entrance to the kitchen and dish cleaning area. To my left, you notice two small reception halls. This is where the church would host their Christmas party, and they would often host kid's parties for the employees. The original purpose for these reception halls was a dining area for the Elk's family staff and a place where the staff could host parties for their own families. Follow me this way."

Claire leads the group farther down the hallway. "Theres's only a few more rooms down this hallway. These rooms include some staff offices, the smoking lounge, the boiler room, and another set of stairs that will take you back to the main floor." As the group gets closer to the end of the hallway and listens to Claire's presentation, Simon notices another double door at the end, which is locked with a sign that says, "No Entry. Dangerous."

Simon asks, "So what's the deal with that door?"

Claire rolls her eyes, looks at Ellie, and says, "Does he always ask so many questions?"

Ellie laughs and says, "Yup. He's always the curious cat."

Neil interjects, "Yeah, we all know what happened to the curious cat."

Liam, Boo, Ellie, and Reggie laugh as Simon says to Neil, "Shut up, scarecrow!"

Will says, "I think I know that door. That's the door that leads to the underground passageway."

Claire smiles. "You're correct, little brother. If I recall, you got into a lot of trouble when Mom went to get change for the soda machine they had in the smoking lounge, and you went for a small exploration of the tunnel on your own. How old were you?"

Will smiles, laughs, and says, "I was about three years old. It's one of my oldest memories."

Claire replies, "Yeah, I remember it well. Mom wasn't too happy with you. This tunnel leads underground to the old staff cottages. Some building engineers from the town inspected it recently and condemned it. Said it wasn't safe and could collapse. Due to no maintenance and old shoring along the ceiling."

Simon says, "Dude, this place is unreal. Grand living rooms, ballrooms, underground passageways… I would have loved to hang out around here when I was a kid."

Reggie says, "Seeing how curious and bright you are since I met you, you wouldn't have made it to puberty before you killed yourself somewhere in here."

The group laughs and Claire hands everyone a printout. "Okay, everyone. I hope you enjoyed your five-cent tour, but now we have work to do. On this printout you will see the list of chores, the names of everyone working on each team, and where you will be working. Your handheld radios have several channels available. Through trial and error, we've found that channel 4 works best around here. We will all plan to work around here until 11:00 a.m. when we will break for lunch. Any questions, please let me know. Let's get to work."

....

CHAPTER 25

LOWER-LEVEL TEAM

Everyone looks at the printout. Liam, Boo, Neil, Ellie, Simon, and Reggie gather together in a huddle to discuss their plan of action. Simon looks at Liam and says, "What's the plan, monster slayer?"

Liam looks at his printout as he reads off the assignments saying, "Let's see. We have Boo working on the lower level here with Marcus, Katie, and Mom. I'll be on the main floor with Aunt Claire, Ellie and Anton. Neil will be on the upper level with Uncle Pete and Dad. And the grounds will be covered by Simon and Reggie. First off, communications. I always hear my dad talking about how important communications are with the fire department. Let's have a plan on how to reach each other quickly."

Simon replies, "Good thinking, dude." Simon looks at his handheld radio and says, "It looks like we have up to four different channels to choose from on these radios. Let's plan on using channel 3. That way we are on a different frequency than the grown-ups. We can plan to do a radio check when we branch off into our groups."

Reggie says, "That's a good idea. Let's also plan to have each other on a group text message feed as a backup."

Ellie says, "That's a great idea. I'll make the group feed now."

Boo interjects, "I still don't know what our main objectives are in this whole thing. Can someone please explain that to me?"

Simon says to Liam, "It's your show, monster slayer. You tell us."

Liam says, "There's still a lot we don't know about The Shadow Man. Neil and Ellie have been here several times and swear they've never seen anything out of the ordinary. Isn't that right?"

Ellie says, "Yes."

Neil nods his head in approval.

Liam continues, "While we are doing our chores around here, everyone should sneak around and try to find some more clues that will help solve this mystery. This place and the grounds surrounding the property are massive. We are bound to find something. But also, our main objective is to be there for each other in case anything goes south. Plus, Simon has some paranormal detection stuff in his bag. Right, Simon?"

Simon says, "That's our monster slayer. A fearless leader against the forces of darkness." Simon kneels and opens his backpack. He shows them his ghost detection gear. "I have a voice recorder, a device that measures electrical activity in the atmosphere, and a camera that I can switch into night-vision mode."

Neil says, "You've got to be kidding me."

Simon replies, "Believe it or not, scarecrow, your sister and I picked up a few strange anomalies on these devices. Low-frequency voices and small orbs, which are usually the visual signature that is captured when a ghost is present. Figure while Reggie and I are policing the grounds we can use this stuff and help gather evidence and clues."

Liam responds, "Sounds like a solid plan. A leader maybe. But I'll be honest I'm feeling a little nervous about this whole thing. But we have each other. That's more important than being afraid."

The rest of the grown-ups make their way to their stations as Aunt Claire notices the young group gathered together. She approaches them saying, "Any questions?"

The group breaks from their huddle and Simon replies, "Nope, all set to do some work around here."

Claire replies, "I thought I would never hear you say the word 'work,' Simon. Doesn't seem to be your forte."

The group laughs.

Simon replies, "I'm turning over a new leaf, ma'am. No more lazy slacker Simon from this moment forward."

Claire says, "Okay, everyone. Get to work. Earn that lunch that I spent all morning making for you."

The young group makes their way to their assigned locations. Boo walks down the hallway to meet up with the rest of the group working on the lower level. Boo turns into the room that leads to the dish cleaning area and the kitchen. That's where she sees her mother talking to Marcus and Katie. Annie turns to Boo and says, "There's my little helper. Glad you found us."

Boo approaches her mother, gives her a hug, and says, "I looked at the printout. Looks like you and I will be working on cleaning the floors and removing a lot of dust."

Annie replies, "That's right. Marcus will be doing some electrical work inside the walk-in freezer. Katie will be sorting through old documents that were found in the staff office."

Katie replies, "Yes. During the cleanup, the volunteer group found some old documents left by the Catholic Church. They asked me to look through them and see if anything should be returned or destroyed. Some of the paperwork supposedly included some legal forms, which are right up my alley. So, I'll be down the hallway sorting and shredding my morning away."

Marcus approaches Katie, gives her a hug, and says, "I'm so amazed by this woman. All grown up and doing the lawyer thing. So proud."

Katie smiles. "Yup. Who would have thought?"

Marcus looks at Annie and Boo and says, "I'll be in that old walk-in freezer over there. Claire wanted to see if I could get it to work. If you need anything give me a shout."

Annie replies, "Sounds good."

Katie goes over to the counter and says, "Annie and Boo, here are your cleaning supplies. If you need anything else, you know where I'll be."

Annie says, "Thank you, Katie. Will do."

Annie and Boo gather their cleaning supplies and head down the hallway. Boo asks, "How do you want to do this, Mom?"

Annie answers, "Well, if you work on dusting the old smoking lounge at the end of the hall, I'll work on the floors in the reception halls."

Boo looks down the hallway and is a little apprehensive about being in the far room by herself. She asks, "Can't you stay with me, Mom?"

Annie smiles and replies, "I know it's a little spooky down here, baby. But I'll be just down the hall. If you get spooked just run over to me, okay?"

Boo nods her head as Annie hands her some furniture polish and extra cleaning rags.

As Boo begins to walk down the hallway, Annie is tapped on the shoulder and is startled. She spins around. "Who is— Oh, Claire, sorry didn't expect that."

Claire chuckles. "Sorry, didn't mean to scare you."

"That's okay. What's up?"

"I know it said on the printout that you'll be doing chores here on the lower floor, but I really need more help on the main floor, especially in the art room. Would you mind?"

Annie looks back toward Boo who is walking farther down the hallway. Annie looks back at Claire and says, "You think Boo will be okay?"

Claire smiles and says, "Of course. She'll be okay. Katie and Marcus are down here. Plus, if she needs anything she can ask over the radio." Annie agrees with Claire and follows her up to the main floor with the rest of her team.

Boo continues to walk down the hallway toward the old smoking lounge. As she approaches the door to the smoking lounge, she looks to her right and looks inside the boiler room. The sound of the generator is loud and continuous. She peeks across the threshold and sees the generator working to keep the power running. She's suddenly startled by Marcus who walks right behind her. Boo jumps in surprise as Marcus says, "Oh sorry, honey. Didn't mean to scare you. Just needed to check a couple fuses for the kitchen."

Boo calms herself and says, "It's okay. This place is a little creepy."

Marcus says, "I understand. It's really creepy. Comes with age. In fact, if you want to see something cool, follow me for a second."

Boo follows Marcus into the boiler room. Marcus says, "Be sure not to touch anything, honey, especially that boiler. It's steaming hot."

Boo replies loudly over the boiler, "Is the boiler making all this noise? I thought it was the generator."

Marcus says, "Yes. It's the newer generator that replaced the old one years ago. This thing is an antique, but it still works. But the most interesting thing here is the old generator. Here, let me show you."

Marcus and Boo walk over the section of the boiler room to the old electrical generator where it's slightly quieter. Marcus points to the old generator. "Not sure what you're learning in school nowadays, but this thing is a piece of history."

Boo asks, "Why's that?"

"This generator was one of a kind. You see, this mansion was one of the first in the area to house its own electrical generator. This place was built shortly after Edison won the battle over electrical current. But this generator was custom built by someone overseas when the Elk family was still building the place. The Elk family was still interested in using AC current. So, this generator has the capability to produce AC current to the entire estate. That's if, of course, myself or anyone could ever get it to work again. This old thing hasn't worked in a long time. Right now, the building is being powered, like all things, with direct current."

Boo replies, "Don't know much about alternate and direct current, but it sounds pretty cool."

Marcus smiles and he leads Boo over to the fuse box to check the fuses. "That's because it *is* cool. History is very cool. I'm a total nerd on the subject." Marcus checks the fuse box and says, "Everything looks okay in here. It should work. Maybe I missed something in the freezer. Let me walk you out, honey, so you can begin your work." Marcus leads Boo out of the boiler room. "Now, if you need anything, the adults are right down the hallway. Just give us a call on the radio."

Boo looks at her radio and says, "Okay. Sounds good."

Marcus walks down the hallway toward the kitchen and vanishes around a corner.

Boo looks ahead at the door that leads to the old smoking lounge. She looks inside. It is a modest-sized room complete with old white-and-green patterned wallpaper that is stained brownish yellow from the remains of old cigar smoke. She walks over the threshold into the room and leaves the checkered board-tiled hallway to a green carpeted room and walks past old leather chairs and couches. She pauses briefly as she remembers the idea about the radio and switches to channel 3. The chairs and couches are pointed toward an old lightly colored wooden radio that stands next to an old-fashioned wooden television stand. On the far wall there's a wood-burning fireplace with a five-foot mantel. Inside the fireplace, there's blackened and charred remains of a handful of wood logs resting on a metal catch basin. The room is illuminated by two large lamps in either corner of the room.

Boo looks at her phone. She sees only one bar for reception and thinks it will be hard to listen to music on her phone. She tries to turn on the free-standing radio and thinks, *Maybe I can find a radio station on this old thing. Listen to some tunes while I'm working. But first, how do I turn it on?* She turns the on/volume circular knob clockwise. The radio lights up and the speakers come to life. She locates the circular knob to change and search for stations. She finds a channel that works. Classic rock. *This will be perfect. Dad always listens to classic rock when he's working on a project.*

Boo begins to work. She hears Simon over the radio saying, "Good afternoon, everyone. This is your main man, Simon. Coming to you live from the Elk's Estate. How do I read?"

Boo grabs her radio, presses the talk-to-speak button, and says, "This is Boo. Loud and clear on the lower level." She grabs a light chair and drags it over to the fireplace. She climbs up the chair and begins to dust off the mantel. Boo is facing the mantel as she sprays furniture polish and cleans off the layers of dust. She hears the door close behind her and hears the radio station change and fades in and out until the music is playing at a low volume. The station is playing old jazz music. Next, Boo hears the sounds of a little girl singing behind her. She's unable to hear what the girl is saying. Boo is scared and beginning to shiver. She turns around slowly and sees a little girl glowing white! The little girl is wearing a yellow dress with brown polka dots. She has brunette hair and two pig tails tied with two red bows. The little girl is playing with a doll and a music box.

Boo tries to scream, but she's so scared nothing comes out of her mouth except and quiet plea for help. The little girl turns to Boo and says, "Hi. I'm Misty. Would you like to play with me?" Boo steps back and falls off the chair with a loud thump. Misty says, "You should be careful. That's one way little girls can get hurt around here."

Boo climbs to her feet and walks along the front of the fireplace. She grabs her radio and says, "Liam! Simon! Anyone!" No response. She looks at the radio. Not working. Battery is completely drained. She takes her phone out of her pocket and looks at the screen. No signal.

Misty asks, "What's your name?"

Boo stammers, "I'm Be-Bec-Becca, but everyone calls me Boo."

Misty smiles and says, "I like that name. Boo is such a fun name. Would you like to hear my music box?" Misty winds up her music to play the chimes of a common bedtime song. Misty looks back at Boo and says, "Isn't it lovely? I got it from my Daddy for Christmas last year. I'm happy that you're able to see me. I try to talk to some other people, but they just ignore me."

Boo walks over toward Misty. She shivers in fear. Goose bumps form down her arms, and a chill runs down her spine. The temperature in the room has gone down several degrees in just a few moments. Misty says, "Oh, if you're cold, here, let me help you." Misty points her right hand to the fireplace, and fire reignites from the smoldered old fire logs. Boo looks at the fire, which spontaneously reignites. Misty says, "Don't be afraid to play with me. It's okay. I'll be happy to share my doll. Her name is Vivion. I got her from my Mommy last Christmas too."

Boo sits down next to Misty. Misty's presence gives off a slight white glow from her body. Boo searches her mind for the right thing to say. "Do you live here, Misty?"

"Yup. Sure do. Live here with a lot of people. This is my favorite room. I can always listen to the radio in here. Haven't been able to hear my favorite stories recently."

Boo looks at the closed door and back at Misty. "Misty, why did you close the door?"

Misty replies, "To keep you safe while we play. My grandpa can be mean, and The Shadow Man is even more mean."

The lamps start to flicker, and the sound of indistinguishable voices come over the radio. Boo looks at the flickering lamps, looks at the radio, and then looks back at Misty. "Misty, what's going on?"

Misty says, "Oh. That means that my grandpa has arrived. He's one of the mean ones. Don't worry, you'll be safe with me. Let's play."

CHAPTER 26

....

MAIN LEVEL TEAM

L iam takes the elevator with his group up to the main level of the mansion. He looks at his printout and asks Claire, "It says I'll be vacuuming the rugs in the billiard room and the carpets in the hallway. That's right around the corner, correct?"

Claire replies, "That's right. I have everything in place for you."

Anton interjects, "And if you have any questions, buddy, I'll be working in a utility closet just down that hallway. I'll be replacing one of the main water feeder pipes that goes up to the second floor."

They all exit the elevator. Annie asks Claire, "What do you need from me?"

Claire says, "I really need someone to begin dusting and cleaning off the walls in the art gallery. That room hasn't been touched in a long time. But it needs more work than the old reception halls downstairs. I've been able to coordinate with the Philadelphia Art Museum. They agreed to allow some of the original artwork to remain at the estate after the state agrees to provide the historical landmark status. That will provide enough funds to allow at least a security guard to police the estate around the clock. At least one security guard at all times."

Annie exclaims, "Wow! That's really impressive. You've put in a lot of effort into this project."

Claire replies, "What can I say? I love this place. I want to see it thrive. I'll be in the ballroom with Ellie working on removing and replacing some broken mirrors. If I need help with the installation, I'll give you a call on the radio. All your cleaning supplies are in the art gallery room."

Annie walks toward the art gallery while Claire walks with Liam and Anton. Ellie makes her way over to the ballroom. Claire shows Liam into the billiard room as Anton continues down the hallway toward the utility closet. Claire gives Liam the vacuum, the extension cord, and shows him the location of all the outlets. Liam looks around the billiard room. The dark wood-trimmed room is brightened by two large floor-to-ceiling French windows. The bright summer sun reflects its light on the massive oriental rug that takes up the entire floor space. The dark wood floor is only seen in the far corners and edges of the room. Liam says, "This rug looks old too."

Claire laughs and says, "Sure is. It was left here. Handcrafted and shipped from overseas when the Elk family owned the estate. I set the vacuum to a delicate setting. Don't want to harm the fibers. If you have any questions, you know where to find me."

Liam gets to work vacuuming. He looks down the hallway toward Anton. Liam sees Anton moving items out of the utility closet before he begins his task. Claire walks through the main living room and into the ballroom. The ballroom is a large open space with high ceilings. The walls are covered with paneled mirrors except for the exterior wall, which has floor-to-ceiling French windows that look out toward one of the old rose gardens and the coach house. Light from the bright sunshine outside reflects off the glossy white tiles that make up the floor space. Old fold-up circular wood tables and chairs are carefully preserved in the far corner of the room. A beautiful crystal chandelier hangs from the center of the ceiling. The wall across from the ballroom entrance has a few broken mirrors. Immediately adjacent to the broken mirrors is a ladder and a large plastic trash can, which is Ellie and Claire's workspace. Claire sees Ellie next to the ladder cleaning up some broken mirror pieces off the floor with a dustpan and broom.

Claire walks into the ballroom as her footsteps echo off the walls of this now empty hall. Claire grabs her radio and looks to make sure it's programmed to channel 4. Ellie decides to keep her radio on channel 4 so her mother doesn't overhear the younger group's communications. Claire presses the talk-to-speak button and says, "Hey, everyone. This is Claire doing a radio check. Lower level, how do I read?"

After a brief pause, Katie says, "Loud and clear from the old staff office."

Claire replies, "Great. Upper level, how do I read?"

Will answers, "You read just fine, sis."

Claire responds, "Great. Finally, grounds crew, how do I read?"

There's a brief pause. No answer. Claire again asks, "Grounds crew? How do I read?"

Ellie takes a quick break from her task and grabs her phone out of her pocket. She texts Simon, "Dude! Switch back to channel 4 now! My mom is looking for you!"

Claire waits a few seconds. Ellie can see her mother getting frustrated. Claire says in a low voice, "I knew I should've had an adult with those two boys." She presses the talk-to-speak button again and says, "Grounds crew? Can you hear me? How do I read?"

A few seconds later, Simon says through the radio, "Yeah! Grounds crew to mother hen. All is well here. Sorry, the volume was too low so we can concentrate on working."

Claire rolls her eyes and says to herself, "I'm sure." Claire responds into the radio, "Okay sounds good."

Ellie looks at her phone and sees a text from Simon saying, "Thanks, beautiful. That was a close one."

Ellie smiles and responds, "No worries. I have my radio on channel 4 so my mom doesn't hear us."

Simon replies, "Smart thinking as usual."

Ellie responds, "Where you guys at?"

Simon answers, "Back part of the property near the big Victorian Rose Garden. Want to see if we can get access to that old underground tunnel from the outside. If not, we will be heading out toward the old worker's quarters and the cemetery."

Ellie replies, "Okay. Sounds good. Keep me posted."

Claire climbs the ladder and looks over to Ellie. Claire sees her texting and says, "Ellie, you can have the rest of the day when we get home to play on your phone. Can you get to work please?"

Ellie puts her phone back into her pocket and says, "Yeah, Mom. Sorry."

"It's okay. When you finish picking up those pieces, I'll need help removing the rest of this mirror panel from the wall."

"No problem, Mom. Were you able to order more mirrors to replace these broken ones?"

Claire, who is starting to loosen the mirror panel screws from the wall, replies, "Just a few. Turns out these mirrors are very expensive. Have to wait and hope for the state funding."

Ellie takes the dustpan filled with broken mirror pieces over to the trash can. She hears a chime on her phone. She looks back at Claire who is focused on her task at the moment. Ellie looks at her phone and sees a text from Simon: "This is strange. Didn't hear anything about thunderstorms today. Clouds are rolling in toward us, the wind is picking up, and I just heard thunder in the distance."

Ellie responds, "Supposed to be clear today I thought."

Simon replies, "Reggie just said he heard someone's voice as the wind picked up. Something weird is going on around here! I'll see if we can pick up anything with my equipment!"

Claire gets a call on the radio from Katie. "Hey, Claire. This is Katie in the staff office. Can you hear me?"

Claire takes a break from her current task to answer Katie. "Yeah, Katie. I can hear you. What's up?"

Katie says, "I've found some strange paperwork in the office. It's definitely worth your attention."

"Okay. I'll be down there in a few minutes."

Claire looks at Ellie and exclaims, "I thought we talked about this, Ellie!"

Ellie puts her phone back into her pocket, walks toward Claire, and says, "Sorry, Mom. No excuse."

Claire exhales, takes a deep breath, and says, "It's okay. Grab that pair of gloves off the floor and help me. After I get the mirror away from the wall, I'll hand it down to you."

Ellie reaches down to grab the pair of gloves.

There's a sound from the grandfather clock on the upper floor. The chimes echo throughout the living room and into the ballroom. It chimes eleven times. 11:00 a.m. Claire looks through the mirror and sees the reflection of the entry way behind her. She sees a nun standing along the threshold! Claire screams and loses her grip on the mirror, which then falls and fractures into several pieces across the tile floor. Claire grabs hold of the ladder before she loses her balance. Ellie is startled by her mother screaming and the deafening sound of the mirror hitting the floor. Ellie holds her hands to her ears as she shivers in fright. Claire turns around to look at the entryway. No one is there. She looks back at one of the mirrors on the wall. No reflection of the nun she just saw a moment ago.

Ellie exclaims, "Mom! What happened?"

Claire takes several quick short breaths as she climbs down the ladder. "I just saw Sister Elizabeth standing in the doorway! I swear on my life! But that's impossible. She...."

At that moment, Will says through the radio, "Hey, sis! What was that loud bang? Everyone o—?"

The radio gives a brief moment of static and then it suddenly dies. Claire looks at Ellie and says, "Stay here! I'll be right back." Claire walks toward the entrance of the ballroom and into the main living room. She sees a silhouette of the nun as she vanishes around the corner and down the hallway toward the art gallery. The lights start to flicker throughout the estate. Claire runs through the main living room. Overhead she sees Will, Pete, and Neil looking down from the overlook on the upper floor. Will exclaims, "What the matter, sis? Everything okay?"

Pete shouts down to Claire saying, "We couldn't hear anything on our radios! You won't believe what we found!"

Claire continues to quickly make her way through the main living room as she answers, "Everybody's okay. But something is going on!"

Neil asks, "What's going on, Mom?"

Claire doesn't answer. Instead, she looks down the hallway and sees the nun as she quickly glides down the hallway! Annie hears all the commotion from the art gallery. She takes a break from her duties and walks into the hallway to find out what's happening. As Annie steps out into the hallway, the nun glides past her and screams to Annie, "Father can't stop it! Father can't stop it!" Annie is paralyzed in fear. She looks at the nun's ghostly face as she screams at her. The nun is crying and shaking as she continues to glide past Annie and vanish through one of the walls that lead to the china room!

Annie gathers her thoughts. She screams and breathes quickly. Annie looks down the hall toward Claire and exclaims, "What the hell was that, Claire?"

Claire answers, "I think that was Sister Elizabeth but…"

Annie runs down the hallway straight past Claire.

Claire asks, "Where you are going?"

Annie says, "Getting Liam!"

Liam is finishing vacuuming the oriental rug in the billiard room. Most of the communication over the radio is drowned out by the noise of the vacuum. He pauses when he hears the loud bang come from the direction of the ballroom. He turns off the vacuum and hears a woman scream. Anton hears the loud distraction and comes out of the utility closet. Anton looks down the hallway at Liam and exclaims, "Hey, Liam! What was that? Everything okay?"

Liam responds, "I don't know! I'll try my radio!" Liam grabs his radio, presses the talk-to-speak button, and hears nothing but static through the speaker. Liam says, "Everyone okay? Copy? This is Liam. Can anyone hear me?"

There's a moment of radio static and then the radio dies. Anton checks his radio and tries to hear any communication. Anton inspects his radio. It appears to be dead as well. He tries to turn it off and on again. The radio is still dead.

Anton starts to walk towards Liam saying, "Hey, kid. Is your radio working? Mine just died."

Liam sees Anton walking toward him and responds, "Nope. My radio is dead too, Anton. I don't know what's going on!"

Anton walks into the billiard room and says, "Okay. Stay with me. Let's find Claire."

At that moment, the lights started to flicker in the billiard room and down the hallway. Liam and Anton look at the flickering lights and hear a door open from down the long hallway filled with dozens of closed doors. A tall figure wearing a black head-to-toe shroud steps out of the room and into the hallway! Liam takes a deep breath in fright as the figure begins to glide down the hallway toward him and Anton! Anton grabs ahold of Liam's hand and says, "Okay. Let's get out of here!"

CHAPTER 27

....

UPPER-LEVEL TEAM

After the main floor team gets off the elevator, the upper-level team waits on the lower level as Neil presses the button for the elevator to return. Will says to Neil, "If you don't want to wait for the elevator, I'll race you up the stairs."

Neil laughs and asks, "You serious, Uncle Will?"

Will looks at Neil and replies, "Of course I'm serious. I train five days a week, young man. Plus, the stairs are good for my cardio. Unless you think you'll be beaten by an old man."

Neil says, "Okay you're on." Neil looks at Pete and asks, "You gonna join us?"

Pete laughs and answers, "Nope. My running days are basically over. I'll wait here for the elevator. You kids have fun."

Neil and Will walk over the winding staircase, which is adjacent to the elevator shaft. Neil says, "Now, this staircase will take us all the way to upper level next to the overlook."

Will says, "I remember my way around. I was exploring this place well before your parents even met, kid."

They line up at the bottom landing right below the first step. Neil looks at Will, smiles, and says, "You call it, Uncle Will."

Will grins and says, "Okay. On your mark. Get set. G—"

Neil interjects, "GO!" and starts running up the stairs in a flash! Will says, "Cheater!" Will starts to run up the steps to catch Neil. Neil makes it to the first-floor landing and hears the elevator descend down the shaft toward the lower level. Will is catching up fast and is only a step behind Neil. Will exclaims, "Told you I'll catch up!"

Neil smiles as he breathes heavily and begins the climb up to the upper level. During their mad dash, they hear the elevator rise through the elevator shaft and ascend up toward the upper level. Neil and Will are neck and neck as they make it halfway between the main floor and the upper level. Will begins to climb harder and take two steps at a time. Neil almost stumbles as he tries to keep up with Will who passes him. Will makes his way up to the upper-level landing. Will does a mini celebration and sings the theme song from *Rocky*.

Neil takes the last few steps up to the upper-level landing knowing he's been defeated by his uncle. Neil makes it up to the landing, continues to breath heavily, and says, "Not bad for an old man."

Will smiles at his nephew and replies, "I was doing some training at the art museum. Even the kids couldn't beat me. I told you I still train."

Neil catches his breath, shakes Will's hand, and says, "Okay. Tomorrow. Rematch on the basketball court near my house."

"Are you sure about that? I play basketball once a week back home."

Will and Neil laugh as they make their way over to the overlook to meet up with Pete.

Pete, who has already exited the elevator, is standing near two concrete statues next to the overlook. Both statues are over five feet tall. The finite details of these statues are articulated by their warmth of various shades of gray material that are carved in and out of the structure to create a masterpiece. Next to Pete is a two-wheeled dolly and two ratchet straps on the floor. As Neil and Will approach, Will asks, "I wonder what we have to do with these?"

Neil looks at his printout that he had folded and placed in the back pocket of his cargo shorts. Neil answers, "It says for the upper-level team: Secure statues and clean up the chapel."

Pete turns to Will and Neil as they arrive. "Did you enjoy your cardio session?" Will and Neil smile as Pete continues, "Who won by the way?"

Neil points to Will. "The old man by a nose."

Neil laughs as Will replies, "I'm old but not as old as your dad here."

Pete smiles and says, "I might be getting older, but I haven't let myself go either."

Will chuckles. "Honestly, it's true. Your dad looks the same as the day your mom brought him around to meet the family. He just looks more tired and worn out if you ask me."

Pete says, "That's because I am. Speaking of which, I'll need both of your help to accomplish our mission. Ready?"

Neil asks Pete, "What do we have to do, Dad?"

Pete looks at Neil and then looks at Will as he asks, "First a question. Do you recognize these statues, Will?"

Will looks at them for a moment and says, "I sure do. They were located around the overlook when I was a boy." Will points at the statues. "The one to the left is Saint William, and the one to the right is Saint Martin of Tours."

Neil is surprised. "How did you know that?"

Will answers, "These statues were significant because they represented two of the largest Catholic Church parishes in northeast Philadelphia. At least the two parishes that had the most parishioners attended weekend retreats here when I was a boy. My father went to Saint William's Catholic School. Our family, and your dad, all attended Saint Martin of Tours Catholic School. I'm surprised the church left these here."

Pete says, "Your uncle is right. These were placed on either side of the overlook back when the church ran this place. The parishioners would walk past them before they made their way to the old chapel."

Will asks, "Any reason why the church would leave these here abandoned?"

Pete answers, "From what we were told, these were left by the church along with anything they left in the chapel for preservation. The wedding venue was in the process of moving them somewhere else when they abandoned shop. That's what we were told anyway."

Neil asks Pete, "So what do we have to do, Dad?"

"Your mom has appointed us the tasks to put these on this dolly here, move them over to the chapel, and place them on the old altar. She figures it can be a nice place to display them."

Will asks Pete, "Is that all?"

Pete laughs. "I wish, bro. I wish. Afterward, we have to remove a lot of construction dust that was created by the wedding venue."

Will replies, "Sounds like fun. Well, let's get to it."

The team discusses their plan of action. Neil hears his radio. It's Simon doing a radio check on channel 3. Neil is nervous that his uncle and father will hear Simon on his radio and quickly switches his radio back to channel 4. Pete pauses, looks at Neil, and asks, "Was there something on the radio, son? Was that Simon?"

Neil nervously answers, "Yeah, Dad, he was just doing a radio check. All is good."

Pete looks at Will's radio and says, "That's funny. Will didn't get any transmission over his radio."

Neil quickly comes up with a story. "Yeah, Dad. If the radios are too close together, only one radio will get the transmission. Helps keep the line of communication nice and clear."

Will says, "Sounds about right. We use radios at my work all the time that work the same way."

They decide to have Pete on dolly duty while Neil and Will move and tilt one statue at a time onto the dolly and secure it with the ratchet straps. As Will and Neil struggle to maneuver the statue of Saint William, Will says, "Jesus. These things weigh a ton. How much do you think, Pete?"

Pete, who's holding the dolly in place says, "Have to be hundreds of pounds each. These babies were made from solid concrete."

Will and Neil place the statue onto the dolly safely and secure it with ratchet straps. Neil and Will help push the statue toward Pete as he pulls back on the dolly. As the statue begins to tilt toward Pete, both Neil and Will place themselves on either side of the statue. They begin to roll it over to the grand spiral staircase.

They reach the grand staircase that leads down to the chapel, which is located midway on the far wall between the upper-level and the main level. Neil asks, "So what's the plan now?"

Pete says, "Well, it would be nice to use the elevator, but it only stops on the main levels. The only way to the chapel is using these stairs. Figure it should be easier to bring it downstairs instead of upstairs."

Will approves. "Agreed. We lift and move patients all the time at work. Figure it will be best to have Pete at the top end guiding the dolly down one step at a time while I'm on the receiving end helping to keep it from falling."

Neil asks, "Then where will I be?"

Will answers, "On one of the sides being ready to help your father and me at a moment's notice."

Will looks at Pete and asks, "How're those wheels holding up on this dolly?"

Pete answers, "They are doing what they can, but they are showing signs that they might buckle."

Will replies, "Okay. Let's do what we can and get this done."

Pete, Will, and Neil carefully make their way down the stairs as they take each step with caution. They reach the landing, which leads to the old chapel. They each breathe a sigh of relief. Will investigates the wood-paneled room. Will says to Pete, "Almost there. Let's get this one on the old altar and then grab the other. Then the hard work should be over."

Neil laughs. "Yeah, until Mom finds something else for us to do."

Pete replies, "Isn't that the truth. Well, your Uncle Will is right. Let's get this done and we will be halfway there."

Will asks, "Which side of the altar do we want good ole Saint William?"

Pete says, "Let's put it on the left side." They agree and begin to maneuver the statue and dolly into the chapel.

As they carefully move the dolly further into the chapel, the left wheel starts to get louder and louder. Neil says, "Wow! I guess the squeaky wheel needs some oil, Dad."

Pete replies, "I just hope that this dolly doesn't give out before we d–"

Suddenly, the left wheel on the dolly buckles, and the statue quickly tilts to the left side as they are passing the large Saint Michael painting. Neil and Will try to help Pete, but the weight is too much and the statue falls right into the Saint Michael painting. As the statue falls it breaks through the painting and hits the floor behind the wall with a loud *THUMP!* The calamity reveals a secret entrance to an unknown hallway!

The hallway goes on for approximately ten feet into a dark room. Will, Neil, and Pete are stunned by the events that have just unfolded. They stare into the entrance, wondering where the passage would lead them.

Neil says, "On man. Mom is gonna be so pissed at us for wrecking that painting!"

Pete replies, "Yup. She sure is. I'm surprised that she's not marching her way up here after that loud thump."

Will says, "There's a good chance she didn't hear it. It's strange how sounds and echoes travel in this house. Anyone want to see where it goes?"

Pete replies, "I'm kind of curious. Yeah, I'll go with you."

Neil says, "Screw that! It's dark back there. You don't know what could be hiding down that hallway."

Pete says, "Come on, son! Don't be such a wuss."

Will laughs and says, "Yeah, dude. You're with your Uncle Will and your dad. Plus, we all have flashlights on our phones."

Will and Pete turn on the flashlights on their phones and venture into the dark and mysterious passage. Pete looks back and flashes his light at his son who's standing at the passageway entrance. "Come on, son. How often in your life can you say you went down a secret passageway that leads to a hidden room? They write books about stuff like this."

Neil apprehensively turns on his phone and mutters, "Yeah and in the chapters to come that's when someone from the team dies by being a curious cat."

Pete asks, "What's that, son?"

Neil makes his way into the passage and replies, "Nothing. I'm on my way."

The team uses their phones to guide their way through the dark passage. The walls are made of large dark bricks, stones, and mortar. The smell inside the passage is old and musty. They make their way into the room at the other end of the passage. Will enters the room and turns to the right, while Neil and Pete turn to the left. They shine their lights up, down, off the floor, and off the walls to get an understanding of the room they just discovered. Will notices strange symbols on the walls with faded red paint. Will begins to speak to Pete and Neil, and his voice bounces off the large open high ceiling. "What do you make of this place, lads? This is wild!"

Pete answers, "I'm not sure. But I have a feeling this room wasn't used for anything good. It looks like the ceilings here reach up about twenty feet or so."

Neil shines his light up toward the ceilings and around the room. Neil interjects, "Yeah that sounds about right. This room looks like it's a big circle. The whole room is about twenty feet in diameter as well." Neil shines his light in the center of the room. He sees a small round table and four old wooden chairs that are covered in massive spider webs. Neil shouts, "Hey, Uncle Will! Dad! Shine your light in the center of the room!"

Pete says, "Jesus, kid. You don't have to shout in this room. Seems like noise just bounces and echoes off the walls."

Pete and Will shine their light at the round table. Neil approaches it. He walks alongside the table and notices an old brown leather book in front of one of the chairs and four well-used decaying red candles. Pete and Will approach Neil. Will shines his light onto the table and investigates the contents. Will notices the same strange symbols on the book are identical to the symbols on the wall. Pete asks Will, "What do you make of this, bro?"

Will answers, "Honestly, I have no idea. It doesn't make much sense. At least to us."

Neil walks away from the table and toward the far end of the room. He shines his light around the floor. The floor is nothing more than a concrete slab that is mostly cracked, old, and deteriorated. He bounces his light back and forth along the edges of the floor where the floor meets the walls. He notices a few faded white lines on the floor and follows them back and forth. Pete breaks away from talking to Will while both are still investigating the contents on the round table and asks, "What is it, son? Found something?"

Neil nervously answers, "Dad. Uncle Will. I think it's time we left this place."

Pete asks, "What do you mean, son?"

Neil says, "I've been following these lines back and forth on the floor. It's a large pentagram! I think this place was used to perform some evil shit!"

Just then, Neil's flashlight on his phone goes out. Neil looks at his phone. It's dead! Pete asks, "What's the matter, son?"

Neil answers, "My phone is dead. That doesn't make any sense. I had it fully charged before we left the house."

Pete and Will look at each other and back at their phones. Pete exclaims, "Wow! Mine is almost out of juice."

Will says, "Mine too. Screw it. It's time to go!"

Will, Neil, and Pete make their way back toward the passage that leads back to the old chapel. Will begins to hear some unreadable chatter echo from his radio. Will says, "I guess there's no radio reception in there. Didn't hear anything come out of this thing while we were there. Now I hear some coms as soon as we are a few feet away from the chapel."

Pete asks, "What was the message? I couldn't make it out."

Neil says, "Yeah I could understand it either."

As they reenter the old chapel, they hear the chimes from the grandfather clock echoing upstairs along the overlook indicating the time of 11:00 a.m. Suddenly, they hear a scream and a loud crash come from the main level. Will exclaims, "What the hell was that!"

Pete says, "That sounds like my wife is in trouble. Let's find out what's going on."

Will, Pete, and Neil walk out of the old chapel and up the stairs toward the overlook to get a bird's-eye view and find out what's going on. As they lean over the waist-high marble banister, they see Claire run quickly out of the ballroom and into the main living room. Will and Pete attempt to communicate with Claire. She's vague and distracted as she makes her way down toward the art gallery.

Will tries to use his radio. He hears a quick unreadable message and then static. Will attempts to use it again. He examines the radio. Will says, "Shit. My radio is dead."

Pete exclaims, "Well, I'm going downstairs to talk to my wife and figure out what's going on around here. Come on, Neil!"

Will says, "Sounds like a good plan. I'm coming too."

They make their way to the grand staircase that leads down to the old chapel and the main level. The lights start to flicker. They look down the staircase and begin to hear an unknown voice of a man speak loudly from inside the chapel.

The voice can be heard shouting, "I command you! In the name of the Father! And of the Son! And of the Holy Spirit! Go back from which you came and leave this place!"

Will, Neil, and Pete descend halfway down the stairs, and they see the man inside the chapel walk backward as he faces the entrance of the chapel. The man is wearing a priest uniform and carrying a Bible, a gold holy cross, and a rosary. They all stop where they stand. All of them are paralyzed in fear. They only see a side profile of the priest. He's middle aged and slightly stocky with dark combed-over hair parted on the left side. He looks extremely pale. Almost completely white in complexion. Neil stammers as he asks, "D-Da-Dad? Who the hell is that?"

Pete also stammers in fear as he replies, "I-I-d-don't know, son!"

Will recognizes the priest. "Father McNolty? What the hell is going on?"

The priest doesn't turn toward the team who are bewildered on the staircase. He continues to back up as he resumes his commanding holy readings from his Bible. As the priest backs up, a dense dark mass fills the left side of the old chapel and quickly creeps its way toward Father McNolty. Will exclaims, "Father! What's going on?"

The priest breaks away from his emergent blessings and commands and looks at Will. Will, Pete, and Neil are frightened by the priest's appearance. His eyes are completely black! Father exclaims in a lower and darker voice, "Go, my son! Leave this place! I can't hold it back anymore!"

The black mass surrounds and engulfs the priest as it begins to make its way up their stairs toward Will, Neil, and Pete!

The three run for their lives up the stairs toward the overlook. Will exclaims, "Quickly! Oh God! What the hell? Follow me! We'll take the other sta—"

Will stops in mid-sentence as they all climb up to the upper-level landing and next to the overlook. They look ahead and see the silhouette of a dark figure in front of them as it starts to form and shape into The Shadow Man! The dark figure is standing next to the grandfather clock. The figure forms into its tall and thin shape, wearing a hat and looking back at Liam, Neil, and Pete with its glowing piercing green eyes! Will looks behind himself; the black mass tingles its way up the stairs like a spider curling up its web toward its prey! Will looks back at The Shadow Man as it begins to laugh. Will flashes back to his dream for a moment. Will thinks, *I saw this all in my dream.*

Neil is terrified. "Dad! Uncle Will! What are we gonna do!"

The Shadow Man points his dark arm and finger toward the grandfather clock. He stares at Will, laughs, and says, "It was part of your dream, Will. And please observe the time."

Will looks at the grandfather clock. The time is 11:11 a.m.!

CHAPTER 28

....

THE GROUNDS TEAM

Reggie and Simon grab their trash bags and pickup tools. They make their way out of the mansion from the main entrance and walk down the gray stone circular stairs down to the ground level. Simon and Reggie are carrying one bag each. Reggie is carrying his slinged bag filled with snacks and drinks. Simon is carrying his backpack that contains all his ghost detecting equipment and the books and printouts from the library. Reggie walks with Simon along the outside wall of the south wing of the main house and asks, "How do you want to do this?"

Simon answers, "Good question, my fine sir. I figure that Ellie's mom is keeping a good eye on us. So, let's do our part just for a little while. For all we know, she's probably watching us from one of the hundred windows and openings in that place. At least the windows that are not boarded up."

Reggie agrees with Simon, and they make their way along the south wing of the main house. They pick up trash and dispose of it into their trash bag as they go. They continue to police the area until they reach the far corners of the main house, which faces the Victorian Rose Garden and the pond. Reggie takes a break, throws down his trash bag and pick-up tool, and reaches for a can of soda from his bag. Simon takes a break as well. He smiles as he approaches Reggie. "I like the way you're thinking. Can you pass me one?" Reggie reaches into his bag, grabs a soda, and tosses it over to Simon. Simon pops open the soda can.

They both *clink* their cans together. Simon says, "Cheers, bro. Now let's look at the map."

Reggie looks behind himself toward the main house and says, "You think Ellie's mom is still looking at us?"

Simon is kneeling down with his backpack in front of him. "Not a chance. If I knew Claire, she probably watched us for a few minutes at the beginning. Now she's scope-locked into completing whatever tasks she's doing. Plus, if I remember correctly, she's working with Ellie in the ballroom, which is in the north wing."

Simon finds the map and lays it on the ground. As Simon examines the map, Reggie, who continues to drink his soda, walks behind Simon and says, "Where do you think we should go from here?"

Simon points to indicators on the map. "Okay. We are here. Next to the south wing of the estate. In front of us is the Victorian Rose Garden. Figure I can use my voice recorder and my device that detects any change in electrical activity in that area."

Reggie asks, "What do you want me to use?"

Simon says, "Just the camera I have for now. Figure it's a good way to document our investigation. And it's a good alternative to using the cameras on our phones, which will drain our batteries quicker."

Reggie nods in approval. "Good thinking. So, you think you can catch the voices of ghosts on that thing? And what's with the electrical devise thingy?"

Simon smiles and he looks up to Reggie. "That's the idea. I was able to pick up some low-level voices in some previous investigations. The electrical thingy, as you put it, detects changes in positive electrical energy in the atmosphere. If this baby starts to spike, there's a good chance we will run in to some ghost or other entities." Simon looks back at the map and continues, "I figure we start in the rose garden, make our way to the old tunnel entrance, check out the greenhouse, and then over to the family cemetery on the far corner of the property. Shouldn't take too long and when we're finished with that, we can continue our work along the north wing of the main house just in case Claire starts looking for us."

Reggie and Simon gather up their items. Simon places his map back into his backpack. Reggie turns on the camera and grabs the cleaning supplies. Simon fires up his voice recorder and his electrical activity device. He checks to make sure both of his devices are working properly. Reggie points the camera at Simon and says, "Okay, dude. We are up and running. Do you have anything to say? How do you usually do this?"

Simon laughs. "Ellie is usually the person behind the camera. Just point it toward me and throw in your two cents from time to time, and everything will be fine. I usually start out with a quick intro."

Reggie who's still pointing the camera at Simon says, "Okay. Okay. And Action!"

Simon replies, "Thanks, Reggie. Okay. Hi, everyone. This is your favorite young paranormal researcher, Simon. Today is a little different. I'm not joined by the lovely Ellie today. She's busy with other duties. It's a beautiful day here at the Elk's Estate in Elkins Park, Pennsylvania. I'm joined by my new good friend Reggie. Say hi, Reggie."

Reggie points the camera at himself and says, "Sup, everybody." Reggie points the camera back to Simon.

Simon continues, "Today we are investigating an area that has been plagued by paranormal activity for quite some time. My team has done some research on the area already. We are starting near the main house of Elk's Estate. Get a shot of the house, Reggie."

Reggie points the camera at the main house for a brief moment and then back to Simon as he continues, "We hope to investigate the main house later today. But for now, we are beginning our investigation at the old Victorian Rose Garden, which is just ahead of us. An elegant place about fifty yards long and about thirty yards wide. Home to dozens of rose bushes and a long white Victorian trellis. We have our devices ready, so let's get started."

Reggie and Simon walk toward the rose garden. They enter the white trellis entryway and walk along the large flat stone steps. Reggie, who's still pointing the camera at Simon, asks, "So, Simon. Do I say cut and turn off the camera for a bit or just keep rolling?"

Simon who's looking at his devices as he walks along the dark stone path says, "Better to keep rolling. Never know when activity will spike, or something will be here and gone in a flash."

Reggie replies, "Gotcha. Anything on your devices yet?"

Simon answers, "Nothing yet. No spikes in electrical activity. I usually wait to ask questions on the voice recorder until I have an electrical spike."

They continue to walk along the ill-maintained rose garden. The white paint that covers the long trellis is cracked, peeling, and weathered. Along the high points of the trellis are several rusty wind chimes that tweet back from the slight breeze hitting their surfaces. The rose bushes are incredibly thick and in desperate need of pruning. The grass is long and covers the majority of the flat stone steps along the path. They walk past a few gray stone benches and sitting areas until they reach the end of the trail.

Reggie asks, "Anything on your thingies, dude?"

Simon is getting frustrated. "Nope. Not a damn thing. No spikes. It really feels like this place is dead."

Reggie points the camera away from Simon and pans the camera around the estate pond and over toward several small buildings. He asks, "What do you make of those buildings, dude?"

Simon looks in the direction where Reggie is pointing the camera. "That must be the old cottages that were used by the workers of the estate when the Elk family still ran the place. The entrance to the underground tunnel should be around there. Let's check it out."

Reggie and Simon exit the rose garden and walk across the estate road to the cottages. Reggie points the camera toward the cottages as Simon continues, "These cottages were built for the workers of the estate and property. I'm not too concerned about gaining access to them. Right now, we are looking for the old entrance to an underground tunnel." As they continue to walk past the cottages, Simon has Reggie redirect the camera back toward what he found. Simon says, "Reggie, look! These are the stairs that lead down to the underground tunnel! Let's check it out."

Reggie and Simon walk to the stairs and look down to the door that leads to the tunnel. The ground surrounding the door is covered with an inch of standing water and mud. Reggie says, "Well, that looks like a bust."

Simon asks, "What do you mean?"

Reggie answers, "The area is flooded, man. Plus, my parents just bought me these nice pair of basketball shoes. This place already claimed one of my shoes. I not about to ruin another pair."

Simon laughs. "I'm envious of your shoes, so I understand. Just stand here and I'll see if I can even open the door."

Reggie stands at ground level filming while Simon goes down the few stone steps to the door. Simon stands on the last stone step, which is slightly higher than the free-standing water. Simon leans his entire body and slams his hands into the door to brace himself. He continues to support his weight with this left hand as he attempts to open the door with his right hand. Reggie says, "Be careful, bro. If that thing opens up, you won't be able to fall back, and you'll be taking a swim in that icky water."

Simon smiles as he replies, "The price of glory is high, my friend. It's probably flooded from all those bad storms recently." Simon attempts to open the door but to no avail. "Shit! It's locked. I wonder if anyone has a key. Screw it. Let's continue."

Simon climbs up the stairs back to ground level. The bright sun that has beaten down on the grounds team is starting to fade away into dark cloud cover. Simon does a radio check on channel 3. He hears Boo answer back. Reggie sees the sun duck behind the clouds as the wind begins to pick up. Reggie and Simon look up toward the sky as Simon says, "I didn't know we were supposed to have storms today."

Reggie replies, "I didn't think so either."

Simon receives a text from Ellie saying, "Dude! Switch to channel 4 now! Mom is looking for you!"

Simon communicates with Claire and continues his research.

The wind continues to pick up. Reggie and Simon can feel the cool breeze increase as the windchimes in the rose garden begin to sing loudly and quickly. As Reggie films the change in weather, Simon starts to get a spike on his electrical detection device. Simon says, "Reggie, film this, brother."

Reggie turns back to Simon and asks, "Film what?"

Simon points down to his device. "There's a spike."

Reggie films the device as its needle continues to increase.

As Reggie continues to film, he hears a woman's voice carry in the wind. He can't make out what the woman is saying, but she sounds upset. The hairs on the back of Reggie's neck stand up. Simon looks up at Reggie as Reggie tells him that he's hearing voices. Simon puts his voice recorder in his pocket for a moment. He grabs his radio.

He attempts to talk into it. He hears nothing but static. The battery dies. Simon says, "Shit. Radio is dead. I'll text the group." As Simon texts the group, they hear thunder in the distance. Reggie is pointing his camera toward the rose garden as he sees a woman wearing a long white dress and a veil walk-glide along the stone path!

Reggie exclaims, "Holy shit, dude!"

Simon replies, "Damn right holy shit! The readings of electrical activity are off the charts! I never seen it this high!"

Reggie says, "Screw that, dude! I just saw a woman in a wedding dress walking in the rose garden."

Simon exclaims, "Holy shit!" Simon looks toward the rose garden and sees the woman briefly as she glides between two overgrown rose bushes. Simon continues, "Come on, dude. Let's follow her!"

Reggie says, "Nope. Nope. Nope. Time to leave! Shit is getting real around here!"

Reggie starts to walk backward as Simon grabs him saying, "Dude, I'm here with you. Let's stay together. Just like Liam said."

Reggie briefly calms down and stammers, "Okay. B-bu-but you go first."

The team walks quickly across the road and back toward the rose garden. They see the woman sitting on the ground next to one of the stone benches about twenty yards ahead of them. Simon is in front as Reggie continues to film. Simon turns toward Reggie and says, "Are you getting this on film?"

Reggie says, "I think so."

Simon asks, "What do you mean you think so?"

Reggie answers, "The screen started to act funny. Blinking in and out. And then it just shut down."

Simon exclaims, "What the hell! First the radio now this!"

They break away from their conversation as they hear the woman begin to cry. Reggie asks, "What do we do?"

Simon answers, "Try to help. I don't know."

They continue to approach the woman. The woman is resting her arms and head on the stone bench and breathing heavily as if she were crying hysterically.

They approach within a few yards of the woman as she continues to cry. The woman says in a sobbing muffled voice, "I trusted him. I loved him. But SHE had to have him!"

Reggie and Simon look at each other. They are both nervous about the entire situation. Simon quietly says to Reggie, "What the hell do we say?"

Reggie replies quietly, "I don't know. I'm following your lead."

Simon looks at his electric detection device. The red needle on the device is buzzing all the way to its highest reading possible! Simon says to the woman, "Excuse me, ma'am. Can we help you? Can you tell us what's going on?"

The woman has her back to the boys as she continues to sob on to the bench as if her life depends on it. The woman lifts her head but doesn't turn to the boys. She replies, "Do you know what today is?"

Simon replies, "It's a beautiful summer day, ma'am."

The woman continues to sob. "Today was my wedding day. I just married my best friend. The man I have loved for so long. We came here for our wedding pictures. Us and our wedding party."

Simon looks to Reggie for answers, but Reggie doesn't know what to do. Simon turns back toward the woman and says, "What's your name, ma'am?"

The woman says, "Isabella. My last name changed today, but I'll never live a day with that bastard's name."

Simon asks, "Can you tell us what happened?"

Reggie interjects, "Yes. How can we help you?"

The woman continues to sob as she begins to lift her arms away from the bench. A trail of dark red blood from both her wrists oozes down to the bench and onto the grass! She says, "I married him. Devoted my love to him before my family and the eyes of God. And within an hour, I saw him kissing my maid of honor. My sister of all people! They thought they could run off somewhere in the estate for another rendezvous. They thought no one would see them." Isabella begins to turn toward the boys. Her white veil gives way to reveal beautiful dark curly hair. She's in a crawling position as she continues to turn toward the boys, revealing more of her face. Her face is cyanotic and decaying, and her eyes are completely black! The dark red oozing blood from her wrists begins to stain her pearly white wedding dress. She crawls toward the boys screaming, "He'll never have me! The two will never become one!"

CHAPTER 29

....

THE GREENHOUSE

Both Simon and Reggie scream in terror as they run for their lives away from the rose garden. Thunder and a quick flash of lightning are seen and heard in the distance. Reggie exclaims, "Dude, let's get out of here! Like now!"

Simon replies, "I'm with you!" Simon discovers another stone walkway that leads to another building. "Quick! Let's follow this trail. I think it leads to the greenhouse and the other side of the estate. At least it's in the opposite direction of our crazy mystery lady."

They follow the walkway toward the greenhouse. The greenhouse is thirty feet long and approximately twenty feet wide. As they approach it, Simon sees a woman sitting inside through the foggy glass. Simon says, "Reggie, there's somebody in there. Maybe it's one of the volunteers." They find the entrance. They stand just outside the entryway looking inside the greenhouse. They see rows of red ceramic pots that house several dry dead plants. There's a woman sitting in a wooden chair in the middle of the structure next to a weathered wood table. She sings as she tends to a large green plant with hundreds of tiny white petals. The plant is nesting inside an orange ceramic flowerpot. Patches of dirt are scattered along this table along with a small pearl-colored bowl and a glass of water.

Simon and Reggie look at each other. Simon says, "I don't think she's a volunteer, dude."

Reggie replies, "Nope. Not me either."

The woman hears the two boys talk to each other and breaks away from her task saying, "Oh! Would you look at that. Where are my manners? Please come in, you two."

Simon and Reggie look at the woman. She is small, young, and beautiful. She has blue eyes that are a shade similar to Caribbean waters and are highlighted by her bright red curly hair and perfectly shaped round face. She's wearing an orange flower dress and dark green apron and brown work shoes. She smiles and says, "Please come in and visit with me." Simon and Reggie look at each other and nod in approval to follow her wishes. As they approach her, Simon looks at his electrical detection device. The red needle shakes and peaks to its capacity as they move closer. The woman asks, "Did Father hire you to tend to the grounds and the gardens? They certainly need some attention."

Simon replies, "No, ma'am."

Reggie interjects, "What's your name, miss?"

She looks back at the boys and smiles. Reggie and Simon almost get lost in her beauty. She answers, "I'm sorry. Where are my manners again? My name is Eleanor. And you are?"

Simon stammers, "M-my name is Simon, and this is Reggie."

Eleanor smiles and replies, "Well, it's so nice to meet you. Will you be staying for dinner?"

Simon doesn't know what to say.

Reggie says, "That's a beautiful flower you're working on, Eleanor."

Eleanor picks up her small pair of scissors and continues her work. She answers, "This is a hemlock plant. Grows like a weed if you let it. But if you take care of it, the tiny white petals branch off the stems quite beautifully."

Simon asks, "Have you always liked working with flowers?"

Eleanor answers, "I've always loved pretty flowers and roses. So much so that Father built that rose garden over there. But I have recently learned so much more about other plants and flowers from my love, Abbott. He's the groundskeeper here."

Simon is shocked by what he hears. He begins to connect the dots in his head. "You mean Abbott Michaels?"

Eleanor answers, "Yes. That's him. But I'm supposed to keep that a secret. At least that's what my sister, Margaret, said."

Reggie asks, "Why do you need to keep it a secret, Eleanor?"

Eleanor's smile begins to fade. "Father will never approve of him. He's not from a wealthy family. We are to run away together very soon." Suddenly, there's a bright flash of lightning and a loud crack of thunder from the approaching storm outside. The winds outside begin to increase as loose branches and leaves hit the greenhouse. Simon and Reggie jump from the abrupt rapture. They look back at Eleanor who has put her hands over her face and begins to cry.

Simon asks, "What's the matter, Eleanor?"

"He's gone. He vanished sometime last night during one of Father's gatherings. I asked Father where he went. He said that he abruptly resigned and left in the middle of the night." She continues to cry as she uses her scissors to cut several white petals from the plant. She takes the petals and places them into the bowl resting on the table. She grabs a stick off the floor and uses it to smash the petals into a white paste.

Simon asks, "Eleanor, what are you doing?"

Eleanor continues to cry as she places the pasty white petals from the bowl into the glass of water. She picks up the glass as she answers, "I don't trust Father. His heart has turned evil with the help of those people he invites to our home. But I do feel like my love has been taken away from me. And if I can't live without my love, then what's the point." Eleanor drinks the glass of water and sets the glass on the table. She looks at the boys and says, "That plant is beautiful but also highly poisonous."

Reggie and Simon begin to back up frantically as Eleanor continues to cry and begins to convulse and foam at the mouth! Her beautifully flushed skin fades to a clammy white as her striking blue eyes roll to one side and lose their beauty as her life leaves her body.

The boys ran out of the greenhouse in a panic. They quickly get soaked by the heavy rain being carried by the wind. Reggie exclaims, "That's it. No more! Two suicidal ghosts in one day. That's two too many."

Simon says. "I agree. Let's get to the others and get out of here!"

They run back to the estate road, and Simon says, "Let's just follow this road back to the main entrance."

They pass up the family cemetery in the far corner of the property. The cemetery is secured with a black iron gate with an archway entrance. As they pass, they see a man and a woman crying while looking at a tombstone. Simon slows down for a moment.

Reggie asks, "Dude! What are you doing? Let's go!"

Simon looks closely at the tombstone. He sees the first name "Misty" written on the tombstone. The man and the woman look at Simon.

The woman exclaims, "Leave this place! It only brings death, sorrow, and evil!"

Simon's electronic detection device sparks and shorts out! Simon drops it in the middle of the road. The storm continues to move closer and closer to the estate. Reggie grabs Simon's shoulder and drags him along the road toward the main entrance. "I already lost one friend to this place. I'm not going to lose another. Come on! Let's find the rest of our group!"

CHAPTER 30

....

THE BOTTOM FALLS OUT

Will, Neil, and Pete are almost cornered along the overlook like three flies in a spider's web. The black mass creeps up to the upper-floor landing. Pete looks at Will and Neil. He sees a small opening for his son to run between the banister and the hallway that leads away from the dense mist entrapping them. Pete pushes Neil toward that opening and screams, "Run, son! Go find Mom and get out of here!"

Neil stumbles and picks himself up quickly as he sees the black mass close in on his father and uncle. Neil screams, "Dad! Uncle Will!"

Pete replies, "Go, son! Take the stairway on the far side of the south wing! Uncle Will and I will handle this!"

Neil starts running down the hallway away from the black mass in a panic. He screams, "Mom! Anyone! Ellie! Help!"

Will and Pete are surrounded. The Shadow Man to their right. The black mass to their left. Nothing but the waist-high gray marble banister behind them. Pete nervously asks Will, "Okay, brother. What do we do know?"

Will is speechless and doesn't know what to do. The Shadow Man laughs and looks at his trapped prey. "There's nothing you can do, Will. Welcome to your new home. And of course, there's room for you too, Pete!"

The Shadow Man belts out a booming evil laugh as the black mass engulfs Will and Pete and sends them flying over the banister toward the tiled floor twenty feet below!

The Shadow Man peers over the banister and sees Will and Pete who are motionless at the bottom of a now cracked tiled floor. The Shadow Man hears screaming and shouting echo throughout the mansion. He says, "Sweet music to my ears. Which reminds me! I have other business to attend to." The black mass engulfs The Shadow Man. The two dark forces become one like an evil matrimony as it moves like a conscious and concentrated fog down the stairway near the elevator.

On the main floor, Annie finds Liam and Anton as they are running out of the billiard room. Annie shouts, "Liam! Thank God! Are you okay, honey?"

Annie grabs him and holds him tight as Anton says, "Let's continue the family reunion away from here!"

The lights continue to flicker as the man in the black shroud glides closer to Annie, Liam, and Anton. He enters the billiard room and points his long ugly index finger at them. Anton says, "Come on! Time to go!"

Annie screams, "We have to find Boo! She's downstairs in the old smoking lounge!"

Anton looks at the sinister figure coming closer to him and says, "Come on! The stairs are right around the corner!"

They run together out of the billiard room to the stairs that lead down to the lower level. As they reach the stairs, Liam and Annie are about to begin their descent when Anton exclaims, "Wait! Stop!" The black mass is crawling quickly down the stairs from the upper level! Anton looks at the elevator next to the stairs and says, "Come on! Let's take the elevator instead!" He runs over to the elevator keypad and presses the down button.

Annie exclaims, "Screw this, Anton! There's no time! Let's take our chances on the stairs!"

Just then, there's a bell indicating the elevator has arrived. Anton is standing in front of the elevator door as it begins to open. Anton looks to Liam and Annie as they wait behind him. Anton says, "That's our ride."

Liam and Annie scream as the door opens further. Anton turns back to the elevator only to find the elevator car isn't there. In the hoist way are several floating apparitions! They are all wearing old hospital gowns and robes with blood coming from their mouths!

Anton screams and tries to escape, but the ghastly spirits scream and drag him into the hoist way. The doors close quickly. Liam and Annie are pushed back by the sudden burst of energy and are knocked down to the floor along the back wall. There's a faint horrifying scream for a brief moment and then silence. Anton is gone!

The Shadow Man starts to take shape on the main level as Annie holds on to her son. The shadow begins to glide across the floor closer to Annie and Liam. Annie is shaking. Her primal thought is to protect her son. The Shadow Man glares at them with his glowing green eyes. He laughs and says, "Oh, isn't that so sweet. Two for the price of one. I've been waiting a long time to meet you, Liam."

Liam is scared beyond comprehension. He breathes heavily and thinks of what to do. Beyond his fear, his first reaction is worrying about his little sister. He says, "Mom! We got to get to Boo!"

Annie stands up and steps toward The Shadow Man. She knows she's the last shield of protection between this monster and her son. She turns to Liam and says, "Honey! Go! Get Boo!"

Liam comes to his feet and is leaning up against the back wall. Annie turns back to The Shadow Man. He glides next to her and grabs her throat! Liam exclaims, "No! Mom! Please God help us!"

Annie says in a choking voice, "You can take me, but you're not taking my kids!"

Liam thinks, *God...God...My silver cross!* He pulls out his silver cross from under his shirt, pulls it over his head, and places himself between The Shadow Man and his mother. He places the silver cross on the misty-shaped body of The Shadow Man. He exclaims, "Let go of my mother!"

A bright light shines from the silver cross and begins to make a small smoldering burn on The Shadow Man's body as he lets out a piercing scream. The Shadow Man is startled. He hasn't felt inflicted pain for so long he doesn't remember what it felt like.

He lets go of Annie's throat, backs up, and screams, "No! You little bastard! What did you do to me?" He backs away and retreats down to the stairwell. Annie hits the floor like a bag of bricks. She coughs and begins to control her breathing. Liam runs up and holds his mother. "Mom! Are you okay?"

Annie stops coughing. As she begins to cry she says, "Honey! Thank you! What you did was so brave."

Liam helps his mother to her feet. "There's things that are more important than being afraid, Mom. You and Dad taught me that." Annie thinks about her husband and Boo. Liam and Annie hear two people screaming in the main living room. It's Claire and Ellie!

Claire and Ellie are standing over Will and Pete. Pete is holding his arm and bleeding from the top of his head. Ellie helps him to a chair. Neil runs down from the south wing hallway and toward his father and sister. Neil hugs his father and says, "Oh my God, Dad! Are you gonna be okay?"

Claire kneels next to Will and uses her nursing skills to assess her brother. Annie and Liam quickly run over to Claire. Annie kneels next to her husband. Liam is standing behind his mother. Liam nervously says, "Dad? Dad?"

Annie continues to cry as she grabs Will's hand and says, "Honey? Honey? Wake up, honey!" Annie looks to Claire and asks, "Is he—?"

Claire answers, "He's alive. His breathing is faint and very shallow. He's knocked out." Ellie grabs an old white sheet off a table and uses it to help her father control the bleeding.

Liam interjects, "Mom, we have to get Boo!"

Claire is shaking as she says, "We need to get everyone out of here now! Neil, try to find Reggie and Simon. We're gonna need their help to get Will out of here."

Neil responds, "I'm on it, Mom!"

Neil runs towards the main entrance and the outside staircase. Claire looks at Annie and says, "Go! Find Boo, Katie, and Marcus. I'll stay here with Ellie and help Pete and Will."

Annie approves and replies, "Okay! I'm taking Liam. Liam! We might need your cross son. Come on!"

Claire exclaims, "And where's Anton?"

On the lower level, Marcus has been preoccupied with his work in the deep freezer. He's been unaware of everything that has happened. Other than the light flickering at times, he continues to work repairing some wires alongside the walk-in freezer with the door propped open. The lights flicker again. He thinks, *Damn. I hope that the generator will be okay. I'll go down there in a few minutes to check on it.* The black mass continues to make its way down the stairs after it's run-in with Liam and Annie.

The black mass arrives on the lower level and glides across the floor toward the walk-in freezer. Marcus completes his repairs and walks inside the freezer. The Shadow Man begins to take form just outside the freezer as the lights flicker quickly. With his back to the door, Marcus doesn't see The Shadow Man in the doorway. He only breaks away from his work when the lights flicker off. Marcus turns and sees The Shadow Man standing in the doorway leering at him with his glowing green eyes! The Shadow Man says, "It's been a long time, hasn't it Marcus."

Marcus backs up to the back wall and starts to breathe quickly. He stammers as he begins to panic. "Wh-who-who are you?"

Marcus continues to shake in fright as The Shadow Man answers, "I'm just like you, Marcus. I'm the hired help around here. Welcome home. You'll enjoy your stay."

The door slams shut! The Shadow Man locks the door as Marcus frantically rushes to the door screaming, "What the hell! Let me out! Please let me out!"

The Shadow Man glides over to the temperature control and turns it down to its lowest setting. The Shadow Man says, "Don't worry, Marcus. I can keep this thing running for a while. Cool down and take a break. You and your brother will enjoy your stay."

The freezer continues to cool down as Marcus continues to scream. The temperature quickly reaches below zero as the screams begin to fade and then silence.

Katie is down the hall in the office. She can't hear Marcus's death screams from the tightly sealed walk-in freezer. She's examining some old legal and medical paperwork that she discovered. She tries to communicate with Claire through her radio. She hears nothing. She examines the radio and says, "Damn it. Piece of shit radio." She notices the lights begin to flicker more often. She looks at her phone. She attempts to text Marcus, hoping he can look at the generator. Her phone has only 1% battery life left, and it dies. She gets up from her station and walks outside to the hallway. The overhead lights continue to flicker. She walks into the interchange that leads to either the kitchen and reception halls or the old boiler room, the smoking lounge, and the alternate stairway. She looks down the hallway and sees bright flashes coming from the boiler room.

She starts to walk toward the kitchen to gain Marcus's attention. She enters the kitchen only to be shocked and briefly paralyzed in fear. Inside the kitchen she sees The Shadow Man! Katie screams. The Shadow Man says, "Nice to see you again, Katie. I always enjoyed seeing you come and go down these halls."

Katie stumbles and she falls back onto the floor.

The Shadow Man approaches her, saying, "You'll be a fine addition to the family, Katie."

Katie regains her strength and climbs to her feet. She runs down the hallway toward the interchange. She looks down that hallway only to see a black mass envelope the entire space and engulf it in darkness. She runs down toward the boiler room and tries to reach the stairs. She runs past the entrance of the boiler room and is thrown back to the wall after another bright flash and a small explosion. She looks inside and sees a glowing silver-and-white apparition of a man who's frantically working around the old AC current generator. He has electric waves of energy running in and out of his body. It's an older man with glasses and a finely trimmed beard. He looks at her and says, "I can get it to work longer. I just need your help! Please help me!" He grabs Katie and pulls her toward the energized AC current generator. Katie screams as hundreds of volts of electricity pierces her throughout her body! She's unable to break free as her muscles flex onto the machine while the energy current destroys her body!

Liam and Annie run to the front entrance and turn right. They are heading over to the stairs that lead down to the lower level. When they arrive, they see sudden flashes of light and hear horrible loud screams coming from the lower level. Annie and Liam pause for a moment. The screams continue for a moment and then silence falls. Annie tries to take the cross from Liam and says, "This is crazy. Honey, I'll go. Just help your dad and get out of here! The exit is right over there."

Liam holds a death grip on the cross. "No, Mom! She's my sister. I'm supposed to protect her too. I'm coming with you."

A few tears fall from Annie's face as she peers down the stairway and dreads her next actions. Annie agrees with Liam's proposal, and they quickly descend into the lower level hoping to find Boo.

Boo is still with Misty. She hears all the horror that has unfolded from the other side of the door. She's sitting with Misty who continues to play with her doll. Boo says, "Misty, can you please let me go? I promise to come back here and play with you again."

Misty says, "But I like playing with you, Boo. You're so nice compared to everyone else here. Most people here are mean and scary."

Boo replies, "I bet they are."

Misty says, "And it's not a good idea to go out there with Grandfather playing with his machine. He gets terribly perturbed."

The Shadow Man relishes the screams that are heard at the end of the hall. He says, "There's one more down that doesn't require my attention. Who's next? Oh yes! Will's little girl. I'm coming, dear."

CHAPTER 31

....

TIME TO GO!

The Shadow Man glides down the hall toward Boo, while Annie and Liam run down the stairs to the lower level. They reach the lower level and continue to see flashes of light come from the boiler room. Liam asks, "Where is Boo, Mom?"

Annie says, "God. I hope she's still in that smoking lounge. It's just around the corner."

They cautiously walk along the wall, and Annie peeks around the corner. She sees the charged apparition in the boiler room who's frantically working around the generator turning knobs and flipping switches. The glowing white ghost has electrified blue-and-purple currents running through its misty form. Below him lies the smoldering body of Katie. Annie's jaw drops as she looks back at Liam. Liam says, "Whatever it is, Mom, we have to get Boo."

Annie nods her head. "Okay. You stand right behind me with your cross. I'll try to get Boo. Got it?"

Liam says, "Got it."

They turn the corner slowly as to not draw attention to themselves by the gleaming figure just inside the boiler room.

Liam stands by at the ready, silver cross in hand and arm stretched out. Annie tries to open the door, but it's locked. She tries to push and pull on the doorknob, but the door doesn't budge. She quietly knocks on the door and says, "Boo. Boo. Honey, it's Mommy. Open the door, honey."

Boo runs to the door and says to Misty, "Misty! That's my mom! I must go!"

Misty stops playing with her doll for a moment and turns toward Boo as the lights go out in the room. The room is slightly glowing from the ambient fire that crackles in the fireplace. Misty says, "You can't leave now. The really mean man is nearby."

Boo asks, "What really mean man?"

Liam tries to see through the pitch black. The Shadow Man beams his glowing green eyes toward Liam and Annie. He yells as he charges toward them! Annie pounds on the door and exclaims, "Boo! Boo! Open the door!"

Liam stands in front of his mother in the center of the hallway. The Shadow Man shouts, "It will take a lot more than a small burn to stop me, little boy!"

Liam shakes in fright as The Shadow Man charges within a few feet of him. Liam keeps the cross in front of him. He suddenly feels someone's hand touch his outstretched arm. Instantly, there's a blinding stream of white light that beams out from the cross! It hits The Shadow Man and throws him back several feet down the hallway. He glares his green eyes at Liam as he screams in pain and shouts, "What the hell was that? You little bastard!" The Shadow Man grimaces in pain as he retreats away from Liam and down the hallway.

Misty says, "It seems as though your brother has some good people beside him. You'll be safe, but you must leave quickly before the mean man returns."

There's a sound from the mechanism in the door, which is now unlocked. Boo opens the door to find Annie and Liam. Annie and Liam give Boo a hug. Annie is incredibly relieved to find her daughter. Annie says, "Oh thank God, honey!"

Boo looks back at Misty and says, "Thank you, Misty, for trying to help me."

Misty smiles and replies, "You're welcome. Thank you for playing with me."

Annie looks behind Boo but only the glowing lights from the small smoldering flames slightly illuminate this vacant room. Annie asks, "Who were you talking to, honey?"

Boo looks back and points to Misty who is still sitting there smiling. Boo says, "That little girl right there. Misty. She protected me."

Annie looks again, shakes her head, and says, "Honey, no one is there."

The lights flicker back on. The white glowing apparition is seen still working around the generator. The figure is distracted and doesn't notice Annie and her kids. He says, "I can get it work! Then we can begin again!"

Annie grabs both kids and says, "Let's get out of here. Quietly."

Liam, Boo, and Annie sneak around the corner and quickly run up the stairs toward the main floor. Annie looks at Liam and says, "Honey, when the dust settles, you'll have to tell me how you made that bright light happen."

Still running up the stairs to the main floor landing, Liam says, "I don't know, Mom. It felt like I got help from someone."

They reach the main floor and run into the living room. Neil runs back inside with Simon and Reggie. The surviving members from the group are all gathered in the living room. Before Simon sees Will and Pete, he says, "Holy shit, guys! You wouldn't believe what we saw out there!"

Neil says, "Yeah, well we ran into some serious shit in here too. Come on!"

Reggie and Simon run with Neil over to Will and Claire. Simon looks at Liam and says, "What happened to your pops, dude?"

Pete stands up with the assistance of Ellie. His one arm is wrapped around Ellie's shoulder while the other arm holds direct pressure over his bleeding forehead. Pete says, "I'm fine too, Simon. Thanks for asking."

Simon looks at Pete and asks, "Damn! Who cleaned your clock?"

Reggie looks toward the far end of the living room. He sees a black mass starting to creep its way down the stairs from the old chapel. Reggie shakes as he points at the black mass. "I bet it was that!"

Liam looks at Simon and Reggie and says, "Dad's passed out. We need your help to get him out of here!"

Simon says, "Okay, but we'll need Neil's help too."

Neil runs over to Will.

Claire asks Annie, "Wait! Where's Katie, Anton, and Marcus?"

Annie shakes her head. "I think they're gone!"

Claire puts her hands to her face and says, "Oh my God!"

The black mass makes its way into the living room and begins to take form. Liam says, "We don't have much time. Let's move!"

Claire goes to her husband's aid and helps Ellie move Pete out of the living room to the main entrance. Neil grabs Will's shirt under his shoulders with both hands. Reggie and Simon each take a leg. Neil says, "Okay. Lift on 3."

Reggie says, "Screw that! Lift! Lift!" They lift Will and quickly work together toward the entrance. Annie grabs Liam's and Boo's hands and they run ahead of Simon, Neil, and Reggie. Liam looks back as The Shadow Man takes form, and his eyes gleam at him. The Shadow Man says, "Your father is going to stay here with me!"

They all make their way down the outside circular stairs. Those helping Will and Pete take slightly longer as they try not to slip on the wet surface of the stairs. Rain is pouring down. Thunder and lightning crash, and the wind blows through the trees. Claire shouts, "I'll drive my car to the hospital! Elkins Memorial! I got Pete and Ellie! You get the rest!"

Annie runs over to her husband's side and grabs the van keys out of his pocket. She presses the button to open the rear hatch door. It springs open as Neil, Simon, and Reggie try to carefully place Will into the rear of the van. Annie opens the driver's side door and fires up the van. Boo gets into the back. Neil shouts to Liam as he continues to hold Will with Simon and Reggie saying, "Liam! Fold down the back row seats!"

Liam jumps into the back and follows Neil's instructions. He throws Boo's scooter and Ellie's skateboard up toward the front row of seats. The Shadow Man moves toward the main entrance and peers down at the group. Reggie looks up and sees The Shadow Man through the falling rain drops and shouts, "Quickly, dude!"

Liam finishes his task, and the boys load Will into the rear storage area. Neil, Simon, and Reggie all hop into the back through the rear hatch. Claire is in her vehicle. She hits the gas and spins it around quickly toward the iron gated entrance. Water and mud thrust backward in an ugly wave as Claire speeds to the exit. Annie shouts, "Are we ready?"

Neil says, "Yeah just go, Aunt Annie!"

Annie spins the van around quickly, making it fishtail due to the water plain. Annie races to the exit but forgets to close the rear hatch. Neil, Simon, and Reggie grab hold of Will before the momentum forces him out of the car. Neil shouts, "Aunt Annie! Close the hatch!" But Annie is distracted as she speeds toward the exit. In front of her are dozens of ghostly figures! All of them were wearing hospital gowns and robes. They are full-bodied apparitions that are a mixture of transparent and a glowing gray color. They look dead with dark circles around their eyes and dark oozing blood coming from their mouths. Annie shouts, "What the hell are those things?"

Liam looks ahead and says, "Just drive straight through them, Mom!"

Annie hits the gas harder, which springs the van faster through the spine-chilling ghosts. The apparitions glide out of the way and begin to speed up to catch the van! The ghouls glide on the wings of the stormy winds to the open rear hatch. The eerie ghosts scream and shout with their arms and hands pointed outward to grab the boys. The boys scream as they continue to hold on to Will. Neil screams, "Annie! Close the damn hatch!"

Annie looks in her rearview mirror and sees the sinister spirits move closer to the rear hatch. She exclaims, "Holy shit! Sorry, boys!" Annie hits the button to close the hatch. It closes as the van reaches the iron gates and the half-circle entrance. Annie doesn't slow down. The ghastly ghouls stop their pursuit as they reach the end of the estate. Annie hits the road at full speed and almost goes off the road as she tries to avoid another vehicle approaching the estate. She gains control of the car and asks Reggie for directions to the hospital.

CHAPTER 32

....

IS THERE ANYTHING YOU CAN DO?

A nnie continues to speed away from the estate. She looks in her rearview mirror and sees the boys looking through the rear hatch window. Annie asks, "Do you see anything following us?"

Simon, Neil and Reggie start to calm down and control their breathing, look at each other, and shake their heads. Neil answers, "No, Aunt Annie. Looks like we are in the clear."

Annie slows the vehicle down as she approaches a red traffic light for Route 611. Traffic is heavy, and rain continues to fall. She contemplates running the red light but doesn't want to endanger her precious cargo. Annie asks, "Reggie! I couldn't hear you the first time. Which way to the hospital?"

Reggie answers, "Turn left and head north for about a mile. When you reach the top of the hill, you'll see another traffic light and the hospital signs. It's off to the right-hand side."

The light turns green, and Annie hits the gas, spinning the wheels over the saturated pavement. She follows Reggie's instructions and says, "Thank you, honey. How's Will doing, guys?"

Simon replies, "I don't know. Never had to do this before."

Liam turns around and says, "I'll show you."

Simon looks at Liam saying, "You know how to do this, monster slayer?"

Liam answers, "Yes. Learned it through the Boy Scouts. Dad runs the merit badge for first aid. Just raise his head and put your ear to his mouth. See if he still breathing."

Simon follows his instructions and says, "Yeah. He's breathing, but it doesn't seem like a lot."

Liam looks at Reggie who is close to Will's right arm and says, "Reggie, take your fingers and press them hard against his wrist just below his hands and see if you can get a pulse."

Reggie follows suit and answers, "The heart is pumping. I can feel it."

Annie speeds up the hill and sees the signs for Elkins Park Memorial Hospital. The rain begins to weaken as she turns at the traffic light and follows the hospital's access road to the emergency room. She pulls behind Claire who is coming out of the ER entrance with a wheelchair as Ellie helps her father out of the car. Claire helps Pete into the wheelchair. She points to the entrance and instructs Ellie to wheel her father toward the awaiting staff. Claire comes over to Annie who's exiting her vehicle. She asks, "Did Will wake up?"

Annie says, "No. The boys checked him on the ride over. He's still breathing and has a pulse."

Claire instructs Annie to follow her. Annie shouts back to everyone back in the van saying, "It's okay! We're getting help!"

Annie and Claire run to the ER entrance and through the motion-activated double-glass doors. The hospital staff is preoccupied with assisting Pete. Annie asks, "What do we do, Claire?"

Claire looks around and finds an empty room. Inside the freshly cleaned hospital ER room is an unoccupied ambulance stretcher. She runs over to the side of the stretcher and unlocks the brakes. She instructs Annie to stay at the foot of the stretcher as she starts to push it toward the ER entrance. A nurse at the front counter sees Annie and Claire as they push the stretcher. The nurse is young for her position—within her first year of practice after graduating with her nursing degree. She's pretty with short blonde hair and pink hospital scrubs. She's on the phone but abruptly finishes her phone call as she recognizes Claire and says, "Claire! What's going on? Is someone else hurt?"

Quickly walking past the nurse's station, Claire says, "Hey, Amy! Yes! My brother is hurt, and we can use some help!"

Amy leaves her station and joins Annie and Claire as they make their way to the van. Liam and Boo have already exited the van. Liam runs to the back of the van and opens the back hatch. Liam looks over his shoulder to see help coming. He instructs Neil, Simon, and Reggie to be ready to help lift his father out of the van.

Amy approaches the van and sees Will lying on his back. Amy asks Claire, "Jesus, Claire! What happened to your brother?"

Claire answers as she places the stretcher perpendicular to the back hatch. "He fell with Pete over the side of the banister over at the Elk's Estate. It's approximately a twenty-foot drop. Don't know if he hit his head or not. He was unconscious but breathing regularly, and his vitals seemed okay when we left. Have to consider spinal precautions."

Everyone works together to move Will from the van onto the stretcher and into the ER. They all help push the stretcher to the entrance. Liam is close to his father's right side near his head. He looks over at his father and palpates for a pulse along his neck. He tries to keep track of the rhythm but it's difficult. Will's pulse seems weak.

They enter the previously unoccupied ER room and help transfer Will over to the hospital bed. Claire instructs everyone to leave the room as she tries to assess her brother. Amy leaves the room quickly to get help from the hospital staff as Claire closes the curtains. Everyone waits outside the hospital room in the hallway. Boo walks over to Annie, gives her mother a hug, and begins to cry. She asks, "Mom, is Dad going to be okay?"

Annie gets choked up. "Daddy will be okay, baby. He'll be okay. He's one of the toughest people I know."

Liam is filled with emotion. He's never seen his father so vulnerable in his life. He begins to cry as he thinks about the possibility of losing his father. Neil comes to Liam's side and gives him a hug. Liam says, "Neil, I'm scared. Dad's pulse wasn't too good when I checked it."

Neil replies, "He's gonna be fine, buddy. Here comes help now."

Amy returns with another nurse, an ER technician, and a doctor. They throw open the curtains to enter the room. The group can see

Claire doing what she was trained to do. She has opened Will's shirt, attached some electrodes to his chest, and applied a cervical collar around his neck. The doctor closes the curtains as he begins to assess Will and ask Claire some questions. The group can hear the commotion back and forth, and they begin to hear the heart monitor. Will's pulse is slow but regular. Simon quietly asks Reggie, "What do you think of all of this, buddy?"

Reggie says in a low voice, "I think we should all be grateful that we made it out of there alive. I don't know anything about medicine, but I saw how Claire reacted when she saw her brother. She knows he's not doing too good. That's why she's with him."

Neil looks at the group and says, "Hey, let's go check on my dad. He should be down the hall."

Annie nods her head as she looks at Liam and Boo. "That's a good idea. Let's give the staff and Aunt Claire time to patch up your father."

The group walks over to the room where Pete is being treated. Ellie is with him. She's sitting in a chair near her father. She looks tired and withdrawn. She hasn't cleaned off some of the blood that got on her arms from helping her father. A nurse is alongside Pete who is lying supine in the hospital bed with a cervical collar applied to his neck. The nurse is cleaning Pete's wounds and preparing to apply stiches. Neil walks in first and kneels next to his sister. They each give each other a hug. The rest of the group waits just outside the threshold. Neil helps Ellie stand up and walks her over to the sink so she can clean up. Neil then walks over to his father's side and holds his hand.

Pete tries to look toward the entrance to the room to see the rest of the group. Pete exclaims, "Is Annie over there?"

Annie walks into the room and answers, "Yeah, Pete. I'm right here." Annie continues to walk toward Pete. "How's everything going with you?"

Pete smiles and coughs for a moment. The coughs are painful, which is reflected by Pete's contorted red face. Pete answers, "Doing okay. Looks like I took on a few rounds with the heavyweight champion. Doc said I probably have a concussion. Need a few stiches and I did a number on my knees and back. Other than that, I'm doing just peachy. How's Will?"

Annie looks back toward the rest of the group. She asks Neil, "Neil, honey, why don't you, Ellie, and the rest of the group find a waiting room while we figure this whole thing out." The group agrees and makes their way down the hall. They find a sign along a door reading: "Waiting Room." They walk inside and find an empty waiting room with over a dozen chairs, a TV, and a few vending machines. Simon says, "Thank God. I'm starving."

Reggie says, "I hear you. I'll get the soda if you get some munchies."

Annie watches the group enter the waiting room from the threshold of Pete's room. She looks back at Pete and begins to walk back toward him. Annie is still choked up and a few tears fall from her eyes. Pete asks, "Oh God! Is he—"

Annie grabs Pete's hand and answers, "No. No. He's still with us. Claire and the rest of the staff are with him now. But he doesn't look good, Pete. I don't know what I'll do if—"

Pete interjects, "Hey! No need to think like that. Will is made of the same stuff as his old man. That man was tough as nails." Pete takes a good look at Annie and then looks at the nurse who's ready to begin the stiches. He asks the nurse to wait a minute. She agrees. Pete looks back at Annie and asks, "You never got to meet Will's dad, did you?"

Annie shakes her head. "No. He died before Will and I started dating."

Pete holds Annie's hand. "If I knew anything about Will's old man, I can tell you that he's looking out for us and watching over Will, especially right now. You don't need to worry. Will's in good hands."

Back inside Will's hospital room, Claire helps the staff in any way that she can. The doctor asks what happened. Claire tells the doctor that her group was attacked by something or someone at the estate. Claire tries to replay the events in her head but can't comprehend or make sense of the matter. The doctor asks if there's anyone else hurt at the estate. Claire takes a deep breath and panics as she thinks about her friends. Claire backs up next to the wall and says, "Oh God! Why didn't I call for help before we left?"

The doctor looks at Claire and asks, "What is it, Claire?"

Claire answers, "We need to send help over to the estate right now. There's three people from my group that were not accounted for when we left."

The doctor looks at Amy and says, "Amy, get on the phone with 911. Tell them about the situation."

Amy nods her head, takes off her examination gloves, washes her hands, and quickly makes her way over to the nurse's station.

Amy looks at her phone on the counter and decides to call her husband who's on duty as a police officer with the Elkins Park Police Department. She calls her husband who answers, "Hey, honey. How are things at the ER? Hopefully a nice and slow afternoon."

Amy answers, "On the contrary. That's why I'm calling you."

Ethan, Amy's husband, asks, "What do you mean, honey?"

Amy says, "I'm here with Claire. The nurse who trained me."

Ethan says, "Yeah. I remember her. What's going on?"

"They came in with two people severally hurt. One of the victims is Claire's brother. The other is her husband. She said that she was attacked by someone at the estate."

Ethan exclaims, "No shit! When did this happen?"

"Within the last hour. She said that there were three people in her group that may be in trouble. She said they are unaccounted for."

Ethan says, "Okay, honey. I'm in my police cruiser. Kenny is back at the station with Detective Rhinelander. I'll call them, put myself en route, and request an ambulance to stand by."

Amy says, "Sounds good, honey. Please be safe. Love you."

Ethan replies, "Love you too, honey. Always."

Amy heads back to help with her new patient.

Ethan calls dispatch. "Car 4 to dispatch."

Dispatch answers, "Go ahead Car 4."

Ethan turns the police cruiser around and begins to head to Elk's Estate. He answers, "Yeah dispatch. Put me en route for a disturbance at the old Elk's Estate. Can I have Car 3 respond along with a standby ambulance?"

There's a moment of silence over the radio. Then Dispatch replies, "Okay Car 4. We will put you en route to the Elk's Estate. We will notify Car 3 and have an ambulance en route."

✦ ✦ ✦

Back at the Elkins Park Police Station, there's a ring on the main line that's directly linked to dispatch. Kenny, who's at the watch desk, answers, "This is Kenny. Go ahead, Dispatch."

Dispatch replies, "Kenny, we have Car 4 en route to the Elk's Estate to investigate a possible disturbance. He requested backup and an ambulance."

Kenny says, "No problem, Dispatch. You can put me en route." Kenny grabs his coffee off the desk and heads to the front door.

Detective Rhinelander sees Kenny on the move. He steps outside his office and says, "Hey, Kenny! What you got?"

Kenny turns to Detective Rhinelander and says, "Oh sorry, Eric. Ethan is on his way to Elk's Estate. Something happened there."

Detective Rhinelander says, "Okay. Keep me in the loop."

Kenny answers, "Will do," as he makes his way to his squad car.

There's a ring coming from the phone inside the detective's office. The main line box is illuminated and blinking as he answers the phone. "Go ahead, Dispatch."

Dispatch says, "Hey, Detective. We have reports of some people involved in an assault. They're being treated at Elkins Park Memorial. Can we put you en route to the hospital to investigate?"

Eric looks frustrated. "It's probably that damn volunteer group. Yeah, that's fine, Dispatch. Put me en route." Eric takes a long sip of his coffee, gathers some supplies from his desk including a manila envelope from his file cabinet, and heads out of the station. As he walks to his undercover vehicle, he sees Kenny heading down the road in his squad car with lights and sirens activated. Eric feels raindrops on top of his head. He looks up at the clouds. The clouds are dark gray and moving quickly into the area. He hears thunder in the distance. He gets into his vehicle, turns on his lights and sirens, and heads to the hospital to question the group and investigate the incident.

Back at the hospital, the group waits inside the waiting room discussing things amongst themselves. Annie walks down the hallway to her husband's hospital room. She sees the staff moving Will in his hospital bed out of the room and down the hallway. Annie walks quickly toward the staff who are heading in her direction. Claire is the first one to intercept Annie. Annie sees her husband is intubated. She looks at Claire in horror and asks, "Oh God! Claire! What's going on with Will?"

Claire grabs hold of Annie as the staff continues to wheel Will past her. Annie looks over Claire's shoulder at her husband and exclaims, "Will! Honey!"

No answer. His eyes are closed, and he remains motionless. Annie looks at Claire and asks, "What the hell is going on with my husband? Where are they taking him?"

Claire looks down to the floor and answers, "They are rushing him over to do an MRI and CT scan."

Annie replies, "Claire, what's going on?"

Claire looks up to Annie and says, "Annie, Will is in a coma."

CHAPTER 33

....

DAD?

"Will? Will? Come on, kid. Pull it together now. I've got you," says a familiar voice that Will hasn't heard in a long time. Will sees nothing. Darkness is ahead of him and surrounds him like an inescapable prison. His hearing is the only sense that seems to be working. Will is scared beyond any capacity he's ever experienced before. But he doesn't feel his body shake nor his heartbeat pound against his chest. The familiar voice says, "Come on, son. No need to be afraid. I gotcha, kid. Come on. Time to get up." Will tries to open his eyes. He doesn't feel his eyes move or the several blinks he attempts with his eyelids. His sight starts to come back into focus. His vision transitions from complete darkness into a white light. The familiar voice says, "That's it, son. That's it. Don't worry. I'm here." Like waking up in the morning, Will's vision is blurry at first and then becomes more into focus. Will looks around. He's in a room. The room is only illuminated by a small radiating fire that burns from a fireplace along the inner wall. The environment is enshrouded in a bleak and misty fog like driving through a thick fog on a cool evening.

Will begins to hear music coming from the old-fashioned standing radio. Vocal jazz music plays through the radio speakers and echoes at a low volume through the room. He looks down and sees a girl sitting near the radio. The little girl is wearing a yellow dress with brown polka dots. She has brown hair and two pigtails tied with two red bows. She's playing with a doll and a music box. It's Misty.

Will doesn't feel the hand that is touching his back. He remembers the voice that has been guiding him through this uncharted transition. The voice is inescapable. It's his father, Bill. Bill reaches his hand down and touches the back of Will's shoulder. A small bright light shimmers from Will's shoulder as the two make contact with each other. Will turns toward the light and sees the smiling face of his father. Will exclaims, "Dad! Dad? Is this one of my dreams? Or am I dead? Oh God! I'm dead, aren't I? Where are we?"

Bill smiles back at him with his bright blue eyes, which are not covered by his old pair of glasses. His smile highlights his dimpled face that's slightly covered by his brown bushy mustache. Bill's father looks younger than the last time Will saw him. Bill looks healthy and fit while sporting his favorite fire department jacket, a button-down shirt, and a pair of jeans.

Will's father died of cancer many years ago. The cancer aged his battle-ridden father who fought bravely to survive. His father looks like what Will remembered when he was a boy. The transparent silhouette of his younger and healthier father is astounding to Will. The stress, pain, and deterioration, which was the result of Bill's struggle during the last year of his life, had simply been washed away. Bill says, "Yeah, it's me, kid. Told you I was going to be there to catch you when you fell."

Will replies, "Wha-wait. That was *you* in my dreams? Dad, what's going on?"

Bill answers, "Don't worry. I'll explain everything. We have time. But first let me help you stand so you can try out your new pair of sea legs." Bill reaches down for Will's hand. Will reaches out his hand and notices his hand is also transparent! Will looks through the outline of his hand and sees the fire glowing from the other side of it.

Bill says, "It's okay, kid. Really. Let me help you up. That first step is a real trip."

Will grabs hold of Bill's hand. The hands interlock and glistening white light shines between their hands. Will is pulled up and tries to stand. But he doesn't feel his feet on the ground. Will stumbles at first, but Bill catches him again. Bill says, "Wow, kid. That's the second time I caught you in a single day. Haven't done that since you were a little kid playing in your uncle's pool. Just hold on to me and try to get your bearings." Within a brief moment, Will is able to stand on his own, and his father lets go.

Bill looks over to Misty and says, "See? What'd I tell ya, kid. He'll do just fine."

Will looks over to Misty as she turns and smiles. Will asks, "Dad? Who is that?"

Misty interjects, "Hi! I'm Misty. Bill says you're Boo's father. She's so nice."

Will exclaims, "How do you know my daughter? Is she—"

Bill puts his hand on Will's shoulder to provide comfort and says, "Don't worry, son. Boo is with everyone over at the hospital. She isn't hurt. She's alive and well. Along with Liam, Claire, and the rest of the family. You're with me at the estate. I was able to catch you and get you down here before that bastard got ahold of you." Bill points to Misty as he continues, "Misty here really helped us out by keeping Boo in this room. Honestly, I wasn't sure how I was going to keep everyone safe. Thanks, Misty."

Misty smiles and continues to play with her music box. Bill looks at Will who is still in shock and bewilderment. Bill points to the closed door that leads out to the hallway and says, "Here, son. Let me show you what I'm talking about." Will and Bill glide over to the door. Bill moves faster than Will at first. Bill looks back and says, "See, you're getting better. It's kind of like trying to run in a dream. Kind of a pain in the ass, but you'll get the hang of it." Will meets his father at the doorway and points upward to several black chalky markings along the upper door frame. Bill says, "Misty let me know about this room. She always felt safe here, but she didn't know why. These markings were made by an old priest who used to reside here. Those markings are made from a collection of ashes from burnt Easter palms, which are blessed by the Church. Figure it like a safe room."

Will looks at his father and says, "Dad? What's happened to me."

Bill answers, "I was just getting to that. I mentioned that the family is at the hospital. They are there for a couple of reasons. One being Pete who is doing just fine last time I checked. He'll heal up nicely. The more serious matter is you, son. When that bastard knocked you and Pete off that balcony, it left you all banged up and in a deep coma. And that bastard figured out a way to keep your soul here while your poor family waits in anguish at the hospital."

Will doesn't seem to understand this astonishing revelation. Bill looks over to the radio and says, "You look confused. Don't worry, I understand. This whole place is confusing. Took me a while to figure it out after I left that nursing home the night I died. Follow me. Let me try to explain."

They glide together over to the radio. Misty says, "Please don't change the radio station. I like listening to this station."

Bill replies, "Don't worry, sweetheart. I promise not to change it. Just want to use it to explain the situation to my son." Bill looks down and points to the radio's control module. Bill looks at his son and says, "You see this thing here? It's called a-ah-ah... whatchamacallit..."

Will answers, "A frequency range, Dad."

Bill replies, "That's it. Thanks, son. Look at this frequency range. You see how the red dial is right in the middle at 90?"

"Yup. Sure do."

"And you see the range of channels you have here? The range of channels goes all the way up to 170 and all the way down to below 60. I want you to think of that range as where your soul lives between the living world, the afterlife, and all the different planes in between."

Will looks puzzled. "Okay?"

Bill continues, "Now picture 170 is you in the living world. Going about your day. Going to work, running errands, and of course paying your damn taxes. Now, going down in the numbers. The 140s is when your consciousness is altered. Figure it like daydreaming. The 120s is when you're sleeping. The 110s a very deep sleep. Like those post-shift naps after a long day at work. The 100s is when someone has passed out due to an injury. Bad concussion, maybe a coma for a short while. That red dial sitting right in the middle at 90 is you right now, son. You're in a deep coma. Annie and the kids got your body out of here, but that shadow guy was able to keep your soul imprisoned here."

Will looks at his dad and exclaims, "How the hell was be able to do that?"

Bill answers, "Not too sure. I know he's a powerful bastard. Has a lot of help from all those poor souls roaming around this estate. He and his gang of ghouls are stuck in the 70 range, unable to cross over completely. They are either trying to relive the last few moments of their physical lives over and over or terrified of going to a place more awful than their death. When someone goes down in their frequency, it allows people like me to push through open doors that were once closed. Kind of like hearing a blend of two radio stations at the same time. But not to worry. We have some good people on our side. Which reminds me. It's about that time. I have to run a few errands. You stay here and keep Misty company and remember, don't leave this room. You're safe here."

Bill glides toward the door that leads to the hallway. Will glides toward him and tries to catch up to his father.

Will exclaims, "Dad, wait please!"

Bill stops, turns toward his son, and asks, "What is it, son?"

"Dad! Please don't leave me! I have so many questions. How are you able to be here? And why didn't you stop The Shadow Man before he was able to hurt the family?"

Bill smiles, rubs his right hand along his left arm, and answers, "Figure it like this, kid. It had to happen this way. That's what I was told anyway. And as for me being here. Well, figure as if I'm on a special assignment."

"A special assignment? What, like you're an angel or something?"

Bill smiles back at his son. "Don't worry, kid. We will have time to go over a lot of things later. But right now. I'm needed elsewhere. I'll see you in a bit." Bill glides out of the room through the closed door as Will and Misty wait in the slightly lit room listening to the music on the radio.

CHAPTER 34

....

DUDE, WE NEED SOME BACKUP

Liam, Boo, Neil, Ellie, Simon, and Reggie are all gathered in the waiting room. Simon and Reggie share snacks together while Boo sits with Liam on a gray couch. Simon chews on a candy bar while Reggie finishes off a bag of potato chips. Simon looks at Reggie and says, "I failed to mention that I'm a stress eater."

Reggie laughs and replies, "Yeah. I wear my emotions on my sleeve and around my waist too. I'm right there with you."

Boo is snuggled up next to Liam. Her head is on his shoulder, and she continues to sob slightly. Tears slowly make their way from her eyes onto Liam's T-shirt. Liam has his left arm wrapped around his sister. He looks down at Boo and says, "It's okay, sis. Everything will be okay." Liam thinks, *I have to be strong for Boo. But I don't know if everything is going to be okay. How is this whole thing going to work out? What if I lose my dad? I'll be lost without Dad being there. And what about Mom?*

Neil walks over to his sister who's sitting along in a row of blue chairs. He sits down next to his sister and wraps his arms around Ellie. Ellie rests her head on Neil's shoulder. Neil says, "Looks like Dad is going to be okay."

Ellie replies, "I'm not worried about Dad. He'll pull through. But what about Uncle Will? Look at Liam and Boo." Ellie and Neil look at Liam and Boo as Ellie continues, "They both look lost without their dad. What are they gonna do? What are we gonna do?"

Neil says, "We're family. They're family. We will be there for them. No matter what. We'll figure this out together."

Simon looks to Liam and says, "Any good ideas, monster slayer?"

Ellie interjects and says, "Not right now, Simon! Leave Liam alone! He's been through enough."

Simon replies, "Hey, don't jump down my back. I'm just looking for a plan. Even if that plan is sitting here until we know more about their old man. Just looking for some guidance."

Boo moves her head away from her brother. She clears the tears from her eyes and says, "Simon's right. We have to think of something. What are we gonna do?"

Liam gives his sister a kiss on her forehead and stands up. Everyone is focused on Liam. "I'm gonna use the restroom. I'll be right back."

Liam walks over to the small alcove along the far wall of the waiting room that leads to the restrooms. Liam enters, feeling sick to his stomach with worry. He waves his hands in front of the automatic sink. He gets his hands wet and rubs the water up and down his face. He continues to feel sick to his stomach. He turns and enters a bathroom stall and closes and locks the door behind him. He collapses in front of the door and begins to cry. The pain and worry he feels for his family is overwhelming. He continues to cry for a few moments. Liam is curled up in a ball with his hands resting on his face. He looks down and sees the silver cross glimmering slightly from the restroom light reflecting off the white glossy tiles. Liam puts his hands together and begins to pray. In a soft and stammering voice, he says, "Dear, God. I need your help. My family needs your help, especially Dad. I don't want to lose him. I can't lose him." Liam collects his thoughts and continues to pray. "Please help me figure this out. I don't care what happens to me. I only want my family to go home together."

The light shimmering off Liam's silver cross reflects into his eyes. Neil enters the bathroom and walks over to the closed stall. He knocks on the door and says, "Hey, Liam. You okay, buddy? The group has a plan. We want to discuss it with you."

Liam clears the tears from his eyes and looks up to the light in the ceiling and says in soft praying voice, "Thank you. I got the message."

Neil says, "You say something, buddy?"

Liam stands up and replies, "It's nothing. I'm coming out." Liam unlocks the door and walks to Neil.

Neil gives him a hug. "It's okay, buddy. You don't have to do this on your own. Come on."

Liam and Neil exit the restroom and meet the group who are facing them and standing in a semicircle. Liam looks at everyone and asks, "Okay. So, what's the plan?"

Ellie says, "We figure we should go over and talk to that old lady."

Reggie interjects, "The lady who lives down the street from me? Jerald's grandmother, Dotty Rose?"

Simon says, "She seems to be some type of psychic medium. She has a wealth of knowledge about the estate, and she's in touch with the world beyond. We figure we start there."

Ellie says, "What do you think, Liam?"

Liam looks at Boo and asks, "What do you think, sis?"

Boo answers, "My Spidey-senses are saying that this is the right move. What do we have to lose?"

Liam looks at the group and says, "Okay. Let's do it. But how are we gonna get there?"

Neil says, "I think I have that covered. All of you gather your things and meet me by Aunt Annie's van. I'll be there in a minute."

The group moves down the hallway toward the exit. Claire and Annie are standing in the hallway and see the group on the move. They both move toward Neil who's approaching them. Claire asks, "Where's everyone going, son?"

Neil answers, "I told them I can drive them home. Figure it would be best. I can drop off Reggie on the way back to Doylestown. The rest of us can wait back home until we find out more."

Claire looks at Annie and asks, "What do you think, Annie?"

Annie, still visibly emotional, wipes tears away from her bloodshot eyes. "I think that would be best. Get the kids home safely. They need rest. Here." Annie hands Neil the van key and continues, "Take the van. You can't fit everyone in your mom's car. I can get a ride back from your mom."

Neil takes the key and asks, "Any news on Uncle Will?"

Annie looks at Claire. She doesn't know what to say. Claire interjects, "Uncle Will is doing okay, honey. Not to worry. He's been taken to another section of the hospital to run some tests. Now when you get home, text me and stay with Liam, Boo, and your sister. You're in charge until we come home. I'll text you if anything new develops."

Neil says, "Thanks, Mom. Will do. I'll text you as soon as we get home."

Claire and Annie watch Neil head toward the exit. Annie says, "Thank you. I don't want the kids to know until we know more."

Claire says, "I agree. No worries. Figure less is more. They're kids, after all. No need to make them worry any more than they already are."

Neil exits the hospital to find the group waiting outside the family's van. The rain has stopped temporarily it seems. It's no longer raining, but it's still cloudy and the smell of moisture fills the outside air. He unlocks the van, and everyone hops aboard. Simon and Reggie unfold the back row and take their seats. Neil gets into the driver's seat and fires up the ignition. Ellie is riding shotgun and fastens her seat belt. "What did you say to Mom and Aunt Annie?"

Neil puts the van into drive. "Whatever they needed to hear in order to get the van keys. Remind me to text Mom in about thirty minutes. I told her we were on our way home."

Ellie grabs her phone out of her pocket, sets a timer for thirty minutes, and says, "Done. Good thinking, scarecrow."

Neil smiles as he drives toward the main exit. "Next stop, that old lady's place."

As they make their way to Mrs. Rose's residence, Neil looks back at Reggie and asks, "Hey, Reggie? Before we get deeper into the weeds with this thing, do you need to check in with your folks?"

Reggie answers, "Not yet. But maybe soon. They're still at work."

Neil replies, "Okay. No worries. Which apartment building is it, Reggie?" Neil continues to drive down Ashbourne Road toward the apartment buildings. They see the estate linger in the gloomy background as they pass by it. The house seems dark and mysterious as it hides behind its tall stone walls. Neil says to the group, "You guys see anything moving around in there?"

The rest of the group examines the grounds as they drive past the main entrance. Simon says, "Nothing. Not a damn thing."

Reggie interjects, "Yeah. It's like no one has been there for ages."

Ellie says, "Yeah, except the cars of the poor people who didn't make it out of there."

Liam looks ahead and sees glowing red-and-blue lights coming down the road. Liam says, "Neil, looks like we have cops inbound."

Neil answers, "Yeah, I see them."

Simon says, "Oh shit! Do you think they're out looking for us?"

Ellie says, "No, you idiot. Just chill. As far as anyone knows, we are on our way home."

Neil pulls the van over to the shoulder as the two police cars drive past them with lights and sirens blasting.

The front police car doesn't take notice of the occupants of the van as he drives past. Liam takes notice of the officer and says, "Looks like he's talking on the radio with someone."

Neil watches through his driver's side mirror as the rest of the group observes from the rear windows. The police cars turn and enter the estate. Reggie asks Simon, "What do you think we should do? Should we help them or something?"

Simon answers, "Not sure if we can. Even if we tried, what would they say?"

Boo answers, "They would probably laugh at us and tell us to get lost."

Simon replies, "Yeah. Really. 'Excuse me, Officers. Don't go into the spooky old mansion. There's a bunch of frightening ghosts and a homicidal black mass in there. Enter at your own risk.'"

Neil looks through the rearview mirror at Liam and asks, "What do you think, Liam? What should we do?"

Liam thinks and answers, "I agree with all of you. The police won't believe us. They'll go in and do their job regardless. Our best bet is to talk to Mrs. Rose first. Maybe we can convince her to go over there with us so she can talk to the police. Hopefully, Mrs. Rose will be able to explain things better than we can. Plus, she's an adult. Things sound better coming from an adult."

Neil says, "Agreed. We're moving. Which building is it, Reggie?"

Reggie answers, "It's the third building on the right."

Neil turns into the driveway and into the parking lot. There are a couple of extra cars in the lot. Reggie says, "Looks like someone has some company."

Neil replies, "Looks that way. All the guest spots are taken. Screw it. I'll just double-park for now." Neil parks the van behind the occupied guest parking spots. The group exits the van and runs up to the apartment building's security door.

Simon is the first one to the outer door. He opens it, holds it open for Ellie, and says, "After you, my dear."

Ellie says, "Thanks," as she looks for the correct button to press. She says, "Okay, which one? Mrs. Rose." Before she presses the button, there's a vibrating buzz coming from the security door.

Over the buzz, a voice loudly says over the speaker, "Come on in, honey! We've been expecting you!"

Ellie grabs the doorknob and opens the security door as she looks back at Simon. Simon says, "Did I hear that old lady say that she's been expecting us? Damn! A chill just went down my spine."

Ellie answers, "You got most of that right. She said that 'we,' meaning plural, 'have been expecting you.'"

Simon replies, "Now I got chills down my spine and goose bumps crawling down my arms. Thanks."

Ellie says to everyone, "Come on! Let's find out what's going on."

Everyone begins their assent up to Mrs. Rose's apartment. Reggie starts to breathe heavily and says, "Just what I need today. More cardio."

Simon turns to look back at Reggie. "You and me both, buddy. My heart hasn't worked this hard since the last Presidential Fitness Test at school. I dread that day more so than the first day of school."

Ellie is the first to reach the top of the stairs. She's surprised to see a younger woman waiting and holding Dotty's apartment door open. She's a slighter older middle-aged woman with dark curly hair. She's strikingly pretty. Her perfectly innocent smile matches her large brown eyes and a round tender face. The woman says, "You must be Ellie. Nice to meet you."

Ellie asks, "Who are you?"

The woman smiles. "Sorry. I'm Rachel. I'm an old friend of Dotty's. Please come inside."

The group enters Dotty's apartment. The windows are open, and the moist breeze flows through the window curtains in the living room. The group piles into the living room and sees Dotty sitting in the kitchen with an older gentleman wearing a traditional priest uniform. Dotty says, "Like I said, honey, we've been expecting you." Dotty looks at Simon and asks, "What's your name again? Simon, right? Does my place still smell like old lady?"

Simon stammers, "N-n-no, ma'am. Smells like wet summer grass. Definitely an upgrade."

Dotty looks over and sees Reggie. She says, "It's about time you come and visit me, Reggie. Come over here and give me hug."

Reggie walks over to Dotty as the man sitting next to her stands up and helps Dotty stand with her walker. The man has a large black satchel with a white cross stitched on the side draped over his left hip. Reggie gives Dotty a hug. Dotty says, "You didn't have to be afraid of me, honey. I don't blame you for Jerald. He made his own decisions."

Reggie replies, "I'm still feeling horrible though. And somewhat responsible. I'm so sorry."

Dotty replies, "It's okay, honey. It will all work out in the end. Now, let's all gather in the dining room. The table is nice and big, and we can grab some extra chairs from the kitchen here." Dotty walks with her walker as the man in the priest uniform walks behind her slowly carrying his chair. He's short but has an athletic build. His neatly trimmed bushy mustache matches his long, combed-back white hair. Dotty says, "Please excuse me for not moving fast enough. And where are my manners? I haven't introduced you to my guest."

Rachel interjects, "It's okay, Dotty. I introduced myself to the group."

The older gentleman says, "But I haven't. Sorry. I'm Father Patrick. Nice to meet everyone."

Father Patrick shakes everyone's hand before they sit at the dining room table. They each take turns introducing themselves. Liam and Boo are the only ones who haven't made their proper introductions. Father Patrick shakes Boo's hand and says, "From what Dotty told me, you must be Boo. Very nice to meet you, dear." Father Patrick looks over, approaches Liam, and shakes his hand saying, "And the man of the hour. You must be Liam. Nice to finally meet you, son. Now, where's that silver cross you used to wound that bastard?"

Looking confused, Liam reaches into his T-shirt collar and grabs the silver cross and pulls it into full view.

Father Patrick says, "That's excellent, son. Glad you stung the bastard. I bet you he wasn't expecting that."

Liam asks, "Father, how do you know about my silv—"

Father Patrick interjects, "Dotty told me all about it. I'm sure you have a lot of questions. But don't worry, son. Dotty, Sister Rachel, and I are here to help you and your family."

CHAPTER 35

....

OKAY, SO WHAT'S THE PLAN?

"So, kids," Father Patrick says as he rubs his hands together, "it sounds like you had a real run-in with all of the residents from the estate over there."

Liam looks to Father Patrick and asks, "Father, how did you know what happened at the estate?"

Father Patrick looks over to Dotty and says, "The boy is asking a good question, Dotty. Mind taking this one?"

Dotty looks at Liam, smiles, and says, "You know about my abilities, honey. Let's just say that someone visited me and told me all about your encounter with The Shadow Man. He also informed me that your father is safe for now."

Liam replies, "Of course my father's safe. We got him out of that place before The Shadow Man could finish him off."

Dotty asks, "Do you remember what The Shadow Man said to you before you left the main house?"

Liam answers, "Yeah. He said something like, 'Your father is staying here with me.'"

Dotty answers, "Yup. That's correct. And he wasn't lying."

Simon interjects, "There's something you're not telling us. This isn't adding up."

Dotty looks at Rachel.

Rachel says, "Just be honest with them. There's no sugar-coating this thing."

Dotty takes a deep breath, and her eyes wander off to her left side for a moment as she continues, "When your father fell over that banister and hit the floor, he went into a deep coma. Since his consciousness, his state of being, slipped far down along the plane, The Shadow Man was able to imprison his soul at the estate."

Boo exclaims, "Wait! What! Is Dad dead?"

Father Patrick says, "No, honey. No, he's not dead. Try to explain it better, Dotty."

Dotty continues, "Right now, our bodies and souls are here in this room. Except for a few exceptions, the doors to the other planes are closed. When we dream, our consciousness (essentially our soul) is susceptible to the different planes. Doors open, and that's how some souls from the other side communicate with us. Loved ones try to send messages to us in our dreams. But these doors to the other side stay open longer on occasions, like with your father. He's farther along the path to the other side."

Father Patrick interjects, "Kids, think of it as being one floor above Purgatory."

Neil asks, "So you're telling us that Uncle Will's soul is trapped in that place while his body is miles away at the hospital?"

Father Patrick answers, "That's exactly right, young man."

Neil asks, "So what do we have to do to get Uncle Will out of there?"

Everyone looks to Father Patrick for answers.

Father Patrick stands up and paces back and forth for a moment while he rubs his hand along his chin. He answers, "That's where things get tricky. You see, Sister Rachel and I were assigned to the estate by the Catholic Church many years before Dotty and the rest of her friends were hired as cleaning ladies. When old man Arthur Elk built that place, he lost his wife from tuberculosis."

Simon interjects, "Yeah, we know the history of the family. We did some research already."

Father Patrick replies, "Good. I can skip that part. So, anyway, he brought in someone who was experimenting with AC as a power source. Being a man of wealth and power, there were a few shady characters lingering around Mr. Elk. One of them was a man who specialized in performing seances. Mr. Elk watched one of his shows at one of the theaters in downtown Philadelphia. He was impressed by the man's magical powers and requested his audience. Mr. Elk told the man that he lost his wife and would pay anything to see her again. From what we were told, this man convinced Mr. Elk that his estate can serve as a gateway to the other side using his seances and homing in energy by the use of AC current. Mr. Elk agreed and worked with this man and the architect of the estate to create a spiritual beacon. They used large magnetic stones to create that big ugly wall that surrounds the property. The AC generator would charge these walls and create a highly charged atmosphere, which created a perfect environment for spiritual activity. Spirits need energy from the surrounding environment to take form. They can't create energy on their own. That highly charged atmosphere is the reason the area around Elk's Estate is constantly being hit by severe storms. That energy acts as a catalyst with the atmosphere."

Ellie asks, "So was Mr. Elk successful in being reunited with his wife?"

Father Patrick answers, "The way the legend goes…no. He was never reunited with his wife. Several seances were performed during their time at the estate. But all these factors opened a door to all of the bad shit that should have remained buried and closed. Mr. Elk didn't know that this magician practiced in the dark arts and had several followers. They worshiped evil, and the demons answered back by walking right through that open door. After the Elk's family was out of the picture, the Catholic Church was brought in to seal the door and make sure it remained locked."

Liam asks, "Were you able to close the door?"

Father Patrick answered, "I thought so. We all thought so anyway. I was a young priest. Just got my first assignment over at Saint Martin of Tours in the city. We spiritually cleansed that séance room, put a blessed painting of Saint Michael in front of the doorway, and built the altar at its entrance to work as a shield."

Ellie asks, "Where did it all go wrong then?"

"We had it well under control for years. There were always members of the church on the premises. Things went quiet for a long time. The church occupied that estate for over fifty years. We turned that place around and enjoyed many years there. But the estate was getting older. The amount of people reserving the estate for retreats dramatically decreased over time. Eventually, the church was looking for ways to save money."

Liam recalls the police cars going into the estate. Liam interjects, "Excuse me, Father Patrick. I appreciate the background story, but there's something happening right now."

Father Patrick asks, "What's that, Liam?"

Liam answers, "On the way over here, there were two police cars heading into the estate."

Father Patrick replies, "Oh yes. I heard them going down the street. They were pulling into the estate?"

Neil answers, "Yes, Father. We saw them pull into the circle entrance."

Sister Rachel interjects, "The officers' lives are in grave danger!"

Dotty says, "I agree. Poor guys are probably investigating what happened there today. Rachel, honey, please hand me my phone."

Sister Rachel walks over to the kitchen counter, grabs Dotty's phone, and hands it to her. Dotty says, "Thanks, honey."

Father Patrick asks, "Who you gonna call, Dotty?"

"That Elkins Park detective. I was in communication with him when Jerald died." Dotty calls Detective Rhinelander.

He answers, "Detective Rhinelander. Go ahead."

Dotty replies, "Hello, Detective. This is Mrs. Rose. Jerald's grandmother."

"Oh hey, Dotty. How can I help you today?"

"I heard some police cars heading to the estate. Is everything okay? Are your officers, okay?"

"Yeah, they're investigating a disturbance with the volunteer group. Other than the initial report from one of my officers that they'd arrived on scene, nothing else to report. Why do you ask?"

"Detective, I told you about my abilities and my personal history with the estate. I know that you're not a believer, but…I'm afraid for their safety."

"Yeah you got that right. I don't believe in crystal balls and all the other stuff you're into. But rest assured that my officers are well-trained, and I will be in communication with them while they investigate. Now, if you'll excuse me, ma'am, I'm at the hospital to interview some witnesses. Talk to you later."

Detective Rhinelander is walking into the ER entrance with his notebook binder and the manila envelope from his office. He stops and thinks about Dotty's phone call. He grabs his radio from his side belt, pushes the press-to-talk button, and says, "Car 2 to Car 3 or 4. Come in."

Kenny answers, "Car 2. This is Car 3. Go ahead."

Detective Rhinelander answers, "What you got over there, Kenny?"

Kenny replies, "Ethan and I just drove around the entire estate. No movement. Nothing going on. There are two vehicles that were left behind near the front entrance. We checked the coach house. Nothing there. We were about to check the main building. Hold on a minute, sir."

Detective Rhinelander waits a minute for a reply and asks, "What's going on, Kenny?"

Kenny replies, "Oh sorry. Nothing, sir. Thought I heard someone. I told Ethan to run the two vehicle plates on scene."

Detective Rhinelander says, "Okay sounds good, Kenny. If you need anything, give me a call right away."

"Yes, sir."

Detective Rhinelander replies, "Message received. Be careful." He then walks to the ER front desk and asks for the location of the volunteers.

✦ ✦ ✦

Back at Dotty's residence, the group discusses their plan of action. Simon has his map of the estate blanketed over the dining room table. The entire group is huddled around the map. Simon says, "Okay, Father Patrick, looking at the map, what are your thoughts?"

Father Patrick points to items on the map and says, "Okay. Here are my thoughts. I figure that The Shadow Man will be expecting us to go through the front gate."

Simon says, "Yeah, so let's ex that plan."

Father Patrick replies, "On the contrary, young man! We will give him just that. But only a few of us."

Ellie asks, "What do you mean?"

Father Patrick answers, "We're gonna drive right up to that front entrance. Neil and Dotty will be in Sister Rachel's car. The rest of the group will enter through that underground street sewer on the other end of the estate. We'll use your van to get over there. We will make our way to the back of the estate and use the underground tunnel. The entrance is over near the old workers' quarters."

Reggie interjects, "Yeah we saw that entrance, but it was locked."

Simon says, "Yeah. Unless Liam and Boo's dad left one of his Halligan bars from work in the van, we'll have a hard time opening it. The door is old, strong, and heavy."

Father Patrick answers, "Not to worry. No need for heavy tools 'cause I have a key." Father Patrick pulls out a chained necklace from under his shirt. On the chain there's a silver cross and a golden key.

Liam says, "That cross looks like mine."

Father Patrick smiles and replies, "Sure does. You're not the only one who has a silver shield against that mean old bastard. Plus, I have a golden key. Now Neil, you'll be in Sister Rachel's car. She'll drive you and Dotty over to that coach house along the road. Dotty's gonna set up shop there. Sister Rachel knows her assignment."

Sister Rachel says, "Sure do. After you two get out of the car. I'll be heading up to the front entrance of the main house. Don't worry about me."

Father Patrick looks at Neil and continues, "Just stay with Dotty and wait until someone tells you what to do next. The rest of the group. Let's see…that will be myself, Liam, Boo, Ellie, Reggie, and Simon. You'll be with me. We enter the main building through the underground tunnel. Liam and Boo, you head to that office where I understand a young lady found some important documents about the estate."

Father Patrick looks over to Dotty. She replies, "That's right. Those documents might give us the location of The Shadow Man's remains."

Ellie asks, "Why are you sending Liam and Boo on this task? Why not one of the older kids?"

Father Patrick looks over to Dotty and says, "Another good question, Dotty. Wanna take it?"

Dotty answers, "Because Boo has been in contact with the little girl spirit, Misty."

Liam looks at Boo and asks, "Is that the little girl you were talking about, Boo?"

Boo answers, "Sure was. She was so nice. But also, very alone and sad. She protected me."

Sister Rachel interjects, "Liam, your sister has the gift."

Boo says, "What gift?"

Dotty answers, "She has the gift of pure empathy. She was able to see and interact with Misty."

Simon says, "So what if she was able to see and interact with a little girl ghost. We saw plenty of ghosts and even got chased by a bunch of pissed-off ghosts on our way out of the estate."

Sister Rachel answers, "That's different, dear."

Simon asks, "How's that different?"

Dotty answers, "Those are miserable trapped spirits. They feed off the energy of the estate and feed off your negative energy. Kind of like misery loves company. When you're a ghost, all you have is time and all you want is energy. Misty is a pure spirit, trapped by The Shadow Man. Like Will's situation. Boo has the gift to communicate and see pure spirits."

Father Patrick continues, "We want Liam and Boo on that assignment. Liam can protect Boo with his silver cross plus some other stuff I'll be handing out. Liam and Boo will find the documents. Misty spoke to our mutual friend and let Dotty know that she will be alongside Boo the entire time. We know that The Shadow Man loves to drain our communication devices, so radios and cell phones are out. But he can't stop Dotty and Boo. Boo will relay the information to Misty, and Misty will relay to Dotty."

Ellie looks at Reggie and Simon and nervously asks, "What do you have in mind for us?"

Father Patrick answers, "Ellie, I need you to run a diversion away from both Liam and Boo and myself. While Liam and Boo venture down the hallway on the lower level, I will be heading up to the main floor."

Ellie says, "So you want me as ghost bait. Great!"

Reggie mutters, "Sucks to be you I guess."

Ellie continues, "Well, I'm not much of a runner."

Simon looks at Ellie and says, "Don't you have your skateboard?"

Ellie thinks and says, "I think it's still in the van."

Reggie answers, "Sure is! Had to move it out of my way while we were loading Will in the back."

Simon says, "You're a lot faster on that board than you are on your feet."

Ellie smiles and replies, "You're right. Okay. I'm the skateboarding ghost bait chick. Got it."

Father Patrick says, "Now, Simon and Reggie. You seem like a couple of very bright young lads."

Simon says, "Thanks, Father."

Reggie smiles and says, "Glad my talents are obvious."

Father Patrick asks, "By any chance do either of you have access or currently in possession of some explosives?"

Simon and Reggie look at each other in shock. Simon says, "Jesus, Father. I'm not *that* devious."

Reggie answers, "I might be."

Simon replies, "Dude! You have explosives?"

Reggie replies, "Kind of. Fireworks. My older cousin from Indiana visited me earlier in the summer. Hooked me up for the Fourth of July."

Father Patrick asks, "What kind of fireworks are we talking here, son?"

Reggie answers, "A shit ton. Apparently, you can buy anything in Indiana. Anything you want."

Father Patrick asks, "Can you and Simon gather all those fireworks together and make them go boom at once? With enough time for you to get out of course."

Simon says, "I'm a big fan of fireworks and chemistry. I'm sure we can come up with something. What are you thinking, Father?"

Father Patrick answers, "Figure you two lads light up that AC generator in the basement and shut down the energy field around this place."

Simon and Reggie look at each other, nod in approval, and shake each other's hand. Simon says, "You got a demo crew, Father."

Father Patrick laughs. "That's the spirit, boys!"

Neil asks, "Any other assignments for me, Father?"

Father Patrick looks at Neil and answers, "You'll stand by with Dotty, son. I have a shovel for you. If Dotty tells you where to dig, start digging." Father Patrick points at the map between the coach house and the carriage house. He continues, "Any of you pay much attention to this open field here?"

The group looks at the map.

Simon says, "Nope. Not really."

Reggie says, "Yeah, I've ventured through that field a couple of times. There're these flat stones on the ground with numbers on them."

Father Patrick smiles and says, "Good, lad. Those stones are markers for graves."

Neil says, "Are you kidding me?"

Father Patrick answers, "No, young man. That's where they buried some of the poor people who died on site during the TB epidemic. We never found the records of which person corresponds to a particular number. We figured that young lady found those records hidden in the office. I also figure that they buried The Shadow Man somewhere in that field, and those records can tell us his location. Let's get started."

Simon asks, "Father Patrick? You mentioned some stuff you have for protection. What do you have?"

Father Patrick reaches for his black bag. "Ha! Glad you asked. Look at what I got here."

CHAPTER 36

....

CAR 3 TO CAR 4:
COME IN, ETHAN!

Ethan and Kenny make their way up the stairs of the main building. The long day has dragged from the late afternoon into the early evening. The setting sun drifts and peeks in and out of view from the overcast sky. The wind begins to pick up, and a cold breeze bends and twists the heavily leafed branches along the property.

Ethan looks up at the sky and asks, "Hey, Kenny. Are they calling for more storms today?"

Kenny answers, "Not that I know of. Did you run those vehicles' license plates?"

"Sure did. Waiting to get the word from dispatch."

"Okay sounds good."

They continue to walk up the stairs. Both front doors are closed. Ethan looks at his senior officer. Kenny says, "Go on! Try the doorknob first before we try to break in."

Ethan nods as he reaches for the doorknob. It turns and the door swings open. The estate is dark. Ethan grabs his large flashlight off his duty belt. He turns it on and releases the safety clip on his department-issued weapon. He looks back at Kenny. Kenny turns on his flashlight and says, "It's okay. Search to the left, and I'll search to the right."

Ethan says, "Ready? Go!"

Ethan springs inside and begins searching down to the left. He makes sure to check the corners. He moves quickly and with purpose as he shouts, "Hello! Elkins Park Police! Anyone here?"

Kenny starts searching down the long hallway to the right. He also scans the room for movement. Kenny shouts, "Elkins Park PD! If anyone's here, don't hide! We're investigating a possible assault! Anyone hurt?"

They continue their search. Ethan makes his way to the stairs that lead down to the basement. He peers down the steps into a pool of darkness and shines his light to investigate. Ethan uses the radio hand device located on his collar to contact Kenny. Ethan says, "Hey, Kenny. You got anything?"

Kenny answers, "Not yet. Looks like no one is home."

Ethan replies, "Right. I'm gonna search the lower level."

"Copy. I'll keep searching the main floor. After you search the lower level, meet up with me so we can check out the upper level together."

Ethan says, "Copy."

Dispatch calls into the radios and says, "Dispatch to Car 3 and 4."

Kenny reaches for his speaker. "Yeah, Dispatch, this is Car 3. Go ahead."

Dispatch replies, "Yeah. Car 3. Ran the plates. Both vehicles match the names of the volunteer group. No missing person reports yet. Both records are clean. EMS is busy handling other calls. They can't have an ambulance sitting there standing by. Let us know if they're needed."

Kenny replies, "Copy that. Did you hear that, Ethan?" There's a pause and some static on the line. Kenny repeats, "Ethan, do you copy?"

Ethan answers, "Yeah, I copy. Having a hard time hearing you. Maybe due to the lower level. Making my way down the stairs now."

Kenny replies, "Copy that. Still searching the main floor."

Ethan enters the lower level. His flashlight is the only illumination that fills an otherwise dark and empty hallway. There's a slight foggy mist in the air and a smell of something burning. Ethan gets a nose full of the air and begins to cough lightly. Ethan thinks, *Jesus. Smells like someone was burning some hair down here or something.* Ethan pans his flashlight beam back and forth as he enters the alcove and searches down the main hallway. He sees light flashing farther down the hallway and the sound of a generator coming to life. He heads toward the direction of the disturbance. He calls out, "Hello? Police department!"

Kenny continues his search. So far, it's negative. He enters the ballroom. His light reflects off the several mirrors on the wall and the large windows that reveal the birth of blue twilight in the early evening as a fast-moving storm approaches. He checks the corners. He calls out, "Hello! Police department! Anyone here?" His voice echoing off the high ceilings is the only response he hears. He steps further into the ballroom. He moves his light along the unoccupied tables and chairs. He steps on some broken glass, and the crackling noise echoes through the room. Kenny looks down and inspects the sharp broken glass with his flashlight. Kenny thinks, *I guess no one is home. God, I hate this place.* Suddenly, he hears someone's voice echo off the ballroom walls. He spins around, using his light to help detect the location of the sound. He draws his weapon out of his duty belt, and he begins to breathe heavily as his heart rate skyrockets. He points his flashlight and weapon toward the entrance of the ballroom. He sees a shadow move past the entrance. He yells, "Hold it! Police department! Don't move!" He moves quickly toward the entrance. He stands at the threshold between the ballroom and the main living room.

Kenny scans the large open area with his flashlight. His hands are starting to shake. He places his flashlight onto the floor for a moment to use his radio. He presses the talk-to-speak button and says, "Ethan! Ethan! Come in, Ethan! I think I have something on the main floor! Need assistance." There is a moment of heavy static on the line. Then the radio goes dead before Kenny can get a response. Kenny presses the button again and says, "Ethan! Ethan! Shit!" He looks at his radio. It's dead. Kenny hears another echo of someone's voice coming from inside the ballroom. He grabs his flashlight and spins around, pointing his weapon at the mirrors on the far wall that reveal a dark figure with two glowing green eyes!

Kenny exclaims, "Oh shit!" He fires several rounds at the object as it hits the mirrors and shatters the sharp broken glass, which falls onto the floor with several loud crashes. Not sure if he hit anything, Kenny moves forward. His breathing and heart rate have increased dramatically. He shines his light on the floor hoping to see someone, only to find broken pieces of mirrored glass. He shines his light at the other mirror on the far wall. It reveals The Shadow Man standing at the threshold behind him! He spins around, but it's too late. Suddenly, a violent rush of wind enters the room, and Kenny is picked up off his feet. He loses his flashlight and weapon as he's turned upside down! The pieces of glass float off the floor with their sharp edges pointed upward toward Kenny. Kenny shouts, "Jesus Christ! What the hell? Who the hell are you?"

The Shadow Man laughs. "I'm always looking for more security for my home. You'll fit in nicely around here."

Kenny screams, "Please! Put me down! Please, put me down!"

The Shadow Man replies, "As you wish."

Kenny falls headfirst onto the sharp pieces of mirrored glass. There is a quick burst of screaming followed by silence as The Shadow Man claims another victim.

Ethan is entering the boiler room as he hears gunfire coming from the floor above. Ethan says to himself, "Oh shit!" He presses the talk button on his radio and exclaims, "Kenny? Kenny? What you got!" No reply. A brief moment of static. Ethan attempts to change to his dispatch radio channel. He presses the button and says, "Car 4 to Dispatch. Car 4 to Dispatch! Emergency! Shots fired. Repeat, shots fired!" He doesn't hear any acknowledgment. He inspects his radio; it's completely dead! He draws his weapon out of his duty belt. He shines his light and weapon around the corner and across the threshold of the boiler room. The generator begins to vibrate. There are bright flashes coming from around the generator. He thinks he sees someone on the other side. Ethan shouts, "Police department! Come out with your hands up!" There's no answer.

Ethan runs quickly to the other side of the generator. He maneuvers around a large drum. He looks at the label reading: "Mineral Oil." He shines his light ahead of him and discovers Katie's charred body! Mr. Elk stands along the generator as blue electric bursts of energy radiant throughout his ghostly silhouette! Ethan exclaims, "What the hell? Holy shit!"

Mr. Elk looks at Ethan and exclaims, "I have to keep the machine working! We are so very close." Mr. Elk looks down at the smoldering remains of Katie and continues, "My assistant should be here any moment. I sent her on an errand."

Ethan's breathing and heart rate are racing. He backs away from Mr. Elk with his flashlight and weapon still pointing at the center of his possible target. He maneuvers around the large drum and exits the boiler room as quickly as possible. Ethan thinks, *Oh Jesus. Kenny!*

I've got to get to him! He begins to walk down the main hallway toward the stairs he used to get down to the lower level. He shines his flashlight and weapon down the hallway. The light beams a few yards down the hallway and bounces off a black foggy mist. Ethan says, "Oh shit! Great! Now there's a fire to deal with too."

The black mist reveals two glowing green eyes in the center of its mass as The Shadow Man begins to take form! Ethan stops dead in his tracks. The Shadow Man says, "No need to worry about a fire, young man. But I *would* worry about other things if I were you."

Ethan is frozen. He can't believe what has manifested in front of his eyes. The Shadow Man starts to move toward Ethan. Ethan backs up and reaches the end of the hallway. He looks inside the boiler room and sees Mr. Elk standing there smiling at him! Ethan shines his light down the hallway. He sees the charred ghostly figure of a woman gliding toward him screaming, "Please! Help me!" Ethan is trapped! His flashlight flickers and goes dead. He drops his flashlight on the tile floor.

Ethan points his weapon down the hall at The Shadow Man. Ethan takes a standing firing stance and begins emptying the magazine from his gun. The bullet casings bounce off the tile floor while the bullets pierce right through The Shadow Man to no avail. Ethan says, "Screw it. Rather go out swinging." He quickly pulls another loaded magazine from his duty belt. Ethan chambers the magazine and fires the entire magazine as The Shadow Man gets within arm's reach of him.

The Shadow Man reaches for Ethan saying, "You think those weapons would have any effect of me, boy? Come here!" The Shadow Man picks up Ethan by his vest. Suddenly, a bright flash comes from underneath the vest, hurting The Shadow Man as he begins to burn from his reaching outstretched hand. The Shadow Man drops Ethan as he screams out in pain. The Shadow Man exclaims, "What the hell do you have that can hurt me?"

Ethan scrambles to his feet. He looks down at his badge. He remembers he got it blessed by his priest the day he graduated. In an instant, there's a rush of wind coming down the hallway. The Shadow Man looks at Ethan with his radiant eyes and says, "Let's see if your badge can protect you from this!" The powerful wind picks Ethan up off his feet and throws him into the masonry wall behind him. His head bounces off the wall with a loud thud as he hits the tile floor hard, rendering him unconscious.

The Shadow Man examines his prey like a hawk flying over a mouse. "I'll have fun with you later. Right now, I must prepare for company." The Shadow Man glides down the hallway and fades into the black mass as it travels up the stairs and out of sight.

CHAPTER 37

....

GAME TIME

As the group prepares, Simon and Reggie run over to Reggie's place to get the fireworks. Simon asks, "Dude, what will we say to your parents?"

Reggie answers, "Not to worry. They're still at work. Won't be home till' after we leave."

Simon and Reggie arrive back at Dotty's apartment. Father Patrick asks, "Success, boys?"

Reggie nods in approval as Simon says, "Yes, sir. Got it in my trusty bag. Packed some extra matches just in case."

Reggie adds, "Yup. Found some PVC pipe that my dad had left over from one of his handyman jobs. All set."

The group gathers and looks inside Father Patrick's black bag. It's filled with plastic squirt bottles, a Bible, silver chains with crosses, rosaries, a glass container filled with a yellow oil, several glass cigar containers filled with ash and capped with cork tops, and a small silver box. He begins to pass out the silver necklaces and crosses and says, "Here you go! Don't worry, there's plenty to go around. And each of you take a rosary as secondary weapon." He throws everyone a rosary made from small pieces of wood and says, "This is good stuff here. These rosaries were made at the Holy Land and blessed by all the bishops and a few cardinals at this thing I attended. Got all of them while I visited the Vatican on official conference."

Simon says, "Sounds like getting your football signed by the whole team. More bang for your buck."

Father Patrick answers, "Ha. That's about right, kid. And everyone, take one of the squirt bottles. You run into any of those icky TB ghosts, spray them with a little bit of this and they'll leave you alone. Believe me."

Reggie grabs the squirt bottle and says, "This should fit nicely in my cargo shorts pocket. What's in here? Holy water?"

Father Patrick smiles and says, "Not just holy water. It's a little pissed-off-ghost-cocktail that I put together in my free time. Holy water, frankincense, Eucharistic wine, salt, sage, and garlic. They hate all that stuff. Now Neil, you'll need these little cigar containers."

Neil asks, "What do I need these for, Father?"

"I'll get to that in just a second." Father Patrick looks at Liam and Boo and says, "Now you two. When you get inside that office, look over those documents. If you find the grave marker list, you let little Misty know right away. She'll be right there with you. She will glide as fast as she can to Dotty's side and let her know." Father Patrick looks back at Neil as he continues, "That's your cue to start doing the grunt work and dig up that grave. When you get to that bastard's body, open these vials and sprinkle this stuff on top of him. It's ashes from burnt Easter palms that were left over from the church. We use this stuff to bless houses and ward off evil spirits."

Father Patrick looks at Simon and Reggie and says, "My demo crew. After you complete your task, run back to the coach house and help Neil with anything he needs to do."

Reggie says, "Yes, sir."

Simon says, "We got it covered, Padre."

Father Patrick reaches into his black bag and pulls out the silver box. He opens it and reveals a small, splintered piece of wood. Sister Rachel blesses herself with the sign of the cross.

Ellie asks, "I'm guessing that thing is important?"

Father Patrick answers, "Right you are, young lady. That, boys and girls, is a piece from the true cross."

Neil says, "Whoa!"

Simon asks, "No pun intended, but where the hell did you get that?"

Father Patrick answers, "Got it on the same trip that I got the rosaries. Had a buddy who works in the Vatican archive. It's amazing what friends overseas are willing to do for a case of top shelf American bourbon." Father Patrick hands the piece to Neil and says, "Neil, after you sprinkle that other stuff on the remains, you top it off with this. That's the grand finale."

They all look over the map on the dining room table one last time. Father Patrick says, "Now, does anyone have any questions before we get this party underway?"

The group all looks at each other. Simon looks at Liam and asks, "Do you think this will work, monster slayer?"

Liam answers, "If everything goes according to plan...yeah, maybe."

Sister Rachel says, "You have nothing to worry about, Liam. And this goes for all of you. We'll be there right with you. We will do everything in our power to not let anything happen to any of you."

Father Patrick notices Dotty looking over to her side. He asks, "Dotty? Anything to add?"

Dotty answers, "Oh sorry, honey. My contact on the inside had to make a quick exit over to the hospital. It's time. I just need Neil's help to get going."

Ellie looks at Neil and asks, "You ready?"

Neil looks at his sister with a serious look and asks, "Is it okay to be scared? Because I am."

Ellie gives her brother a hug.

Liam interjects, "Of course it's okay to be scared. We are all scared."

Father Patrick says, "You got that right, kid."

Liam continues, "But there are more important things than being scared."

Simon says, "Hell, yeah. Let's get Liam and Boo's dad back!"

Reggie says, "And maybe some revenge for Jerald."

Dotty nods in approval. "For our Jerald."

Neil adds, "Maybe some for my dad lying in a hospital bed."

Ellie says, "And definitely for my mom's friends."

Father Patrick gives the sign of the cross over the whole group. Boo asks, "You okay, Father?"

Father Patrick finishes his prayer, ends with the sign of the cross, and says, "Oh, yeah. Just fine, honey. Figure I would give a blessing over the whole group. Neil, hand over those van keys. You're with Dotty and Sister Rachel. Let's head out."

The timer goes off. Ellie tells Neil to text their mom saying they are home.

CHAPTER 38

....

PUTTING THE PLAN
INTO ACTION

The two vehicles exit the parking lot and drive onto Ashbourne Road. The day has marched onward. Evening dusk transforms into a stormy twilight evening. Rain, thunder, and lightning keep the group company as they head to different sides of the estate. Sister Rachel turns onto the half-circle drive and drives past the Elk's Estate iron gates. She pauses briefly and brings her vehicle to a full stop. The main house stands and waits ahead of them. Lights flicker through the sides of the boarded-up openings and aged windows. Neil looks around as he waits impatiently in the back seat. Neil asks, "What are you doing, Sister Rachel?"

Sister Rachel answers, "Just sizing up the situation, my dear."

Neil scans the outside through the wet tempered glass and says, "I don't see anything. No ghost, ghouls, Shadow Man, nothing."

Sister Rachel replies, "Oh he's around. He's just waiting."

Dotty says, "I agree, honey. Let's get up to that coach house. And Neil, I have a bag and my walker in the trunk. Be a doll and grab them when we stop."

Sister Rachel creeps slowly up to the coach house and gets ready to drop off her passengers.

Father Patrick drives down the road and comes to a stop just before the underground street sewer. The group sees the large stone wall running parallel along the side of the van. Father Patrick says, "Okay, kids. This is our stop. Looks like we're gonna get a little wet."

Everyone exits the van as Father Patrick opens the rear hatch. The group gathers everything they need, and they begin their descent down the ditch toward the mouth of the street sewer.

Simon opens his backpack and grabs his flashlight. He turns it on as he looks at the depth of the rainwater and says, "Well, shit. I hate wet feet."

Reggie replies, "How do you think I feel? This Shadow Man is costing my parents a fortune in new shoes."

Father Patrick interjects, "All right, you two. Let's get moving. Simon, you stay at the rear of the group and hold that flashlight. I'll be on point and lead the way."

Reggie turns to Simon and says, "Good call on the flashlight."

Simon replies, "Always be prepared. We didn't use it on our last run."

Reggie replies, "Probably the only reason the battery isn't drained yet."

The group enters the sewer as they walk in a single straight line to the other side. Father Patrick pushes a wagon out of the way. As they enter the inner perimeter of the estate, Liam asks, "Okay, Father. Where to next?"

Father looks back at the group and says, "Simon, shine your light on that stream over here." As Simon shines his light, Father Patrick points at the stream and continues, "We're gonna follow this stream all the way to the pond. From there, we'll be really close to the tunnel entrance."

The group follows Father Patrick and makes their way along the stream. Boo holds on to her brother's hand as he provides comfort and a sense of protection for his sister. She holds on to him tighter as loud cracks of thunder rage over the estate. Liam looks around and assesses his surroundings as rain continues to fall and saturate his clothes. A few flashes of lightning help illuminate the path ahead.

Simon asks, "What do you think, monster slayer? Do you think he knows we're here?"

Liam looks back and answers, "I guess we'll find out soon enough."

Reggie says, "Damn. I don't like that answer."

Ellie, using her skateboard as an umbrella, interjects, "For two manly men like yourselves, you sure sound like a couple of scared little babies."

They arrive at the pond and follow the driving path to the cottages.

Reggie thinks about Ellie's remarks and says, "Hey look. While you were with the whole gang inside the estate, Reggie and I were running around here dodging some crazy ghost ladies. Shit got real out here really quick."

As Simon scans the area with his flashlight, Ellie asks, "Ghost ladies? What kind of ghost ladies?"

Reggie answers, "There was this one wearing a—"

Simon interjects, "Wedding dress lady."

Reggie replies, "Yeah, she was wearing a wedding dress."

Simon adds, "No, Reggie. The wedding dress lady. She's right over there. Guys, we've got company!"

The group pauses and turns to Simon. Simon is directing his light toward the Victorian Rose Garden as thousands of raindrops fill the void between them. A flash of lightning reveals her full form. She begins to glide quickly toward the group; blood oozes down from her wrists and drips onto the saturated grass. She screams, "Where's my husband? Either he'll pay for this or someone else will!"

Ellie exclaims, "Holy shit!"

Reggie says, "Oh, who's the baby now!"

Simon says, "Run!"

Father Patrick runs toward the ghostly figure as he exclaims, "Everyone! Head to the workers' cottages. I'll be there in a minute."

Liam grabs Boo's hand firmly and says, "Come on, Boo. We have to move!"

The group follows Father Patrick's instructions. Father Patrick grabs a squirt bottle out of his black bag. The ghostly figure drifts quickly toward the priest and says, "Where's my husband? Did you marry us? You did this to me!"

The ghastly figure reaches for Father Patrick as he sprays her with the liquid from the bottle and says, "I don't know where your husband is, lady! Nor do I care! Back!"

The liquid flows through the air and hits the ghost across her wedding dress. The silhouette of her wedding dress begins to burn as she screams out in pain, "Ahhh! Damn you!" She immediately glides quickly in the opposite direction away from Father Patrick.

Father Patrick shouts, "Damn me? I'm not the idiot who took my own life over some guy! Get the hell out of here!"

Sister Rachel pulls up to the coach house. The brakes squeal as Neil hops out of the back seat. He walks to the back of the vehicle and taps on the trunk. Sister Rachel pops the trunk open as Neil grabs Dotty's bag, her walker, and a shovel. He tucks his head as he attempts to dodge raindrops. Neil walks over to the passenger side to open Dotty's door. Dotty reaches out her hand and says, "Thank you, honey. Be a doll and help me stand."

Neil helps pull Dotty out of the car. Concerned, Neil asks, "Do you have an umbrella, Mrs. Rose?"

Dotty begins to walk up the path to the coach house as she answers, "I'm not worried about getting wet or getting a cold, honey. Just help me up these steps."

Sister Rachel looks at Dotty and Neil. She blesses herself with the sign of the cross and continues to drive up to the main building.

Liam and Boo's group make it to the workers' cottages. Ellie asks, "So um quick question. Did you run into any spooky spirits around the cottages?"

Reggie, catching his breath, answers, "No. This area seemed okay. Just don't go into the greenhouse."

Liam asks, "What's in the greenhouse?"

Reggie answers, "Must you ask? Just take our word for it, okay?"

Liam looks at Simon and asks, "Where's the entrance to the underground tunnel?"

Simon shines his flashlight just past the cottages and answers, "Yeah. It's this way."

Suddenly, there's a lot of movement coming from the pond. The group hears a large splash and a wave of water hitting the shoreline. Simon turns with his flashlight and asks, "What the hell was that?"

The group follows his light over to the pond where it reveals a spectral image of a bloated man tied up in vines! The ghastly apparition drags itself out of the water and toward the group screaming, "Help me!"

Simon exclaims, "Who the hell is that?"

Reggie looks closely and answers, "Holy shit! I think it's Crazy Old Man Jack!"

Ellie asks, "Who?"

Reggie answers, "Never mind that! Time to go! Run!"

The group runs past the cottages. Simon is on point leading the way to the entrance of the tunnel. He exclaims, "Come on! This way!"

Reggie's at the end of the pack. He trips and falls. He looks back as Crazy Old Man Jack quickly drifts closer to him. Ellie looks back and shouts, "Reggie! Come on!" Reggie stumbles as he gets back on his feet. Simon leads the group down the stairs toward the tunnel entrance. The floor of the entrance is bathed in a pool of rainwater.

Simon splashes through the pool of water and tries to open the door. "It's locked!" Simon exclaims, "Oh shit! I forgot. Father Patrick has the key!"

Reggie is the last to arrive at the tunnel steps. Rainwater flows down the steps like tiny waterfalls. Reggie exclaims, "Simon! Open the door!"

Simon says, "I can't. Father Patrick has the key!"

In a flash of lightning, a vine grabs hold of Reggie's foot and pulls him backward causing him to fall on his face! Reggie looks back and screams, "Help! Someone help!"

Reggie tries to grab the squirt bottle in his cargo pants pocket. He grabs ahold of it, but a violent jerk of the vine makes Reggie lose his grip. Crazy Old Man Jack says, "You can help me first. The Shadow Man said if I find someone to take my place, he'll let me go. You'll do just fine!"

Liam asks Simon, "Do you have a knife in that bag?"

Simon says, "Yeah. My utility knife. Front pocket!"

Liam reaches into Simon's bag and grabs the knife. Liam looks at Boo and says, "Boo, grab your squirt bottle and follow me. Ellie, help Simon and try to break open that door!"

Liam and Boo run up the stairs. Boo slips over the running water, but she catches herself. Reggie is being pulled closer to the pond! He looks back and sees Liam and Boo running toward him. He screams, "Please help me!"

Liam rushes forward, catching every raindrop in his path. He makes it to the vine that's pulling Reggie, grabs it, and begins cutting. The vine breaks loose as Crazy Old Man Jack spins around and lunges at Liam and Reggie! Boo aims her squirt bottle at the ghostly figure and sprays him with its contents. He screams out in pain as the contents begin to sizzle his ghastly figure. Crazy Old Man Jack glides quickly back to the pond as Father Patrick runs up to assist the crew.

Neil helps Dotty up the stairs. They enter the dark and damp coach house. Neil asks Dotty, "Okay, Mrs. Rose. What do you need?"

Dotty looks around and sees an old table and couple of chairs in one of the rooms. She answers, "Not too much, honey. Just drop my bag off on that table over there and I'll take care of the rest."

Neil follows Dotty's instructions. She sets the walker next to the chair and takes a seat. She opens her bag and pulls out a couple of candles, a notepad, a black marker, and a lighter. Neil asks, "Is that it? That's all you need?"

Dotty smiles as she lights up the candles and answers, "That's it, honey. Low-tech stuff here. The candles will help me communicate with Little Misty."

As she investigates the flames from the candles, she writes down a few symbols on her notepad and says, "Neil, honey. Be a doll and take one of the cigar containers out of your pocket."

Neil grabs one of the containers out of his side cargo pants pocket and says, "Okay. What do you need?"

Dotty answers, "We have company coming, honey. Dip your hand into the container and smear these symbols over the threshold of the front door and the back door."

Neil looks out the window and sees the same ghostly figures that chased him and the rest of the group out of the estate. They glide across the grass coughing up blood and screaming as they move closer to the coach house.

Neil moves quickly, grabs Dotty's notepad, dips his fingers into the container, and smears the symbols from her notepad over the front and back doors. He runs back into the room where Dotty is sitting. He is shocked to see a ghostly apparition standing in the room with Dotty! Dotty says, "Sorry, honey. I didn't tell you fast enough. This is my grandson, Jerald."

Jerald's apparition turns toward Neil to reveal his mangled face and crooked neck that he suffered in his traumatic death.

CHAPTER 39

....

THE CONNECTION

Annie waits impatiently in Will's hospital room. She's waiting for Will to return from his tests. Claire walks in with Detective Rhinelander and knocks along the side of the threshold to gain Annie's attention—her imagination is running wild. Claire says, "Annie? Annie?"

Annie comes back to reality and sees the two guests waiting for her response. "Yeah. Sorry. Didn't see you there."

Claire replies, "It's okay."

Detective Rhinelander walks across the threshold carrying his paperwork in one hand and extending his other hand. "Hello. Annie, is it? Detective Rhinelander, Elkins Park Police."

Annie shakes his hand. "Nice to meet you, Detective. How can I help you?"

Detective Rhinelander answers, "I'm here to gather information about your husband's assault."

Annie replies, "Okay? What would you like to know?"

Detective Rhinelander says, "Good question. I've spent a good amount of time today interviewing hospital staff that took care of your husband and Claire's husband." He looks at Claire and continues speaking to Annie, "I've also spent a good amount of time talking to Claire and her husband and getting their statements about the incident. Sounds like a very outlandish story."

Annie looks at Claire then looks at Detective Rhinelander. "What have they told you?"

Claire interjects, "Only what makes sense, Annie."

Annie replies, "Nothing about this makes sense, Claire! Our family and Claire's friends were attacked! Attacked by something evil in that house!"

Detective Rhinelander finds an open seat and pulls it next to Annie. He asks, "Annie, can I get you anything? Water? Coffee?"

Annie answers, "No. I'm fine, Detective. Just worried about my husband."

Detective Rhinelander sits down, crosses his legs, and opens his folder containing the manilla envelope. "Now. You asked a good question just a moment ago. You asked what Claire and Pete said in their statement." Annie nods her head as Detective Rhinelander continues, "In Claire's statement, they said they were attacked by hooded figures wearing dark shrouds. One in particular had glowing green eyes." Detective Rhinelander looks up at Claire and asks, "Is there anything else you would like to add to your official statement, Claire?" Claire shakes her head as Detective Rhinelander opens the manilla envelope.

Father Patrick helps Reggie to his feet as Crazy Old Man Jack descends into the black abyss of the pond. Father Patrick moves past the group and opens the door to the underground tunnel with his key. He says, "Sorry. I don't move as fast as you young people. Looks like Liam and Boo were on the case with that blobby mess."

Reggie pats Liam and Boo on the shoulder as he catches his breath. "Thanks, Liam and Boo. I didn't know which way that was going to go."

Liam replies "Sounds like you recognized that thing."

Reggie answers, "Yeah. Looked like Crazy Old Man Jack. Local hobo. Nobody's seen him for a few days. We figured he bailed or was dead somewhere."

Simon walks into the underground tunnel and stops to examine something. Father Patrick shouts to Simon, "Got anything down there, kid?"

Simon shines his light on the contents on the floors. "Looks like Reggie is right. That homeless dude was camping out right here when The Shadow Man got to him." Simon beams his light down the tunnel and says, "Looks like we are in the clear from here."

Father Patrick moves up to the front. "Come on. Let's go."

✦✦✦

Sister Rachel walks up the gray stone stairs to the front entrance. Her rosary swings back and forth in between her hands. She holds a small holy book and reads from it as she walks through the two open oak doors. She continues to pray as she walks through the foyer and enters the main living room. The overhead lights shimmer on and off throughout the estate. At the far end of the room stands The Shadow Man! His eyes glow and glare back at her. He says, "Well, well, well. It's been a long time, Sister."

Sister Rachel replies, "Yes. It has been a long time, Abbott."

The Shadow Man replies, "Don't call me that, you old bitch!"

"The only bitch I see here is you. Working for the masters of darkness. Doing their bidding like a lapdog."

The Shadow Man shouts, "I *am* the master of darkness! I've harnessed and controlled the powers of evil and collected souls along the way! What do you have that can possibly stand in my way?"

Sister Rachel raises her right hand holding the rosary and says, "I have God on my side. That's all I need."

✦✦✦

Neil is frozen in fright as he sees the unholy figure of Jerald, who appears more enraged than he looks deformed. Neil grabs his squirt bottle out of his pocket, but Dotty interjects, "Wait! Let me handle this, honey. Jerald!"

Jerald looks at Dotty and says, "You must come with us! He has plans for you."

Dotty grabs her rosary from out her pocket and holds it in front of Jerald. He shrieks and attempts to attack Dotty! Dotty shouts, "I command you by the power of the Holy Spirit! Release Jerald's soul from this evil!"

A bright light flashes as Jerald attempts to grab Dotty and touches the rosary. He screams out in pain as his ghostly presence is jolted to the end of the room! He staggers as he attempts to raise his phantom mass off the floor. He says, "Why did you do this to me, Grandma? I'm your grandson! Please help me!"

Dotty looks to Neil and says, "Believe me. This is the best way to help him. The Shadow Man is working through that poor boy's soul. If he moves, hit him with the stuff from your bottle."

Neil nods his head, gets in between Dotty and Jerald, and stands at the ready. Dotty turns and focuses on the flickering flames of the candles.

✦ ✦ ✦

The underground group reaches the other end of the tunnel. There's a door in front of them. Father Patrick turns the doorknob. It's unlocked. Simon's flashlight starts to flicker into a brown dimmed light. He knocks the flashlight a few times with his hands. It stays on only for a moment. The flashlight goes dead. Simon says, "Shit. Well at least it got us this far."

Father Patrick turns to the group and says, "Okay. After I open this door, there's no going back. This is where everyone branches off to their assignments. Have your weapons ready." The group grabs their squirt bottles and rosaries. Father Patrick asks, "Ready?"

Simon in front looks back at everyone and says, "Ready!"

Father Patrick opens to the door and says, "Go!"

The group is immediately stopped by the unearthly apparition of Katie! Her charred body lunges at the group, and she lets out a horrible scream! The group falls back together and screams as they spray Katie with the holy contents of their bottles. She cries out in pain and retreats away from the group. Reggie exclaims, "This is the last time I hang out with you guys!"

Simon and Reggie walk through the threshold and notice the officer lying on the floor. They run over to check on him. Liam asks, "Is he okay?"

Simon says, "He looks like he took quite a nasty hit. He's unconscious but breathing. Looks like he's coming around too."

Father Patrick looks at Simon and Reggie as they assess the officer and says, "After you light the fuse, make sure you take him with you."

Reggie nods as Father Patrick and Ellie continue to walk down the hallway toward the far stairway.

Liam and Boo make the short walk down the hallway to the smoking lounge. Boo knocks on the door and turns the doorknob.

She opens the door and sees Misty smiling at her. Misty comes up to Boo and tries to give her a hug. Boo feels a cold chill go down her spine as Misty continues to talk to her. Misty says, "I'm so glad you've come. Your father is so nice."

Liam looks at Boo and asks, "You okay, Boo? Your whole body just shook."

Boo answers, "I'm okay. Misty's right here. She says she'll help lead us out of here after we find the documents."

Misty looks at Will who springs past the threshold that previously protected him from the forces of evil and stands alongside his kids. Will says, "I can't sit in there hiding and waiting for my father. I gotta protect my kids."

Boo looks up and sees her father! Boo exclaims, "Dad? Liam! Dad is here!"

Liam looks around and says, "I can't see him, Boo, but I'll take your word for it."

Boo says, "Dad, we have to find out where The Shadow Man is buried!"

Liam looks back and sees lights flicker behind him. He sees Simon and Reggie and the electrified presence of Mr. Elk standing along the threshold of the boiler room! Liam shouts, "Reggie! Simon! Watch out!"

Simon sees the energized apparition and says, "What the hell?! Go, Liam! We got this! Find out where that bastard is buried!"

Liam grabs Boo's hand and asks, "Are you, Misty, and Dad ready?"

Boo looks to her side, smiles and says, "We're ready. Let's go!"

Sister Rachel stands like a soldier holding a shield in battle as The Shadow Man charges toward her. He attempts to grab her, but she blocks him by swinging the rosary at his black mass. She continues to read from her holy book as The Shadow Man circles back and forth trying to figure out his next attack. Two other dark entities immerge from the main floor hallway: the tall figure in a black shroud and the screaming nun!

Father Patrick and Ellie quickly ascend the stairs to the main level. Ellie peeks around the corner. She sees the two phantom spirits move toward Sister Rachel and The Shadow Man as they both engage in spiritual combat! Father Patrick says, "Okay you know what to do, right?"

Ellie answers, "Yeah, keep those evil spirits preoccupied by being live bait. I think I got it."

Father Patrick smiles and says, "Now, have your bottle handy. If they get close, light them up."

Ellie extends her hand to give Father Patrick a fist pump and says, "On your word, Father."

Father Patrick fist pumps back and says, "Go!"

On cue, Ellie runs down the hallway. She throws down her skateboard and darts past the two phantom entities like a ball being shot out of a cannon! She turns back and sprays them with the contents of her bottle and says, "Hey, jagoffs. Catch me if you can!"

The two gloomy spirits scream in pain as they begin to chase Ellie down the hallway. Ellie continues to speed down the black-and-white checkerboard-tiled hallway toward the art gallery. Father Patrick sees the open window and sneaks down the hallway to the séance room.

Simon sees Liam and Boo turn the corner toward the office. Reggie stands over the officer as Mr. Elk glares over the boys. Streaks of blue-and-purple electrical currents travel across the floating apparition. Mr. Elk hovers over Reggie. Reggie reaches for his spray bottle. His pocket is empty! He lost it during his encounter with Crazy Old Man Jack. Reggie grabs hold of his rosary and extends his arm as Mr. Elk lashes down on him! Simon runs in front of Reggie and sprays Mr. Elk with his bottle and says, "Piss off, sparky. Leave my friend alone!"

Mr. Elk screams in terror as he finally feels the sensation of pain. Something he hasn't felt for a long time. Mr. Elk retreats from his attack and dashes back into the boiler room. He screams, "You'll pay dearly for your treachery. Nothing will interrupt my plans!"

Simon replies, "Whatever, dude! Get the hell out of here!"

Reggie gives Simon and fist pump and a hug and says, "Thanks, brother. You got right in front of that dude. You were fearless!"

Simon replies, "Like Liam said, there are more important things than being afraid."

Reggie glances into the boiler room and sees the generator. He adds, "Speaking of Liam. When do you think when we should light the fuse on this bad boy?"

Simon says, "I'll keep an eye out for Liam and Boo. They're right down the hallway. When Liam gives me the thumbs up, we light this cherry and bail." Simon throws Reggie his spray bottle and says, "Here! Hold on to this just in case old sparky decides to strike back."

Liam and Boo enter the office and begin searching for the documents left on the desk by Katie. Will asks, "So what exactly are we looking for?"

Boo answers, "We figure Katie stumbled across some old secret documents that were hidden in the estate. Our hope is that one of those documents will tell us where The Shadow Man is buried."

Liam desperately searches through the documents. He says, "No! No! This is just some old crap concerning the church. Some construction information when they built the chapel and closed the séance room. There's nothing here about The Shadow Man or a burial site!"

Boo asks, "What are we gonna do now?"

Suddenly Will doesn't feel right. Will says to Boo, "Honey, I think something is wrong. I'm feeling different."

Boo asks Misty, "What's happening?"

Will's spirit curls up on the floor. Misty observes Will's behavior and says, "It looks like your father is in the process of crossing over completely!"

CHAPTER 40

....

CODE BLUE

Detective Rhinelander shows Annie the contents inside the manilla envelope and says, "Believe it or not, I believe that paranormal activity has something to do with a cold case I've been investigating."

Annie asks, "What are you talking about?"

Detective Rhinelander pulls out a black-and-white photo and two old legal documents: one document from the medical doctor on location when Elk's Estate was used as a tuberculosis center, the other from the county coroner. He hands the documents to Annie and says, "The man is this picture is Abbott Michaels. Old groundskeeper at the estate. One of Mr. Elk's daughters filed a missing person's report with the police department shortly before taking her own life. In her statement, she believed that Mr. Michaels was murdered by the hands of her father, and his body was dumped somewhere on the grounds of the estate."

Annie asks, "What did the police do after she filed a report?"

Detective Rhinelander answers, "They investigated. Asked Mr. Elk, his family, and the staff members if they knew about his whereabouts. Everyone denied any knowledge. The daughter wasn't so quiet. Mr. Elk was an extraordinarily wealthy man, and the local police wanted to close the books on the case. So, they simply left the case unsolved and moved on. This has been a cold case I've been working on for some time. I believe that he is buried in the same field as the patients who died of TB at the estate."

Annie is shocked over this revelation. "So, you think that… what? That this man has been haunting the estate and causing all these problems over the years?"

Detective Rhinelander answers, "The whole paranormal thing is a huge gray area for the police department. And frankly, I'm a bit of a skeptic myself. I'm more interested in what's black and white. I've been working with the county to exhume the remains from this plot." Detective Rhinelander points to the document from the medical doctor on staff and continues, "Plot number 37. The name was left blank while all the other plots have names along with county coroner reports to match. This is the only plot that doesn't match."

Immediately the lights in the hospital room flicker, and a cold chill fills the room. Claire shivers as she stands next to the doorway and says, "Wow. I just felt a cold chill. That was weird."

Detective Rhinelander looks at the flickering lights and says, "Maybe that storm is getting out of hand outside."

Without pause, there's an overhead page with an alert tone saying, "Code Blue. CT room. Code Blue. CT Room."

Annie gasps. "Oh God! That's my husband. I have a feeling!"

Claire grabs Annie's hand and says, "Come on! Follow me!"

Detective Rhinelander stands up as the two ladies dash down the hallway. He hears his radio saying, "Car 2? Are you out there, Car 2?"

Detective Rhinelander presses the button and says, "Yeah this is Car 2. Go ahead, Dispatch."

Dispatch replies, "Car 2. We've been trying to reach Car 3 and Car 4. They aren't responding."

Detective Rhinelander says, "Okay. Put me en route to the estate to investigate." Detective Rhinelander heads out of the hospital and gets ready to respond.

Annie follows Claire to the window outside the CT room. There they see doctors, nurses, and other hospital staff working together and performing CPR on Will. Annie collapses to the floor and begins to cry. Claire kneels next to Annie and holds her tight. Annie cries to herself, "Please God! Help us! I need my husband!"

✦ ✦ ✦

Liam looks at Boo and asks, "What's going on, Boo?"

Boo answers while tears stream down her face, "It's Dad! Misty's saying he's beginning to cross over completely. We have to free him from this place now!"

Liam runs out to the hallway. The overhead lights continue to flicker as he looks for Simon. Liam shouts, "Simon! Light the fuse. Light it now!"

Simon replies, "Okay! Get Boo and get out of here!" Simon runs back towards Reggie.

Reggie says, "Haven't seen old sparky come back."

Simon exclaims, "Something's wrong. Liam wants this thing lit right now!" Simon grabs the pipe and the lighter out of his bag. He lights the fuse. The fuse sparkles and burns as it works its way down toward the pipe. He rolls the pipe right under the generator. He exclaims, "Time to go! Help me with the cop!"

Boo looks at Will who looks like he's in pain. "What do we do, Dad?"

Will gathers whatever energy he has left and says, "Follow Misty and get out of here. Now!"

Misty looks down at Will and says, "I'll get them out of here. I promise."

Simon and Reggie pick up Officer Adams who is now regaining consciousness. Ethan says, "What the hell happened?"

Simon who has Ethan's arm over his shoulder says, "Please don't arrest us, Officer, but we just lit a homemade bomb next to that old generator."

Ethan exclaims, "You what! Did you notice that huge drum of mineral oil right next to that generator? It could take down half the building!"

Reggie interjects, "Then we have to move faster, Officer. We're leaving through the tunnel. Come on!"

They both help Ethan gather his footing as all three of them run toward the tunnel.

Sister Rachel continues to wage battle against The Shadow Man. So far, he's been wounded with her counterattacks, and he feels his powers are being depleted. He withdraws back to the far wall of the main living room. He calls on the powers of the wind and begins to hurl items from the living space directly at Sister Rachel. A small piece of furniture strikes Sister Rachel on the forehead, and she falls to the ground. She's dizzy and unable to regain her footing. She drops her rosary and her holy book, which get carried away by the powerful wind. The Shadow Man looks up at the large chandelier that's directly over Sister Rachel. He says, "Wind and gravity will do the trick. Welcome home, Sister." He reengages the powers of the wind and begins to twist and turn the cables of the chandelier. The cables break and the chandelier plummets down toward Sister Rachel! There's a sudden shriek of a painful scream and then silence. The Shadow Man claims another victim. He says, "Little lady put up a good fight, I'll give her that. Now to my séance room to regain my strength."

The Shadow Man glides across the room and heads toward the séance room. There he sees Father Patrick standing dead center at the top of the circular steps just outside the chapel. The Shadow Man shouts, "What the hell are you doing here, Priest? I thought I killed you years ago."

Father Patrick says, "You almost killed me, you bastard. Don't even think about going back to that séance room. I worked my magic. That therapy room of yours is closed. Permanently this time."

The Shadow Man screams, "What!"

Suddenly, Dotty gets a message while looking into the glimmering candles. She writes it down quickly. She looks at Neil and says, "Plot number 37. Go! Now!" Neil grabs his shovel and heads outside. Jerald glides over to Dotty and says, "Grandma, please come with me. We can be a family again."

Dotty holds out her rosary like a shield against the forces of evil and says, "Don't get any closer, honey. Somewhere in there is my grandson. But not right now." Jerald backs up as he begins to scream!

The ghastly ghosts glide past Neil and try to grab him as he sprays them with the contents of his bottle. He quickly finds plot 37 and begins to dig. Detective Rhinelander arrives at the estate with lights and sirens blazing. He suddenly stops and skids across the soaked pavement as he encounters a wave of ghastly apparitions.

He gets out of the car holding his flashlight and draws his weapon. He sees Neil struggle to dig the soaked earth while defending against the phantom spirits. He runs to him and says, "Holy shit, kid! What the hell is going on? And what are you doing?" Detective Rhinelander shines his light down. He sees the plot number and says, "That's Abbott Michaels's grave." Several evil spirits hurdle toward Neil and Detective Rhinelander. They scream and extend their arms while blood drips from their mouths. Detective Rhinelander points his weapon at the apparitions and fires. The bullets pass through the ghosts without any effect. Detective Rhinelander says, "Get behind me, kid!"

Neil steps in front of Detective Rhinelander with his bottle and sprays the spirits with its contents. The ghosts squeal in pain and change course away from Neil and the detective. Detective Rhinelander looks at Neil and says, "Thanks, kid. What did you hit them with?"

Neil answers, "Some stuff that Father made. Has holy water, salt, sage, and some other stuff."

Detective Rhinelander looks up and sees several other spirits heading in their direction. He asks Neil, "You said salt, right?"

Neil answers, "Yeah."

Detective Rhinelander says, "Watch my back, kid. I'm grabbing something from my trunk." Detective Rhinelander opens his trunk as the evil phantoms drift quickly toward him. He pulls out a shotgun and a box of shells. He quickly loads his weapon as the spirits try to reach for him. He fires. *BOOM! BOOM!* The spirits scatter, and they are laced with the contents of the shell's explosion. Detective Rhinelander quickly reloads.

Neil says, "Wow! What are you hitting them with?"

Detective Rhinelander answers, "Cases filled with rock salt. Seems to be doing the trick." The detective grabs a shovel from out of his trunk, cocks his shotgun, and says, "Okay, kid. Let's dig and cover each other's back."

Ellie makes it to the art gallery and attempts to turn around and flank the two frightening phantoms. She loses her footing and falls off her skateboard. The skateboard rolls behind her toward the spirits as she rolls her ankle. She stumbles and tries to stand as the evil apparitions close in on her.

Ethan, Simon, and Reggie reach the far end of the tunnel. Ethan asks, "How long did you make that fuse?"

Simon says, "Don't worry. If my calculations are correct, we've got plenty of—" Suddenly, there's a loud *BOOM!* A bright flash of light follows with a violent vibration that shakes the tunnel and causes it to collapse! Reggie, Simon, and Ethan quickly dash out of the tunnel just before the surrounding earth traps them inside. They reach the surface as they desperately climb the stairs.

Instantly, all the trapped spirits begin to be freed from the estate! Each one stops their pursuits as they feel something happening to them. A bluish bright light showers over them as the misty spirits begin to drift up into the sky. Reggie says, "Oh God! I hope everyone made it out okay."

Ethan asks, "Did you guys think of a rallying point?"

Simon answers, "Yeah. After we lit the fuse, we're supposed to head to the open field in the front and help Neil."

Ethan says, "Okay. I'll look around and see if anyone needs help. Go!"

✦✦✦

The Shadow Man charges at Father Patrick and tries to grab ahold of him. The violent blast collapses the floor around Father Patrick, and he hurls into the air and then drops down below the floor into a pool of fire and smoke. The Shadow Man follows Father Patrick into the hellish abyss. The two ghoulish phantoms stop their pursuit of Ellie as they begin to cross over and dissolve into the air above. Ellie stumbles as she makes her way out of the front door and away from danger.

✦✦✦

Will lies in pain as smoke fills the hallways and the office. He feels trapped and not ready to cross over. Suddenly, he feels the presence of his father. He looks up and sees his dad! Bill says, "Come on, kid! Time to go! Got to get you back to the hospital."

Will reaches for his father's hand. A burst of white light erupts as the father and son connect, and Bill escorts his son out of the estate. Bill travels with his son as fast as he can back to the hospital.

✦✦✦

Annie can hear the hospital staff working on her husband. She can hear the counts of the compressions and the call for the staff to clear before a shock is delivered to Will's unresponsive body. Claire holds on to her sister-in-law tightly. Claire begins to cry as she realizes her brother may not come back. Suddenly, Claire hears a heartbeat on the monitor. She stands up. She hears the doctor say, "Hold CPR! Hold compressions! I think we have him back!"

Claire picks up Annie and says, "Annie! Look! They got Will back!"

Annie stands but continues to hold on to Claire. She sees the monitor and immediately is relieved as her husband is brought back to life!

✦ ✦ ✦

Liam and Boo are halfway up the stairs as the explosion occurs. The violent blast knocks them off their feet. Smoke quickly fills the hallways and the stairwells. The radiant flames continue to catch whatever contents it can as it begins to engulf the estate. Liam and Boo start to cough breathing in the toxic smoke. Boo looks and sees Misty. Misty is starting to fade into a brilliant blue light. She says, "Boo! I think I'm starting to cross over!" Misty knows that Liam and Boo are in grave danger and says, "Follow me. I'll show you the way out!"

Liam and Boo quickly make their way to the front door. Fire and smoke continue to destroy the estate. The front door is blocked by The Shadow Man, who glares his menacing green eyes at Liam and Boo. He says, "You think you've won? You're not leaving. You're staying here with me!"

Boo begins to choke from the thick black smoke filling the estate. Liam looks at The Shadow Man and says, "We are leaving this place. My family is going home, and you're going back to whatever place you belong."

✦ ✦ ✦

Reggie and Simon meet up with Neil and Detective Rhinelander. All of them work tirelessly to dig the hole through the saturated earth down to the resting place of The Shadow Man. They reach the infamous remains of Abbott Michaels! Neil stands over the deteriorating wooden box holding The Shadow Man's remains. He uses the working end of the shovel to pry open the upper portion of the coffin. Neil stands over the decaying skeletal frame, opens his cigar containers, and pours the contents. Next, he places the piece of the true cross over the body and gives the sign of the cross by waving his hands.

✦ ✦ ✦

Immediately, The Shadow Man curls up from a burst of extreme pain! He exclaims, "What have you done?" Then a small bright white light in the shape of the holy cross fills The Shadow Man's black mass! His green eyes open wide in fear as he screams out, "NO!!!!" The brilliant light grows and quickly consumes his entire body as it bursts outward. He disappears while turning darkness into light. The Shadow Man is no more.

The turbulent reaction causes another violent vibration that collapses the floor above the main entrance. Liam and Boo are trapped! Boo turns to Misty and says, "What do we do? How can we get out?"

Misty continues to fade and cross over, turns, and says, "I'll get help!" Misty vanishes through the heavy smoke that continues to engulf the estate. There are only a few feet of air between the floor and the black smoke. Liam and Boo drop to their knees.

Boo exclaims, "Liam! What do we do?"

Liam coughs, looks toward a wall, and says, "Do what Dad taught us to do! Find a wall and follow it until you reach an exit. Come on!"

The smoke becomes too much for Liam. He begins to severely cough. The heat and the toxic smoke burn his eyes. He says, "Boo! I can't see!"

Boo looks ahead and sees a firefighter reach out his hand. The firefighter says, "Follow me, kids! I'll get you out of here!"

Boo turns to Liam, grabs his hand, and says, "Help is here, Liam! Just hold my hand. We're getting out of here!"

The firefighter says, "Just follow my light and my voice. You'll be safe!"

Liam and Boo continue to crawl and follow the firefighter until they reach a broken-out window. The firefighter says, "Just climb out this window and you'll be safe. Help will be waiting for you!"

Boo pulls Liam over the windowsill. Ellie sees Liam hanging out of the window and runs to his aid! Liam climbs over the edge of the windowsill and collapses on the other side. Boo looks at the firefighter. The firefighter smiles and says, "Time to go home, Boo!" She climbs and makes her way out the window. Ellie tries to pull up Liam, but he struggles to stand as he continues to cough.

Ethan sees the kids with Ellie. He runs to their aid. He says, "Hey! I see you. It's okay." Ethan picks up Liam and says, "This whole place is going to collapse. Follow me! We gotta go!"

CHAPTER 41

....

I GOT THE MESSAGE

Ethan, Ellie, Liam, and Boo dash away from the mansion as the roof collapses and pushes the walls away from the foundation. Ethan takes notice of Detective Rhinelander's vehicle and heads toward the rest of the group. Dotty carefully walks out of the coach house with the help of her walker. Ellie notices Dotty and runs toward her. Dotty looks at the blazing inferno with tears in her eyes. Ellie asks, "Are you okay, Mrs. Rose?"

Dotty answers, "Doing just fine, honey. Just need help to get down these steps is all."

Ellie helps Dotty as she asks, "And what about Jerald?"

Dotty looks at Ellie and begins to cry. "He's okay, honey. He drifted away and followed my husband into the light. He's home now. Now I can bury him knowing he's at peace."

The massive fire drew several of the neighbors around the property to witness the blaze from across the street. Detective Rhinelander goes over to his vehicle's radio and says, "Dispatch! This is Car 2. We have heavy fire at Elk's Estate. Send the fire department and a few ambulances to my location. I'll get back to you with the rest."

Dispatch says, "Message received, Car 2. The fire department has already been dispatched due to several calls. Were you able to locate Car 3 and 4?"

Detective Rhinelander looks over at Ethan as he stands with the reunited group and says, "Able to locate Car 4. He needs an ambulance. Haven't located Car 3."

The crew is happy and relieved to find each other and be reunited. Ethan comes up to Liam and Boo and says, "I give you two credit. I don't think I could have found my way out of that inferno."

Boo answers, "I felt safe when that firefighter showed us the way out." Boo looks at the estate as the roof continues to collapse. She continues, "Oh God! That firefighter is probably in trouble. We need to get him some help!"

Officer Adams looks at Boo and says, "Sweetheart, the fire department is just arriving now. No one was inside. Here, look."

Ethan points at the arriving fire trucks. Liam and Boo look at each other.

Boo says, "Then who saved us? Do you think…"

Liam coughs, clears his throat, and says, "It was our guardian angel."

Ambulances pull up along the drive. Ethan enters one ambulance while Liam enters another. Before Boo enters the ambulance, she looks over and sees Misty! Misty waves to Boo while she stands next to her parents. The family is happily reunited as they turn away and drift into the blue light. Ethan sees the paramedics and says, "I've never visited my wife at work as a patient. This will be different."

They are seen and assessed by the medics as the rest of the group walks to the open double doors in the back of one of the ambulances. There, they see Liam and Boo. Reggie asks, "How you two doing?"

Boo says, "Okay I think."

Simon looks at Liam and asks, "And how are you doing, monster slayer?"

Liam looks up while sitting on the ambulance bench and receiving oxygen. He smiles and gives the group a thumbs up.

One of the medics climbs down the back step and says, "They'll do just fine. We're taking them over to the hospital now as a precaution." The medic closes the double doors, gets into the driver's seat, and pulls away.

The fire chief walks up to Detective Rhinelander and says, "Hey, Detective! We set up a defensive operation. We'll be throwing water on this place for a long time."

Detective Rhinelander replies, "Thanks, Chief. I'll let my boss know." Detective Rhinelander leans into his patrol car and grabs his radio. He says, "Dispatch, let the chief know that I'll be on scene for the rest of the night with fire department. Have him call in some officers for relief. And have somebody stop by and bring some coffee. In the meantime, any local calls will be directed to county sheriff's office."

Dispatch replies, "Message received, Detective. We'll make all the notifications."

Simon comes up to Ellie who's just finished giving her brother a hug. Simon says, "Well, pretty lady. Looks like—"

Ellie interjects, "You know something. You talk too much." She leans in and gives Simon a big kiss on the lips.

Surprised by the exchange, Reggie says, "Well, I guess I shouldn't be too surprised. They seem to be right for each other. Sometimes you need a little push. Or, in this case, a life and death situation." Reggie gives both Simon and Ellie a hug and asks, "Who's hungry? Let's go back to my place and order some pizzas. I know this late-night pizza joint that never disappoints."

Simon replies, "Sounds perfect!" Simon looks at Neil and asks, "You in, scarecrow?"

Neil smiles and says, "No. You go ahead. I'll follow Liam and Boo over to the hospital. Let Mom know what's really going on."

Ellie smiles and asks, "Want me to come with you? For protection?"

Neil smiles as he looks down at the silver cross around his neck. "Nope. It's all right. I got all the protection I need."

Will, Annie, Liam, and Boo are back home. It's a picture-perfect autumn day. The sun beams over a golden blue sky as they exit their van. They walk across the parking lot. Will is wearing his fire department dress uniform. The brilliant light from the sun reflects off his highly polished black shoes and the silver bugles on his shoulders representing his promotion to lieutenant. He holds Liam's hand. Liam takes in the beauty of a gentle cool breeze that carries the brilliant colors of red, orange, and yellow leaves off nearby trees. Boo holds on to a dozen white roses in one hand and her mother's hand in the other.

The family walks a few yards along the neatly maintained grass and find the resting place of Will's father. The family watches as Boo places the white roses along her grandfather's engraved name on the flat grave marker. Liam looks at his father and asks, "Why haven't we visited his grave before?"

Will looks down and answers, "That's a good question. I always felt that if I needed to talk to my dad, I could say a prayer. Plus, I always felt his presence more in other places."

Boo says, "I know he saved us from that fire. I just know it."

Will replies, "I think you're right, honey. Looks like my dad followed his calling into his next life. He was always meant to serve and protect."

Annie says, "You know, I've learned something during this whole thing."

Will looks at Annie and asks, "What's that, honey?"

"I've learned that when you die, the people that you loved miss you. That love is more powerful than death. It travels with us even after we are gone."

Will smiles. "Beautifully said, honey. I've learned something too."

Liam looks up at his father. "What's that, Dad?"

Will answers, "That it's important to listen to the messages. Thanks, Dad."

The family walks back to the van. Liam looks at Will and asks, "So any plans for next summer? Where are we traveling next?"

Will smiles as he enters the van and fires up the ignition. Will looks at the time on the dashboard: 11:11 a.m. He smiles as he turns on the radio. The radio is playing a song that reminds him of his father. Will smiles even more when he looks at the sky and says, "Got the message, Dad. We love you too."

Boo asks, "Yeah, Dad. Any ideas for next summer?"

Will answers, "Your mother and I were talking. Maybe next summer we will have a nice quiet vacation at home."

The van travels out of the cemetery and onto the main road. Will drives down the road and heads toward the highway signs reading: Chicago: Exit Here.

And that's where our next adventure will take place. Follow Liam and Boo as they stay home and find out what evil and wicked things are flying around their Chicago neighborhood in, *Red-Eyed Flight*. The Liam and Boo Series Book 3.